THE WOMAN IN COACH D

SARAH A. DENZIL

Copyright © 2024 by Sarah A. Denzil

Cover Design by Damonza

All rights reserved.

No part of this book may be reproduced in any form or by any electronic or mechanical means, including information storage and retrieval systems, without written permission from the author, except for the use of brief quotations in a book review.

PROLOGUE

The abyss yawns beneath their toes. Somewhere, deep down in the throat of that black hole, awaits freezing cold water. But the drop is long before their bodies will hit the water. She looks to her friend, terror written starkly across her young features. Skin pulled tight across a quivering jaw, eyes darting along the dark landscape. They clasp hands, both letting out a nervous giggle.

This is the one. The challenge to end it all. This is what they've both been waiting for. And now they've finally dug deep enough to mine out the bravery needed.

Or stupidity.

People have died at this spot. She knows that. It's closed to the public for that very reason. They are trespassing in a place that doesn't belong to them, but they don't care.

She looks at her best friend in the entire world and knows she's doing the right thing. Her friend looks back, long hair flowing in the wind, tears formed in the corners of her eyes. Maybe from the wind, maybe not. They both nod and they say the words.

One, two, three

Dare you, dare me.

Her body trembles, her toes tense around the crumbling edge of the drop.

One, two, three

Let the fear set you free.

She pulls in a deep breath, redirecting her eyes to the hole below them. The cave. The ancient drop where so many others have fallen to their deaths. But not them. They won't die, because they are protected.

One, two, three

Follow you, follow me.

She notices her voice is shaking. So is her entire body. She has never been so terrified in her life. And this isn't the first time she's leapt into the unknown.

One, two, three

Let the fear set you free.

Let the fear set you free.

Her friend steps first. She hesitates. Only for a split second, but she does. And then she bends her knees. She flies into the air. Her fingers come loose from her friend's grip and the darkness swallows them both. She hangs there, for just the briefest of moments, before gravity pulls her into the abyss. And then she's gone.

CHAPTER ONE

December rain taps against the umbrella canopy. Water drips down to my shoes. A steady stream of traffic fills the space around me with the white noise of swooshing of tyres. I take my time approaching the train station. I'm early, which is exactly how I like it.

"Sorry, love."

The sudden knock against my umbrella almost loosens it from my grip. I lift a hand to accept the woman's apology, but she is already ahead of me, hurrying to Harrison Park station. I recognise her from my regular commute into Manchester city centre. She always wears a navy-blue trench coat that complements her olive complexion. She must be catching the earlier train today. If I run, I could get it, too, but I don't. I'd rather wait the extra twenty minutes for my usual train and sit in the seat I always reserve. Coach D, seat 22. If I get the earlier train, my seat reservation won't count, and I could end up standing. Even after 5 p.m., the train into Manchester is busy and I'm not a big fan of crowded spaces.

Harrison Park station is small, just one platform and a ticket office. I know exactly where to stand on the platform to get on the correct carriage. I hang back first, letting the earlier train leave. A few minutes later, I pick my spot to wait.

The rain almost makes me regret letting the earlier train leave. There could be delays. I could end up standing here for an hour. I'm wearing court shoes with a slight heel. I'm usually in flats but I was taking minutes in an important meeting today at work and had to come straight from the office to catch the train.

My ex-boyfriend, Jack, used to laugh at my small feet and the fact I could never find comfortable shoes. Every pair rubbed my skin or squashed my toes or fell off my feet when I walked too fast. Later he'd roll his eyes, sick of it. I should probably have seen the break-up coming at that point, but I loved him so much. Too much. An all-consuming, unhealthy love that can only be born from a trauma bond.

A garbled message comes over the Tanoy sound system, bringing me back to the present. Jack and I are over. I've been single for six months and am renting a small, terraced house. Harry, my housemate, makes me a cup of tea after a nightmare. And, no, we're not having sex, we're just friends, but he still treats me better than my ex. Jack was sympathetic towards my anxiety at first, but then he started wearing ear plugs or headphones so I wouldn't disturb him at night. What at first endeared me to him ended up frustrating him.

I pace the platform, watching familiar faces arrive. A few even nod at me. There's the pink-cheeked man who smokes at the end of the platform. The anorak lady who always clutches her handbag like one of us is going to rob her. The woman with honey-coloured hair and full lips who is almost always in a hurry but still an absolute knockout despite running for the train.

Finally, it screeches up to the platform, and I take my usual seat by the window. I grab my phone and consider checking my work inbox but there's nothing too pressing going on. My boss, Trudy, won't have even read the minutes yet. There's a group of men in suits drinking bottles of Peroni a few seats away from me. Ties are askew, the top button of their shirts undone. It's Friday night and they're heading into the city centre for drinks after work.

My stop approaches. I tug on my winter coat, bracing myself for the biting December wind, and shuffle down the aisle to the door. As the train lurches, my foot catches on someone's bag strap and I pitch forward for a few uneven steps. Then I right myself, turning to apologise to the woman whose bag I accidentally kicked.

"No problem," she says.

Her blue eyes tilt up to mine. She's around my age, I think, in her early thirties, but there are bags under her eyes and her skin is dry and flaky. Her hair hangs limp and greasy, but it's a beautiful golden colour. She wears a large wax jacket that completely swamps her tiny frame.

I double take.

"Have we met?" I ask.

She shakes her head. "I don't think so."

A tremor works its way along her jaw as though she is gritting her teeth, and then those azure eyes turn to the train window. The doors open, and I hurry through the rest of the carriage. A thundering sound echoes through my mind as I step down onto the platform. It takes a moment to realise it's my throbbing pulse.

Cold wind slaps me on the face. I'm soon lost in the crowd. Manchester Piccadilly is a vast, open space that now feels tight and constrained as I'm surrounded by coats and suitcases and shoulders. My chest tightens. I need to get away from these people, away from the sound of trains pulling in, whistles blowing, station staff hollering. There are harsh lights above me, like hospital lights, and then an escalator, and then turnstiles, and all the time my breath is frozen in my lungs, and I can't breathe. I'm sweating. It trickles down my temples. My face feels bloodless, and my hands shake as I search for my ticket to scan.

I know the signs now. I've experienced panic attacks for over a decade. While my body is in flight or fight mode, I force myself to keep going, to move and breathe and follow the flow of the people in front of me.

The arrow glows green on the turnstile and I hurry through, rushing out of the exit as quickly as I can without shoving people out of my way. Even then it takes me a few minutes to find a quiet place, somewhere I can sit on a bench and pull in a deep breath. I use the circular breathing method of holding my breath before releasing it, and then I touch the wood with bare fingertips, grounding myself to this place, this moment.

"Mummy loves you, Jenny. Don't forget that."

Her voice in my mind is what anchors me, pulling away from the attack, and finally letting it go. Mum tucking me in for bed. Making me marmite sandwiches. Wrapping my small body into hers as we watch *The X Factor* in fuzzy socks.

I smile. I'm back. I lived through it. Sometimes panic attacks trick my brain into thinking I'm going to die. Sometimes they fizz and crackle beneath the surface, lasting for hours, or even days.

Then the smile fades from my face. It was the woman, I think. She triggered this. I know her from somewhere, but I just can't remember *where*.

CHAPTER TWO

"Evening, Jenny. Nice weather for ducks tonight." Bob gives me a faux salute.

He waits until I've removed my coat and hung it on the rack by the door before passing me a hot cup of tea. "It's been quiet tonight so far. Have you eaten, love?"

"Not yet. I've got a Snickers bar in my bag."

"There's custard creams in the kitchen," he says. "And Kavi brought doughnuts."

"Great." I flop down in my usual chair before taking a sip.

Bob is an angel amongst men. I've been volunteering at Solace for two years and he always has a cup of tea waiting for me when I arrive for my shift. Many of the volunteers are friendly retirees with time to kill and Bob is exactly that. He has to be in his sixties but walks like a much younger man. He carries his stocky weight like someone who was once fit, healthy and probably very attractive. I picture him as a former boxer. The gentlemanly kind who would never stand for any underhand nonsense. Not a violent man but a sportsman.

He trained me for Solace back when I first joined. I spent

six weeks with a group of new recruits, role playing through all the kinds of calls we'd experience here at the crisis helpline. From sex pests to suicidal teens. After I dropped out of a master's degree in psychology, I wanted to keep a toe in that area in case I decided to go back. I took a job at Trudy's office so that I could shadow her as a psychologist at her counselling centre while volunteering at Solace in my spare time.

"Are you all right, Jenny?"

I glance up at Bob's concerned face. I'd almost forgotten about the panic attack, but I'm sure it has left me looking wan and somewhat shaken. The rain leaving my hair and clothes soggy doesn't help, either.

"Oh yeah, I'm fine. Just a bit tired after work, that's all. I'm sure a few custard creams will sort me right out." I give him my most convincing smile.

"Well, if you need ten minutes in the break room before your shift, that's fine. Just let me know."

"Actually, that would be nice."

"Off you pop, then," he says.

I take the tea into the kitchen first, grabbing a few biscuits and a doughnut, then head into the break room. It's small and sparsely decorated. The charity doesn't have the budget for a lot, but I sit down on the faded sofa, grab a magazine and eat my sugary dinner while decompressing from the train ride.

My thoughts drift back to the woman on the train. She'd barely looked at me. She showed no recognition in her eyes, no hint that we know each other at all. But there was something so familiar about her. I slap the magazine closed, placing it back on the coffee table, and make my way back to my phone. Bob gives me a thumbs up, I respond in kind, and wait for the first call.

It doesn't take long.

"You're through to Solace. My name is Susie and I'm here to listen."

The blood drains from my face.

At Solace, we're trained to use a pseudonym when we answer calls. Privacy is one of the top priorities here. We're protected by our fake names and never record a conversation to respect the privacy of the callers.

I've never used the fake name Susie before. My usual persona is Bella, named after the dog Jack and I adopted years ago. I've never, ever called myself Susie.

I blink myself back to reality. There's still someone on the line, but they haven't spoken yet. That in itself isn't unusual. Sometimes callers don't speak at all. Sometimes they take a few moments to find the courage to speak.

"Take your time. I'm here if you'd like to chat."

I hear a breath. A quiet, soft breath. My mind wanders back to the name Susie, the significance of it, the past coming back to haunt me. Goosebumps erupt along my arms. My scalp prickles. I try to push it down so I can concentrate on the call.

"How has your day been today?" I prompt.

There's a sob on the line. It's so loud it almost makes me jump, but I'm relieved to know I'm not on the line with one of the sexual harassment calls. The people who ring and masturbate until you hang up. I get three or more per shift usually.

"Fucking shit."

"I'm sorry to hear that. What happened?" I ask gently. I keep my voice low and calm on the line, though some callers do tell me I sound patronising. It can be hard to find the right balance.

I focus on the voice. He sounds young, probably a

teenager, though they tend to text the helpline rather than call so perhaps he's in his twenties.

"I... I don't... I can't..."

He's crying now. His voice is choked. I tear up with him because I still haven't managed to turn that instinct off no matter how many calls I take here.

"Take your time. Just know I'm here and I'm listening."

"Thanks," he says.

I sense his chest heaving up and down as he tries to breathe. He's silent for a few moments. I consider using another question, but instead I give him space.

"It was my mate. He... he died."

His voice cracks. His pain seeps into me like I'm an absorbent sponge and his emotions are water.

"I'm so sorry to hear that. He meant a lot to you."

"Yeah, he did. He was my mate. He stopped me from cutting."

"Cutting?"

"Cutting my arms. I... I want to do it now. That's why I called."

"Tell me about your friend," I say. I can't tell him not to cut. I can't offer any advice at all, but I can keep him talking. I can try my best to listen and hope it helps after he hangs up. "Tell me his name."

"Si." He sniffs. "He left me his cat. Cola. She's a good cat. She's sweet."

"What colour is she?"

"Orange. She's one of those ginger cats that climb on everything. She jumps on the bed in the morning and wakes me up."

"It's nice that you're looking after your friend's cat."

"Yeah, I guess." There's a pause and then another sob. "I really miss him."

"I'm so sorry," I say. "You're not alone right now. You can tell me how it feels if that would help."

He lashes out at first. "How do you think it feels? It's shit. It's the worst." Then he softens. "I don't want to go to college because he won't be there. We can't text anymore. I used to tell him when I felt like cutting. Now what can I do?"

"Solace is always here. If you want to call and tell us that you feel like cutting, there will be someone to listen."

"I was on hold for fifteen minutes," he says. "I could've done anything in that time."

I'm never sure how to answer those issues. Solace isn't perfect. There's so much we can't do, and, yes, some callers end up on hold.

"I'm so sorry about that. We do our best."

He sighs. "Yeah, I know. I'm just messed up right now."

I listen to him cry for a few more minutes and try to prompt him to talk more, but he seems to have closed up. After a while he hangs up.

I take a moment to breathe. His call has hit me harder than I expected. I know what it's like to lose a friend at a young age. I went through those same feelings for someone I loved deeply. Someone more like a sister to me. The difference is, my friend didn't die, she vanished. Her name was Susie, and her name slipped out of my mouth in the same way long forgotten lines in a school play can pop into our memories.

At that moment, it all comes together. The panic attack. The woman with her blue eyes. Susie. Long, lost, missing person, Susie.

The woman on the train was Susie, the girl who used to be my best friend before she disappeared. I'm sure of it.

She's back.

CHAPTER THREE

There is a bright, white light shining in front of my eyes. It hurts to look at. My head is pounding, and I have already been sick several times. I'm scared stiff of looking away from the light, because if I do, I see nothing but shadows. If I turn away, I go back. I can never go back.

My feet move. The ground is uneven and I'm not wearing shoes. There are sharp stones penetrating my skin. My balance is off. I keep stumbling and my legs won't do what I want them to do. But there is a voice ahead, guiding me. Relief floods through me. I'm saved. A second emotion creeps up from the depths of my empty stomach. A sadness that has a weight to it. A dread that no child should ever be forced to feel.

I'm leaving her behind.

It's not something I want to do but nevertheless, it's happening. I run towards safety, towards the voice echoing out from the bright light. But Susie isn't running anywhere. She is behind me, lost to the shadows somewhere. If I knew where to find her, I would, but I don't. So I carry on in a straight line, knowing I am about to find sanctuary when my best friend is still lost. I run and I run until a man in uniform wraps a jacket around my shoulders.

And then I wake.

I gulp in air and swipe a hand across my forehead. As always, the pillow is soaked. I'm soaked. My body shivers as the memories slowly fade.

"You're safe," I tell myself. My adult self.

The Jenny in my nightmares is a distant memory and yet it feels so near and almost tangible like I could step right back into those woods. Sometimes, in my dreams, I think I hear Susie's voice behind me, calling me back. Telling me not to go. But I can't tell if it's real or not. I haven't been able to trust my memories for a very long time.

Unpicking what is real and what isn't has become a pastime of mine.

As I place my feet on the cool floorboards, the wood grounds me. I remind myself that these things happened sixteen years ago and I'm in my bedroom now. It has been a long time since I ran out of the woods in a torn, dirty dress.

I pull in a deep breath, focussing my mind, itemising the dream in case there are any new details. I know I ran to safety that night. I know Susie was never found. I know I lost my best friend when I was sixteen years old. It's almost every other detail from that night that eludes me.

Susie's face is so clear in my mind. Last night, after I got home from my shift at the helpline, I went through old photo albums trying to figure out if the woman on the train was definitely her. But sixteen years and the quick flash of a face on a busy train make it hard to know for sure.

I walk through to the bathroom and turn on the shower, aching to wash away the sweat. Forest scents invade my senses. Then I remember the cool fabric of the police officer's jacket as he wrapped it around my shivering shoulders. He'd talked softly to me as he led me out of the woods and into a car. He drove me to the hospital and my parents arrived, tear streaked and panicked. Doctors worked on me, cleaning up blood, checking the wound on the back of my head, shining lights in my eyes.

After stitches, I went for scans. Mum held my hand so tightly, she left white marks on my skin. The hospital stay is blurry, but I remember most of it. I remember the headaches, but I don't remember the seizures that Mum described later.

Sixteen years ago, I went into the woods with my best friend, Susie, and I hit my head. Part of my brain died that night when I suffered a traumatic brain injury. But at least I came out of the woods. Susie never did.

The reason for us being there is also hazy in my mind, but I know it relates to our dares. Susie and I, blood-sworn best friends, chosen sisters, had been young and stupid. We gave each other challenges. Hair-brained, dangerous dares to complete, from cliff jumping to stealing cars. That night was our last dare. We were both sixteen and we had decided to jump into Hangman's Cave, a dangerous spot in the woods outside Chillingham-by-the-Sea, our childhood home.

The rest is fractured, like trying to complete a jigsaw puzzle without all the pieces. The doctors told me I have what's called retrograde amnesia, which means, when I fell and hit my head, I lost many of my memories. Whenever I think about it, I always imagine a child hitting a piggy bank to get the coins out. The harder you hit it, the more coins coming spilling out through the narrow hole. I hit my head pretty hard.

I remember most of my childhood up until my sixteenth year, but from that birthday to the moment the policeman placed the jacket over my shoulders, it's a blur.

My dreams conjure new perspectives of the night, making

me distrust my true memories. Sometimes I know Susie is somewhere behind me. Sometimes I'm afraid that Susie has been captured by a malignant presence in the woods. Other times I'm running away from Susie because she frightens me.

"Hey, Jen. You all right?"

Harry leans against the kitchen counter holding a mug of steaming hot tea. He's in his loose pyjama bottoms and a thin white t-shirt. Somehow, no matter how tired he is, he always looks good. I am aware of the zombie I resemble even after my shower. Restless sleep makes my skin blotch. I feel myself holding my back too straight, still tense from the nightmare.

"Bad night's sleep. Is the kettle still hot?" I force myself to smile.

He nods and steps out of my way. I throw a tea bag in my favourite mug—the one from a family holiday to Whitby. It's decorated with a sketch of the abbey.

"Still getting nightmares?" he asks.

"Yeah." I don't embellish. It's not something I want to go into, and he knows that.

He pats my shoulder and walks away. "I'd best get ready for work. But you know where I am if you want to talk, Jen."

I met Harry two months after Jack—who is alternatively known as the "liar, liar pants on fire"—dropped his flaming underwear for the friend now known as the "great big ho." Tanya is on her birth certificate, I suppose. I'd been living with Jack for over a year before the relationship ended. I ended up browsing ads for housemates wanted and ended up in a two-bedroom terrace in Harrison Park, a Manchester suburb. It's ten minutes from where I work, close to the train station so I can get into the city quickly, and Harry is neat, considerate, has a stable office job, never steals my milk, and, unfortunately for me, utterly gorgeous. A much better prospect than Jack ever was, but one who isn't in the slightest bit interested in me romantically, and someone I can't complicate things with anyway.

But I did have to tell Harry about the nightmares after he burst into my room one night. I'd been screaming the place down and he'd thought there was an intruder. I'll never forget the sight of Harry clutching a golf club at two a.m. with a tight expression of terror masking his features. After I'd calmed down, we both poured a shot of vodka and I told him all about what happened with me and Susie when we were children.

It's not easy telling people that you were once on the news in connection with a missing teenage girl. But Harry took it all in his stride. I let him know that he could throw me out, and I wouldn't hold it against him. Instead, he gave me a hug and told me he was always available to talk.

So far, I haven't taken him up on it. What is there to say? I don't remember half of it. What I do remember comes to me in flashes in my nightmares. It's not something I want to tell people.

I pop some bread into the toaster and add milk to my tea. But my thoughts are all of Susie. Her smile and the blue of her eyes. The way she always smelled like Palmolive soap because her mum couldn't afford nice shower gels. We'd been best friends at school. Inseparable. We played on the rope swing at the bottom of my garden and made mud pies from the field next to our house. We picked bluebells together in spring and went on bike rides with sandwiches in our lunch boxes.

Until she got ill, and everything changed.

CHAPTER FOUR

It was a nationwide story. Two teenage girls went missing in a small, coastal town in North Yorkshire. One survived, one never came home. Our faces sold newspapers and made people cry when they watched the six o'clock news. True crime fans spawned theories, building up cases, discovering villains. It was intensive and often cruel. Our Chillingham came alive with photographers and malicious gossip.

In the end, my parents moved me away from Chillingham about six months after I was found in the woods. We relocated another two times until reporters eventually left us alone. About a year after Susie's disappearance, my dad was even arrested for punching a photographer.

We were the trashy family. The ones with the broad Yorkshire accents who dressed in faded jeans and jumpers pulled out of shape by too many washes. While Susie's family were also from a poor background, her mother spoke softly and always wore her best dress when the press questioned her. In contrast, my dad came across as bullish. His beer belly poked over his cracked, leather belt. His greying beard hid his jowls.

They called him an alcoholic. He wasn't. They pointed out my mum's cousin was in prison. She hadn't seen her cousin for over a decade, and he was in prison for a non-violent crime.

The event occurred around the same time Facebook opened up to the world, allowing conspiracy theories to run rampant. A section of true crime fans started calling themselves Susie Patterson Truthers and set up groups to discuss how my dad kidnapped and murdered my best friend. I've read the foulest, most disgusting theories about my dad being a paedophile. They played out their own sick fantasies, using my father as the main character.

After Facebook groups came blogs and forums. Mum, Dad, and I have all been confronted on the street by amateur sleuths demanding we answer their questions. I grew up knowing these people are out there, watching me. Tracking my every move. Sometimes they send me letters demanding I tell the truth. Then they go on their podcasts and say I'm a liar. They even accuse me of killing Susie. They say I'm faking my amnesia. Some of them say I was in love with Susie and obsessed with her. Others say we were lovers.

Even after sixteen years, Susie's body has never been found but still a villain must be identified. Whether it's my dad or me, it makes these people feel better knowing someone is to blame. Someone snuffed the life out of this beautiful golden-haired girl and that someone could be me.

But that is a thread I hate to pull. I leave it where it belongs, in the deepest, darkest corners of my mind.

What if Susie really is alive? What if I saw her last night on the train? It would put an end to all of it. No more Susie Patterson Truthers rushing towards me with their phones ready to record me answering their questions. Maybe I'd be able to get a date without being ghosted once they've Googled my name.

And I'd finally know. I'd finally have the answers for myself. She was my best friend. I loved her like a sister and spent all of my time with her until she was suddenly not there anymore. It felt like losing a twin. She left a hole in my life that no one has been able to fill since. If it was her on the train... If she's out there... It would never be the same as it was, but I'd at least know she exists in this world, that I'm not alone any longer.

I wave bye to Harry and set off up the hill. I work until two on Saturdays but have Tuesday afternoons off. It's a twenty-minute walk to work but I don't drive. Driving is one aspect of life I refuse to compromise on. I've come to terms with the fact that metal boxes travelling at speed are the way we get around this world, but I don't want to be the person in control of one.

My boss, Trudy, runs a counselling and therapy centre in a small office block on the edge of Harrison Park. Around a dozen counsellors use the space to see some of their client and I manage the building. I create schedules, greet clients and attend meetings between the counsellors. After I completed my BA in psychology, I started a master's degree with the intention of training to become an educational psychologist. There's something about the teenage years that draws me in. I'm not Sigmund Freud, but it's safe to say that experiencing a loss of memories in my sixteenth year has given me a fixation on that time period. I wanted to help teens at school.

But the timing wasn't right. Jack wanted to buy a house and we were saving up for a deposit. I decided to put my studies on hold and get a job. I should have checked whether he was secretly sleeping with my friend first. Hindsight is, and always will be, twenty-twenty.

I wander into the building a little distracted, still replaying the event on the train on my mind.

"Morning, Jen." Trudy bustles over to the reception desk as I'm taking off my coat. "Tristan Coates cancelled again this morning. Shane is sick so can you give his clients a quick call and rearrange their appointments? Maybe go for next week. It's a cold apparently so he should be back fairly soon."

"Sure."

"How was your Friday night?" Trudy smiles, revealing her large teeth. She pushes up the sleeves on her long cardigan. She always wears the kind that float around her calves.

"I was at Solace. But it was fine. Only one guy had a wank down the phone, so, you know, all in all not a bad Friday night."

She laughs. "I volunteered for a crisis line at uni. One guy asked me to send him pictures of my feet."

"Oh, yeah. I've had that, too. He kept telling me about his verruca and asking me if my feet were 'clean'." I shudder.

"You've been doing that for two years now, right?" Trudy leans against the desk, her gold necklace hitting the brochure stand by my computer.

I nod.

"Hon, when are you going to go back to studying?"

I raise a non-committal shoulder. "Soon. Hopefully."

"But why not now? There are evening classes and online courses running right now. You could be working here as one of my counsellors in a few years. God knows you've put the time in at Solace."

"I know, I just..."

"What?"

"I've got a lot going on."

She half steps away from the desk. "There's always something. Just remember that. I don't want you taking minutes for our meetings next year, I want you *in* the meetings. Is that clear?"

"Crystal."

Trudy winks in response and I boot up the computer ready to tackle the day. She's right. She knows I'm holding myself back. I do too, but I don't know how to change.

CHAPTER FIVE

"Jenny, I'd like you to count down from thirty. Can you do that for me?"

I mumble through the numbers as Raj speaks over me in a deep voice, repeating the same mantras he always uses. "You are relaxed and safe." Slowly, I feel my consciousness tugged away, like the tide shifting out to sea. And while I stay aware of my surroundings, I know I'm somewhere else.

Psychologists—or wannabe psychologists like me—are not supposed to believe that lost memories can be recovered through hypnosis. During my undergraduate degree, I attended lectures that provided evidence against the process. And yet no other therapy has helped me with my memories. After my Saturday shifts at work, I see Raj to try and access what I think is buried.

I don't believe there is a medical reason for all my memory loss. I saw the scans at the hospital. I remember doctors pointing at blurry black and white photos, telling me what has happened to my brain. I went through rehabilitation to improve my short-term memory and speech. For a while, words slipped from my mind, and I slurred my speech, often sounding drunk when I tried to hold a conversation. I know that the fall killed cells and interrupted synapses. I know all of that. But I still believe that I have repressed some of my memories and that one day, I might be able to unlock them.

It's all about trauma. I blocked out the most traumatic memories because I couldn't handle them. One day I will get them back.

"You're in the woods," Raj continues. "And you're sixteen years old. You're with your best friend, Susie. This is the last time you saw her. What do you remember?"

I'm immediately freezing cold and there's nothing but darkness around me. My clothes are wet. But I was only wearing a light dress to begin with. I repeat this back to Raj, my voice monotone.

"It feels like I just woke up," I say. "I'm not in the place I expected to be. I'm somewhere else."

I remember. The damp grass is cool beneath my body but it's out of place. The sensation of those soft blades seems unexpected. My head throbs and I want to throw up. Susie is supposed to be with me, but I let go of her.

"I let her go." The moment I utter the words I know I've never said them before, but I don't want to pull myself out of the memory.

"What do you mean you let her go?" Raj asks.

"We were holding hands when we jumped," I say.

"What happened after you jumped?" He asks.

I shake my head. "I don't know. I can't remember. Everything after is black."

"That's okay," he says. "Take your time. You're in a safe space and you can access those memories if you want."

But I try too hard. I force myself to think back to that time.

And then the fear, like a shard of ice, penetrates my heart. I gulp in air. I stumble through the woods calling her name. My vision is blurry. There's an ache thrumming through my head, radiating across my skull. As I run my heart rate picks up and the pain worsens.

I'm terrified but I don't know why. It could be the dark and the fact that I don't know where Susie is. Something deep in my bones tells me it's more than that.

"I don't know who I am. I mean... I do know. I know my name, but I've forgotten the person I am. I don't know why I'm there. All I remember is that I wanted to help Susie, but I couldn't help her anymore."

"That's good, Jenny. Keep going. You're safe."

My upper lip trembles. There are tears on my cheeks. "Jenny died. I created a new one."

And then my eyes fly open, because I see her, Susie, in my mind, and not only is she looking at me with big blue eyes, but she's sitting on that train. She says she doesn't know me. But I know her, and I just tripped over her bag.

"Deep breaths," Raj says. "In with me."

I pull air into my lungs, watching my hypnotherapist as he does the same. We hold in our breath and then slowly let it out. My fingers grip the arms of the chair. We're in a small room, cheaply furnished with white walls and flatpack furniture. I've been in this room dozens of times.

"Another deep breath," he says, and we repeat the process. "Good. Are you okay?"

I nod. My clothes feel too tight, and the air is claustrophobic. I want to get out of the room, but I'm convinced that my legs won't be able to hold my weight.

"I can get you a cup of tea," he says. "If you need a moment."

"Actually, I really need to go," I say. "I'm late. But thanks. It was a productive session today."

"Do you want to talk about it?" he asks. "I feel like we covered new ground today. You mentioned some things you've never mentioned before."

"I'm late for an appointment," I say, gathering my bag from the floor. "We'll talk about it next time."

"Okay," he says.

I've known Raj for a few years now and sense disappointment emanating from his half-closed brown eyes. I just don't know why. Maybe he's excited to have reached a breakthrough with me. Or he's worried his patient is in distress.

All I know is I need to get out of that room.

CHAPTER SIX

It's almost five p.m. I race down to Harrison Park and onto the platform. My heart is jumping around my chest and tension runs tightly through my body.

Raj was right. I did remember more in that last session than I ever have before, but none of that is important now. I know what I need. I need to see my friend. If I can get on the same train to Manchester at the same time as last night, maybe she'll be there.

During that last session, many of the emotions that I've kept at bay came flooding back. All the love and admiration I had for her hit me like a tidal wave.

Oh, Susie. My best friend in the entire world. We were both just seven when she was diagnosed with leukaemia. I used to pull silly pranks and dares to cheer her up. I ate marmite by the spoonful to make her laugh. I slid down the stairs in a cardboard box. I walked on my hands in the park with everyone staring.

After a while, whenever she felt better, Susie used to join in, too. And then our challenges took a different turn. Instead of silly pranks, we chose to face what scared us. I put a worm on my forehead and let it slither down my face. Susie talked back to the most terrifying dinner lady at the school. We hid on the football pitch and tried to skip a lesson. The headteacher found us and told us off, but he never called our parents.

The dares got bigger and bigger. Until we did something really terrifying, and it changed our lives forever.

One, two, three

Dare you, dare me.

I wait on the platform, examining faces as they pass me. It's a long shot. She could be anywhere by now, in another city, on a later train, on an earlier train. But what if she isn't? What if she's on this train with me again?

I have an opportunity to right a sixteen-year-old wrong. To find my long-lost friend and hug her and tell her I'm sorry for never finding her in those woods that night.

The train arrives. I'm the first to reach Coach D, slapping the door release button frantically until it finally opens. Someone shoves past me, trying to get off. I take a step back and examine the faces of those leaving the train. Then I'm inside, and I hurry down the aisle. I need to check every single seat on this four-carriage train. Despite the cold, sweat trickles down my temples. I'm breathing heavily. I must look unhinged to the people around me.

It's busy and the aisle is cramped with people heading to their seats. A familiar surge of claustrophobic panic works its way up from my abdomen as I push through the narrow space, tripping over suitcases and shopping bags. Sweat snakes down my spine, running between taut shoulder blades. I'm breathing heavily. I sense that my skin has paled. I'm bloodless, a limp figure dragging herself between the seats.

Ten minutes into the journey, the aisles become clearer,

but I still have to budge my way through the people sitting on the floor by the toilets. A few faces turn in my direction. I'm attracting attention. I'm sure panic and desperation emanates from me in waves. But there's no time to worry about that now.

I fantasise about finding Susie. This time she'll remember me, and we'll reconcile with a huge hug. Then we'll go for coffee, or I'll take her back to my house. She might cry when she tells me all about where she's been but that's okay because she's my best friend and I know exactly how to comfort her. And then we'll go to the police and the hospital so she can get checked out. I'm sure she has an insane story to tell. Maybe she lost her memories, too. Or she was kidnapped by a man who held her captive. Lastly, I'll hold her hand as I walk her up the drive to her mum's house and, finally, Mrs Patterson will thank me for finding her daughter. For bringing her home.

Susie's mother still sends me letters every few months. Sometimes emails, too. She asks me over and over again if I remember what happened to her daughter. I'm convinced she believes I'm faking my memory loss. Deep down, I think Mrs Patterson, Fiona, believes I hurt Susie that night. Perhaps she even thinks I killed her. The police were suspicious at first, too. But my head injury suggested I could have been unconscious for a long period of time and therefore unable to physically hurt Susie.

There's a woman with blonde hair right at the end of the last train carriage. She has her head down, searching for something inside her bag. I pick up the pace, my fingers gripping the seats as I hurry along the aisle.

"Susie!" I raise my voice. "Susie! It's me, it's Jenny."

The woman looks up. Her expression turns to confusion,

and she glances behind her and then around her, baffled as to why I'm talking to her.

My heart sinks. She isn't Susie. She's no one.

"Sorry," I say. "I thought you were someone else."

CHAPTER SEVEN

Familiar streets become strange and otherworldly. Blood rushes through my ears like the sound of the sea in a shell. But I know not to panic because this is a regular occurrence for me. My first panic attack happened in the hospital about five hours after I realised my memory wasn't working as it should be. The idea of losing a part of myself was so unnerving, I thought I was going to die. For a brief moment, I convinced myself that the fear inside my body would finish me off once and for all.

Anxiety attacks can make the world blurry. Sometimes I don't feel like I'm inside my body, instead I'm an alien in a surreal land, completely detached from reality. Of course, that in itself can be terrifying. It can make me tremble and my chest tight. It's like that now. Christmas lights strung up around the city smudge into unfocused colours. I duck into a shop, find a quiet corner and use breathing techniques to calm myself down.

I came to Manchester city centre just so I could ride the train at the same time again, to see if I saw her. And now I'm here, I have nothing to do. I don't have a shift at Solace. I'm hungry but money is tight, and I don't want to eat out.

But there is one thing I can do. I check Google Maps to make sure I know where to go, and then walk out of the shop.

It's been a long time since I set foot inside a police station. After I was found in the woods, I sat through many police interviews. And then a few years after that, I remember picking up my dad after his first arrest.

There were times during the period that followed Susie's disappearance when I felt my face was instantly recognisable. I'd become infamous. A teenage girl, either innocent or viciously terrifying, depending on which angle the newspaper wanted to spin. But infamous, either way.

Susie remained trapped in amber, a perfectly pure relic of that moment. No one would dig up dirt on a cancer survivor. But that image of an angelic and beautiful innocent wasn't quite the Susie I knew. I knew a flawed human. There were times she wasn't nice to me. There were moments of utter cruelty. I loved her like a sister no matter what.

This time, when I walk into the concrete building, I am anonymous. The world has moved on.

"Can I help you?" the policewoman on the reception desk asks.

"I think I may have seen a missing person," I say. "I'd like to tell someone."

"You can tell me, if you like," she says. "I'll take the details. How long has the person been missing?"

"About sixteen years," I say.

She looks up sharply then. "Oh. Do you know their name?"

"Susie Patterson," I say.

She's quiet for a moment. Then the recognition hits her. "Susie Patterson. Okay, and where did you see her?"

"The five thirty-five train from Harrison Park to Manchester Piccadilly. She was in coach D, I think, sitting near the glass doors that lead to the next carriage. In the aisle seat."

The officer writes it all down. "Can I take a description?"

I nod, and reel off what I remember about what she was wearing and her general appearance. Even though I feel as though the sight of her is etched on my brain, I begin to doubt myself as I offer up the details.

"And your name?" she asks.

"Jenny Woods."

She pauses again. Even though she doesn't react, I know what she's thinking. It's all hitting her at once, the memory of the newspaper cover stories. Pictures of sixteen-year-old me with my arm slung around Susie's shoulders.

She looks up. "Thank you, Ms Woods. If I could just take a phone number, we'll be in touch."

I walk out on unsteady legs with an anti-climactic sense of disappointment settling somewhere deep in my bones. I'm not sure what I expected, but it was more than this.

The promise of a call isn't enough. I want action now. I want it over. I speed up along the street, sweating under my coat. The adrenaline wears off finally. I'm tired. I drag myself back to the train station, onto the next train home, and try searching once more for Susie. She isn't there.

I didn't think she would be, but that doesn't stop my mind from spinning out of control. I think I imagined the whole thing. No one is going to find Susie because I've invented it all. The woman on the train wasn't her at all. It was a random person going home for the night. I'm just the mad cow with half a brain trying desperately to dredge up the past.

Shut up, Jenny, I think.

Trudy would tell me to be kind to myself. "If not you then who? Why wait for the kindness of others, give it to yourself, freely."

I check the train once more on my way down to the train door, and soon I'm back to my local, one platform stop. I hurry home, pink-cheeked from the wind.

Harry is watching a Love Island repeat when I get in. He waves absentmindedly from the sofa. And then he does a double take.

"Jen? You look like you've seen a ghost."

He's so on point that I almost laugh.

"Long day," I say. "And I think I might be coming down with something. Probably just a dodgy prawn or something, you know? Shouldn't have had that biryani at lunch, I guess."

He nods. "We've all been there."

His response is gracious as always, but I hate myself for the ramble I go down while high on anxiety—which by the way, really is like a drug—and back away. "Anyway, I'm going to lie down. See you later."

"Okay," he says, distracted by the drama on the screen. "If you want a glass of water fetching, give me a shout."

I thank him and hurry through to my room. Then I open a window and let the winter air cool my hot skin. It's like the train is still around me, moving under my feet. All those people, all that motion and the stress of the sensory overload. Quickly, I peel away my clothes, drag a make-up remover wipe across my face and slide into the covers, tucking my head underneath the pillow.

Peace.

My mind drifts to the details uncovered from my hypnosis

session. Today was the first time I actually remembered the moment we jumped into Hangman's Cave. I've always known I jumped, but I've never actually remembered the details of it. And yet I still can't trust the memory. My mind may have filled in the gaps for me without giving me the actual moment. I was found close to the cave, and Susie and I had talked about jumping in there for years. Ever since she was first diagnosed with her illness.

Memories of Susie's illness float in and out of my mind. I remember all the adults around us kept bursting into tears. Like they'd already given up.

There's one memory in particular that stands out. The day she got the all clear. It was about two years after she started chemotherapy. We'd snuck out of Susie's house and ran all the way down to the beach. I remember Susie grabbing my hand, pointing up to the cliffs, and whispering in my ear what she wanted me to do.

I remember the thrill of the fear.

"Please, Jenny," she'd said. "I need to do it."

Later, we'd hurried back to Mrs Patterson's house, still soaked through from plunging into the sea. It'd been our scariest dare up to that point, but I'd wanted to do it for Susie.

We were just kids but there was a zealousness inside us that had us both convinced that the dares—that facing these fears—gave us a layer of invincibility. It wasn't the chemotherapy curing Susie, it was the dares.

Mrs Patterson had been so mad with us for running off, but she didn't have a chance to scold us when we returned. She got the call from the doctor almost immediately. Susie had gasped when her mother crumpled in on herself, rushing to be by her side. But Mrs Patterson lifted herself and beamed.

"Mummy?" Susie asked tentatively.

"You're going to be okay, sweetheart," she said. "You're in remission."

She'd scooped us both into hugs, our wet clothes and hair dampening her floral blouse. The scent of her Elizabeth Taylor perfume. A knock off, not even the original White Diamonds. And then the tears.

But what I didn't understand then, is what we did that day on the cliffs became as dangerous as the cancerous cells that had tainted Susie's blood. The dares became our doctrine. Our one belief. We lost ourselves to it.

Jenny died and I created a new one.

I emerged from that dark forest as a new version of myself, leaving the old, fearless version back in the shadows. I'm a pale imitation of that girl. I am both afraid of living and afraid of dying.

Maybe if I can find Susie, I can bring the old me back. I want that more than anything.

CHAPTER EIGHT

There's a crusting drool stain on my pillow when I wake. I groan and stretch out my naked body. When I crawled into bed yesterday evening, I hadn't expected to sleep through the entire night. And now my stomach growls.

I grab a dressing gown and head into the bathroom for a shower. Then I dress, apply mascara and lip gloss, and consider what I'm going to do today. Harry sleeps in on Sundays so I grab a mug of coffee and relax in the quiet kitchen. I pull in a deep breath and centre myself.

After completing the rehabilitation for my brain injury, I made a pact with myself to not allow it or my anxiety to stop me having a normal life. Some days are harder than others, but on the whole, I try to push outside of my comfort zone as often as I can. My body tests me at every turn but I have my coping mechanisms to help.

For instance, I get up early, I spend time alone at the table with a hot drink. If I'm travelling, I get an early train and make sure I'm one of the first to arrive at my appointment so that I can compose myself.

I was not composed yesterday. I ran around like a mad thing, hopping on trains, going to the police station, rushing home with my heart in my mouth.

When I hear the sounds of Harry moving around, I take the rest of my coffee back to my room and open up my laptop. I compose an email to Mrs Patterson in my mind, telling her all about how I've found Susie safe and sound. But every time I think of the police officer taking down the details, that fragment of hope splits into a thousand pieces. What if I'm wrong?

Sitting around doing nothing is driving me crazy. I get dressed, head down to Harrison Park station and sit on the platform, letting train after train go by. I examine the faces of those who get on and off the train, searching for a hint of golden hair. Those blue eyes. I remember what it was like when seven-year-old Susie tearfully told me about her illness, tears swimming, her expression shy. We'd hugged and I felt so helpless.

Jack always asked me why I live in the past. I could never give him an answer. Maybe because so much of it was erased from me. How can I not fixate on that? How do I move on? I lost her in one terrible blur of a night. While I've been able to live my life as normal, she has been gone. In my mind, she was trapped inside the woods. Guilt has gnawed at me, infecting my relationships.

I get on the train and get off at Manchester. I sit there, on the platform, watching the people. There are plenty of blonde heads moving around. After waiting for at least two hours, I decide to call it a day and board the next train home. At least this time there's no panic attack brewing beneath the surface. I check the carriages again, but it's much quieter than last time and I'm able to move up and down with ease.

She isn't here.

I sit down, feeling deflated. Is this all I get after sixteen years? A quick glimpse of my lost best friend followed by the emptiness of wondering if it was really her. A sudden surge of emotion pricks at my eyes and nose. I stare out of the window, letting my eyes burn but not allowing the tears to fall. Once I've cleared my throat, they're finally under control.

The train stops at Harrison Park, and I disembark. I glance behind me, checking one more time. And then I mentally let it go. I've done what I can. Now it's up to the police to check whether I was right or not. If I did see her, then maybe they'll find her on CCTV and follow the trail until the mystery of where she's been is cleared up. If I didn't see her, then that will be discovered, too. There's no need for me to email Mrs Patterson and get her hopes up. All I need to do is live my life as well as I can.

It's a reassuring thought but not one that erases all the complexities of the situation. Of course, I'm going to think about my friend. A lot, knowing me and my overanalysing brain. But when I step into the house, I feel lighter than the day before. That counts for something.

"Jen," Harry says, smiling. He stirs sauce on the stove. "Hope you don't mind, but I've got a date tonight. She's coming round about seven."

"Course not," I reply. "What are you cooking?"

"Beef bourguignon," he says.

I take a step closer and groan. "It smells so good."

"I made way too much," he says. "We could probably have some leftovers tomorrow night."

"Great." The smile on my face does a terrible job of hiding the disappointment. No doubt there'll be a gorgeous woman eating Harry's delicious beef bourguignon tonight while I'll get the leftovers tomorrow.

"You received a letter by the way," he says, gesturing to

the rack where we put the post. "It must have come yesterday and got mixed up with the spam."

"Another bill? Pizza menu? Actually, I hope it's a pizza menu, I'm starving."

"Don't think so," he says.

I grab the envelope, kick off my shoes and head into my room to hide away from Harry's romantic date. The envelope is A4 size with a printed label on the front. The postmark tells me it's from Whitby. That gives me pause. Whitby was close to Chillingham, where Susie and I grew up. I tear open the envelope and remove what feels like a few sheets of thin paper. I'm confused at first. The papers seem old and torn, like they've been ripped from a notebook.

And then I half collapse onto my bed.

> *You are reading the diary of Jenny Woods aged 7 and you need to <u>STOP READING RIGHT NOW</u>. This is private!!!*

I blink, then throw the papers onto my bed like they burned my fingers. And then I'm on my feet, pacing the small space of my bedroom.

"What the fuck?" I say out loud.

I place one hand on my chest, still walking up and down, wearing a track into the carpet fibres. This can't be real. Can it?

Almost as suddenly as I tossed the papers down, I snatch them back up and read on.

CHAPTER NINE
JENNY'S DIARY

You are reading the diary of Jenny Woods aged 7 and you need to <u>STOP READING RIGHT NOW</u>. This is private!!!

Seriously.

Go away.

Mum, that means you.

Dad, that means you.

I'll shout at you if you read this, and I won't do my chores for a week. I won't even go to school anymore, that's how serious I am. Because today was the worst day ever. If you read this, then it gets even worse.

There is no one at school that I like apart from Susie Patterson. She's my best friend in the whole world. All the other girls are horrible, and they make up stupid songs about me and Susie just because we like hanging out together. Like: Jenny and Susie weirdoooes. Creepy from their head to their toooes.

Ugh.

And today I got told the worst news ever! I don't know if I can even write it down. Maybe if I write it really small it won't look so horrible.

This is my really small writing. My friend has cancer.

No, that didn't help. I might as well write it big. MY FRIEND HAS CANCER.

~~lookemea~~
~~lukeemia~~
~~lookeemeea~~

It's in her blood. My best friend has stuff in her blood that's making her sick, and I can't do anything about it. Mrs Patterson told me that the doctors are working really hard to make her better. If they don't, I'm going to go and shout at them because Susie is my best friend and I really don't want anything to happen to her. Mrs Patterson told me I could pray for Susie and I've done that. But Dad always says that it doesn't do anything and it's a waste of time because there isn't a man with a beard in the sky.

Why don't adults know what to do? Isn't that what they're supposed to do? If they don't know, what's the point of having parents?

After Mrs Patterson told me about Susie being ill, I wanted to take her to the cove to cheer her up. We aren't allowed to go on our own but Mrs Patterson always goes with us. She likes it there too. We pick up seashells and smooth stones. Some of them are so shiny. I have them along my windowsill. But Mrs

Patterson wouldn't let us go today. She said Susie had to rest. Susie said she was fine and she got upset. She started crying and then I started crying and my mum had to come and pick me up.

Mrs Patterson said I upset Susie.

That hurt my feelings a little bit.

Why would she say that? I don't want to upset Susie. I just wanted to cheer her up. It was the adults who upset her. They make everything worse. Which is why they're not allowed to read my diary.

I don't want people to know I'm still upset. I don't like that. I just want Susie to be better. She's nice and she's pretty and she lends me her books.

It's not fair that she's poorly and it's not fair that she might not get better.

CHAPTER TEN

I turn the page over. There's a message:

It was so good to see you on the train, Jenny.
Do you remember this day? The one from your diary? You were so upset. I'm sorry about that. Children should be protected from things like cancer, shouldn't they? In an ideal world, anyway.
Are you ready to play our game again? It all started on this day, didn't it? Well, it took a little while to get going but it started there. You were always so funny trying to cheer me up. I loved it. And you. I love you, Jenny.
And I want to start it again. I need it and I think you do, too.
So, your challenge is this.
It's very simple.
On Monday 11th December, at 1 p.m., go to the

block of flats opposite your work building. Go right up on the roof and walk to the edge. I want you to look down at the road below. It's fifteen floors. Easy peasy.

Let the fear set you free, Jenny.

I read the note again. My breath bursts from my chest in a rapid staccato. Every time I read the words, I feel like I'm imagining them, that they're some sort of hallucination. But they aren't. And this diary is real. These are my words from when I was seven years old. I remember the day I found out Susie had cancer as clear as it was yesterday. The brain injury didn't rob me of it.

After Susie found out she was in remission our dares became a monthly challenge. One terrifying stunt every four weeks to keep Susie in remission. We really believed they worked.

Until they didn't.

This piece of paper in my hand is proof that she didn't die in the woods. Susie is alive and well and still testing me.

My best friend is out there. I'm filled with anxious energy and get on my feet to pace again. I press the papers from my diary to my chest, trying to calm my quickening pulse. Susie is out there, and I need to do what she says. I have to go to the roof of the apartment block in one week. And I have to look down. My stomach squirms at the thought. I hate heights these days. But then it hits me. Susie will need to be there to see me do it. If I go, she'll come with me. I'll finally be reunited with my best friend after all these years.

Before Harry's date begins, I grab the diary pages along with the envelope and shove it in my handbag. I'm going to have to go back to the police station and hand this in. It's evidence, and it could help find Susie. I have to consider the scenario that Susie doesn't turn up to the challenge she has set. Or the more unlikely scenario that she didn't send me this diary at all and someone else did. Of course I want to believe she'll be there, but what if I'm wrong? What if this is all some sort of prank?

On the train, after I perform a quick scan of the passengers, I take some quick photographs of both the diary pages and the note. The police will probably take this from me. It's late. I should get there just before the station closes up for the night. This is too important not to go right away. *Susie Patterson.* She was in the news for months. Even now, journalists write maudlin articles about the unsolved case every anniversary of her disappearance. The police will want to see me right away. I know they will.

It's about a ten-minute walk from the train station, which I do briskly, trying to keep warm in the cold December air. The receptionist audibly sighs as I walk in. But it isn't the same officer as before. I hurry up to the desk and explain the situation, still out of breath and talking too quickly for them to follow. The officer stares at me for a moment.

"Wait, did you say Susie Patterson?" he asks.

"Yes," I say.

"And you're Jenny Woods."

"Yes."

"Okay. Um, hold on a moment."

He picks up the phone to make a call. I wipe the sweat from my forehead and remove a scarf. About a minute or so later, a different man walks up. He's in his thirties with dark, closely cropped hair and warm hazel eyes. He smiles at me when he approaches, but it's guarded.

"Nice to meet you, Ms Woods," he says. "I'm DS Harding. Would you like to come through? We'll have a chat in private."

"Okay." I follow him as he politely guides me through the station. Almost immediately, my body tenses because I've done this walk before. I remember tall men leaning against desks, smiling and offering me hot chocolate before tearing into me until I sobbed the same thing over and over again. *I don't remember what happened to Susie.* The older men would narrow their piggy eyes at me, not believing a word I was saying. I don't wish to relive those moments.

"Would you like a glass of water?" he asks, directing me into an interview room.

"No, thank you," I say. "Can we just get on with it?"

"Sure, take a seat."

I don't like him or his handsome face. It's disarming. I wonder how he's going to try to lure me in. I'm not sixteen anymore but somehow, I've always remained an open book, despite everything that has happened.

"Thanks." I watch him sit opposite me. He smiles politely, waiting for me to begin.

I clear my throat and retrieve the envelope with trembling fingers. "I received this." I spread the diary pages out on the table between us. "Pages from my diary."

DS Harding frowns. "What do you mean you received it?"

"Exactly that," I say. "It was sent to me in the post."

He frowns. "So someone sent you your own diary. Why would someone else have your diary? Did you know it was missing?"

"I thought I'd lost it," I say. "I kept it sporadically all through my childhood and after..." I swallow, wishing I'd accepted that glass of water. "After my friend went missing, and I suffered my head injury, I forgot all about it."

"You forgot?"

"Haven't you read my file?" I snap. Then I shake my head. "Sorry. I'm just used to everyone knowing everything about me. I had what is called a traumatic brain injury, or a TBI. It caused some retrograde amnesia, which means I don't remember much in the months running up to the accident. Well, it's mainly related to events close to the accident, but many aspects of my childhood are blurry, too. It's not like I completely forgot about keeping a diary, I just..." I shrug, trying to find the words to describe what I mean. "I guess I forgot where it was. My family moved and I never really thought about it when I was packing."

DS Harding leans back in his chair and reads the pages.

"Hey," I say. "Can you not do that in front of me?" I'm suddenly flooded with embarrassment that he'll read my seven-year-old-girl thoughts.

"I'm going to have to study them. You know that," he says, lifting an eyebrow.

"Look, turn the page. That's the important part. Susie left me a message."

He turns the paper over and rubs the stubble along his jawline as he reads the challenge.

"Whoever wrote this makes it sound like you performed a lot of dares as a child," he says.

I fold my arms across my chest and let out a sardonic laugh. "No shit, Sherlock."

He places the paper down. "You do realise you're speaking to a police officer. Some respect would go a long way."

I sigh. "The whole reason I did those challenges was to keep her safe. But every police officer I met treated me like I was the one who hurt her."

"What does that mean?" he asks, immediately pouncing on my wording. "Keep her safe?"

"Look, it was silly kid stuff, but it meant a lot to us. If I explain it all, you have to promise not to judge me as some crazy person, okay?"

"I make no such promise," he says. "But go ahead."

"Susie was diagnosed with leukaemia when we were both seven. I thought my friend was going to die and I just wanted to cheer her up, you know. So I started doing these dares. Stupid kid shit. Holding spiders or trying a cigarette, that kind of thing." I lick my lips, suddenly overcome with emotion. "Susie got sicker and sicker, and our dares got bigger and bigger. We... we started to think that being scared of something but doing it anyway kept her alive." I wipe moisture from my nose, surprised by the tears. "So, yes. I am more than familiar with dares."

"How long did they go on for?" he asks.

"Until she went missing."

He nods. "I think I remember reading about it."

"What were you, about ten?"

"No," he says, amused. "But thank you. I was seventeen."

"So I guess you're a year older than me."

His hazel eyes meet mine. "I guess I am."

"Did you want to become a police officer so you could lock me up? Everyone thought I was guilty. Either me or my dad, anyway."

He shakes his head. "I did not become a police officer to lock you up."

I notice that he doesn't say he thought I was innocent. That's interesting.

"Look, just find Susie. Please. That's all I came here to ask. You have the envelope so do your tests or whatever and figure out where she's hiding."

"Right," he says. "You want to clear your name."

I shrug. "I want my friend back."

He watches me with narrowed eyes as I stand and collect my bag. Then he nods gently as I thank him for seeing me. As I'm on my way out, he clears his throat and asks one more question.

"Are you going to do it?"

"Do what?" I ask.

"Are you going to go up to the roof of the building she mentioned and look down?"

"Yes," I say without hesitation.

CHAPTER ELEVEN

When I return, I find myself wandering into the house during an awkward moment. Harry and his date are kissing next to an untouched bowl of beef bourguignon.

"Sorry," I mutter. "Don't mind me!"

I tip toe up the stairs to my room and quietly close the door. Neither of them even paused for a moment. Maybe they didn't see me. How embarrassing to be a thirty-two-year-old woman with a housemate. I guess that's what happens when you let your boyfriend talk you out of finishing your master's.

I met Jack when I was nineteen. It was my first year at university after going through rehabilitation and retaking my exams. I'd expected to fail, but I didn't. I even managed to get into one of the better universities and ended up studying psychology at Birmingham. Jack was twenty. He'd taken a few years to go travelling. His mum and dad funded most of it, but he was already in debt when we met. Of course, back then neither of us really cared about money. We scraped by. I worked in bars and restaurants all through university and Jack took shifts in the local supermarket. We lived in the same shared house, managed to pay our rent and had a little left over for nights out.

Jack took me away from everything related to Susie and her disappearance. He introduced me to another world. One with friends and parties. But while he was addictive to be around, Jack suffered with addictions himself. There were times I had to hold his hand through months, even years, of alcohol issues. Now, when I look back, I see that we were co-dependent. But at the time it felt like us against the world.

When he cheated, it was like my world imploded. I didn't just lose Jack, I lost my friends, too, because we were a unit. I never made my own friends; I just adopted his. Even though I still resent him for everything, when I think about it now, I understand why he did what he did. It was an act of cowardice. He wanted out, and he didn't know how to tell me, so he showed me instead.

I flop down on the bed. Today has been quite a day. The most intense of days I can remember for a long time and the vein running across my temple throbs. When I'm tired, words fall out of my head, and I find I can't think straight. I'm like that now. Tired but filled with adrenaline. A crawling sensation spreads over my skin when I think about DS Harding reading the pages from my diary.

After Susie went missing, the police officers dug through every room in our house searching for evidence. Remembering it makes my scalp itch. The complete lack of privacy. Knowing that they are trying their best to prove that I, or my dad, had something to do with Susie's disappearance.

They wanted a murder conviction. But they never found that evidence and they never found a body. The most common theory is that Susie fell into the body of water beneath Hangman's Cave, died, and floated out to sea. It had been raining in the weeks leading up to our disastrous stunt. Hangman's Cave is connected to the river that joins the sea. The high levels of the water could have taken her body quickly but her being pushed out to the river would have speeded up the process which is why so many Susie Patterson Truthers think I was involved.

I hate thinking about her body in the water. Bloated and decomposed. Instead, I try to figure out why Susie would have my diary now. I can't remember giving it to her, but that's hardly surprising considering the huge gaps in my memory. But if I did, why? Maybe I wanted to show her how much I valued her friendship, or maybe I gave it to her for safe keeping. It's clear that I was paranoid about my parents reading it, or I wouldn't have left those warnings on the first page.

I reach into the back of my wardrobe and pull down a large box. A door closes somewhere else in the house, and I know Harry and his date have gone into his room. Before I tip out the contents, I put on headphones and play my early 2000s pop mix. If I'm delving into old memories, I'd may as well do it right. The playlists kicks off with Beautiful by Christina Aguilera which I remember Susie and I butchering in her bedroom. The CD player blasting, us holding hairbrushes in front of our faces.

We were babies in some ways. In others, we were older than our years. Susie spent a chunk of her childhood in hospital going through hell to beat cancer. I saw her on the bad days and held her hair when she threw up. I saw the IV drips and listened to the hum of the machines feeding her medicine. I lived with a ball of tension in my stomach anxious that I would lose my friend.

I reach for the photo albums first. I need to see Susie's face again. Every now and then I have this awful feeling that it wasn't her on the train that day. Sixteen years could be nothing or everything. She may have barely aged; she could be unrecognisable.

I flick through the sticker covered albums. The overzealous flash of my mum's camera bleaches our young skin. We grin, holding each other's hands, wearing pink t-shirts and pigtails. Susie's bright blue eyes sparkle, making my hazel ones seem dull in comparison. After turning a few pages, I suck in a breath through my teeth. It's always a shock to see her in the hospital. I'm sitting next to her on the bed and there's birthday wrapping paper on the linens. Mrs Patterson allowed just one friend to visit that day. I remember washing my hands and making sure I didn't have a cold. I'd been so scared to see her like that, with the bruises under her eyes and the hollow of her cheeks.

She's so thin, barely there under the bedding. Her eyelids are half closed. But it's the baldness of her head that stands out. I know her lovely hair regrew, but it's still shocking to see, and my heart skips a beat. I don't linger on the page, I flick forward, trying to push down the emotions rising to the surface. I need to be analytical now. Emotions can't play into this. I need to assess whether the woman on the train really was Susie.

But it took just twenty seconds or less to trip over the train woman's bag and apologise. How am I supposed to hold those few seconds in my mind? There's no way to be sure I haven't altered her facial features in some way. Looking through the old photographs of Susie only makes it worse. By the end I'm convinced that I'm somehow putting Susie's features onto this random woman.

I close the book and run my fingers over the stickers on the cover. Hello Kitty and love hearts and a bright colourful "best friends forever". I'm not crazy. It has to be her. Why else would I have received the diary so soon after? And how does she know where I live? Where I work?

Susie has been watching me. She planned the meeting on the train. She knew my carriage and the reserved seat. She did this because she wanted to reach out to me, but she wasn't ready to walk up to me and talk to me.

I flick open the album one more time. It turns to a page from when we were teenagers. I'm not sure how old we are, maybe fifteen. We're smiling. There's glitter along my cheekbones. It could be the night of the school disco. Susie is wearing my purple halter neck dress because she hated the one her mum had picked for her. I'd bought that dress especially for the disco and now I remember giving it to her because I wanted her to have it. Susie grew accustomed to getting her own way. People treated her differently after her diagnosis. Now that I think about it, she got away with a lot.

I try to imagine her fully grown. What kind of adult is she now? I think about the psyche of a person who pretends to be dead for sixteen years. A person who emerges mysteriously by faking a chance encounter, followed by sending instructions scribbled on the back of a stolen diary entry. I can't deny that it's strange behaviour. Perhaps she's afraid of returning to her old life. Maybe she's building up the courage to see me, the girl she left injured all those years ago. Alternatively, she isn't the girl I used to know.

Who is Susie Patterson?
Is she dangerous?
Am I in danger?

CHAPTER TWELVE

I look up from the reception desk as Trudy limps into the building.

"Hey," I say. "How was spin class?"

"Fuuuuucking kill me now." She rolls her eyes. "I don't know why I do it to myself."

I shake my head. "Me neither. Endorphins?"

"They don't fucking work, either." Trudy is the most soothing person once she puts on her therapist persona, but outside of that, she has a filthy mouth. "How was your weekend?

I hesitate, considering whether to tell her everything. In the end, I just shake my head slightly. "Harry had a date at the house, so awkward."

"Hot Harry? Oh no! I told you to make a move."

"I can't. He's my housemate."

"So." She raises an eyebrow.

"It'd mess everything up!"

"Or it could be, you know, a meaningful relationship between two consenting adults." Trudy taps the reception desk with long, purple fingernails. "And a lot of fun."

I frown and hand her the notes for her next client. "Sure. Because that's what always happens."

Trudy starts to turn back towards her office but then hesitates. She places a hand on my arm. "Look, I know I push you a little bit—"

"A little!" I say with a playful tone.

She laughs. "Okay, I nag you about furthering your career. But it's because I care about you. You're like a slightly younger sister to me."

I laugh. She grins.

"Seriously," she says. "I'd like to see you putting yourself out there a bit more. You spent all your twenties with one man. And a controlling man at that. You haven't had a chance to experiment, to find yourself, to figure out what you want in a partner."

"I know," I say softly.

What she's skirting around the edges at is my TBI. The fact that I met Jack so close to the end of my rehabilitation and never put in the work to find myself while single. And, yes, she has a point. I could be doing more to figure out what I want in life.

"I'm still healing, Trudy," I remind her.

She gives me a quick hug and heads into her office. For some reason, when I sit back down, DS Harding's hazel eyes pop into my mind.

"Oh no," I whisper to myself. "Do not go there."

I spend the rest of the day busy with phone calls, scheduling and filing. But the entire time, I debate whether to tell Mrs Patterson about the latest developments. There's no easy answer to this. Both options presented to me seem cruel. If I tell her about the diary and it somehow turns out that it didn't come from Susie, then I've needlessly raised her expectations. If I don't tell her then it feels like I'm withholding information.

In the end, I decide to wait. DS Harding can make that call.

Instead, I make an emergency appointment with Raj for after work. With the new diary entry coming into my life, I'm excited to slip back into my subconscious.

At university, a professor told me that weak people bend to the will of the hypnotist. The patient can become so susceptible to the guided instructions that their mind may invent past events. False memories can be implanted by someone with an agenda. But I've developed enough trust with Raj to feel sure that isn't the case here. Accessing my subconscious is the only way I feel safe enough to search the hidden parts of my past. There are days where I have my concerns about hypnosis, but on the whole I've decided to trust the process.

The day goes by quickly and as soon as work ends, I hop on the bus to the other side of Harrison Park. Still determined to uncover new memories, I stride purposefully into Raj's office.

"Is everything okay today, Jenny?" he asks.

As always, he sits in his grey armchair, one leg crossed over the other with his glasses dangling from his long fingers. He's in the usual checked shirt with the collar button undone. He's an attractive man, though I've never thought of him that way. I'm here for treatment and I'm focused on that. Still, I've always appreciated the calmness of his brown eyes.

"Yes," I say. "I just felt like I needed an extra session this week."

He nods.

Sometimes Raj likes to ask me questions before the

session begins but he picks up on my energy and dives right in. I settle back into the supple leather of the recliner, closing my eyes.

"Count backwards from thirty," he says.

30

29

28

Let the fear set you free.

I continue on, but it's Susie's voice counting down the numbers. We're next to a long stretch of train tracks running through Chillingham. She stares at me, her expression stern as she counts. Her hair is long and bleached by the hot summer we'd been having. There are freckles across the bridge of her nose. Her rose-pink lips form an "O."

"One," she says. "Go."

But I don't.

I stare at the great hunks of iron running parallel to each other through the grass. "I don't know if I can do this."

"Yes, you can," she says. "You know there's nothing coming. We checked the timetables." She folds her arms. "Come on, Jen, don't be such a sap."

I glare at her.

"It's going to be fine! Look, I'll count down again. But this time you *have* to do it. Okay?"

"Okay," I say reluctantly.

Susie's voice is loud and firm. "Ten. Nine. Eight..."

The train tracks snake through all the small coastal towns on the east, running along the cliffs. We use them to go shopping, hopping on at our tiny local stop to get to Whitby. The trains come every hour or so. We know there isn't one due for another thirty minutes, but I keep thinking about freight trains or carrier trains or whatever they are. What if one comes zooming down at any moment? What if my foot touches the metal and I get an electric shock? I gaze out at the sea beyond, and my legs feel like jelly.

"One," Susie says again.

We run. I squeal in fear as I hop over the first rail, step on the boards, then hop over the last rail. We run halfway up the bank on the other side, then turn around and do it all again in the opposite direction. And then we keep running, screaming into the wind, our arms stretched out. The sea breeze feels cool between my fingers and reeds of grass hit my shins.

Adrenaline gushes through my limbs, making me sprint faster than I've ever gone before. The nothingness of our dare hits me. Four quick hops and it was over. Why was I even afraid?

"We did it, Jen." Susie grabs my shoulders. "We did it! We're invincible."

I pull away slightly because I'm not sure I believe her. The word "invincible" makes my stomach squirm. Sometimes it's like Susie loses sight of why we're doing this. This is our ritual, our prayer, and even though, deep down, I know it doesn't keep the leukaemia away, I feel like it's necessary. But if we do something so reckless that we die, that's the opposite of what we're trying to do. We can't just go around saying we're invincible and doing whatever we want.

"We need to go bigger next time." Susie's cheeks are flushed, and her eyes are bright. "That was cool, but I don't think we were in much danger. Next time we need to really feel it."

"I don't know," I say. My voice sounds whiny in comparison to Susie's. "That was plenty dangerous for me." I let out a nervous laugh.

But Susie isn't listening. She turns away from me and runs through the long grass. I glance out at the sea, watching it chop and churn. I can't deny what we did made me feel good, but she's taking it in a direction that makes me uncomfortable. As much as I hate to admit it, I think I'm growing out of this now. I want to live a normal life and I'm not sure we're doing that.

"Where are you, Jenny?" Raj asks.

"At a crossroads," I say.

CHAPTER THIRTEEN

The brain injury didn't take that memory from me. It was something else. My biased mind didn't want me to remember that Susie and I had our issues. We were close and we loved each other, but we had disagreements, too. Of course we did; we were teenagers. All this time, I've looked back with rose-tinted glasses.

The truth is, not long before Susie disappeared, she'd begun spiralling out of control. She wanted the challenges to be bigger, scarier occasions, but I saw it as childish. Putting ourselves in dodgy situations didn't stop the cancer coming back.

Yet... I hadn't completely given it up. At least not that day at train tracks. I felt the exhilaration, the sudden burst of adrenaline. I walk faster towards the bus stop, my skin thrumming as though I'd actually hopped the train tracks in real life. I don't feel the cold at all. Every now and then, a smile spreads across my lips when I think about us running through that field with our arms stretched open.

No, I hadn't given the challenges up, but I wasn't a zealot about them like Susie.

My mind spins on the bus. I notice a tall, thin man staring at me, but when our eyes meet, he glances away. Perhaps I'm more noticeable with my cheeks flushed, the teenage version of me at the forefront of my memory. Trudy did tell me to put myself out there, but this man is older and not attractive to me. I avert my gaze as I get off at my usual stop.

Back home, Harry walks in as I'm cooking.

"Oh, sorry, Jen. I forgot to say there's leftovers in the fridge," he says.

I shake my head, thinking about him and his date kissing at the table. "That's okay. I fancied pasta. Actually, I made enough for you too if you want some."

"That's brilliant," he says. "Let me grab a plate. I don't want beef again either."

"So I saw the date went well."

"Oh, crap, sorry. Yeah, I heard you come in." He grins, revealing two small dimples in his cheeks.

"Are you seeing her again?"

He nods. "Yeah. I think we're going to go rock climbing together." Harry places two plates down next to my pan of pasta and I begin portioning it out.

I raise my eyebrows. "Nice!" I can't help but wonder what it's like to be fit and confident enough to casually go on a rock-climbing date. Then I push the thought away and add grated cheese to my meal.

"Do you want to catch up with Love Island with me?" he asks, reaching for the cheese grater.

"Actually, I just had a hypnosis session and I'm really tired," I say, feeling guilty about not wanting to stay and watch TV with him. "I think I might go up to my room with dinner tonight."

"No probs." He grates cheddar onto his pasta. "Thanks for

making tea tonight. I'll throw together a casserole this weekend if you're around."

"That sounds great." I smile and hurry out of the kitchen.

Harry and I tend to eat together when we're both in. Sometimes we plan proper meals together, other times we cobble something together, reheat leftovers or order a takeaway. I feel bad slipping away to my room, but it's what my body needs. I eat half of the pasta, wash up my bowl, then go straight to bed.

For the next few days, I throw myself into work, trying to distract myself from all things relating to Susie. I have a shift at Solace on Tuesday. It's a day shift rather than a night one. Day shifts are quieter. The night is when our most desperate thoughts and feelings rise to the surface. The night prompts the weary and afraid to call us in their darkest hour. Some people find themselves in crisis in the daytime, too, but it's rarer. I find myself drinking tea with Bob more than taking calls.

The counselling centre is busy, too. I make hot drinks for clients, pass out tissues and schedule appointments. Sometimes I even take the train into Manchester for no reason, just to check each carriage and make sure Susie isn't there. Of course, she never is.

On Saturday, I cancel my usual hypnosis session and go straight home after work. The house is empty. Harry is busy in the throes of his new relationship. While I can't deny my own tingle of resentment, and, let's face it, jealousy, I'm happy for him. One of us should be out there getting it. Good for him. And good for her. Harry is a catch.

I slip off my shoes, unbutton my blazer and pour out a large glass of wine. That's when the doorbell jolts through the quiet. I glance at the app on my phone and let out a long sigh.

A short woman with blonde hair cut into a blunt bob

stands by the door anxiously scratching her wrist. Fiona Patterson, Susie's mother, is waiting for me to answer the door. DS Harding must have been in touch with her. *Shit.*

I get another wine glass from the cupboard ready and quickly tidy away a few papers, letters, and other debris. Then I smooth my hair. What is it about seeing the parent of a childhood friend that makes me feel shy again? I take my time moving through the house, prolonging the moment before I let her in.

"Hi, Jenny," she says. "Sorry to turn up like this."

Fiona is still just as well put together as always. She wears cheap but clean and neatly ironed clothes. Jeans that fit just-so. A cardigan buttoned up to the neck. I lead her through to the kitchen.

"Would you like a glass of wine?" I offer.

Her nervous eyes regard the bottle and then find my gaze. "Yes, I think I would. I'm not leaving Manchester until tomorrow morning, so why not?"

I quickly pour a glass and hand it to her. Then we both sit. She crosses one leg over the other in a way I'd started to see Susie copy after turning thirteen.

"You came all the way from Chillingham?" I ask.

She nods. She looks tired. "I booked a hotel."

Guilt hits my stomach as sourly as the wine. "That must be expensive—"

"It's okay," she says.

"Look, I'm sorry it came from the police officer," I blurt out. "I was going to tell you, but I really didn't want to get your hopes up."

"Is it her?" Fiona's eyebrows shoot up her forehead.

I flinch away from the hopeful expression on her face.

"I can't know for certain," I admit. "I want it to be her. More than anything. You believe that, right?"

She nods. "Yes. I think I do." She takes a long sip of wine and wipes her mouth. "Tell me everything you know. Please."

I launch into the story, starting with the day on the train. She leans towards me, transfixed by my words. Occasionally her eyes close slowly, as though she's in pain. By the time I stop talking, Fiona is almost out of wine.

"It's happening on Monday," I say. "That's when I go to the roof of the apartment building. But I think I should go alone."

Her hand rises to her mouth. "What if it's her? What if she's *there*?"

"I'll convince her to talk to you. But she may want to do that in her own time. If we both go up, it might spook her," I say. "There has to be a reason for her disappearing for so long. I don't know what it is, but there must be something. Maybe a... I don't know, a psychological issue."

Fiona winces. I place a hand on her arm.

There's a catch in her throat when she says, "I can trust you, can't I, Jenny?"

"Of course you can," I say.

"Over the years, so many people have said I can't trust you, that I'm stupid for standing by you. I've always told them they're wrong. There may have been moments where I've worried that... that I've made a mistake." Her voice wobbles but she sniffs loudly and continues. "But I don't think I have. Have I?"

"No," I say. "I loved her. You know that. I believe she's alive. I really do."

Her eyes fill with determination. She straightens her back and squares her shoulders. "Then bring her back to me."

CHAPTER FOURTEEN

The promise lies bloated inside my body as I show her out. It isn't fair of her to lay the responsibility at my feet, but then it isn't fair that she lost her daughter, either.

I take the bottle of wine into the lounge to finish it alone. On Monday, I may see Susie for the first time in sixteen years and I need to figure out how to handle that. There'll be great relief, I know that. But also resentment and anger. If she has been in hiding all this time, then she left me, my family, and her mother to the wolves. I had to defend myself, to prove I was innocent. At any point she could have walked into a police station and made it all go away.

Why didn't she?

Perhaps the answer lies in the memories I can't access yet.

My phone rings halfway through a *Friends* repeat. It's a number I don't recognise, but maybe it's the police. I answer right away.

"Ms Woods? It's DS Harding. I wanted to give you an update—"

"Let me guess," I say. "You spoke to Fiona Patterson."

"She got in touch?" he asks.

"Yep. Well done, DS Harding, now she's made me promise to bring her daughter home to her. And she wants to come to my office on the day of the dare."

"About that," he says. "We need to organise it properly. We could have a wire—"

"Nope," I say.

He lets out a frustrated, humourless laugh. "You don't know what Susie has been doing all this time. She might be dangerous."

I blow air through my lips. "Yeah, right."

"She won't be the same person, you know. A lot of time has passed. I think at the very least, I should be there. I can be discreet. If you want, I won't be on the roof. I'll arrange to be somewhere nearby. You can wear a very small listening device so that I can intervene if there are any problems. We can use a code word. Whatever you want."

"You can arrange all that?"

"Yes," he says. "I think I can."

I think about it for a moment. As much as I hate to admit it, DS Harding is right. I don't know what Susie is like after sixteen years.

I nod. "All right. But nothing too crazy. We can't scare her away."

"That's not what I want to do," he says. "Can you come to the station tomorrow? I can talk you through everything. And you'll need to have a word with your boss about the operation."

"It's not a sting," I say. "You're not going to have to clear the building, are you?"

"I don't think so," he says. "She's not wanted for a crime, and she hasn't been associated with any criminals, as far as we know. I am curious as to how she's going to get to the roof of the apartment building, though. How are you going to do it?"

"Actually, my boss lives there. She forgot her phone once and I had to go into her apartment to get it while she had an appointment. So I know the building code. Maybe Susie is going to get in touch with me on Monday morning. I can let her in."

"That seems a little anticlimactic for a woman about to come out of hiding. With the diary pages and the challenge, you'd think she'd want to make a grand entrance," he says. "Emerge from some shadowy part of the roof or something."

"It's not like she's going to pop up from the fire escape to say hello," I say. "She's not a meerkat."

"Well, you need to prepare yourself for every possibility," he says.

I can't tell if he's trying to be funny or not.

"I read up on the case last night, Jenny," DS Harding says. Him using my first name takes me by surprise. "You've been through a lot. I'm sorry."

"Yeah, well. Shit happens."

He laughs. "No kidding. Anyway, I'd better go."

"Got a date with the wife?" I joke.

"More like a date with a food ordering service. I'll see you tomorrow morning. Get here as early as you can. I'll be around."

"Okay. Bye."

As soon as I hang up the phone, I feel like I just left a voicemail for a boy I like at school. He's a *police officer*. He's pretty much the enemy as far as I'm concerned. And yet, against my will, I'm beginning to warm to DS Harding.

CHAPTER FIFTEEN

The next morning, I rise, shower, make boiled eggs with soldiers and browse through the headlines on my phone. Then I see it resting on the doormat. Another A4 envelope with a label stuck to the outside. I grab it, staggering back into the kitchen, and sit down on a chair by the table.

My pulse quickens. I reach into the envelope and pull out the sheets of paper inside. There are two more pages from my diary. I scan over them, cringing at young me and my view of the world, and then I check the back for any messages.

I hope you haven't forgotten, Jenny. I can't wait to see you again. S

This is the confirmation I need. She's coming. As long as I hold my nerve, I'm going to be face to face with the girl who went missing sixteen years ago. The thought makes me nauseous with anticipation and fear and everything in between. DS Harding warned me that Susie may not be the same girl she was. I'm not the same girl, either. I'm not strong and fearless anymore. I'm a tepid copy, a broken imitation. And no amount of kintsugi will put me back together.

I place the envelope in my handbag and force myself to my feet. There's no point moping around in the house. It's time to get to the police station. At least I can hand in another piece of evidence while I'm at it.

I'm taken through to an office this time. DS Harding grabs a small cardboard box from his desk. "This is it. If you can, wear loose clothing on the day so that I can tape the device to your chest."

I nod, trying not to imagine DS Harding running a wire down my chest, touching my skin. He opens the box and shows me the device.

"It's very easy to fit," he says. "And it doesn't show."

"Okay. I need to tell you something." I place my bag on the desk and Harding sighs.

"Careful. That's my inbox," he says, nodding at my bag.

"Are you seriously complaining at me for messing this up? You have papers everywhere. Literally, everywhere. Even on the floor." I gesture to the many mounds of old files, letters and reports all over the room.

"It's a system!" he protests.

I roll my eyes and pull the envelope from my bag.

"More diary entries?" he asks.

I nod. "Yep, more of the same. I received it this morning."

"Excellent," he says. "I've really been enjoying Little Jenny's story."

"Wow. Watch your fucking mouth," I snap. And then I tense, realising I just swore at a police officer. "Sorry."

His eyes go cold. "You'd better be sorry."

My hands begin to shake. The change in his tone catapults me back to sixteen years ago, terrified the police were going to charge me for Susie's murder. "Are you going to arrest me?"

His expression softens. "No, of course not. But you can't speak to me like that."

"Maybe don't make fun of my memories, then. Don't you have a code of conduct? Ethics? This is all very difficult for me." I stare down at my hands, willing them to stop shaking. "Memories are precious when you know what it's like to lose them."

Harding's gaze trails down to my hands. He lets out a deep sigh. "I'm so sorry. You're right." Then he shakes his head and gives me a slight smile. "You're a tricky one, Ms Woods. I swear I'm much more professional when dealing with the rest of the Great British public."

"Why?" I ask.

He's quiet for a moment and his eyes travel over me, almost imperceptibly fast, as though he's trying to figure out how to answer that. He clears his throat. "Thank you for dropping this evidence off. It'll be tagged and stored for safekeeping. I'll get the lab to run the usual tests. Now, if you want to sit down in the... hold on, I'll clear that for you." He removes a backpack from his chair, and I take a seat.

"I called the building manager and we have an area to set you up with the wire tomorrow morning. It's a supply closet on the third floor, so it's not super glamorous. Have you told your boss what's going on?" He sits down at his desk and threads his fingers.

"Not yet," I say.

"Are you all right, Jenny?" he asks. His head tilts slightly to the right.

A familiar surge of anxiety heightens my senses. Every muscle in my body shivers. The detective's office, with all of his paraphernalia, closes in on me. I reach out to the leather strap of my bag to give myself something to touch. I'm desperate for it to ground me, but it doesn't work.

"Jenny?" he asks again. "Are you sure you're okay? Do you want a glass of water?"

"That would be nice, thanks."

It's hellish when an anxiety attack takes hold of me in public. My face stretches into a smile to reassure DS Harding that I'm okay. Smiling and nodding and saying I'm okay is one of my typical coping mechanisms during the throes of anxiety. If there's one thing worse than the attack making my chest constrict, it's the idea of everyone knowing how afraid I feel.

He gets up from his desk and leaves the room. I pull my collar away from my throat and lift the ponytail from the back of my neck. Every part of my body is clammy.

"Here," he says, placing a cup of water down in front of me. "Take a deep breath."

I sip the water first, then breathe deeply.

DS Harding moves back to behind his desk. "My sister has an anxiety disorder. I can always tell when she's not feeling well. She always goes very pale."

"Am I pale?" I ask.

He laughs. "Right now, you're Casper the ghost."

"Oh," I say, and then I laugh, too.

"You don't have to do this, you know. We can try and track Susie Patterson down another way." He laces his fingers and regards me.

I shake my head. "She's my best friend. I need to see her."

"Okay, but only if you're sure."

I take another sip of my water. "I can do this."

He smiles and it's surprisingly warm, making his eyes brighten. The left corner of his lips twitch and I'm suddenly drawn to his mouth. He's either impressed with my determination, or there's something he knows that I don't. I'm just not sure which it is.

CHAPTER SIXTEEN
JENNY'S DIARY

Susie thinks I'm funny. No one else thinks I am but Susie does and she's who matters. We went out into her mum's garden and I put a worm on my head! It was gross but it made her laugh. She doesn't smile or mess around as much now that she's having chemotherapy. Her hair is falling out and she doesn't like it.

I wouldn't like it, either. I think my hair is pretty. I think Susie's hair is pretty, too. Hers is bright like the sun and mine is like chocolate. At least that's what Susie says.

She feels poorly a lot of the time and sometimes her mum doesn't want me to go round to theirs. But I think I should go because I cheer Susie up. Like the time I ate marmite straight from the jar with a spoon!

Everyone at school is being really nice to Susie, but they weren't nice to her before. I don't like that.

What if Susie decides she likes them better now? What if she likes them better than me?

Okay, so I'm really going to make her laugh at school. I'm going to hang from the bars like a monkey for as long as I can.

I did it. At school today, I went on the playground, and I hung on the bar until my arms hurt. Ms Hunter came running out to get me down and Susie was really disappointed. She was counting and wanted to see how long I could stay.

We did this thing at school. We had an egg and we had to build a cage around it with ice lolly sticks and cotton wool and stuff. Then Ms Hunter dropped them all while she was standing on a chair. Susie did something that I didn't understand. She put her egg carefully in the pocket of her backpack. And then she told Ms Hunter that we didn't have one. I didn't say anything. But we got another egg.

Our egg came second to last in the competition. The one that won didn't break at all! I didn't like the way Ms Hunter told us we could do better. And I really didn't like the way she leaned down and went awwwww nevermind to Susie.

We're allowed to walk home as long as we stick with Billy's mum up until Sea View Close, which is where Billy and his mum turn off. We walk along the *close, then I turn left to go home. Susie lives right on the corner and my mum waits for me there.*

Ms Hunter lives in a house along Sea View Close. We know which one because we've seen her go in.

We walked down the road when Susie grabbed my hand. She grinned but I didn't know why. Then she told me her idea and I said no because we'd get in trouble. But Susie said so what. I guess she thought since she was ill, she could get away with things and I knew then that she was right. She pointed to Ms Hunter's house and said how her car wasn't there. Then she got the egg out of her bag.

Susie told me she wanted to do dares, too. It was funny when I did it, so she wanted to join in. She ran right up to the house and threw the egg at the door. Then her face lit all up and she ran back to me, laughing her head off. I was scared at first, but then I laughed, too, and we walked home in giggles. Mum asked me why I was laughing but I said it was something Susie did that was silly. She didn't say anything more.

Susie looked really tired after. Her face went white and I didn't like it.

Mum made me fish fingers with the smiley faced potato things I like. Then I did my homework and watched cartoons for a bit. I heard Mum talking on the phone and she said Susie's name, so I snuck down to the stairs to listen. That's when I heard her talking about how Susie is going to be too sick to go to school soon. It must have been Susie's mum. That means *I'll be all alone at school.*

CHAPTER SEVENTEEN

First thing Monday morning, when I knock on Trudy's office door, my heart pounds. This is such a bizarre thing to tell your boss. She calls me in, and I sense sweat beading on my upper lip.

"How was your weekend?" she asks.

"Well, I was in a police station," I admit. It feels good to get straight to the point.

She sits up straighter. "Oh. I hope there's nothing bad going on."

I take a seat in front of her desk. "Look, you know about my past, don't you? We never talk about it, but I know you know."

Her throat works as she swallows hard. I get the impression that Trudy tries not to think about me and the fact my best friend went missing all those years ago. Perhaps she worries if she does think about it, she'll start to think I had something to do with it.

"I know some of it," she says.

"I... I may have received a letter in the post from Susie," I say. "The girl who went missing."

"Wow. That's... huge." Trudy's eyes widen.

I nod. "Yeah, it's been a weird few days." Then I launch into the explanation. The woman on the train, the diary entries, and DS Harding with the idea for the surveillance.

"So you're meeting a missing person and a police officer in my apartment building?" she asks.

"Yep. Pretty much."

Trudy leans back in her chair. She lifts her eyes to the ceiling and lets out a long exhale. "Well, I did not expect this. You really do keep work interesting, Jenny." She sets herself upright again. "Okay. I mean, whatever you need. We're all about helping people here, aren't we? Susie obviously needs our help."

"I think she does," I admit. "Thank you so much. I really hope this will be the end of it all now."

"So do I, Jen."

There's sadness in Trudy's eyes when she smiles. I can't help but wonder what she's thinking. It almost felt like she was doubtful. I walk back to my desk on unsteady legs. I keep wondering how Susie is even going to get into the building. Because if she can't get in, we won't meet. And then all of this will be for nothing. No one will believe me. They'll assume I'm crazy and I'm making it all up for attention. People will believe I'm sending the pages of the diary to myself.

I skipped breakfast this morning—too worried I wouldn't keep it down. Every blond-headed person caught my eye on the walk here. As I make my way across to the apartment building, I do the same thing, scanning every face, searching for her. It's like I'm ghost hunting.

"Jenny."

Hearing my name makes my muscles clench. But it's just DS Harding waiting for me outside the building.

"Hi," I say.

"Are you ready for this?" His tone makes the words sound doubtful.

In a way, his lack of faith is exactly what I need. I punch the door code in with extra force. "Yes. I'm ready."

I snatch open the door and head in, making sure to hold it open for him. Then we make our way to the lifts and head up to the third floor.

"Do you often work in supply closets, DS Harding?" I ask, ensuring I use the most condescending tone.

"Oh, I work everywhere," he says in a husky voice. "I'm not afraid of getting my hands dirty."

The blood rushes to my cheeks. The word "dirty" has never had an effect on me before, but then I've never heard DS Harding say it.

"This way," he says.

The room is tiny. I knock over a mop on the way in and then a sponge falls off the shelf when I turn.

"Watch it," he says, this time with humour in his voice. "Bloody hell, you're wrecking the joint. I'll have you for vandalism."

He grins but doesn't bother picking up the sponge. "Right. Come on then. Let's get you fitted."

"Do I... do I need to remove my blouse?" I ask.

DS Harding clears his throat as he opens the box containing the wire, breaking the brief moment of silence that followed my question. "No. But you will need to unbutton it." He doesn't look at me and I notice his broad shoulders tense.

He places the open box on a shelf and his gaze finally meets mine. "Is that okay? I could call in and see if my female colleague is free?"

"We're all grown-ups here," I say. And yet my fingers tremble as I unbutton the shirt.

It reveals my blue t-shirt bra. It's possibly my least flattering bra, because when I was getting ready this morning, I refused to allow myself to gussy-up for him.

DS Harding takes a step forward with the wire in his hands. His hazel eyes are open wide, fixed on the area above my chest, and there's a tense smile stretched across his face.

"I'm going to have to tape this here. Is that okay?"

"Sure," I say. "That's fine."

His fingers are long, I notice, as attaches the microphone just under my collar bone. And then he cuts a few strips of tape and applies them gently to the device. Every stroke of his fingers makes my skin thrum with electricity. I stop looking at him and stare at the shelves behind his head instead.

I don't understand why this is so exciting. Or why my body responds to each brush of his fingertips. And then I realise I haven't had sex in a very, very long time.

"I'm sorry about this," he says. "It's the oldest bit of equipment we have. Everything else was already checked out."

"It's fine," I say, my heart hammering.

"How are you feeling?" he asks.

I button up my blouse. "I have no idea. I don't think the world prepares you for this sort of... thing." I make sure to button it up to the collar so that Susie doesn't notice the microphone when she arrives. "What time is it?"

"Just after twelve. You have less than an hour now." He takes a laptop out of his bag and sets it up awkwardly on a shelf with a bucket on it.

"Maybe I should wait outside the building for her," I say.

"Okay," he says. "Try to stay nice and relaxed, okay, Jenny?"

I open my mouth to say something smart about him talking to me like I'm going to bust a drug deal, but then I think about what it will be like to see Susie again, and I don't feel like being smart anymore. So I nod, and then I take the lift down to the ground floor. But Susie isn't there. I head back up to the supply closet.

"She's not coming," I say, walking in without knocking.

"It's only 12:43," he says. "She said 1 p.m., remember? Look, I wonder if you need to go up on the roof and wait for her there. She might have a plan about how to get around the passcode issue. Or maybe she's watching from a different building in the area."

"If she's in another building, I won't know," I say, panicking at the thought of not actually meeting her today. "There are like five other apartment blocks around here. And if she's in one of them, that means she has no intention of meeting me. Of putting all of this to rest and making things right." I'm filled with excess energy. I pace back and forth, wringing my hands.

DS Harding glances away. He seems sympathetic. Pitying even. "No, maybe she doesn't. There's a chance she's messing with you."

I turn sharply towards him. "What? Why?"

"I don't know." He shrugs. "Perhaps it's some sort of test. If you do as she asks now, she'll be more willing to meet you later."

I consider this for a moment. Maybe he's right.

"Like she's testing the water to make sure I'm up for the challenge."

That does sound like Susie. She never made anything easy.

"Exactly that," DS Harding says.

"I should just go up there and do it then?" I ask.

"If you want to."

It's such a loaded statement. Why would I want to do any

of this? The old me would find looking down at a long drop to be baby stuff. We would have done this easily when we were seven years old. I think of us running away from Ms Hunter's house. The yolk trickling down the blue paint.

I still have to try.

"I want to," I finally say.

"Okay," he says. "Take your time. Be careful. Remember to breathe. Choose a spot on the roof where you feel comfortable and safe. I'm right here if you need me."

"What if I see Susie?"

"Keep her talking," he says.

"Okay," I say.

It all sounds so simple.

CHAPTER EIGHTEEN

The fire escape door weighs heavy against my palms. And then the winter wind hits me square in the face, taking my breath away. I gasp and pull a strand of hair from the corner of my mouth.

Tugging the collar of my coat closer to my throat, I step out onto the roof and take in the sight. Nerves tingle in the pit of my stomach. Anxious thoughts flood my mind. What if the listening device doesn't pick up our voices under my coat? It's too cold to take it off. I walk towards the centre of the roof and the Harrison Park suburb stretches before me, criss-crossed with lines of terraced houses and bare trees, the occasional supermarket or car park sprawling out until a patchwork of concrete and glass marks Manchester itself. For a moment, I close my eyes and pretend I'm back at Chillingham-by-the-Sea, able to taste the salt in the air. I picture seagulls circling above, their raucous song ringing in my ears. I feel Susie's small hand in mine.

My eyes snap open. I take a few steps forward and it's as though my soul leaves my body. I'm a ghost watching my body move around the roof. The world blurs at the corners like a damaged VHS tape.

Susie is not here.

Old leaves and a torn crisp packet travel across the roof with the breeze. Up ahead there's a flimsy-looking metal barrier to stop someone stepping off the edge of the building by accident. No one is supposed to be up here aside from construction workers or engineers.

I remember DS Harding down in the supply closet and decide to give him some information. "It's windy and empty up here. I can't see Susie." I rub my arms. "It's so cold."

I take a few tentative steps towards the barrier, my chest tightening. When the world tilts and a rush of dizziness washes over me, I pause and pull in five deep breaths. Then I scan the windows of the building opposite. There's no way I can see her from here, but maybe she's watching me.

The wind stings my eyes and I feel tears forming. I glance back towards the fire escape door, willing it to open.

Let the fear set you free.

I don't remember the day we made up the rhyme. No doubt we were messing around with Susie's recording set, singing Spice Girls songs and dancing. Sometimes we invented silly lyrics and screamed them into the microphone. All I know is the rhyme became part of the ritual.

One, two, three.
Dare you, Dare me.
One, two, three.
Let the fear set you free.
One, two, three,
Follow you, follow me.
One, two, three.
Let the fear set you free.

Words are powerful. A manifesto can change the world.

Our mantra changed us from timid schoolgirls into reckless, wild teens.

Susie internalised the meaning fervently. She had so much more at stake. The dares were her way of taking back control, of acting like the cancer didn't own her. I think I knew that even as a child—on a subconscious, instinctual level rather than intellectually. Now I know how to articulate it. I understand the need for Susie, made powerless by her illness, to reclaim that power.

Where are you, Susie?

The closest building is another apartment block identical to this one. Owned by the same company no doubt. Many of the windows are visible, but I don't see anyone standing at them.

And then I hear a whirring sound over the wind. A head rises up from the side of the building, emerging, shockingly, not unlike the meerkat imagery DS Harding put into my mind. I gasp. And then I realise it isn't a head at all, but it is small and round. It's white and plastic and wobbles slightly in the wind. It hovers above the building, staring at me. A drone.

"Fuck," I blurt out. "Susie?"

I realise that I need to describe to DS Harding what's going on.

"There's a drone on the roof," I say out loud. "I guess it's the kind with a camera and is here to record me doing the dare." I swallow. This means I have to do it.

"Susie?" I shout over the wind. "Can you hear me?"

I know nothing about drones. But if they have cameras, they might also have microphones, right? It's a long shot.

I try to take a step forward, but my knees feel weak. "Susie, I can't do this." I take a deep breath, trying to remember the circular breathing that calms me when I feel a panic attack coming on. Anxiety pulls every muscle taut, squeezing me, like my entire body is in a vice. "Susie, I'm not the same person anymore. I can't..."

The barrier is about an arm's distance from me now. I reach out and my fingertips brush the cold metal. They tremble, my fingernails blue from the cold.

"I don't want to fail. I really don't." It feels completely ridiculous talking to a drone, but here I am, in the midst of a panic attack, telling a chunk of floating plastic that I'm absolutely scared shitless. "Fuck. Fuck. Fuck."

I stagger back, tripping over a ridge. I land on my backside with a smack and place my head between my knees for a moment. The rooftop sways under my body while the whirring drone and whistling wind circles me.

"This is ridiculous, Jenny. All you have to do is look down. There's a barrier for God's sake. Do it. Just fucking do it." I climb to my feet and take two steps forward. This time I'm close enough that my hands can wrap around the barrier. "Just look down. It's not that bad. *Look down!*"

On instinct, my left-hand flexes and reaches out from my side. I half expect Susie's hand to entwine with mine. And then I feel the soft touch of skin against my fingertips. When I sharply turn my head, instead of my missing friend, DS Harding is standing next to me.

"You can do this, Jenny," he says.

His hazel eyes are warm against the pale, cloudy sky that stretches across the horizon. Strands of his chestnut hair fly around his face. I never noticed how tall he is, and I certainly didn't notice the solidity of his body, the broadness of his chest. His hand is warm in mine and that warmth chases some of the panic away.

I take another step. Tears stream down my cheeks, but I don't care. I bend my knees and duck down. If I'm going to do this, I'm going to do it right. DS Harding's grip tightens. He has me. I can do this. I push my head between the top and middle barrier, careful not to lean my full weight against the metal. I do not trust a structure that was built on a roof without access to the general public.

And then I look down.

The length of the building swoops like a treacherous ski slope. There at the bottom is the pavement and the parked cars dotted along the road. People go about their day, completely oblivious to the anxiety-filled woman completing a ridiculous dare.

I pull my head back and sit down.

"I did it," I say, my voice a quiet rasp stolen by the wind.

"You did it," DS Harding repeats. He crouches down to my height and smiles. Then he turns towards the drone. But before DS Harding can do anything, it disappears from sight. "Come on, let's get you inside."

I nod, allowing him to pull me to my feet. In one last desperate attempt to see my long-lost friend, I allow my gaze to roam the empty roof, but she isn't there. She isn't ready to reveal herself yet.

CHAPTER NINETEEN

"Well, I'm afraid I can't search the apartment building," DS Harding says. "The flats are private property, obviously, and I'd need a warrant. She may know someone who lives in the building and is operating the drone from a room nearby."

I'm bundled up in my coat with a mug of steaming hot tea in my hands. Trudy has leant us her office while she's with a client in a meeting room. The familiarity of the setting comforts me.

He glances at his watch. "I'm sorry to ditch you but I have to get back to the station."

I shake my head. "Of course. You have proper work to do. You can't spend all day on a wild goose chase with me."

He raises his eyebrows when I say that. "Do you mind if I level with you, Jenny?"

"Level away." I lift a hand to demonstrate levelling.

"Susie Patterson's disappearance was huge news and finding her would be a great boon for our department. It would close a case that has been open for sixteen years. But she isn't a criminal, as far as we know, so I have to tread carefully here. I can't overstep. And, yes, I have other cases to take care of."

"That's good to know," I say. "Thank you for the tea." It surprises me to hear the note of disappointment in my voice. The stupid, lizard part of my brain might have thought that he prioritised this because he liked me, not because he wanted to close an old case. I think about his fingers in mine. But it was friendly support, nothing more. A young detective eager to see if the famous Susie Patterson really was going to turn up.

"I could put in a few calls to the police officers who handled the case in Chillingham if—"

"No," I say. My fingers tighten around the mug.

"You didn't have a good experience with them, did you?"

The stark interrogation room pops into my mind. Tears falling on the desk. My mum arguing with the police officers. Me, scared of my broken brain, willing it to work, to remember. Praying to God that I would just remember what happened to Susie.

"I'm sorry," he says. "And I'm sorry she didn't turn up today."

"Deep down I knew she wouldn't. Deep, deep down." I sip the tea, letting its warmth spread through my body.

DS Harding leaves and there's not much else for me to do except go back to work. Trudy asks me a few questions at the end of the day, but I mostly fob her off with non-committal responses. Still, she's not a psychologist for nothing, so I can tell she reads between the lines.

It takes a while to shake the anxiety from being on the roof. For the rest of the day, my stomach is in knots, and I barely eat a thing. Later I'll binge on something and feel even worse. But at least now I've learned that's my coping mechanism. And tomorrow I can do something good for my body. Or at least try. That's the idea.

The anxiety is harder to shake than usual. Perhaps it's because I'm playing the waiting game. Unless Susie is offended by the fact that DS Harding joined me, she's probably going to send me another portion of my diary along with a second challenge. The next challenge will be harder than the first. I don't know what she'll have in store for me but it's going to be worse than looking down from a great height.

I wonder if she enjoys this, in a sick and twisted way. She knows the kind of responsibility she's laying on my shoulders. If I perform her challenges, then I may be able to reunite a lost daughter with the woman who has spent sixteen years asking me for answers. If I don't, Susie remains a ghost. She's dead to the world. A murder victim. And I will remain the murderer to the Susie Patterson Truthers. Me or my father, anyway.

She knew which train I took to Solace, and she knows where I work. What else does she know about me? That I've had anxiety issues since she disappeared? That my boyfriend cheated on me? That I'm a mess? Maybe this is her fucked up way of fixing me.

As soon as the clock hits five, I grab my coat and leave.

My body loosens as I walk the last ten minutes home. Freezing rain pelts down from the black sky, hitting my hood with a pattering sound. Back at home, I shrug away the coat and uncoil the last of the tension in my limbs. It's pizza night for me. I need carbs. And while I wait, I go through all my old photos again. None of it helps. Nothing jumps out at me. I wish I had the diary pages in my hand instead of the photographed versions. Even the touch and smell of them could jog something.

The pizza arrives and shortly after, Harry arrives home. He walks into the house still in his own world, whistling a romantic tune. God, I hate being around people who have recently fallen in love.

"Would you like a slice?" I ask.

"I'm good," he says. "I ate at Hannah's."

"Cool." I'm secretly relieved. I hate sharing takeaways.

"Everything okay?" he asks. "Sorry I haven't been around much."

"Actually, I have a lot going on right now," I say.

"Oh." He flops down on the sofa next to me. "Wanna talk about it?"

I fold the box over the pizza and place it to one side. DS Harding has not sworn me to secrecy. But on the other hand, neither of us would want any of this getting out into the media. I cringe, thinking about the circus that would ensue, along with it, the possibility of those letters starting up again.

"It's something serious, isn't it?" He frowns before tentatively placing a hand on my arm. "Oh, God. You're not ill, are you?"

I laugh. "No. I'm fine. Well, apart from the usual memory stuff."

There's a chance that some of the warm feelings I've built up about Harry influence my decision, but at that moment, I decide to trust him. I tell him all about the diary pages and the challenges. Even to my ears, it sounds unbelievable in a bad way. Harry simply listens quietly before nodding his head.

"Wow," he says.

"I know."

"Wow," he says again, leaning against the sofa.

"Yup."

"Jenny, you have lived the most extraordinary life."

The words make me tingle all over, as though I've listened to a hauntingly beautiful piece of music. Extraordinary is not a word I would ever say about myself, but I can't deny that many strange things have happened to me.

"Are you sure this person is a friend? Because it doesn't seem like she is."

With that one line, I splinter in two.

"What do you mean?" I ask breathlessly.

"It seems as though she's toying with you," he replies.

"N-no," I say. "She... she was my... my best friend."

His expression turns from awe to pity and that fleeting moment of self-possession slips away. I'm butter on a hot knife melting onto the floor.

"She must know what she's doing to you," he continues. "She knows what she's putting you through, right? She disappears for sixteen years and then comes back to send you snippets of your diaries and make you perform like a... like a dancing bear."

I frown. "I... I don't know if she realises how anxious I am now. I wasn't like that before. We did this kind of thing all the time—"

"But if she watched you through the drone, she saw your panic attack. And she made you do it anyway. That's messed up."

I hadn't thought about it like that.

"Well, maybe it was too late by then," I say. But the words sound hollow even to me.

Harry continues. "If she asks you to do more than this one challenge, or if she holds all of this over your head, then... I don't know, I just don't think that's a very friend-like thing to do." He lifts his palms. "I don't like her or what she's doing to you."

"You don't know her," I snap. "And you don't know our friendship."

He flinches slightly. "Hey, I know. I'm sorry, I overstepped."

"No, I'm sorry." I let out a long exhale and shake my head. "I think you might have hit a nerve. DS Harding mentioned that Susie might not be the same person."

"He's right," Harry says. "Honestly, all of this feels incredibly cruel, and I don't believe a good person would do this."

I pick at the edge of the pizza box. "It's fine. I swear. It's just repeating old kids' stuff. Like an inside joke."

His expression is tight. I can tell he doesn't believe that at all. "Please promise me that you'll be careful. Don't underestimate this person."

I flash him a wide grin. "I promise."

But I'm not sure I'm telling the truth.

CHAPTER TWENTY

In the end, I do take Harry's advice. I try my best not to focus on Susie, even though every time the phone rings I hope it's going to be DS Harding. I fantasise about her walking into the nearest police station, or even coming to the house.

I spend Tuesday afternoon at Solace answering calls. With Christmas just a few weeks away, there are many calls from lonely people. I spend an hour on the phone with a widow with nowhere to go at Christmas. Then I speak to a teenager who feels alienated from her religious parents because she doesn't share their beliefs. Family arguments are already ramping up due to the stress of December. Inevitably, it makes me think about my own parents.

Mum, worn down by the media attention after Susie's disappearance, growing weaker with stress. Dad turning to drink. It was a painful time. I try to pull my thoughts away from the past and focus on the present. At the end of my shift, I book in another extra session with Raj to try and ground myself.

When I first started hypnosis, I was full of nervous anticipation of what I might uncover. I imagined all kinds of morbid memories rising to the surface. But after years of uncovering nothing, arriving at Raj's office became a dull, monotonous routine. I'd often cancel appointments, considering them pointless. Jack always said I was wasting my money. That I'd may as well flush it down the toilet. And yet I never gave them up because all I need is *one* session. One moment of clarity where it all comes flooding back to me.

The nerves return, prickling my belly. There's a chance now. I'm closer to the past than I have been for a very long time. The answers are coming but I don't know what form they'll take. It could be today, in this session. Or it could be next week. Or it could be when Susie reveals herself to me.

I'm in a daze on the journey there. I'm swift among the shadowed streets peppered by Christmas lights. My trainers slip on the damp pavements. A fluttering heart won't settle beneath layers of wool and cotton and skin and meat and bone. I drag my fingers through my damp hair when he lets me in. We say hello and then head through to our usual room.

Raj is as relaxed as always on his chair. He nods to the recliner. "Get yourself comfortable. Take some deep breaths." His voice slows as he talks. "I want you to count backwards..."

He goes on.

I sink into the leather.

My body is resistant at first but as I recite the numbers backwards, the room melts away. Susie is usually the first thing on my mind, but this time I find myself on the roof with DS Harding's fingers entwined in mine. There's the barest citrus scent in the air, his aftershave. Pinpricks move up and down my arms as I force the memory away. I'm here to think about Susie, not another crush that's going nowhere.

Instead, I imagine myself sitting on the carpet next to Susie's bed. She has her Barbie dolls lined up on the duvet and is giving one a haircut. We draw love hearts on her face in red ink. Susie colours what's left of her white-blonde hair with a purple felt pen.

"I don't want to die," she says. "Daddy died. I hate him for it."

Then we're older. Thirteen maybe. Years after she beat the cancer and stayed in remission. We're in a car alone. Susie is driving even though she doesn't know how to. She presses her foot against the accelerator, and I yelp her name in terror. We're on a back road. We stole it from the yard of some old farm near our house. Whenever we'd walk past, Susie would always say the owner never locked it and sometimes left the key in the ignition. It had been our challenge that month.

"I don't like it!" I shout over the sound of the engine.

It's an old car. It has eighties plates, I think. It goes faster and faster until it makes a weird noise.

"You have to change gear!" I shout.

"How do I do that?" She shouts.

"The clutch! Push it in!"

Susie rams the clutch pedal down and I move the gear stick into second gear. The car goes even faster.

"Slow down!" I scream.

She laughs. It's not normal. It's like a hyena with gleeful braying. We're all over the road, unable to stay in a straight line. Susie keeps veering into the opposite lane and if a car—or God forbid a van or tractor—comes around the bend, we're fucked.

"I'm serious now," I shout. "Slow down or we're going to die."

She pushes the accelerator harder. The car races around a corner and my stomach flies up to my heart and back down again.

"Not until you enjoy it," Susie says.

I screw my eyes closed as we careen around another bend. But when I open them again, we're on a long stretch of straight road with nothing ahead. The sea stretches out to my left, far away in the distance. It's a beautiful spring day and the windows are open. I shove my head out of the window and let out a primal scream to no one.

"Yes, Jenny!" she yells.

She changes gear and the car jolts. And then she screams, too. I laugh, pulling my head back into the car and putting my feet up on the dashboard. Susie lifts her hands from the wheel and for the briefest of seconds, the sense of immortality washes over us both.

Let the fear set you free.

We believed every word. But we were young and stupid.

She finally stops the car because the petrol needle hits low, and we don't want something bad to happen. And then we have to walk all the way home in the bright sunshine. By the time we reach the town, it's dark and our shins are dusty. My dad screams at me when I walk through the door.

"You're not going to that girl's house ever again!" he shouts. "She's a bad influence."

"Whatever." I sneer. And then I run up the stairs and slam the door.

Downstairs Mum and Dad argue about what to do with me. My schoolwork is suffering. I spend too much time with Susie. Our parents can't keep track of us. We sneak out of our rooms before breakfast. We return with dirty or wet clothes from walking along the beach or running through the fields.

"She's out of control, Dee," Dad says in a whining, woeful voice.

When I flop on the bed and pull on my headphones, I wonder if he's right. It makes me sad. I love Susie and I want to make her happy, but I love my parents, too. They're not happy with me. We are wild. We stole a car, and, at that moment, I didn't care if we got caught. I don't care about the consequences anymore. Neither does Susie. We started out doing things that scared us, but nothing scares her anymore.

PJ Harvey wails into my ears. Susie told me to check her out and said she's better than the boy bands at number one. She's right. Susie is always right.

I should just trust my best friend. Shouldn't I?

But as I'm about to pull myself from the hypnotic state, a new sensation squirms under my skin. Like snakes nested in my abdomen, wriggling and writhing. My skin blasts hot, like I've stepped into a blazing sauna, and I grip hold of the arm rests of Raj's leather recliner.

"You're in a safe space, Jenny," Raj says, his voice soft and soothing. "I'd like you to count down from ten and then open your eyes. Gently peel away from wherever you are."

"No," I say.

I don't know why I say it. All I know is that my body rejects his suggestion. Someone lets out a low, heartbreaking whimper, like a wounded baby animal. It's me. I'm making that sound.

"Jenny, take a deep breath. Breathe with me. In... 1... 2... 3... 4."

I pitch forward, landing on the carpet by the chair. And then my stomach lurches and I purge.

He hurries towards me and places a hand on my back. "You're okay." There's a tremor in his voice. He's concerned but desperately trying to hide it. "Everything is okay. This is a safe space."

My abdomen contracts and the last of my lunch comes out of me. Appalled, I fall back, trying to get away from my vomit. "God. I'm so sorry. I don't know why..." I trail off.

There's a sheen of sweat spreading all over my freezing cold body.

Raj disappears for a moment and returns with two towels and a glass of water. He places one towel over the sick, and gives me the other, along with the water.

"It's okay, Jenny. Take your time. Would you like to sit on the chair?"

I shake my head.

"What about my chair?" he asks.

"Okay."

After I drink a little water, Raj lifts me back on my feet and helps me settle into his chair. He disappears from the room again and I get the impression he's cancelling his next appointment.

"Sorry," I say. "I'm being a hassle."

"Don't be sorry. I should apologise for not bringing you back sooner. You seemed so comfortable. You described being in the car. And then your parents arguing. Is that what frightened you? Hearing the argument between your parents?"

I shake my head. "I don't remember what it was. Something shifted."

"A new memory, perhaps?" he asks.

"I don't know." I sip the water again, trying to rid my mouth of the foul taste.

"Breathe with me," he says and guides me through meditation.

At the end, I close my eyes. I see it. Just a flash. I pull in a sharp gasp.

"Jenny? Are you okay?" Raj asks.

"I'm fine," I lie. "I'm so sorry for the mess. I think I need to go home now."

He nods. He offers me an arm to cling onto as I stand.

His brown eyes regard me steadily. He doesn't know what

I saw. The churning water, bubbling and thrashing. Dark, inky water, the kind that has a depth to it, that hides all manner of dangers underneath its surface.

I am connected to that water. I know that water. Something happened in that water.

Something I don't remember.

CHAPTER TWENTY-ONE

With the past coming back to haunt me, I feel as though I'm a teenage girl again. It's not a place I feel comfortable with, but it might be where I need to live in order to survive what I'm about to face.

After a sleepless night, I spend an hour trying to reach my GP the morning after my hypnosis session. It's been a long time since I took anxiety medication, but I need it now. Even being in bed, my heart races. Every time I close my eyes, I see the same churning waters that invaded my mind during hypnosis. It seems important and it definitely seems familiar, but I don't even know if it's real. It could be a figment of my own imagination for all I know. It could be a nightmare.

I call in sick.

Outside my bedroom window, tiny snowflakes dance in the air. There's a frigidness to the white sky. I'm still in my pyjamas after giving up on the doctor's appointment. I climb back into bed and turn on the television.

A few hours into mindless reality TV, my phone rings. I'm about to cancel the call when I recognise DS Harding's number. Not wanting to miss any new developments, I reluctantly answer.

"Hello."

"Hi... um, are you okay, Ms Woods."

I balk slightly at the "Ms Woods" I had hoped I was Jenny by now. "I'm fine. Why?"

"Nothing, you just sound a little..."

"Tired?" I suggest.

"Perhaps." He clears his throat. "Is it a convenient time to talk about the case?"

"Yes," I say, willing him to say more. "Have you found her?"

"No," he replies. "But I do have some CCTV images I'd like you to look at. That way we can eliminate people matching the description who aren't Susie Patterson. When can you come into the station."

I sigh. "In about an hour, I guess."

"Well, I wouldn't want to put you out," he says, his tone slightly huffy.

"You're not," I reply.

"Good. So I guess I'll see you in an hour."

"Yep. That's what I said. One hour. Great comprehension skills."

I hang up.

I'm definitely going to end up being arrested by that man one of these days.

I take twenty minutes longer than I estimated. Part of that is due to rail delays. The other is me dragging my feet. The journey is unpleasant. My heart won't calm, and I sense my body is in flight or fight mode the entire time. Anxiety is an exhausting condition. I go about my regular tasks and the whole time my body acts like I'm in the fight of my life. That spike of adrenaline, the catch in my breath, the tightness in my chest, the sense of not pulling enough oxygen into my body.

At least now I know what to expect when I walk into a police station. DS Harding waits by the reception desk and leads me through to this messy office.

"I see you tidied up for company," I say sarcastically.

He lets out a derisive snort and places a set of photos on the desk.

I squint. "Can't you make these less blurry? You know, enhance them? Like they do on the TV shows." I smirk to myself when he pulls a face. Teasing DS Harding makes my crappy days a little brighter.

I'm not sure what it is about this detective that brings out my dry sense of humour, but for some reason, he does. With all the stressful events going on surrounding Susie and the past, it's a nice change of pace.

"You know, police work is not like TV. This isn't Luther, Jenny." His voice is stern and dry but there's a definite glint in his eyes.

Him using my first name makes me smile. But that isn't a road I want to go down. I force myself to concentrate. Finding Susie is what matters.

"I think this could be her," I say, pointing to a slim figure in dark clothing. "It's hard to tell because she's wearing a hat here and it's mostly covering her hair. But the jacket looks right. And the shape of her nose is... familiar."

"And you think this is Susie Patterson?" he asks. "And you're sure it was her on the train? Sixteen years is a long time."

"I mean, it has to be," I say. "This all started when I saw

her on the train. Who else would send me my diary piece by piece?"

He takes the photograph from my fingers in complete silence.

"Oh," I say, and my heart sinks. "You think I'm doing this to myself?" I lean back against the chair, floored by this sudden realisation. DS Harding's expression remains impassive, but I know it on an instinctual level, and I have to say it hurts a lot. It hurts enough to make my eyes burn. "Do you think I'm crazy?"

"No," he says quietly.

"Well, that sounds convincing." I get to my feet. I'm on the brink of losing my emotional shit and I don't want him to see it. "You know what? I'm going to leave. I don't want to be around someone who doesn't believe me."

"Jenny, wait. I'm sorry." He lifts his palms, placating me. "I'm a detective, I have to keep my mind open to all possibilities. I don't think you're crazy at all." He holds out one arm as though he wants to reach out and take my hand. But then it drops to the desk. "Have you eaten today?"

I shake my head.

"Can I buy you a sandwich?"

The offer takes me aback, but I just blink and say, "Okay."

CHAPTER TWENTY-TWO

"I think I'm going to go with the tuna melt. What about you?" he asks.

I still feel on the backfoot and feeling uncertain about this odd lunch date. Especially considering he's the detective helping me find Susie but also a man I'm developing unprofessional feelings for.

"The hummus salad bowl, please." I smile at the waitress and hand over the menu.

The place is nice. When he asked me to go for a sandwich, I figured it would be a convenience shop sandwich or a café. Instead, we ended up in a decent Gastro pub close to the police station.

"Look, I know this is unusual," he says. "Trust me. I do not make it a habit inviting… um…" He searches for the word.

"Suspects?" I offer.

He smiles. "No. I wasn't going to say that."

"I'm either a victim or a suspect. Those are the two choices."

His eyes narrow. "Do you really believe that? With all the

complexities in the world? You think you're either a victim or a suspect and nothing in between?"

"Why do you sound so confident that I'd know how the world works?" I place both arms on the table and lean towards him, interested in what he has to say.

"No one could go through the things you've been through and not come out the other side without reassessing their view of the world. I guess that's one thing coppers and the people involved in a crime have in common. Perspective."

"Yeah, but that's assuming someone is willing to change their view on the world. Loads of people go through a life changing event and are too stubborn to change."

He shakes his head. "Not you."

The waitress brings over two diet Cokes. DS Harding takes a sip.

"I suffered a brain injury," I point out. "Maybe it stunted my growth."

He frowns. "But you went to university. You volunteer as well as work a full-time job. That doesn't sound like someone whose injury held them back."

"No, I suppose not." I sigh. Then I wag a finger at him. "You know an awful lot about me. Have you been keeping an eye on me, DS Harding?"

He shrugs. "I'm a detective, what do you expect?"

"I guess."

He's quiet for a moment. I suspect that he's waiting for me to fill the silence. It's probably a trick that police officers use during interrogation. It works.

"I just wish I could remember everything," I blurt. "That's what holds me back. The missing piece of the puzzle. The part of me that no longer exists is also the part that could tell me what happened to Susie."

"I'm sorry, that must be hard," he says.

I raise an eyebrow. "Well, if this is going where I think it's going, Susie will—eventually—tell me herself."

DS Harding says nothing. I can't shake the feeling that he's assessing me. There's a chance this lunch is a way for him to figure out if I'm telling the truth, or if I'm a big fat liar.

"What's your first name?" I ask, hoping it might interrupt his train of thought.

He grins.

"It's only fair," I say. "You've been calling me Jenny for a while now."

"Liam," he says.

"DS Liam Harding," I say. "I like it."

"What, do you want my middle name, too?"

"Why not?"

"Victor."

"Oh no. Really? Liam Victor Harding."

He laughs. "That's right. My mum's favourite book is Les Misérables."

"And musical?" I ask.

"Yes, she likes that, too."

"Well, now I know quite a lot about DS Harding."

"Yes," he says. "You do."

The waitress is back with our meals. I suddenly feel self-conscious about eating in front of him. But DS Harding—Liam—tucks straight in and I do the same. My mind overflows with racing thoughts. Our relationship has become something unusual. Maybe I'm deluded and he hopes I'll drop my guard and blurt out a confession. Getting Jenny Woods to confess to the murder of Susie Patterson all these years later would certainly be a career changing event for any officer of the law.

"You look deep in thought," he says.

I swallow. "I suppose I wonder why you brought me here."

"It's a fair question," he says. "Honestly, you looked stressed, and I thought you needed some food. When I get anxious, I find eating a decent meal always helps."

"Do you get anxious a lot?" I ask.

He shrugs. "It comes with the job."

"How do you deal with it? The job, I mean."

He places his sandwich down and regards me. "It used to be booze. These days it's eight hours of sleep a night and a multivitamin."

"I go to hypnotherapy," I say. "Though it's not for my anxiety. It's to help me remember."

"Does it work?" he asks.

"It wasn't working." I glance down at my salad, pushing hummus and grated carrot around the bowl. "Until I saw her on the train. Now I keep getting these memories, but none of them are useful." I think of the dark, swirling water. I drop my fork.

"What's wrong?" Liam asks.

I shake my head. "Nothing."

He doesn't push it. We continue eating and our conversation moves onto the case. He doesn't reveal too much information but lets me know they're working hard to find a lead on Susie's whereabouts. They're currently checking the area where the envelope was posted. And checking for drone users who requested permission to fly in the Harrison Park area. But the longer he talks, the more I think what they're doing is worthless. Susie won't come out of hiding until she's ready.

At the end, I offer to pay but Liam won't hear of it. So I thank him and tell him to stay in touch with me about the case.

"Of course I will," he says. "I know how much this means to you."

His voice is so tender that I replay the words over and over in my mind all the way home. Snowflakes coat my eyelashes, but I don't mind. It cools my hot skin. I almost forget to check every seat on the train just in case I see *her* one more time.

The giddy distraction means I'm completely unprepared for what I find on the doormat. Harry hasn't been home yet today, so the post waits for me. There's the usual. Bills. A clothing catalogue I never signed up for. Takeaway menus. And a large brown envelope with a printed label on the front.

Susie.

CHAPTER TWENTY-THREE
JENNY'S DIARY

We did it, we did it, we did it.
Aaaahhhh!!
I don't even know where to begin.
So today is Saturday the 14th April 2001. It's almost five and I'll have to go downstairs for tea soon, but I want to write down everything that happened because today was the best day ever.

I didn't even want to do it, but Susie said we should. We had to sneak out of her house without her mum noticing. And then we ran all the way to the cliff that overlooks the bay. We've been there so many times but never on our own. We're not allowed there on our own.

It was so scary.

Susie is still a bit bald from all the chemo, but there's some hair coming through. It's like sunshine-blonde now. It's really pretty. It was so warm today.

We took our cardigans off and carried them all the way there.

I asked Susie if we were really going to do this. The cliff is so high up. People jump off it all the time but they're usually so much older than us. She said she had to. And then we sat down next to the cliff, and we made up a rhyme to make ourselves feel better.

When we stood up and took off our shoes and walked up to the edge of the cliff, Susie held my hand. She looked so brave. She is brave. She went through all those tests and surgeries and took all the medicine. She said it hurt so much and made her sick everywhere. So I had to be brave, too. It's only fair.

I agreed because I haven't taken any medicine or had a needle in my arm. I've been fine, haven't I? And that isn't fair because Susie hurts a lot and I haven't hurt at all. I need to make it right.

We stood at the edge, and it was scary. The water looked so far away. It was kinda dark. And it moved around a lot. Susie asked me if I was ready and then we counted down from ten. My voice was all shaky.

My tummy felt funny when we jumped off. Like it flipped over. And then we fell, and I screamed so loud! The water was so cold! I had to remember to paddle with my feet and hands like they showed us at school, but it was so cold, I could hardly move. I couldn't see Susie. I shouted her name, but I couldn't see her anywhere.

I splashed around in the sea shouting her name. There was water everywhere. Up my nose, in my eyes. I saw it moving, like splashing and spraying all over. I thought Susie had died and I started to cry. I kept shouting her name. Then she popped up from the water. She coughed and I grabbed her arms to make sure she didn't drift off. Once she stopped coughing, she laughed, and I was really mad because I'd thought she'd died. I was so scared, but she wasn't scared at all. She thought it was funny!

We paddled our way to the beach and sat there for a minute in the sun, trying to dry off. Then we had to walk all the way back around to the top of the cliff to get our shoes. I felt strange, like I'd done something that should make me feel different. And maybe I did feel different, but I wasn't sure. Susie kept grinning and laughing and grabbing my hand. She kept saying that we'd done it. Like it was this big thing. Like getting full marks in a test at school.

And then I realised we were going to be in sooooo much trouble. Our clothes were soaking wet! What were our parents going to say? Susie didn't seem to care.

I dragged my feet on the way home, super scared. Maybe someone saw us jump off the cliff. We planned to tell Susie's mum that we paddled on the beach and fell over. She'd be so mad if she knew the truth. There was no way Mrs Patterson would let me play with Susie if she knew.

When we walked down the drive towards Susie's house, Mrs Patterson came running out at full speed. My heart started beating super fast and I thought I was going to have a heart attack! But then she slowed down and stopped right before us. Susie said something really quiet, like I think she asked if her mum was okay.

Mrs Patterson asked us where we'd been, and we started lying about what we'd done. Then Mrs Patterson interrupted us and told us it didn't matter. I thought she was about to yell at us. Susie held my hand. I stared down at my wet shoes and the puddle on the driveway. I figured she'd ring my mum to tell her how naughty I was. But she didn't do any of that.

She pulled Susie into this big hug, and she started crying and she wouldn't let her go. And then she hugged me, too. And then she stood up straight and she told us today is a good day because Susie doesn't have cancer anymore.

Susie isn't going to die! She's better! She's finally better!

Mrs Patterson dried our hair and clothes and we put on pyjamas and watched a movie until it was time for me to go home.

I'm so happy! My bestest friend is okay again!

But when I was leaving, Susie said something weird.

She said that it was because we jumped into the

sea. She said we made it happen. She said that when we did something scary, it made her better.

I hope we did because that would be cool.

It's a bit weird, though, because Susie almost drowned. She isn't going to make me do that again, is she? I don't think I liked it.

CHAPTER TWENTY-FOUR

I stop reading. The memories come flooding back. The fear, the cold, the way my teeth chattered in the sea when I called Susie's name, and then the soft towel at the Patterson's house followed by hot soup and The Goonies on VHS.

The dark water. It's strange that the image of water came into my mind during hypnosis and then I received this diary entry. Maybe I'm anticipating some sort of pattern to all this.

I skim over the words again. It's still strange to see these entries. To hear my nine-year-old voice. Even back then, I had my doubts about mine and Susie's pact. Susie decided right from the start that our challenges were interlinked with her health. But I see now that I never believed it. Okay, that's not quite true. I think I came to believe it for a while after this, but the conviction was never quite as strong as hers.

And that was the day we worked out our rhyme. I'd pictured us doing it in Susie's bedroom, messing around with her tape recorder. Perhaps that came later. I definitely remember us recording the rhyme at some point. But it was on the cliffs, staring down at the sea below, that the words came to us.

I close my eyes and imagine the scent of salt, the sound of seagulls up ahead. Yes, I hear our voices now. *Let the fear set you free.* This wasn't long after Susie's miserable hospital birthday. It's such an odd thing for nine-year-olds to say. But Susie stared death right in the face. Doctors told her to be brave. They told her not to be scared. It all makes sense in that context.

I turn the page and check the message on the back.

> We are the agitators.
> We do not let fear win.
> We let it set us free.
> Meet us at the Stonecliffe Quarry on the 20th December. After dark.
> You have been invited.

I read it again. It's completely different in tone to Susie's first message. It doesn't even appear to be from her.

I wander through to the living room and slump down onto the sofa, my body limp and my mind confused. *We are the agitators.* Who is we? That tiny word changes everything. Susie is part of a *we*.

The front door opens, and I hear Harry coming in. But I don't want to make small talk now. I want to find out what the hell is going on. Before he enters the living room, I slip into my bedroom and grab my laptop. He shouts out a "hey" and I call my own back. Thankfully he doesn't come to my room for a chat. I sit back down on the bed, propping myself up with pillows.

I put the laptop on my knee, closed. Then I read the note again. *We are the agitators. We do not let fear win. We let it set us free.* It's a mantra and it's extremely similar to the mantra Susie and I developed on the edge of that cliff. Whoever is part of this group took the time to sit down and develop this short statement.

But it could be two people. It could literally be Susie and some random person. Or it could be a bigger, more organised group. I place the diary entry to one side and open my laptop. I type "we are the agitators" into the browser search bar.

There's an indie rock band called The Agitators and a few books with that title. I also come across some historical facts about rebellions and the people who lead them. At first, I feel like it's a dead end, until I discover a logline for a strange website. I click on the link. "We are the agitators" appears in the centre of a blank page. In the address bar, the site is shown as free.dm.

I click on the words across the screen and the website unfolds before me like a piece of origami opening up. Black and grey shapes move and converge until they become one flat black screen. "We are the agitators" is replaced by FREEDM.

Underneath, more words scroll across the screen. "We are the agitators. We do not let fear win."

The background turns blood red leaving one last message: "Invitation only."

I see a login link at the top of the page, but I don't have a username or password and there's no "sign up" option. Unless something in the message I received is the password. I check my diary page again. It could be something simple. I try my name as the username and then go through every significant word in the message as the password, from agitator to Stonecliffe. None of them work.

Frustrated, I close my laptop lid and lie down on the bed. There is some organisation behind this. Again, I don't know who is a part of this. For all I know, Susie set this website up on her own, but it's at least trying to make me think there's more going on than just Susie sending me challenges.

If Susie belongs to some sort of organisation, then this whole thing is bigger than I initially thought.

I close my eyes. If I'm right, it might help explain where she's been for the last sixteen years. What's fuzzier is why or how. I walk through everything I know, trying to piece it together. Susie and I went into the woods. We jumped into Hangman's Cave, hitting the water below. The next thing I remember is running towards the police officer with the torch. Susie must have run away and carried on running. How does she get from homeless and alone to part of a group using our old rhyme as some sort of mantra?

FREEDM

It sounds like an app. The kind that blocks social media to let you do some work without distractions. I even check the app store on my phone to see if it comes up. It doesn't. Not under this spelling, anyway.

I don't like this. From the branded website to the name to the mantra, it's creepy and cult-like. I learned a little about cults at university. From the charismatic leaders to the psychological reprogramming to the cognitive dissonance that make people stay, cults are dangerous. Cult leaders strip away their follower's sense of identity and replace it with their own agenda.

We do not let fear win.
We let it set us free.

I feel sick. It's so similar to the silly rhyme Susie and I made up when we were kids. The one about us using fear to make Susie better. I toss the diary page onto my duvet and place both hands over my mouth. I want to scream.

Meet us at Stonecliffe Quarry...

Meet us. Us.
If I go, who am I going to meet? And how do I know I'll be safe?

CHAPTER TWENTY-FIVE

For the first time since I met DS Liam Harding, I don't take the evidence to him right away. Instead, I sleep on it. Maybe I don't want him to draw the same conclusions as me. I want to feel like another solution is the most probable.

I keep telling myself that anyone can set up a professional website. There are templates out there that allow you to do it in minutes. Susie's "group", whoever they are, could be tiny. Or they could be vast. I have no idea.

It takes me a long time to finally fall asleep, but once I do, it's dreamless. I wake feeling like I only just closed my eyes. Susie is still on my mind. Her bright blue eyes and freckled nose. The way she counted down from ten before we jumped off the cliff. The red website and its ominous use of the word "we."

I call Trudy and tell her I need the rest of the week off.

"Is everything okay, Jen?" she asks. There's nothing but concern in her voice and as always, I'm grateful for having a boss who cares about me.

"Yeah. I... I've been trying to get a doctor's appointment for my anxiety."

"Ah," she says. "I can try to get you in with my psychiatrist friend if you like? She can prescribe you meds, if that's what you need."

"Thanks," I say. "That's so kind. I think I want to see my doctor, though. They understand everything about my TBI."

"Sure. That makes sense. All right, well I'll see you Monday unless you still feel poorly."

"Thanks, see you Monday."

I hang up wondering if I even want the meds. They don't take the thoughts away, just the panic attacks. I'll still worry about Susie, so what's the point? I get up, shower, and call Liam. It feels so strange to think of him as *Liam*, but I guess we're sort of friends now.

"DS Harding," he says, ruining my mental perception of him as Liam.

"It's Jenny Woods," I say.

"Good morning, Jenny Woods," he replies. I feel like I hear the smirk on his face.

"I got another envelope from Susie," I say. "And... well, there's more to it this time."

"Want to meet for breakfast? Where do you live?"

I give him directions. "There's a café a few streets down. On the corner of Emerald Avenue."

"I'll be there in about forty minutes. I'll have toast and a cappuccino. Thanks, Jenny."

The man is such a damn oddball. First lunch, now breakfast, and that cocky but down-to-earth way he speaks to me. Every conversation I have with Liam Victor Harding messes with my head. I wish I could figure out if he has an agenda, or whether he's just bad at setting boundaries between him as a police officer and me as a general member of the public.

I don't know. All I know is that I apply lipstick before I leave the house.

Liam arrives five minutes after his toast. "One white, one wholemeal. Excellent."

"I got both because I don't know your preference. And a few different jams." I push the tiny jars across the table.

"You're so thoughtful." He grins. "Here, try this. Wholemeal and marmalade for the first slice. White and strawberry jam for the second. It's like the main course and the dessert."

I shake my head. "And you call yourself a serious man of the law."

He spreads the butter. "A serious man of the law with hidden depths."

I can't help but laugh.

"So," he says. "What did you bring?"

I put the diary pages in a plastic sheath before leaving the house. I place it down on the table so that Liam can read the message from the agitators.

He bites down on a piece of toast. "Okay, put it back in your bag so we don't get crumbs on it. And the diary entry? What was it about?"

"When we were about eight years old, we snuck out of her mum's house and ran down to the coast. There's this spot at Chillingham where people cliff dive. It's about fifteen feet. It's safe for adults, but not so much for children. We jumped it that day."

"Wow," he says. "Were you hurt?"

"No." I grab a knife and spread marmalade on my toast. "Susie went under for a few seconds, and I was terrified she'd drowned. But she was fine. When we got back to her mum's house, we found out she was cancer-free."

"Oh," he says. "That must have been quite a defining moment for a kid."

"It was. It's pretty clear reading the diary entry that she connected the two things in her head. From what she said to me back then, I mean. She thought facing her fears kept her safe from cancer." I take a bite. It's good marmalade with proper orange peel. "So I put that phrase, you know, the "we are the agitators" thing, into Google last night. It came up with this weird website. It's called FREEDM."

Liam hands me his unlocked phone. "Show me."

I type the address into the browser and hand it back.

"This is some weird shit." He places his toast back down on the plate. From the expression on his face, I see him trying to make sense of it, too. "So I guess she isn't the only one obsessed with your childhood dares. Unless the "we" is unrelated in some way. I've seen cases where people refer to themselves as more than one person."

"Like Dissociative Identity Disorder?" I ask.

"Not necessarily. It's more like they associate with certain groups and assume they share the same values. For instance, lone gunmen or terrorists who assume various subcultures approve of whatever violent shit they pull. Often the organised groups or subcultures have never heard of the guy, but he still sees himself as part of them."

I nod, thinking how bizarre that would be for Susie.

"It's getting worse with the internet." He takes a bite of his toast. "There's a tonne of deluded people out there."

I fiddle with my knife and fork, trying to make sense of it all. "Susie was never like that."

"You don't think that the girl who thought jumping off a cliff cured her cancer had delusions?"

My cheeks warm as anger floods through me. "We both believed that. We were nine years old!"

Liam holds up his palms in surrender. "Sorry. I know you were both very young. But she also believed it when you were sixteen, right?"

"I... I can't know for sure because I don't remember much about that year. We were still doing the challenges, though. So I guess she did believe it. I... Well, I don't think I did by then, but I kept doing them anyway."

"Why?" he asks.

"Because... I... Well, I don't know."

"You can't blame your brain injury on this one, Jenny. You know. Deep down you know why you kept doing it."

I want him to shut up. I fix him a glare that says as much. But he doesn't. He keeps pushing.

"You weren't a little girl when you jumped into Hangman's Cave. You were sixteen years old. Almost an adult. You could stand up to her if you wanted. So why didn't you?"

"She was my friend. I wanted her to be happy."

He regards me. I feel like he's taking it all in. My weak voice, my rounded shoulders huddled over my frame. His questions make me feel bad, make my stomach flip. He asks the questions that I've asked myself for a long time. Uncomfortable questions.

"You loved her," Liam says.

The words hang there for a moment.

"She was like a sister to me," I say. "We were both only children. Her dad died of cancer when she was a toddler. My mum wasn't able to conceive after my birth. We found each other and I suppose we bonded over that. It was a strong bond. One that was difficult to break. Which is what my parents discovered when they said Susie was a bad influence on me." I stare unhappily down at my toast. I don't quite understand why these things are so difficult to admit, but they are.

"I'm not judging you," he says.

"Why does it feel like you are?"

"Because you're embarrassed," he says. "We're all embarrassed of shit we did as teenagers. Trust me, I've come across teenagers doing way worse stuff than what you and Susie got up to."

I shrug. "So?"

"I just want to understand, that's all. I'm trying to figure out the dynamic between you and Susie."

"You don't believe she's part of some sort of organisation? Like a cult?"

He breathes in through his teeth. "If she is, it makes all of this much, much trickier." He frowns. "There may not be much I can do going forward. If Susie is alive and well but choosing to live with a cult, there's not going to be much for a police officer to investigate."

"What do you mean?"

"If the evidence points to Susie living the life she wants to lead. If it suggests she isn't in any danger, I'd have to leave her alone."

"Don't you want to clear my name?" I ask.

"You were never charged with Susie's murder," he says.

"But in the court of public opinion—"

"I get it," he says. "But it's not a legal matter anymore. There's no reason for me to investigate anything. I could try and close the missing person's report if you like, but I can't waste resources if Susie is just living her life."

"Okay, but what if she is in a cult and they're up to illegal activities?" I ask.

"I'd need evidence. I can't investigate a crime that *may* happen. I can't assume they're going to do something bad.

Look, I don't like cults. They prey on vulnerable people. But you may be jumping to conclusions here." He must see the disappointment on my face because he adds a hasty, "I'm sorry, Jenny."

"It's okay," I say. "I... I guess in my head everything got a hundred times more dangerous and I just figured you'd help me."

He falls silent. The sounds of the café envelope us. The milk steamer hisses until I can hardly stand it. Even the delicious marmalade seems unappetising to me. I place the toast back down on my plate. Liam's usually warm hazel eyes seem cold.

"I should go," I say. "The toast and the drink is paid for. Thank you for everything you've done and for lunch the other day."

"Jenny, wait," he says, half rising.

But I don't stop. I'm out of the door and walking up the road. It's only when I reach my street that I dare to glance behind me. It's naïve of me to believe he might have followed me out of the café, but I've always been that hopeful. Of course, the pavements are empty.

CHAPTER TWENTY-SIX

"Oh, hi, you must be Jenny!" A petite strawberry blonde woman with smudges of flour on her cheeks extends a hand as I walk into the house. "I'm Hannah. I've been dying to meet you."

It turns out Hannah and Harry are making brownies in the kitchen. I shake Hannah's warm hand and glance at the bowl of brownie mix, my mouth watering.

"Sorry for taking over," Harry says. "We both have the day off and thought why the hell not. Do you have the day off too?"

"Oh, fun!" Hannah says, smiling so broadly it lights up her face. "Hang with us, Jen. Go on, say you will."

I have to admit, Harry is punching above his weight here. And, yes, Harry is gorgeous but Hannah is luminous. I'm suddenly aware of my windswept hair and blotchy cheeks from the cold.

"Okay, sure," I say.

At least it'll take my mind off Susie. I shed my coat, wash my hands and roll up my sleeves. Hannah passes me a bag of white chocolate chips and I tip them into the mixture.

"I phoned in sick," I admit. "I'm not sick... well..." I shake my head. It seems a little soon to blurt out all my anxiety issues to a stranger. Though it is something I've been known to do. Social anxiety works in weird and wonderful ways, which occasionally means oversharing.

"Hey, mental health days are important," Hannah says smiling kindly.

I feel like the awkward third wheel in a Hallmark movie. Or the friend of the hot couple who gets invited for a threesome at the end of the movie. The thought makes me blush and I hope neither of them figure out where my mind just went. Where did that even come from? I make a mental note to tell Trudy and make her laugh on Monday. It's the least I can do for leaving her in the lurch this week.

Hannah tips the mixture into a tin and places it in the preheated oven. She moves around our kitchen like she lives here. I wonder how many times she's been here without me noticing. Maybe I spend way too much time in my room recently, avoiding life.

"Where did you go this morning?" Harry asks.

"For a walk," I lie. I don't feel like explaining to Hannah why I met a detective for breakfast.

"Don't you think that a good walk makes things seem so much better?" Hannah asks. She pulls off the oven gloves and rinses her hands. "That's why I love to get out in the countryside as often as I can. Especially Saddleworth. It's so beautiful."

I shiver slightly, because all I ever associate Saddleworth Moor is with the Moors Murders. Hannah seems like the sort of person who only sees beauty. I can't shake the violent past.

"Harry, don't you think Jenny should come with us on Sunday?"

Harry glances over at me. "If she wants to." I can tell he's dubious.

"Where are you going?" I ask.

"Go Ape," she says. "They have ten ziplines and a load of rock-climbing walls." She grabs the kettle and fills it with water. "Rope bridges. Tree houses. Everything. And it's only an hour away. I've been three times now, but this is Harry's first go. It would be amazing if you came with us."

I laugh, much louder and harder than I intend. Then I realise she's serious and rearrange my expression. "Thanks, but it's not really my thing. Ask Harry."

"Yeah, it's not her thing," Harry agrees.

"I have a panic attack getting on the train every morning," I say. "Let alone being twenty feet up on a wire." A blast of childhood memories hit me like a hurricane. Running along the train tracks. Leaping into the sea. Throwing the egg. The dark churning waters...

"I used to be anxious, too," Hannah says. "That's why I like to take myself out of my comfort zone."

"I just remembered. I'm meeting someone for lunch," I say.

"Oh, but I just put the kettle on. I thought we could have tea with the brownies." Hannah jabs a thumb at the oven door.

"Just save me one." I hurry over to the hall, grab my coat and rush out of the house.

Listening to her brightness, watching the two of them gaze fondly at each other, smelling the cloying scent of chocolate, it's all too much. I need fresh air. I need to get out of that place.

I walk for hours until I reach the two lines of shops in Harrison Park. Miniature Christmas trees hang from each shop front. White stars glinting against the dark sky. I can't stop thinking about the circumstances that brought me to this junction in my life.

But my life is not a tragedy. I love my job and my volunteer work. While daily anxiety is a challenge, it doesn't stop me from living. Before seeing Susie on the train that day, I'd been relatively content. Maybe somewhat resentful at times, but aside from that, fine.

Eventually I decide to turn back and head towards the house, a sense of calm washing over me. I hate to admit that Hannah is right about the walk.

The walk has clarified a few things for me. I'm going to move out of the house I share with Harry and see if I can afford a one-bedroom apartment in the city. I want to start over. If Liam Harding thinks Susie Patterson doesn't want any help, then I can leave it all behind with a clear conscience. I can hand all of this over to Fiona and let her find her daughter. There's nothing holding me back. I don't owe Susie anything, especially if she really did run away and let me deal with the aftermath of her disappearance.

Susie owes *me*. She owes me my memories and the last sixteen years of dealing with her heartbroken mother. She had a hand in the police interviews and the news articles and as I think about it, my fists clench. My father would never have punched that reporter if she hadn't gone missing. I would never have seen my mother crying over the kitchen sink as she did the washing up.

"Excuse me?"

I glance back, surprised to see that the voice is directed at me. I even jab a finger towards my chest.

"Are you Jenny Woods?"

The man is tall, reedy and over fifty. He's wearing a beige

jacket with a grey collar that blends with his hair. He's one of the true crime fanatics. I can feel it. I turn away and quicken my pace.

"I... I need to speak to you." His voice sounds breathless as he tries to catch up with me. "It won't take long."

I'm away from the shopping area and on a residential street now. There's no one around and the streetlights flicker above my head. Almost every curtain is closed. I hurry, almost breaking into a run.

"I'm sorry," he says. "I don't want to upset you, but I have something important to tell you. I... I'm part of a community. We've put sixteen years into figuring out what happened to Susie Patterson."

"Please stay away from me."

I try not to look back. I keep going. I can't interact with this man. At the end of the road, I take a right. The street name is unfamiliar to me, but I keep going anyway.

"Why did you go to the police station?" he calls.

A tingling sensation spreads through my abdomen. These people are watching me. They follow my movements. I wrap my arms around my body and stare down at the pavement making sure I don't trip.

"Has something happened? Is it Susie? Has she contacted you?"

He sounds closer. We move uphill now and my thighs ache. I slow down but he doesn't. I cross the street and head back down. He does the same, but this time, I really do run. He's older, surely he won't be able to keep up.

"I'm not going to hurt you! Please stop!"

I sprint as fast as I can. I take a left and then another right, making sure I'm going down the hill each time. *My knees will last longer than yours,* I think. Fuck this guy.

We do this for five minutes or so before I realise I'm alone. I lost him on the hills somewhere. But it's not until I find a bus stop that I finally catch my breath.

The vultures are circling, ready to pick the meat from my bones.

CHAPTER TWENTY-SEVEN

I almost don't go to my shift at Solace on Saturday morning, but the guy chasing me down the street obviously knows my whereabouts, and I don't want to give the toothpick-looking weirdo the satisfaction of knowing he's rattled me. I don't want these Susie Patterson Truthers seeing me change my habits. Especially as I spent most of Friday in my PJs moping around.

As I get on the train, I search for two people: Susie or her true crime obsessive. There's no sight of her golden hair or his tall, lanky frame. I sit down in my usual seat in Coach D and try to relax.

If I thought the Susie Patterson Truthers could actually find her, I'd be tempted to call some sort of truce and work with them. But I don't trust them. That's one reason to ignore them. The other is that after sixteen years they've found absolutely zero leads. I'm not even convinced they're looking for her. It's more fun for them to believe Susie is dead. That there's a villain deserving justice. They've never been interested in tracking Susie down. They crave the morbid outcome. They're spectators in the Pantheon braying for blood.

The train stops at Piccadilly station. I alight, stepping onto the platform in the exact spot that I had my panic attack two weeks ago. As I make my way through the city, I glance over my shoulder, expecting to see the toothpick man. I imagine him shoving a phone in my face, trying to catch me out. *Did you murder Susie Patterson?*

By the time I reach the call centre, I'm coiled up. A spring waiting to release.

"Morning, Jenny," Bob calls. "The kettle's hot if you'd like a cuppa."

"Cheers." I peel away my coat, plump up my hair and then shake out my fingers like I'm shedding the outside.

"I'll brew. Get yourself sat down." His chair squeaks as he leaves for the kitchen.

Given what we do here, it should make me tense walking in. But it has the opposite effect. I uncoil slightly. I put on my headset and lean back in my chair. By the time Bob returns with the cup of tea—made with just the right amount of milk—I'm on a call.

"You're through to Solace. My name is Bella and I'm here to listen."

"Hello, dear, I'm Frank. You have a lovely voice."

"That's kind of you." I try to shift the conversation along quickly, in case the older man on the line turns our conversation into something inappropriate. "Would you like to tell me about your day?"

His tone shifts, losing the lightness from before. "My day was the same as it has been for three years. I woke up alone. I made myself a slice of toast and then I sat down. I didn't move for seven hours. I just sat there. No one visited. No one called.

I sat there and I watched TV." He sighs before going quiet. I give him some time in case he has more to say. "The thing is, Bella, I can't go out anymore. My legs... you know... they aren't as strong as before. Elsie—that was my wife's name before she died—used to help me. But now there's no one."

"I'm so sorry. That must be difficult."

"It is, love." He sighs again. "Oh, you do have a nice voice. Could you talk to me a little."

"Well, I'm really here to listen."

"Please talk a little. I haven't heard anyone's voice for three days."

"All right," I say. And then I tell him about a book I like. It's what I always do when a caller wants me to speak. I never give them any personal details. This time I talk about Jane Eyre. He's soon invested in the plot, asking me to carry on.

"Does she marry him?"

"Yes," I say.

"Good."

Frank ends the call and I drink the last of my lukewarm tea. Sometimes the lonely callers get to me more than the callers going through emotional turmoil. It's the aching sadness in their voices. But most sound lighter by the end of the call. The next call comes from a young woman in tears. There's a screaming child in the background. She tells me her worst thoughts. The deepest, darkest, most shocking thoughts about her child. And then she hangs up abruptly.

I'm still decompressing when the next call comes in. This one is nothing but a man breathing heavily. When I suspect he's calling to make me listen to his orgasm, I hang up. The lines are quiet for a few minutes. I nip to the toilet, then head into the kitchen for a glass of water. I notice someone has brought in Jammy Dodgers, so I take a couple back to my desk.

The phone rings.

"You're through to Solace. My name is Bella and I'm here to listen."

There's silence on the other end. I let it linger for a moment. The caller still doesn't speak.

"Take your time," I prompt. "I'm here, ready to listen."

"It's done."

The voice is that of a young woman. My arms and legs immediately feel cold because of the finality in her words.

"What is?" I ask.

"The decision. I made it. It's done." The breath she lets out is shivering. It reverberates through the speaker, distorting it eerily. "I called because I didn't want to be alone when..."

I grip the edge of my desk. "When what?"

"When I die."

No, I think. *No. Not one of these calls. No, no, no.*

I choose my words carefully. "When you die?"

"It shouldn't be long now. I took all the pills."

I lower my head. She knows I can't intervene. She called here because she knows that. Solace listeners do not offer advice and cannot trace calls unless asked. She knows I can't stop her from killing herself. She just wants the comfort of knowing I'm there and now I have to give her that.

"What led you to this decision?" I ask.

"Many, many things," she says.

"Things that can be changed?" I ask. "Things that can be improved?"

"No," she says.

"There's still time to change your mind," I say. "All you have to do is give me your name and address and I will call an ambulance for you. Or you can call one for yourself. But that is your decision to make."

"I know," she says. "I don't want to do that."

"Would you like to talk about some of the things that made you do this?" I ask.

"No," she says. "I just want you to be on the line. I'm going to lie down now. I feel tired."

"Okay. I'll be here. You're not alone. I'm listening." I try once more. "Remember, all you need to do is give me your name and—"

"I won't."

She's quiet then. I'm quiet, too. I hear her breathing. I hear the rasp of her voice. I hear a soft snore. My fingers clasp the desk so hard that they turn white. A tear rolls down my nose and splashes against the glass of water by my hands. I don't want her to hear me crying so I choke down a sob. I clasp a hand over my mouth. There's blood whooshing through my ears. She's still breathing.

And then nothing.

Shaking, I hang up. I pull off the headset and throw it onto the desk like it's red hot. Numbness spreads out through my body. It's like someone has pumped me full of anaesthesia. I sense the other listeners looking at me. Bob is over at my desk in a second, his expression tight with concern.

"Jenny?"

"I have to go," I say.

"That last call... was it..."

"It was a suicide."

He rubs my shoulder. "Go."

I walk out. There's a sharp pain lodged in my chest. Pain for the woman on the phone. A nameless, bodiless voice telling me that she's had enough. She has made her choice, and I can't do anything about it. Pain for me, too. For believing DS Harding would help me. For thinking Susie wanted to make amends. For thinking I could make a difference in this world. How did I expect to make a difference in other people's lives when I can't fix myself?

I'm on the train before I know what I'm doing. I get off at one of the tiny stops in between the city and the open countryside. I walk and walk in my impractical shoes that catch on every stone on the uneven ground. And then I face the train tracks. I stand on the bank, staring down at them.

They aren't the same train tracks Susie and I ran across, but they look similar.

I wonder if Susie had the right idea by running away. When you're alone, you make your own family. If I'm right about FREEDM, she found her people. I stare down at the tracks, tears running down my nose. And then I do something I haven't done in many years. I call my dad.

"What?" he answers.

My shoulders sag. His voice is slurred and it's not even lunchtime. Unless he's on medication affecting his speech patterns, he's already drunk.

"It's Jenny."

I hear a shuffling sound as though he's repositioning himself. I imagine him sitting upright on his chair or pulling his feet onto the sofa.

"Jenny." His voice softens. "It's good to hear your voice, love. How are you?"

"Fine," I lie.

"You don't sound fine, sweetheart."

I close my eyes. The last time I saw my dad was in prison and I was so angry. He'd never been able to shake the labels the press gave him. He ended up becoming what they said he was because he was too weak to fight it. I hated him for that. I hated him because I thought I might do the same thing.

Mum couldn't cope on her own. Not with the Susie Patterson Truthers hounding us day and night.

"I've had a bad day. At the helpline."

"What happened, sweetheart?"

"A woman committed suicide," I say.

"Oh, Jenny," he says. "I'm sorry. I hope you're not blaming yourself."

I don't say a word.

"Of course you are." He sighs. "You always did, love. You know, your mother got you wrong. She thought you were... oh, I don't know. A little cold. I told her that wasn't the case. It was that you felt too much. Isn't that right, love?"

"I don't know, Dad," I say.

"Why don't you come and see me? Today even. You know I'm only a few hours away."

"I think Susie is alive," I say. "She's been in contact."

"Has she?" There's another shuffle. "That's good. Isn't it?"

"I don't know who she is anymore. She could be a bad person."

He's quiet for a moment. "Jenny, I know you loved that girl. But she was never as good as you thought she was. She had a mean streak in her."

"She didn't," I say. "Not before the cancer, anyway."

"No, it was always there," he says. "Come over and we'll chat about it. We haven't talked in so long. We haven't talked about your mum for—"

"I... I can't, Dad. Not right now. But soon."

He sighs. "Okay. Soon. Take care of yourself. I love you."

"Love you, too, Dad."

I hang up and then I step onto the tracks.

CHAPTER TWENTY-EIGHT

A rush of adrenaline hits me like a tidal wave. I'm on the tracks for two or three heartbeats, and then I run across them to the other side. My shoes slip as I climb up the bank, using my hands and knees when I fall. By the time I reach the top, there's sweat pouring down my temples, but the view up here is spectacular. Or maybe it's not, but I feel spectacular. Fields roll away into sentry lines of terraced houses. They're so small from I'm up here. Above me the peaks of the hills are dusted with snow, like icing sugar on macaroons.

The ground beneath my feet shudders and I turn around to look down from where I came. The train thunders past in the blink of an eye. I sit down in the mud and watch it disappear along the tracks.

"Susie, what have you done to me?"

Every muscle in my body trembles. I think of the woman on the phone. *It's done.* Her words, so final. I contemplate whether I might ever reach breaking point like that. The strength it must take to face that moment. It's hard to live. It's hard to die. There's no other choice to make.

It begins to snow.

Back when Mum had just had her first stroke, and I was almost eighteen, we were with Dad in Boots buying hand cream for her dry, cracked skin. It hadn't been a good day. Mum still struggled to communicate at that point, and everything took longer than before. A stranger walked right up to us and pointed his finger at me.

"Murderer!" he'd screamed. "You should be locked up! What did you do with Susie's body? Where did you bury her?"

Dad gave him a broken nose and a concussion before serving a few years in prison for it. My grandparents moved in to help with Mum's rehabilitation as well as take care of me. I failed my A-Levels that year. Mum died nine months later, and on the day I retook my exams, someone threw red paint at me outside the exam hall.

Three women screamed, "murderer!" before running away.

Dad left prison to attend Mum's funeral. I applied to university. I met Jack. The Earth continued to revolve around the sun and those obsessive Susie Patterson Truthers slowly faded into the background.

Every now and then someone will track down my work email address and send me messages. *I know what you did.*

I ignore them. But there are times when I'm tempted to reply back and ask them what they know. Because I don't even remember myself.

I've often wondered if they're right, that I did kill Susie. And there have been times over the years when I became so convinced, I thought the world might be a better place without me in it.

But that's impossible now. Susie is alive. I haven't killed anyone.

So why do I still feel guilty?

Harry stares at me completely dumbfounded as I walk into the apartment with mud on my skirt and a scraped knee. Locks of my hair lie flat against my skin with the combination of snow and sweat. It's late. I had to walk to the nearest town and book an Uber. I spent a fortune getting home during the brief snowstorm, but I made it here alive and well.

"Jenny?"

I hang up my coat and rake my fingers through the soggy strands across my forehead. I'll absolutely be sinking into a hot bath as soon as he stops talking to me. But I suppose he deserves an explanation.

"I got stranded," I say. "Because of the snow."

"But... it barely settled," he says.

I shrug. "You know what city drivers are like when there's an inch of snow on the ground."

"And the mud?"

"I fell on a grass verge. Look, I don't appreciate this third degree. I'm not your girlfriend, Harry. You have a girlfriend who's a whole other person other than me so maybe you should just shut up. I want a bath."

"S-sorry," he stutters. "Sorry... I... Okay, well I guess I'll go to my room."

I know I should apologise but I also know that if I do that, I'll start to cry and then God knows what will spill out of my big mouth. Maybe I'll end up admitting my crush on him, or my crush on Liam Harding, or even Hannah, for God's sake, and then whatever deep dark secrets lurk inside my soul. Luckily, he walks away, and I head through to the bathroom to run water so hot, it's going to turn my skin lobster red.

My problems are not his fault. Tomorrow, when I have a

better handle on it all, I'll apologise, but for now I just need to warm up.

I peel damp clothing away from shaking legs. Did I really stand in the middle of a working train track? When I close my eyes, I feel the rumble of the ground, the din of the train as it passed. I know how close I was to being flattened by that train. A second surge of adrenaline shoots through me. I haven't felt anything like it since before the night at Hangman's Cave.

It felt good.

The water envelopes me like a scalding hot hug. It finds the chill in the marrow of my bones and chases it away.

Stepping onto the train tracks didn't solve all my problems but it did do something to me. It took me out of the world, even for a second. *Let the fear set you free.* You were right, Susie. All this time, you were right. But this isn't any way to live.

I grab my phone and check all the messages I've ignored. There's one from Bob asking me if I'm okay. I fire off a quick text to let him know I'm fine and will be back for my next shift.

And that's it.

I'm disappointed because in my heart of hearts, I have to admit that I'd hoped for a message from Liam. Part of me wants him to tell me he's going to continue helping me. Because how am I going to find Susie on my own?

I bring up the website again. FREEDM. It could be a wellness brand. Or a yoga retreat.

There's no denying that the Susie I knew was wild and free. To an extreme extent. To the point where it made her dangerous to be around. How many times did I put myself in harm's way for her?

I consider my dad's words. I'm not sure if he meant them as a warning, but that's the spirit in which I've taken them. *She had a mean streak in her.* If that's true, then I need to watch my back.

CHAPTER TWENTY-NINE

The drizzling sleet lasts for another three days. I get up in the dark, go to work, and travel home in the dark. Pathetically damp snowflakes wet my eyelashes and sting my cheeks. There's nothing as quietly miserable as an English winter.

It is Wednesday 20th of December, the day I'm supposed to go to the quarry. I'm at work unable to concentrate on anything. I brought the diary pages with me and have them out next to my keyboard. I can't stop touching them. My fingers graze the words written on the back.

> *We are the agitators.*
> *We do not let fear win.*
> *We let it set us free.*
> *You have been invited.*

Invited to what and by whom? Societal agitators are people who disrupt norms. Rebels raging against the system. I have no idea if these people are protesting something or whether they choose to live in a dramatically unusual way. Though it could mean nothing. If Susie is in some sort of cult, then often the message is little more than a garbled manifesto created by drug-addled brains. Charles Manson convinced his followers that a race war was coming, and they had to instigate violence to save the world.

I lean back in my office chair. Of course, I'm going to the quarry. I have to. As soon as the clock hits 5 p.m., I say goodbye to Trudy, get changed in the toilets and hurry outside. I book a taxi while standing outside the office. It takes me a little while to figure out where the entrance of the quarry is on the map. Then I pace back and forth in the cold waiting for the white Vauxhall to arrive.

The journey is quiet. We don't make small talk, instead the driver puts the radio on and I close my eyes, half-listening to telephone callers complaining about football managers. My mind drifts back to the call at Solace. The woman on the line wasn't the first person to tell me they are going to kill themselves. But she was the first to do it while I was on the call with her.

"Is this the place?"

I open my eyes to see the driver's face staring at me from the rearview mirror.

"Yeah," I say. "It's... um... it's a rave. You know, one of those illegal, hush-hush ones."

He frowns. I'm clearly over thirty and probably not the kind of woman who would go to a rave by herself. "In December?"

I don't reply to that because I don't have a decent come-back. Instead, I thank him and slip out of the car.

It's pitch black here away from the city. The outfit I changed into in the office toilets is much more appropriate for walking around a quarry. I'm wearing sensible boots, jeans and a wax coat with a hood.

There's a gravel path in front of me. Tapping the torch function on my phone—which I charged fully before leaving—I see the locked gate and frown. What am I supposed to do here? Swinging the beam left and right, I check for a way in. And that's when I see it. An envelope taped to the fence. I grab it and rip it open, almost dropping my phone in the process.

Find a way in.

"Thanks for the tip," I mutter, laughing slightly.

Well, I'm no cat burglar but surely it can't be that difficult. I walk carefully around the perimeter searching for something I can duck under or climb over. The fence is high, over six feet, and there doesn't appear to be any weak spots. That is, until I come to an older section that's almost completely covered in some sort of thorny weed. Here, the fence leans inwards, as though it's been partially blown down by wind. If I kick it hard enough, I might be able to get in.

I shove my boot against the slanted panels, throwing my weight against them. The fence creaks but barely budges. It's clear I don't have the physical strength to knock this thing over. Perhaps I have the right idea, but not the right approach. I shine the torchlight around the fence, searching for another weakness. And that's when I find the gap.

Where the old fence meets the new fence, there's a slim space just big enough to try and force my way through. The old fence is pitched forwards while the new wooden panels stand straight up. The main issue will be the thorny weed.

I kick my foot as high as possible and bring the heel down on the weeds, attempting to break them up. Thorns snag my jeans but don't penetrate the fabric, which is a relief. I stamp down as much of the plant as I can, sweat breaking out along my forehead and upper lip.

"You'd better bloody be here, Susie Patterson," I mumble, forcing my way through the space between the two fences.

This is a hell of a lot of work to go through for nothing. If Susie doesn't show up today, she's seriously wearing my patience.

The pocket of my coat catches on a protruding nail. I pull it free and the stitches snap. Another inch through the gap and a thorn scratches my cheek. I push once more and tumble to the ground, landing heavily on my knees and elbows. Cursing Susie, I scramble back to my feet, letting out a sigh of relief, and dust down my jeans.

Then it hits me. I'm in. But the note didn't give me any further directions. This can't be it. Susie wouldn't bring me all the way out here to climb through a fence and then go home. What would be the point in that?

My body jolts when a blindingly bright yellow light illuminates the hollow quarried space. I gaze up at it, positioned high up on the far cliff above the gaping hole in the ground. The hole I'm standing in right now.

Someone turned that light on and they're most likely looking at me right now. I'm not alone.

The freezing cold December breeze lifts the hair on the back of my scalp. I rub gloved hands together, feeling the chill through my coat. This place is in the middle of nowhere. Even the taxi driver seemed reluctant to let me out. Just like at the train tracks, adrenaline rushes through my veins and I like it. It chases away the panic and anxiety that usually plagues me.

I'm such an anxious person that I could have a panic attack lying in bed. Yet here I am in the middle of nowhere. Here I am standing alone in the dark. I just broke into private property. This is me finally telling the world that I am alive, and I am not scared.

If Susie arranged all of this just for me, I'm not too proud to admit that it makes me feel special. But I am also not too proud to admit how fucked up that thought is. My father's warning pops into my mind, followed by DS Harding's many words of caution about my childhood friend. Even Harry had an opinion on who Susie might be. She could be a terrible person. And yet I don't care. As if, after all these years, I'm going to come this far and then turn back because I'm afraid.

No. Fuck that.

I'm going to find her.

CHAPTER THIRTY

I squint into the shadows surrounding the spotlight. From the way it's positioned right up above the quarry hole, I suspect Susie wants me to find a way across and up the other side. She wants me up on that cliff. It's about heights again, as it often was with her. They tended to be her weakness. And mine.

There's only one thing for it. I stride towards the light, hoping I'll find a path on the approach. It's a beacon, directing me. The ground is relatively smooth beneath my feet and I'm glad not to trip on anything. On the other hand, with the cold weather and frost, it might become slippery underfoot once I begin the incline.

If only the light was behind me so that it lit my way. The closer I get, the more of a hindrance it becomes. I shield my eyes from it, while, using my phone light, I search the shadows for a path.

With each step, I imagine eyes watching me in the distance. Whoever turned on the light must be there somewhere, and I am completely visible with this spotlight trained on me. I reach the other side of the quarry and come to the path I need to climb. It's not going to be easy. The path is cut into the stone, most likely built for vehicles to move up and down. But it's incredibly steep and high. I make a start.

About halfway up, my muscles complain. I've never been the most athletic person in the world, but I do walk a lot. I'm accustomed to hills, but this is one of the steepest inclines I've ever attempted. My calves ache, then my thighs, and then my back aches, too. The ground has a layer of frost on it that makes my boots slip and slide every so often. Without any sort of handrail, I'm worried I might fall over the edge. The drop gapes below. Fifteen feet. Then twenty. Soon, fifty. The path narrows. The blinding light hurts my retinas. Fear grips my chest. I drop to my hands and knees with the cold air shuddering in and out of tired lungs. Tiny stones dig into the leather of my gloves.

When the ground levels out, I scurry across the gravel, still moving towards the white glow. Sweat drops down onto the dirt beneath me, and I take a moment to catch my breath before climbing to my feet. I need water but didn't think to bring any.

I walk quickly over to the spotlight. I haven't caught my breath yet and my chest heaves up and down, but I'm determined to find her. As soon as I'm close to the spotlight, I search for the shape of a person. I could be up here with anyone. I might be in this quarry with a complete stranger. But there are no figures silhouetted against the brightness.

I wipe sweat from my forehead, disappointed, then place my hands on my hips. She isn't here. Yet again, I've completed a challenge for her, and she hasn't bothered to turn up. Anger surges through me. I take a step towards the light, tempted to shove the thing down into the quarry. But as I approach, I find an envelope taped to the metal frame. I snatch it and tear open the paper.

Walk into the trees.

"What?" I say out loud.

What trees?

I grab my phone and turn the torch back on. Then I perform a 360 angle slow spin to check my surroundings. When I see the woods behind me, I realise this isn't over. Not even close.

"You've got to be kidding me," I mumble.

As the cold fist of dread finally eases off, righteous anger builds up from my belly.

"Are you kidding me, Susie?" I shout. "All this and you want more? After all this time? After everything you've done?"

"Hey."

The voice makes me yelp. I spin on my heel, every sense heightened, my heart percussive. My fist reaches out and connects with a hard shoulder. Then I recognise the citrus aftershave. Liam.

"What the fuck?" I yell.

He rubs his shoulder. "You just assaulted a police officer. I should arrest you."

I know he's joking, but the words leave me with a sense of unease. I like this man, but he just came out of nowhere. After our conversation at the café, he made it clear he wasn't going to help me. Yet here he is, in a dark, empty quarry with me. Why? He either followed me here or set this entire thing up.

"I think it was justified," I say. "What are you doing here?"

"I thought you might need some help," he says. "Look, I was a bit of a dick in the café the other day. I saw all the information on your diary page, and I had a feeling you'd come here and do it on your own. It seemed dangerous so I wanted to make sure you were okay."

"And you didn't feel the need to tell me about any of this?"

"I only decided to come about an hour ago," he says. "Check your phone."

I do check it. I'd been so busy concentrating on getting across the quarry that I hadn't seen my notifications. Sure enough there's a text from Liam letting me know he's coming.

"Oh," I say.

"What's the challenge?" he asks. "That climb was a killer." If I'm not mistaken, there's a hint of exhilaration in his voice. Perhaps I'm not the only one catching the adrenaline bug.

I turn around and point to the trees. "She wants me to go into those woods."

"She?" he asks. "You're still sure it's Susie?"

I glare at him. "I was until you showed up. How do I know you're not behind all this? It's pretty weird you being here."

"Do you want me to leave?" he asks.

"You didn't answer my question." I fold my arms and lift my chin. The idea of Liam, a detective, setting up this whole thing, is faintly ridiculous. But I can't let it go until he answers.

He squares his shoulder and lifts his brows. "Jenny, I did not lug a huge spotlight and set it up to a generator to trick you into thinking your missing best friend wants you to perform a dare." He pulls in a long breath. "Happy now?"

"I think so. Come on. Let's find out what's in these woods."

CHAPTER THIRTY-ONE

Freezing cold rain tumbles down from the black sky. We don't speak as we inch our way towards the woods. Both of us have our hoods up and our coats rustle with every step. I edge a glance at him. He's focused on the trees. I wonder if his brain is in detective mode, assessing all possible dangers. But that's the point of Susie's challenges. We're supposed to know what we're doing is reckless and do it anyway.

"Stay close," he says as we're about to step into the trees. "I don't want either of us to end up lost." He grabs a torch from his pocket and hits the on switch.

My shoulder bumps his as we drift closer. The pitter-patter of rain is the only sound breaking the silence as we step into the woods. There's no discernible path here and the trees are thickset. This isn't a place to go for a hike on a Sunday afternoon, it's a wild, untamed forest. I turn sideways to follow Liam as he helps me through the tangled area.

"What now?" Liam says. "We're here. Where do we go?"

But I have no idea. There were no further instructions and I'm at a loss. "Maybe we should stop."

"Do you want to stop?" Liam asks. "Do you want to turn back?" He shines the light in my direction to see my facial expression. I hear an audible sigh. "Stay close to me. There are hundreds of places for an assailant to hide in these woods. Not to mention the fact that the longer we walk, the harder it'll be to find our way—"

He's cut off by a high-pitched giggle and my hand flies up to my throat. For half a heartbeat I'm convinced the sound fluttered out of my own body. But the giggle continues, and I hear the tell-tale scratchy, fuzzy sounds from a tape recording.

Liam stops dead. I forget to breathe. He passes the torchlight over the area. Every hair on the back of my neck stands up as I watch the yellow beam pick out tree roots, bushes, and gnarled branches. I wait for a pair of eyes to meet us in the dark. There's nothing.

Whispers float through the trees.

"What the fuck?" Liam mumbles.

I shush him, listening to the voice. It's then I realise there is more than one person on the recording, and they are growing louder. My pulse races. Blood thumps hard through my body. All around us, two high-pitched, almost squeaky voices are talking and laughing.

My voice finally comes back, raspy from fear. "It's a recording. Listen."

We stand there as still as statues. It takes a moment for me to redirect my concentration from my terror to the sounds echoing through the trees. As soon as I understand what's happening, I gasp.

"It's me. That's my voice." My nose tingles. Tears flood my eyes. I clear my throat and pull myself together. "We... Susie and I... made tapes when we were little. Susie had this recording device with a microphone, so we made silly tapes of us saying stupid things."

The fear will set you free, we say eerily through whatever speaker is blasting our voices through the trees. It's followed by childish giggles.

Then Susie says, *I dare you to always be my best friend. To never betray me and always do the challenges when I ask.*

I accept the dare, says my tinny voice. *Let's say the rhyme again.*

We speak together.
One, two, three
Dare you, dare me.
One, two, three
Let the fear set you free.
One, two, three
Follow you, follow me.
One, two, three
Let the fear set you free.
Let the fear set you free.
More giggles.
And then it starts again.

Air shudders out of my body. Every part of me is freezing cold, like my body is turning into ice. I want to run to her, but I can't move.

"Jenny?" Liam places a hand on my arm. "Are you all right?"

I can't move and I can't speak. It's too much. I don't want to go back to these memories anymore. An urge to run seizes my body, but I ignore it.

"Breathe, Jenny," he says. "Look at me."

I lift my face until I gaze into his hazel eyes. The torch is between us, looking up, so that we're both bathed in its light. His chest rises and falls, and I try to match the same rhythm.

"Do you want to go back?" he asks.

I shake my head. "I've come this far."

He holds out a hand and I take it willingly.

"We need to figure out which direction the sound is coming from," Liam says. "I think we need to walk through those elms."

"Okay," I say, beginning to get the feeling back in my limbs again.

He casts a quick glance at me, as though figuring out if I'm fit to walk, and then we set off. My childhood giggles echo around us. I want to throw my hands over my ears and block out the sound. Why is she doing this to me?

"Still with me, Jenny?" Liam asks.

"I'm okay," I say, and this time my voice actually carries conviction. *I am okay. I am going to do this and I'm going to survive.* "I kinda wish you had a gun, though."

"Me, too," he admits.

"Let's hope Susie isn't a serial killer these—"

He shushes me. I'm immediately silent and then we both stop walking. I strain to hear what Liam must have noticed over the sound of the tape. I whip my head to the right, catching the slight rustle of movement through bushes. Liam sets off first, the torchlight bouncing as he sprints. I have to hurry to keep up, my boots tripping over tree roots and weeds. Susie's childish voice asks me to never betray her as I run through the trees, keeping my gaze fixed on Liam's back. I can't lose him. These woods will swallow me whole.

But I don't need to worry about the woods. Twenty more strides and they open up into a vast expanse of field. Liam, about twenty feet ahead now, comes to a stop, moving the torch from left to right, and then places his hands on his knees. A moment later, he jogs back to me.

"Are you all right?" he asks.

"I have a stitch, but yes, I'm fine. You?"

He nods. "I saw someone. A figure, running through the woods. But they were too fast. Fuck." He tosses the torch to the grass in anger.

"Susie?"

He shakes his head. "I don't know. It was too dark to see. Come on. Let's see what they left for you."

I'm breathless and sweating as we head back towards the trees. But it doesn't take long to find the huge speaker hooked up to another generator. Liam unplugs it and the giggles stop abruptly. My body jolts as soon as the recording ends. I let out a shuddering breath and help Liam search for more clues, but this is it. It's over.

"I guess my challenge was walking through the woods with the tape on loop," I say. And then my heart sinks. "Maybe Susie ran away when she saw you. Maybe she would have stayed to talk to me."

"You might be right," he says.

"I'm not sure I would have made it through the woods without you," I say.

The words hang in the cold air between us. Our hot bodies produce steam floating up towards the trees looming over us. I'm the first to look away.

Liam clears his throat. "Someone needs to come and collect this gear. We could wait until morning and find out who's coming. Or we could leave now and come back first thing in the morning. If you don't mind sleeping at my house. My car is back near the quarry."

"All right then," I say. "Let's do that. The second option."

CHAPTER THIRTY-TWO

"We're probably only going to get a few hours kip," Liam says. "But at least you can dry out your clothes and warm up."

"Sure," I say.

I've learned a few new things about Liam Harding. Firstly, he drives a Mini. Nothing wrong with that, I'm just surprised. He also keeps a tidy house, which shouldn't be a surprise for a man living alone, but often is, as I've found out through a few bad Tinder dates.

"I'll take the sofa," he says. "If you leave your wet things in a pile, I'll put them on the radiator to—"

I cut him off with a kiss. A short, tentative one. The kind that tests the waters. And then I back away.

"Sorry," I say. "You don't... I mean, it's okay if—"

He cuts me off with a second kiss. I sink into it, touching his chest. And then he pulls us apart.

I stand there in my wet clothes, suddenly freezing cold and shivering, while he runs his hands through his hair.

"Sorry," he says. "I can't do this. I can't." He backs away.

I pull my fingers through my knotted hair, working

through the tangles, staring at the ground, anything to avoid his eyes.

"We can't do this. It's not right," he says. "I'm—"

I hold up a hand. "You don't have to explain yourself. I know. You're a police officer and I'm..." I trail off because we still haven't established if I'm a victim or a suspect yet.

"I'll get the bedding for the sofa." He doesn't look at me as he leaves the room.

I pace back and forth, shaking my arms out like I can shake off the embarrassment. All I can think is *fuck you, Susie. Fuck you for making me vulnerable. Fuck you for making me hear those tapes. Fuck you for all of this.*

If she hadn't turned up on the train and sent me my diary pages then I wouldn't be standing here shivering, my lips on fire from a kiss that shouldn't have happened. He went in for a second kiss. I saw him lean into me. I felt his hands on my waist. But then his professional side took over and now I feel like a fucking idiot. I put him in an uncomfortable position. I initiated the first kiss. Talk about a terrible idea.

But the worst part is... every inch of my body aches for him, for his touch. The warmth of his body pressed against mine. The softness of his lips, the slight scrape of the stubble against my cheek. It was over too soon. Before it even began.

Liam returns, dumping the bedding on the sofa, and then shows me to his room. Barely looking at me, he tells me to leave my clothes outside the room and hands me a t-shirt to wear in bed. The door closes and I'm alone.

There's still adrenaline in my veins and I know I won't be able to sleep. I pace back and forth staring at his double bed. The décor is dark and masculine. Forest green walls and mahogany furniture. There are no personal items, no photographs, no trinkets. The room reminds me of those staged IKEA areas with fake books stacked next to a plastic plant. I sink down on top of the plush duvet. There's no way I'll learn anything more about Liam Harding here.

In the end, I drift off. I'm back in the woods, following the light. The police officer is up ahead but when he opens his mouth, Susie's giggle spills from his throat. I open my eyes with a start, waking on top of a damp pillowcase, the sound of soft knocking coming from the door.

"Yeah?" I call, feeling too self-conscious to open the door in Liam's t-shirt.

"It's me." He pauses, probably feeling stupid for revealing the obvious. "Just to let you know, it's getting light so we might want to—"

"Okay, I'll just get dressed."

"Your clothes are out here in the hall. I dried them as best I could."

"Thanks."

When I hear the sound of his footsteps moving away from the door, I hurry over, peek into the hall and grab my folded clothes. They'll do, despite the fact that they're slightly damp. My hair is too, but from sweat, not rain. I check the room for a hairdryer or even a hairbrush but can't see anything. I pull on my clothes, tie my hair back and step into the hall, wondering where the bathroom is.

In the end, I wander into the living room to find Liam standing awkwardly next to the sofa. He has a backpack on his shoulder ready to go.

"You ready?" he asks.

"I need the loo."

He shakes his head slightly. "Sorry. I should have told you

where it is. Back up the stairs, down the hall, second door on the left."

"Thanks."

There is a hairbrush in the bathroom so I'm able to make myself look more respectable. I squirt on some of his deodorant, which is better than nothing, I decide, and rub toothpaste onto my teeth.

This is the first time I've stayed at a man's house in months, and he rejected me. And I look like shit. Well, there's no point dwelling on it. Susie and FREEDM are more important.

"Ready," I say brightly.

I step past him towards the front door, pulling on my coat, wishing I hadn't agreed to stay here at all. We probably won't even find Susie. But while ever there's a chance, I'll take it.

On the way back to the quarry, I rest my head against the car window and Liam turns the radio on. We don't speak.

"The spotlight is still on." He pulls the car over into layby. "Looks like we came back in time."

I'm out of the car immediately, glad to be away from the hum of the air conditioner and the loud jazz music. He comes around to stand by my side, staying around two feet away from me, as though he doesn't trust himself to be close to me. Whatever he's doing, it doesn't work. The electricity between us builds until I wrap my arms around my chest.

"We can't get too close," he warns.

"How are we supposed to see who takes the spotlight away?" I ask.

He grins, allowing his usual confidence to creep in, then pulls a pair of binoculars from his backpack. I'm impressed he's so well prepared.

"They'll work better once the sun comes up," he says. "But I see the spotlight at least."

I button my coat right up to my chin and thrust my hands in my pocket. My nose goes numb as we wait.

"Maybe I should have made a flask of tea," Liam says. "We could be here for a while."

I lift my eyebrows. Now is a perfect time to have a conversation about what happened last night—well, a few hours ago—but the itching at the pit of my stomach is relentless. I'm too chicken-shit to do it.

"Do you see anything?" I ask instead.

"Nothing."

And then we wait. At one point I sit on the damp ground, because my legs ache. And then I pace around. The sun rises in a flash of burnt orange that quickly morphs into an ominous grey.

"It's going to snow," I say, staring grimly up at the sky.

Not long after, as the first flakes hit my hood, the quarry workers turn up and it's our cue to leave. No one from FREEDM is coming back for the spotlight, and we don't want to be connected to the abandoned equipment ourselves. We pile back into Liam's Mini.

"She left them there," I say. "Maybe she knew we'd be waiting."

"Maybe," he says. He picks a piece of lint from his jeans and avoids my gaze.

"Can't you dust the spotlight for prints?" I ask.

He shakes his head. "I'm not here as a police officer."

"You're not?"

Liam strokes the stubble along his chin. "I'm not sure why I'm here."

"You don't have to be," I snap. "I was fine on my own." The words tumbling out of my mouth are not true, but I'm too raw and exhausted to think straight, let alone allow myself to be vulnerable enough to say how I feel.

"Well, thank me very much."

He pulls the car out of the lay-by and turns it around too fast and using too much pedal. I grip the arm rest and hold my breath.

"I'll take you home," he says.

"You don't have to do that. Just drop me off at the nearest bus stop."

"Is that what you want?" he asks.

"Why wouldn't it be?"

He glares at me. "You know, I get the impression that by doing the right thing and *not* taking advantage of you last night, I've somehow done something wrong."

"Taking advantage of me? What do you think I am? Some broken woman-child incapable of making my own decisions?"

"That's not what I said. Or what I meant." He takes the next left so fast, my fingers clamp harder. He looks at me for a long time. If only I could read his thoughts because his expression is completely unreadable. And then his brow creases.

"Would you look at the road?" I snap.

"I'll do whatever you want," he retorts.

He drives in silence for ten minutes before pulling over at the next bus stop. Without saying a word, I step out of the car and watch him drive away.

CHAPTER THIRTY-THREE

I'm late to work by almost an hour, but I get there. Trudy isn't in the centre, which makes things easier. Somehow, I manage to get away with being late and looking like I haven't slept. Later, when I crawl into my bed and pull the covers over my head, it all sinks in for the first time. I was so close to seeing Susie. If Liam hadn't been there, she might have revealed herself to me. Do I know that for certain? No, I don't. Perhaps it's a tall tale that I'm lying to myself in order to feel better about all this. Because what happened out there was anything but normal.

I fall asleep wondering who I can trust and why Liam turned up to the quarry.

In my dreams, I'm in the woods by the quarry listening to a tape of Fiona Patterson telling us that Susie is cancer free. Then Liam pops out from nowhere, a faceless woman in his grip. She's blonde, but there are no features on her face. No eyes, no mouth, no eyebrows, nothing.

The last Friday before Christmas—and our last day of work—is quiet. The counselling centre is finally winding down. It feels like everyone that walks in does so with the same lack of energy. Even Trudy seems sleepy today.

With so little going on, I decide to take a long lunch. I treat myself to a pub meal and then walk around the block to try to clear my head. It has been a few days since the incident at the quarry. My thighs still ache from the incline and every now and then I hear the sounds of mine and Susie's giggles in my mind. Susie has not been in touch since. Neither has Liam.

"Jenny Woods?"

I turn my head to see Toothpick Man running towards me. *Shit.*

"Don't go! Please!" he calls.

I take a sharp left, trying to keep my wits about me, to move in the direction of work rather than panic and run down an unfamiliar road.

"Get away from me!" I shout.

He's quick this time. Somehow, he's only a few steps behind. I glance around me, searching for help but the road is empty.

"Jenny, please. It's about Susie and it's important."

"Like fuck it is! You lot do nothing but accuse me and my father." I come to a halt and face the man pursuing me. If I can't outrun him, I at least won't allow him to see how afraid I am.

He stops, too. He holds up both palms. "I'm not like them. I swear. I did used to post on the Susie Patterson forum, but this isn't about that. It's about this."

He reaches into his coat pocket, and I flinch away, half expecting him to pull out a knife or even a gun, but he doesn't, he pulls out a small pamphlet. Bemusement replaces fear. Is this guy trying to save my soul by getting me to accept Jesus Christ as my Lord and saviour?

He holds it out. Tentatively, I take the leaflet.

Let the fear set you free.

I gasp when I see the words on the cover. I open up the booklet and there on the first page is the word FREEDM. Below it is written: A Guide to Helping You Find Your Wings.

I regard Toothpick Man. "Where did you get this?"

He lets out a long sigh, and I get the feeling he has carried this leaflet around for a long time. "I was given it."

"By who?"

"By someone in FREEDM." He glances over his shoulder as though he's afraid we'll be overheard. "Can we go somewhere and talk? Please?"

I check the time on my phone. "Okay but I don't have a lot of time."

"This won't take a lot of time," he says.

"All right. Let's go back to the Red Lion, it's just around the corner."

On the way back to the pub he says, "I'm Kevin, by the way."

"I've been calling you Toothpick Man in my head," I blurt out.

He frowns, then laughs. "I suppose I am tall and thin."

"Sorry, I probably shouldn't have said that."

"It's okay," he says.

Up close, he reminds me of one of my mum's uncles. Someone I met briefly as a child. A tall, thin man who always wore shell suit jackets despite them being out of fashion. Kevin is in an anorak and wears thick rimmed glasses.

"How did you get into the true crime game, Kevin?" I hold the door open for him as we step into the pub.

"My sister went missing when I was twelve."

My heart sinks. Sadness washes over me. What the Susie Patterson Truthers have done to me over the years has been invasive and unpleasant, but I wouldn't wish that on my worst enemy. I ask Kevin what he'd like to drink. It feels strange to buy my stalker a drink but it has been a really weird month.

We both get Cokes and take them over to a quiet table away from the windows. He removes his anorak and places it on his knee. I hang my coat over the back of my chair.

"I'm sorry about your sister," I say. "How long has she been missing?"

"Forty-three years," he says. "She isn't alive anymore. We were twins. I'd feel it if she was." He sips the Coke. "But Susie is alive."

"I know," I say.

"You've seen her?"

"Yes... I think so. On a train." I don't offer any more information, waiting for him to tell me what all of this is about.

"Susie is behind this, isn't she?" he asks, pointing at the leaflet again. "You two had some sort of pact when you were children. The newspapers reported on it. The two of you jumped into Hangman's Cave because you thought your childish dares kept her cancer away."

"Well, it was in the newspapers, so it must be true."

He tilts his head slightly, trying to figure out if I'm affirming his beliefs or not. In the end, I nod.

"Yes, we had a pact." I place my finger on the word "fear". "This used to be our mantra."

His eyes open wide. "So it's true! She is alive and she's a cult leader."

The word "cult" makes my heart skip a beat. I close my fingers around the cool glass of Coke in front of me.

"Tell me everything you know about FREEDM," I say.

CHAPTER THIRTY-FOUR

Bob passes me a cup of tea as soon as I walk in. His skin seems pulled tight, like he's had a bit too much Botox.

"It's good to see you, Jenny," he says.

I take the tea. "Thanks."

"Let's have a chat," he says.

I follow him into his office and close the door behind us. I place the tea on the desk and hang my bag on the back of the chair before sitting down.

"Am I in trouble?" I ask.

"What? No, of course not. You're not the first volunteer to walk out in the middle of a shift. Besides, I know you. I know you didn't do it for no reason. You had a hard call, didn't you?"

I nod.

"Would you like to talk about it?"

I feel like the person on the other end of a call with Bob. I'm the one in crisis.

"Not really," I say. "I'm okay, I swear. There's just a lot going on right now."

"You know where I am if you need a chat."

"Thanks." I stand. "Sorry for walking out like that. I've never let it bother me before."

He waves a hand to say it's no big deal. Grabbing the tea, I make my way back to my usual desk and boot up the old computer. It whirrs to life, and I wait for the system to load. The computers here have to be twenty years old.

In between calls, I decide to research FREEDM as best I can. I've already read the vague pamphlet Kevin gave me. He told me about a seminar he attended that ended with these small booklets being handed out to everyone in the audience. I'm still getting my head around the fact that FREEDM is big enough to set up seminars in the first place.

The seminar had been advertised as a self-improvement exercise for anxious people. Kevin told me he went to support a friend. He may have been lying but I don't care either way, it's the organisation I want information on. Unfortunately, he had very little aside from the pamphlet. He described the seminar as a motivational TED talk with a charismatic speaker who talked about facing her fears. She hadn't been Susie, he was sure of that. She was too young.

There's an email address included in the pamphlet, but I haven't contacted them yet. I want to see what else I can find online. I try typing different phrases into Google that I think Susie might have incorporated into her organisation. *Dare me, dare you*. And *follow me, follow you*.

After a few different combinations, I uncover a few Facebook comments that warrant further investigation. And then I click into some social media profiles, jotting down names as I go. Maybe these people are cult members. It's hard to tell when most profiles are set to private. Still, there are trails from public group comments that lead me in different directions and it's interesting to see where they go. I take some screenshots, too.

What am I going to do with these? If he's still speaking to me, I could ask Liam to look up these people, but they haven't done anything wrong, as far as I know. I'm not sure he can pry into people's records without a reason. Susie's cult also doesn't seem to have done anything wrong. I've never seen anything in the news about it.

But if Susie has based her cult on the risky dares she and I did as children, then surely there is some element of danger involved in joining. This cult is all about facing your fears. Does Susie make these people perform challenges like she's making me perform them?

Before I consider that idea further, I have several phone calls back to back. A man in the middle of a divorce, an old woman frustrated by local teens breaking into her shed, a sex pervert asking me about my feet, and finally, a young woman with a recent cancer diagnosis.

"It's terminal," she says. "Stage four."

"I'm so sorry to hear that. How are you feeling?"

"Physically, I'm okay. I know that will change soon." She sighs. "I have a lot of people to take care of."

"A big family?" I ask.

"Yes. I don't want to leave them."

"That's more than understandable," I say. "Would it be a comfort to know they can carry on without you?"

"Yes, it would. They need someone to replace me, you see. I just don't know who."

It's an odd thought, but I get it. She sounds like a mother terrified that her children won't have a mother figure.

"I'm sure you can't be replaced, but your children will find peace in their memories of you."

"Oh, they aren't my children," she says. "Not biologically, anyway."

"I'm so sorry for the confusion."

"It's okay. They are my children in a sense."

"I see—"

"Thank you so much for talking to me. I feel a lot better now."

"I'm so glad I could—"

The line goes dead. Bob lifts an arm and points at his watch. It's the end of my shift and time for me to go home. I give him a nod, then remove my headset.

CHAPTER THIRTY-FIVE

I thumb through the FREEDM pamphlet again on the train home. Many of the pages are a blood red colour, with one mysterious line printed on the page. *We are the agitators. Let the fear set you free. Don't let fear hold you back.* But there are also some pictures of happy people holding hands towards the back of the booklet.

There's no coincidence here. The FREEDM organisation is based on mine and Susie's pact. My best friend and the woman who has been missing for sixteen years started a cult. She is a cult leader.

It all falls into place. Of course, this was where Susie ended up. I saw the signs all the way back to when we were seven. I saw it all happen. From the moment when she threw that egg at our teacher's house, to the way she seemed so convinced that us jumping into the sea cured her cancer. To the day when she forced me across the train tracks. Her commitment to it all remained devout throughout our childhood.

While Susie did have a good childhood and a great mum who gave her everything she could, I also know the toll prolonged illnesses takes on a child. She may have had complex PTSD issues that weren't understood by the adults around us at the time. Susie developed leukaemia right before the millennium when a lot of psychological issues could be missed or ignored.

Maybe she disappeared because she wanted to start again. She wanted to become this… this leader of disciples. She created a whole new persona to avoid the trauma she experienced as a child.

I pick up my phone and scroll through the contacts until I see DS Liam Harding's number. We left things on a terrible note. But I'm not sure how to continue this without telling him everything I know. I have proof that Susie is part of an organised cult. One that, if it's based on our childhood dares, must involve asking members to perform dangerous stunts. At some point, this cult must have broken the law. With all these people performing risky challenges, I'm surprised there hasn't been any unusual deaths somewhere along the way.

Unless there have been, but because they're accidental, nothing has come of it. The police might not have known about the cult being involved.

Harrison Park station comes into view, and I shove the leaflet back in my bag before hurrying down the aisle. I've given up searching for Susie on the train. She's not going to be here; I know that now.

The wind takes my breath away as I make my way home. I keep my head down, eyes on the pavement, my mind whirring. I'm trying to think of a way to ensure the police have to get involved. This is a tricky area. On the one hand, unless any of the members are minors, I assume they consented to be part of whatever challenge Susie set for them. But cults can be coercive. Especially if there's a charismatic leader.

I step into the house expecting to hear the television on in the living room, but the kitchen light is off and the house is silent.

"Harry? You in?"

There's no call from his room. I shrug and pour out a small glass of wine before settling on the sofa. The house is a sanctuary away from the chaos outside. Part of me hopes Harry might move in with Hannah soon. After putting a little money away in a savings account for the last few months, I might just be able to afford a deposit for a small flat in the city centre. I should be nervous about living alone after the strange things that have happened to me this month, but I'm not. The idea brings with it a sense of comfort. For thirty-two years, I have felt uncomfortable in my own skin but now, I'm beginning to enjoy it.

Just as I'm thinking of him, Harry sends me a text.

> Hey. Sorry I haven't been home much. I'm at Hannah's but wanted to check you're okay?

I reply back:

> All good here. Got my Pinot and a takeaway menu. Ready for a rock and roll night!

He responds:

> Great stuff! Enjoy! And have a good Chrimbo. I'm staying with Hannah up until Xmas eve and then going to her family's house in the Peak District.

> Ooh, sounds lovely, I reply. Have a great time!

I realise that Harry has left without giving me a card or present. He's usually thoughtful about these things and makes sure to get my favourite chocolates on my birthday. I've been so caught up in everything that I didn't even get him anything. Maybe he saw I was too distracted and didn't want to embarrass me.

> Almost forgot. There's another letter for you. I put it on the desk in your room. Xx

My fingers tighten around my phone. I sense it's from her without even seeing the familiar envelope and address label. When I leap up off the sofa, I almost knock the wine glass from the coffee table. Swearing, I right it, and leave the dribble of Pinot Grigio that spilled from the glass. Then I hurry into my room and snatch up the packet. This one doesn't have a postage mark on it, but aside from that it's the same.

Susie hand delivered it to the house. Or *someone* did, at least.

I rip it open, and I flip over the last page to read Susie's challenge.

> *You did well in the woods, but then you had DS Harding's hand to hold. I think you should do the next one alone. On Christmas Day. I know you don't have anything better to do.*
>
> *There is a lake ten miles east of where you live. Get there alone at midday. It will be frozen over. The forecast is below freezing. But the ice will be thin.*
>
> *Wear a wetsuit.*
> *Jump in the ice.*
> *Swim under the ice.*
> *Then come back up.*

I lift a hand to my throat. Susie knows that I have a fear of being trapped under ice. When I was four, I was walking in the park with my father when a dog jumped into an icy pond and got stuck under the surface. Even though the adults present managed to get the dog out before he drowned, I remember the panic in the poor creature's eyes. It gave me nightmares for weeks.

But the message here is clear. She wants me to face my biggest fear and she wants me to do it alone.

CHAPTER THIRTY-SIX
JENNY'S DIARY

It must be a miracle, or maybe hell has frozen over, because Mum let me buy a bikini last week. I even wore it down at the beach with Susie. Mum reckons that now I'm sixteen, I can make my own decisions. I mean, duh. I've been telling her this forever, but she never listened before. I don't know why parents think turning sixteen is like this magical number but I'm not complaining.

We jumped off the cliff together again. This time I was scared about losing my bikini top, not about the actual jump. But Susie said it'd be fine. She's always in bikini tops these days. Maybe her mum isn't a great big prude like mine.

Anyway. We kinda muttered the words, but I guess I don't say them as often now. We did do that big challenge the other month, though. We jumped off the higher point at Breaker's Bay. What Susie really wants to do is Hangman's Cave, but I'm not sure about that. It's supposed to be dangerous.

Anyway, we jumped into Breaker's Bay, and then we swam to the beach and sunbathed for a bit. There were these lads there. I didn't recognise them from school. I guess they must be older. They kept looking at us. They'd look, and then turn away and laugh. I thought they might be saying mean things about us, but then they came over to talk to us.

"You two looked pretty good jumping from up there," one guy said. He was blocking my sun, and I wasn't happy about that. I guess he was kinda good-looking. Susie sat up and took notice right away.

"Oh yeah?" Susie said.

He nods. "Most girls wouldn't jump that. Are you local?"

I was annoyed when she told him we were. We don't know these boys. They definitely don't need to know where we live. What if they follow us home? I know I'm supposed to be brave with these challenges and stuff, but it made me uneasy to see her chatting to strangers so casually. They were older than us and I didn't like the way the guy's eyes kept drifting down below our collar bones.

"What's your names, anyway?" he asked. "I'm Owen."

Susie introduced us and Owen shook both of our hands. Then he asked if we wanted to join his group for the afternoon. They had a portable barbecue and some beers. Obviously, Susie got really excited about this because it felt like such a grown up thing to do. But as we walked over, I pulled her aside.

"I'm not sure we should stay," I said. "We don't know them. They don't even go to our school. And they're older."

She just shrugged. "Why are you so boring, Jen? Get a life, okay?"

I gave her my best dead eye, but she laughed at me.

"Look, if you do this, it'll count as our challenge for the month. Come on! I wanna try a beer!" She pouted at me until I relented.

Owen patted the sand next to him and we walked over. It made me feel a bit better that there were some girls in the group, too. They all told me their names. I think there were about ten of them. Some were couples, with the girls sitting on the boys' laps. I only remember a few of them now. Owen, who talked to Susie the whole time. Then there was Nicky, Laila and Max. I can't remember the others. They were friendly, though, and super tanned from being on the beach all day.

Once the beer got passed around, Susie and Owen started kissing and I felt a bit nervous and out of place. You hear all sorts of stories about drink spiking and drugs and peer pressure. But then Max talked to me, and I felt better. We have loads in common. Like loving Stephen King novels and watching Buffy repeats on TV. And then I found out that we both want to study psychology. We talked for ages about

Freud, it was so cool! Susie isn't usually interested. But Max thinks Freud's dream interpretation theory is cool and for once, I didn't feel like a great big nerd.

Anyway. We left when the sun went down. Susie threw up on the way home and I had to hold her hair back. We argued about it because she was super annoying talking about Owen non-stop. And then I had to make her coffee at my house to sober her up. I hope her mum didn't see how drunk she was. Mrs Patterson already thinks I'm a bad influence.

She's wrong, though.

It's the other way around. I get the blame for ev-er-y-thing but it's literally always Susie pushing us to do stuff. She gets mad when I hang out with anyone else at school, too. Like when I had a crush on Greg and he sent me notes, she read them out and made fun of me. I felt so weird about it, I didn't reply to them. Susie made Greg seem really lame and thinking about it now. I wish I hadn't listened.

But what am I going to do? She's my best friend. Oh, and—okay this sounds really bad—but everyone feels sorry for Susie because she had cancer. Like, she gets her own way all the time. I overheard Dad say that she was a little so-and-so before the cancer. He said, "Problem is, everyone feels sorry for her now, so they say nothing! Meanwhile our Jenny gets it in the neck from the teachers for breathing."

I kinda liked hearing him speak up for me. He tells me that I should speak up for myself, that I should look out for number one and stop being such a pushover. But I don't think I'm a pushover. Susie is super bossy, I know that. But most of the time, I actually want to do what she suggests, I just feel a bit nervous about it, that's all.

Anyway, I've decided that I'm not going to let Susie make fun of Max and ruin it all. We exchanged numbers so we're gonna text. It's so cool!

CHAPTER THIRTY-SEVEN

I don't remember the latest diary entry. Nothing about it even rings a bell in my mind. I have no recollection of the boys on the beach. I had a whole conversation with a boy—and exchanged numbers with him—that is completely gone from my mind.

My sleep is restless. Saturday comes before I've had enough sleep. It has been a while since I've been so starkly reminded of my brain injury. I'm not too proud to admit that it rattles me deep down to my bones. Every time I reach inside to try and remember, I'm greeted with a sucking void that leaves me ice cold.

It's Christmas Day on Monday. It won't be about family and presents this year, it will be about surviving a swim in an icy lake. I have to hurry out to a sports shop in Manchester to buy a wetsuit before the stunt. I get a text from Trudy asking if I want to go out for a drink later, seeing as I missed drinks with the counsellors due to my shift at Solace. I tell her I have a headache and can't make it.

Back at home, I decide to do some research into Owen and the group from the beach. Whoever they were, they must have lived in Chillingham. It's not exactly a tourist town. In my diary entry, I mentioned that this group didn't go to our school. But Susie and I were sixteen at the time so they may have been older boys who had already left. I'm a member of the Chillingham Secondary School Facebook group, so I scroll through looking for posts by members a few years older than me.

I refer back to the diary pages. Sixteen-year-old me doesn't go into much detail but I assume the kids were around eighteen to twenty years old. They would have graduated about 2005. I search the group members for anyone called Owen—there are nine—and then check out their bios to see if they have their ages listed. After an hour or so of research, I have a few potential Owens, but I don't feel confident about them. I'm not even sure what I'm going to do. Is the Owen from the beach going to remember some random encounter from sixteen years ago?

Then I move onto Max, but I don't find anyone the right age called Max at all.

Feeling deflated, I head into the kitchen to make dinner. It's not so much the FOMO of not having that big family to sit around a huge dining table, it's the fact that I should care more. At least, I think I should. Maybe society thinks I should.

Can we talk?

I stare at the message on my phone. It's from Liam. I pull on my coat and slip my phone into my pocket without answering. For some reason, I imagine him sitting in a busy bar, nursing a whisky, rowdy police officers celebrating Christmas all around him.

But Liam isn't that type. He's not tortured like the TV cops. He's more... solid than that. A safe pair of hands. That is, unless you begin to query his decision to meet me at the quarry. I can't deny it was odd.

Then I picture the expression on his face as he let me out of the car. Did I judge him too harshly? The rejection really hit me hard and there's a good chance I was a jangle of exposed nerves, raw and angry, not thinking straight enough to say what I felt. I have a part to play in our fight.

I decide to text him back.

OK, I type.

> Are you free tonight? I can meet at seven. What's that pub on the end of your street called?

The Dancing Bear? I respond.

> Yep. Are you free?

I so desperately want to leave him hanging. But he could help me, and I actually do want to show him the leaflet Kevin gave me.

> All right. I'll meet you there.

I place the phone on the coffee table. I didn't tell him about the latest diary entry, and I can't decide whether to tell him later. Susie asked me to go to the lake alone. If I have any chance of finding her and finally getting the answers I deserve, I have to do what she says.

CHAPTER THIRTY-EIGHT

There's a reason The Dancing Bear isn't my favourite pub. Right now, it's packed to the rafters with Christmas revellers. A drunk woman in a pencil skirt and an askew blouse is singing *Flowers* by Miley Cyrus on the karaoke machine.

Liam walks in and sheds his coat. He looks at the singer and lets out a low whistle between his teeth. "Ye Gads."

"What's your karaoke song?" I ask as he sits opposite me on the tiny table in the darkest corner of the pub.

"Silence. Not Silence is Golden, but complete silence. I don't do karaoke."

"Are you sure? I can see you singing Elvis or something like that," I say. "Or rapping. Actually, yes, I can see you rapping *Bodak Yellow*. Maybe with some twerking."

He lifts an eyebrow. "I feel like this might be your own private fantasy."

Without thinking, I grab his arm. "Oh, let's do *WAP* as a duet."

Liam shakes his head. "You are way too perky for a woman with a dark past."

As soon as the laughter ends, an uncomfortable silence stretches between us. We're probably both thinking about the fight we had in the car. I know I am.

"Do you want a drink?" he asks, motioning to the bar.

I shake my head, watching him walk away. I'm nursing a red wine, hoping to keep a clear head throughout this entire exchange. I need his help, but there are also things I don't want to divulge. But my heart is galloping, and I'm as disarmed by him as always.

I watch him walk back to the table with his pint. There's nothing relaxed about his posture. He walks like someone constantly checking his exits, with his eyes roaming and his spine rigid. A man constantly observing. I hate to think what he has observed about me.

"So you wanted to talk?" I ask.

He places the pint down and sits. "Yes." His mouth opens and closes and his eyes drift away from mine.

"Well, I think you may have to actually speak," I say. "Otherwise, this is going to be a wasted endeavour."

"All right, give me a minute," he says. For once, I see that he is actually grappling with his emotions. I sit back and chew on a thumbnail, giving him time to gather his thoughts. "Jenny, I do like you. But while I'm helping you find Susie Patterson, nothing can happen between us. There's a professional barrier here. Susie Patterson is still a missing person. Until she is not, this is off the table." He takes a long drink of lager after speaking.

"Okay," I say.

His eyes narrow. "Is that all you have to say in return?"

I pick at a thread on my sleeve. "Yes."

"Great." He glances up at the next karaoke singer, a middle-aged man singing *Disco 2000* by Pulp. "So has she been in contact again?"

"Actually, I was given this by someone else." I place the pamphlet Kevin gave me on the table. My palms are sweating, and not just from the hot air inside the pub. I don't want to lie to Liam, especially not after his pleasant speech.

"Who?" he asks.

"A man called Kevin. He's a Susie Patterson Truther, or in other words, he's one of the true crime obsessives who has stalked me and my family for the last sixteen years. But he did correctly identify the language used by FREEDM. Look." I point to some of the statements used inside the small booklet. "The exact same words Susie and I spoke before we performed our challenges."

"Where did he get this?"

"From a seminar," I say. "One of those self-help type places. A TED Talk for cultists recruiting their next members. I'm sure Kevin is a perfect candidate. His sister went missing years ago and he still seems broken by it. Then these fuckers swoop in and break his brain even more."

By the time I stop talking, I realise my fists are clenched. I hadn't realised how passionate I felt about the subject until I opened my mouth. But as someone with a broken brain, I can't stand the conditioning used at these places.

"Susie is one of those fuckers," he says. "How do you feel about that?"

"She's not just one of them. She's the leader. Look how the entire mission statement is built around our childhood." I shake my head. "I can't hate her. I'm sorry, but I just can't. I know what pushed her to this. I understand her better than anyone."

"That isn't true, though, is it? You haven't seen her for sixteen years."

"It is true. I was there for her formative years. I don't care what has happened since then, I know the core of who she is."

I finger the rim of my wine glass. "I know she isn't a good person. As much as I love her and the memory of her, I'm also furious at her. So mad, it physically hurts at times. But I can never hate her."

Liam lets out a long, loud sigh that even the woman on the next table hears. "What can I do to help?"

Some of the tension in my body finally releases. "I was hoping you'd say that." I point at the booklet again. "The dares. They have to be a main part of this cult. Jumping from cliffs, scaling buildings, bungee jumping, whatever. Susie loves that stuff, and she would want her acolytes doing all of that. I don't know how big this cult is, but even if a few dozen people are jumping from buildings and racing cars, or whatever, that there would be some accidental injuries or even deaths linked to this organisation. I wondered if you could try and find a pattern. I don't know where the cult operates from yet. There's an email address in here that—"

"Whoa, hold on a moment. You're not going to contact them?"

"Of course, I am. You really think I'm going to let a lead like that slip through my fingers?"

He shakes his head. "Cults are dangerous. You should stay away."

"I can't stay away. I have to see Susie, and if that means worming my way into her cult, then so be it."

"You have no idea what you're doing, Jenny."

"I've done okay so far."

Even to me, my voice sounds childishly high. There's nothing convincing or commanding about the weak tone. It feels like I'm back in Chillingham arguing about going out with Susie. A little girl stamping her foot and demanding freedom that hasn't yet been earned, pulling her weight against the ever-tightening lasso of adolescence.

"Look, I'm sorry to say this, but I don't like your friend," Liam says. "And you're a fool to think you can get any kind of closure with her."

"At least that's better than you believing I murdered her."

A ripple works up his jawline and his voice hardens. "I never thought that."

I snort. "Don't lie to me. Everyone does." I tap my wine glass against his pint and say sarcastically, "Here's to a new beginning. Us getting off on the right foot knowing I'm not a cold-blooded murderer. Now I'm just an incapable fool."

"I swear, Jenny, I never thought you murdered that girl. I'm a detective, I keep my mind completely open."

I take a swig of the wine, no longer trying to pace myself.

"It's true," he insists. "Come on, let's not argue again. I do want to help, I promise."

I put the wine down and lean back in my chair. "So what *do* you make of all this? What's your theory?"

He shrugs. "Basically, until proven otherwise, the most logical answer is usually the right one. That's the principle I work on. If I look at the evidence here, someone is sending you pages from your diary. It has to be someone who was close to you when you were young, or you yourself."

I wince slightly.

"At least that was what I thought at first. Now that I've been present to two of the challenges this person set up, it seems to me that there's a bigger team behind it all. The drone, the spotlight and the loudspeaker point to that. Unless you're the cult leader. But in that case, it wouldn't make much sense for you to come to the police." He pulls in a deep breath. "The most obvious solution is that Susie Patterson, the girl who went missing sixteen years ago, who has a history of recruiting others to take part in dangerous challenges, has set up some sort of organisation and now—for reasons unknown—she wants to recruit you." He points at my chest. "While she has clearly managed to fly under the radar for all of these years, she's now growing bolder. Even the fact that you went to the police doesn't seem to have bothered her. I wouldn't be surprised to learn she has some sort of security within her group. Cults tend to cultivate a fear of the establishment, including law enforcement. It's one of the ways they control their subjects. Susie hasn't shied away from you after you involved me. That says a lot."

His eyes sparkle. I can tell he loves his job and using his mind for this kind of investigation.

"What does it say?" I ask.

"That she thinks she's untouchable. And that makes her, and the rest of this cult, extremely dangerous."

CHAPTER THIRTY-NINE

Liam walks me home. It's two minutes of strangeness, the world so quiet after the loud pub. Tiny snowflakes land on my nose. My ears ring. Song lyrics from karaoke songs play on a loop through my mind. There's a moment at the door when I think he might lean in to kiss me, but it never happens.

"Have a good Christmas, Jenny," he says. And then he reaches into his pocket and produces a small box wrapped in a bow. "I got you something. It's not a big deal."

"Oh." I take the gift and stare at it. "I didn't get you anything."

He laughs. "That's okay, I didn't expect you to." He waves a hand. "It's nothing. It's... It's just a small gesture. I thought you might need cheering up or something."

"Thanks."

"I'll be in touch if I discover anything that might be of interest."

"Okay. Um... have a good Christmas." I raise a hand to say goodbye.

There's no hug, no contact between us, but the gift in my

hands makes me feel like we did embrace in some way. I don't understand it. Why would he give me a present?

I wait there for a moment outside my house, considering calling his name. I watch him melt into the shadows before I head inside. A dusting of snow hits the hallway floor. Damp flakes follow me into the living room where I flop down on the sofa woozily, the alcohol still making me dizzy.

A nagging sensation pulls at my stomach. Liam was open and honest with me tonight. He told me exactly what he thought about Susie and FREEDM. But I lied to him.

Technically, it wasn't a lie. Deep down, I know not telling someone important information is lying. I will be heading to the frozen lake in a few days, but Liam knows nothing about it. We're investigating this together and I didn't tell him because I know he won't approve.

I tear into the wrapping paper. It opens up to a red box. I quickly pull that open and retrieve the gift. A small snow globe. It's pretty and feminine in a quaint, precious way, depicting an ice skater on an icy lake. She's in an arabesque position, her cheeks rosy pink. I shake it up. Snow gathers inside, the burgeoning of a storm. And then I place it down on the table, my body cold all over.

Is it a coincidence? Of course it is. Snow globes always depict a wintery scene. Icy lakes are wintery. It doesn't mean he knows about the challenge. Does it?

On Christmas Eve, I research the lake in question and find some not particularly comforting information. Two people have died trying to walk on the ice. One in 2005 and the other in 2018. It tends to ice over but not enough for it to hold a person's weight. Susie doesn't actually want me to walk on the ice. She wants me underneath it. I shiver at the thought.

Liam is right not to like Susie. There's an element of cruelty about this challenge. She knows me and knows my fear. I told her about the dog I saw fall into the icy water and now she's using it against me. But then it wouldn't be a challenge if it wasn't easy, would it?

I pre-book a very expensive Uber for Christmas Day. Then I eat a whole box of mince pies and watch Home Alone. Susie and I had a crush on Macaulay Culkin the first time we watched it. That was when we were six, before everything went sideways.

I think about calling Dad again. But what am I going to say? He didn't even send me a card. I guess I didn't send him one, either. He'd sounded pleased to hear from me when I last called, but not enough to reach out to me again. Either he's stubbornly waiting for me to go back to him, or he cares less than he makes out, or he's given up. Though, I have no idea what to do about it if I figure out which it is.

Sleep doesn't come easy. As my eyes drift closed, I hear giggling. I'm back in the woods with Liam, listening to the tapes. *Dare me, dare you. Follow me, follow you.* She always wanted followers. I was her first.

I wake before my alarm on Christmas Day. This is it. Every part of my body is numb. I pull on my new wetsuit and layer it up with warm clothes over the top. I choose boots that are easy to lace and layers I can peel away. I pack a towel and a flask of scorching hot tea. There's no eating breakfast, I'm too worried I'll throw it back up. Then I get into the taxi.

"Happy Christmas," the driver says. "Are you going to meet family?"

"Yes," I lie. "We have a family tradition. We meet by the

lake every Christmas day for a nice walk. Only my car needs new tyres."

"Nightmare," he says.

I get lost in my story. "Yeah. I ran over a nail on the road. It's going to cost a fortune. My dad's lending me the money, though, so it's all good."

A strange kind of thrill runs through me. It's similar to the spike in adrenaline I had when Susie and I stole the car, or when I ran over the train tracks. I'm bolder and braver than I once was. I'm finding her again, the Jenny that died at Hangman's Cave.

The taxi driver concentrates on his Sat Nav. I get the impression he's done with small talk. I browse my phone. I even pull up the lake on Google Images. It is quite isolated and we're meeting at the time most people sit down for their Christmas dinner. I still can't help wondering if there will be walkers around to see me do this. Perhaps they'll be lucky enough to watch me drown.

As the driver stops the car, I'm sweating under the wetsuit and far from prepared for what I'm about to do. I clear my throat to thank him before getting out.

"Have a good one," he calls.

"You, too," I say back, my voice cracking.

The weather is stark but beautiful. A spattering of snow clings to tree branches like icing sugar but the sky is bright blue, allowing me to see the city miles away in the distance. I look down at the frozen lake and my stomach lurches.

"Susie, you'd better be here," I mumble.

If I go ahead with this challenge, I don't have a way back. I'll be cold—freezing cold—with no car. Just a towel and a flask of hot tea. I'm relying on Susie being here this time. She needs to save me.

"I'm trusting you," I shout to no one. A bird flies from a branch, causing snow to tumble down to the cold ground.

I pull my attention to the long, thin lake. There's something unpleasant about it. The shape isn't aesthetically pleasing like a nice, rounded lake is. Light glistens and bounces across the thin layer of ice coating the surface. Patchy ice. The kind that breaks when you poke it with your toe. I think of the two people who died in this spot. Did they die because they weren't prepared for it to crack? At least I know what to expect.

I dump my bag on the frozen ground and look around me. The area is deserted. There's a small copse of trees at my back. I sigh, and remove my coat, imagining myself being watched from a distance.

"This is insane," I say quietly to myself. "Completely and utterly insane. I can't believe I'm doing this for you. Again. You've put me through hell, Susie, and yet here I still am."

I picture her face. From an innocent seven-year-old, to the bald-headed, pale faced child going through chemotherapy, to the precocious sixteen-year-old with the hard glint in her eye. Then I remove my woollen jumper and turn around to face the trees.

A figure approaches.

CHAPTER FORTY

The world tilts on its axis and I disassociate from my own body. I'm looking down, numbly watching my own body as my jaw drops open and the figure—the woman—strides towards me. She walks with her back straight and her head held high. She's blonde, and she's wearing a long coat that reaches below her knees.

There's no way to know for sure. But who else would it be? This is it. I followed her instructions to the letter, and she's come to reward me. *Susie*. All my resentment falls away and I just want to know she's alive. I want to see her and hug her and pretend we're seven again. That isn't too much to ask, is it? I deserve this gift from the universe after everything else I've been through.

And then she comes closer. My fingers tighten into fists. It grounds me, pulling me back to reality. As she approaches, and I get my first glimpse of her face, my reaction is one of confusion. She doesn't look like the woman I saw on the train. She's younger. Her features are petite. Her hair is a darker blonde, more ash than straw. It's like all of my organs are torn from my body at the same time. This isn't Susie. The person walking towards me is only around twenty-five years old.

"Hi," she calls, waving a gloved hand. "I'm Mia. Susie sent me."

"Where is Susie?" My tone is abrupt, rude even, but I can't hide the disappointment. I came all this way here.

"She said she'll see you very soon," Mia says. When she reaches me, she stands a couple of feet away and shrugs off her coat. "I'm here to do the challenge with you. Susie understands she's given you a difficult one."

Her words bring me back to the task at hand. Swimming under the ice. My heartbeat quickens. "It's my worst fear."

Mia nods. "Our leader always gives us the hardest challenges before we become part of the group."

"Are you part of the group?" I ask.

"I am. For six months now."

"What was your indoctrination?"

"I had to let a tarantula crawl across my face." She smiles. "I had a horrible fear of them. For years, if there were spiders in my room, I'd run away screaming. I'd have panic attacks. Nightmares. But Susie changed all that." She places a hand on my shoulder. "I'm sure you understand." Her tone is knowing, referencing my history with Susie. "We call her Agnes because it means pure. But she told me you'd know her name from before."

"Before what? Before this cult? Before she ran away?" I regard this young woman before me, with her knowing smile and shining grey eyes. I see no trace of darkness in her. No sense of a troubled soul.

"Before she was reborn, I suppose. We are all reborn after we face our worst nightmares." Mia stares out at the lake. "Would you like to plan your journey through the ice? I've been in this lake before. It's deep so if you're not careful you can drift way below from the surface. You need to find the thinnest patches to break through."

"You've swum under the ice here?" I ask.

She shakes her head. "I've only been here in summer. But I'm confident we can figure out your best route. Come on." She takes my hand and leads me down to the water's edge.

I respond to her quiet confidence. She's pretty and petite, but what makes her special is her composure. She walks with her head held high, her hair blowing behind her like an ethereal creature from a fantasy movie. Mia's skin does not tremble like mine does. She's still smiling, not grimacing in utter terror.

"I will be honoured to recite the words with one of the original creators. You are special to us, Jenny Woods. A beacon."

"Me?" I gaze out at the lake, every muscle in my body shaking in fear. My knees are weak and about to buckle under my weight. "I'm not the person you think I am."

I could tell her that I can't even drive a car here because I'm so afraid, or that I routinely experience panic attacks. Or that I'm once again outside of my own body, too terrified and too cowardly to live in my own fear.

"It wouldn't be a challenge if you weren't afraid," Mia says. "You're the strong one. The innovator. You belong with us." She gestures to the lake. "The water is cleansing, and you can be reborn. I believe in you."

Her words are quiet against the chattering of my teeth. She lets go of my hand and peels away her layers. At the same time, she points out the best entry point into the ice and possible exit points.

"You might not be able to see very well," she says. "Stay close to the surface. Feel with your hands and punch through."

I nod. I remove my layers of clothing. Mia helps me when I shake too hard.

"You're all set," she says, smiling. I notice that she's doing this without a wetsuit. She's down to her underwear and barely seems bothered by the freezing air around us.

In contrast, there's no blood in my body. I'm sure of it. I can only imagine the pallor of my skin. Teeth chattering, limbs shaking, I fear that I'm already too cold to survive this. I grab my flask and gulp down a few mouthfuls of hot tea. Mia drinks, too.

She grabs my hand again. And we recite Susie's poem.

One, two, three
Dare you, dare me.
One, two, three
Let the fear set you free.
One, two, three
Follow you, follow me.
One, two, three
Let the fear set you free.
Let the fear set you free.

Mia turns to me, staring deep into my eyes. "Let the fear set you free."

She pulls me closer to the water. Sharp stones jab into the soles of my feet. I've never understood those who seek out pain. Piercings, extreme spicy food, tattoos and so on. There's an addictive quality to it, but I'm too avoidant to try. This is so far out of my comfort zone, I'm on another planet.

"Ready?" Mia asks.

I'm not, but I nod anyway. I want answers and I want to know Susie is alive.

I want to know, once and for all, that I'm not a murderer.

Because sometimes I think I might be.

CHAPTER FORTY-ONE

As soon as I break the surface of the freezing cold water my body enters survival mode. Both Mia and I gasp involuntarily, shocked by the sudden chill. I can't imagine doing this without a wetsuit. Mia must have nerves of steel. We break thin ice with each step. Panting, we continue into the lake, which surprises me by how deep it becomes so quickly.

Mia stops and grasps my hand. "Now we go under the ice. Are you ready?"

I nod, but my thoughts swirl with uncertainty. She lets go of my hand and I turn to her, picturing Susie in her place, the two of us at eight years old standing at the top of the cliff. A smile spreads across my mouth. Adrenaline surges through my veins. I want to do this. I want to feel this.

Then I'm under the ice in one swift arc of my body. The cold hits my bones and I convulse, hands groping up towards the surface. All I want to do is gasp for breath. I kick my feet and hold my breath, turning to look for Mia. The water is black and blurry like the liquid from my nightmares. There's a shape somewhere in the distance—Mia, I think—but I can't tell how far away she is. Then my head bumps against the ice and I'm surprised by its solidity. Remembering what Mia said, I try to turn over, so that I'm belly up. But I can't.

The water is dark, almost pitch black. I know Mia is somewhere nearby, but I can't see her. It takes me back to that moment when Susie and I jumped from the cliff, the terrifying seconds of thinking she'd drowned. Only this time it's me underneath the surface, paddling and holding my breath, trying not to panic.

Something touches my foot. A weed. Algae. Debris. I don't know. I kick out, making sure it doesn't wrap around my ankle and pull me down. I need to come up for air. I have no idea which direction I started swimming, even though I had a location in mind. As soon as the cold water hit my body, all rational thought went out of my head.

Groping upwards, I feel for the ice again. Mia told me it would be easy to break but it's firm. I'm flailing, bashing against the surface. Every time I make a dent, I keep floating away. I can't seem to hit the same spot more than once.

Panic sets in. My lungs burn. I need to breathe. I'm going to die. Something hits my foot again. Not a plant, but an object. Could it be Mia? There's no way to find out when I drift along another couple of feet. I release air bubbles and force myself to open my eyes as wide as they'll go. I've never been a strong swimmer. I won't survive this. The number of times I almost died for Susie and now it's actually happening.

Dark, cold, thrashing water. Churning, bubbling, deep and black as night. What if the image of churning water wasn't a memory but an omen?

And then it hits me. The real reason I'm doing all of this. The morbid motivation that I keep buried all the way down inside. I've told myself that I'm doing this for answers. A desire to find out what happened to my best friend once and for all. To find those pieces of my memory that I lost, that have made me feel less than whole for the last sixteen years. But all of that is bullshit. I'm doing these challenges because I think I have nothing to live for.

I built my life on rocky foundations that eventually split apart. Since Jack dumped me for his mistress, I've lived without purpose, believing life will come crumbling down around me. But all I need to do is go back to those foundations and make them stronger.

I'm down but I'm not out. I'm not alone. I have a father and while ever we're both alive, we can reconcile. It might not be easy but it's an option. Harry might not have fallen at my feet but he's a good friend. So is Trudy, even though she's my boss. And then there's Liam.

I want to fucking live.

My arms swing back, beating the ice. There's a crack, I roar as I throw my weight back, the base of my skull hitting a weak spot. It gives, finally, and I thrust myself up. I fill my lungs with air. Tremors shudder through my body and I can't see anything for a moment, but I can breathe at long last. But my body is weak, and I could fall back under the ice at any moment. I need to figure out where I am.

Once I blink away the water, everything comes into focus. There's Mia, standing on the edge of the lake, a group of people gathered around her, towels over her slim body. We're not alone and we haven't been this entire time. I'm not sure if that's unnerving or some sort of comfort.

They applaud as soon as my head emerges from the ice. Mia jumps up and down, clapping her hands. Someone shouts my name.

I'm right in the middle of the lake which isn't good. There's another twenty feet or more to swim and it's all ice.

Maybe I can try to crawl across, but if I fall, I'd have less control over my body.

I smash the ice directly in front of me. I've done my swim beneath the surface for Susie, now I need warmth and safety. It's slow going, but I manage to stay afloat and continue smashing the ice as I travel across the lake. Bit by bit. Broken shards float alongside me, bumping into my body. Up ahead, the faces of the people come into view. These are the members of FREEDM. I note that they're a diverse group of people, from young, like Mia, to those with greying hair and wrinkles. Susie has reached all of these people somehow. Her influence reaches far and wide.

Three of them run down the bank. They grasp hold of my elbows and help me out. Their warm bodies feel strange next to my numb limbs. Someone wraps a towel around me. Another pushes a hot drink into my hand. Someone else unzips my wetsuit and removes it from my wet skin.

Mia approaches. She's shivering, but aside from that, her composure is as self-possessed as before. "You are reborn, Jenny Woods. Welcome to our family."

The group repeats mine and Susie's childhood mantra in unison. *Let the fear set you free.*

And I do feel free.

CHAPTER FORTY-TWO

I'm bundled into a car wrapped in towels. Someone has retrieved my bag from the other side of the lake to bring with us, wherever it is we're going. A woman with olive skin and brown eyes rubs the towel against my shoulders while a man in glasses dries my hair. It's bizarre sitting in a car in my underwear with strangers all around me, keeping me warm, rubbing my wet skin. My teeth chatter so hard, I can't speak. I can't even ask where we're going. All I care about is getting warm. The driver, an older man with grey hair, cranks up the heating and I bask in the hot air.

We could be in the car for fifteen minutes or two hours. I'd believe both. By the time we pull up outside a cosy cottage, I'm so out of it that two of the cult members carry me through, my half naked body held close to a chest I've never touched before.

Once inside, I try to keep my bearings, paying attention to what I see. It's a big house with a large front garden without any other houses surrounding it. I'm taken into a living room, passing three, maybe four people on the way. Then I'm placed gently down on the carpet in front of a roaring fire. A few people sit on the sofas and chairs around me. They smile but stay quiet.

"Hey, Jenny."

It's Mia, crouching down to me. She passes me my bag and clothes. She asks the others to leave and gives me a few moments to quickly change. She returns to the room in comfy jogging bottoms and a hoody. Her hair is almost dry now.

"How are you doing?" Mia asks.

"Very. Very cold," I reply. I grab my flask and take a sip of tea.

Mia grabs hold of my feet, which are now in thick socks, and rubs them. It's oddly intimate but the friction helps.

A few minutes later, one of the men from the car brings me a bowl of hot soup. He places the tray down near me on the carpet. It's tomato. Not my favourite, but I don't care. After I wolf it down, my stomach churns and I lie down, staring up at the beams.

"Where am I?" I say.

Mia pushes a cushion under my head. "In one of our safe spaces."

I notice the phrasing. *One of*. FREEDM owns—or rents—multiple properties. Does that mean Susie is rich? I've never known a cult leader to not profit from their subjects.

"Are we close to the lake?" I ask. I sit up and lean against a chair. "How many people are in this... organisation?" I manage to stop myself saying cult.

Mia pats my arm. "We'll talk about all of that later. Just enjoy yourself. You faced your biggest fear and came out the other side." She moves closer, her face near mine, her hands on my legs. "You are a force to be reckoned with."

"It's time," someone shouts.

Mia grins. She helps me up and throws an arm over my shoulder.

"Time for what?" I ask.

"You'll see," she says, leading me through the house.

We come to a dining room where there's a long, wooden table laid out with roast turkey and all the usual trimmings. Despite the soup, my mouth waters.

"A proper Christmas Dinner," I say.

"Sit," Mia instructs. "As the newest member, you're at the head of the table and you get to pull the first cracker."

Mia moves away, heading somewhere further down the table. I feel awkward for a moment. But then people introduce themselves to me. There's a David and a Rachel and a Priti and a Jabari. There's no way I'll remember everyone. But I pull a cracker with one of them and then people pass me bowls of food. Someone hands me a glass of mulled wine. Everyone congratulates me.

"You did it and you're part of the family now," Priti, sitting to my left, says. She passes me the potatoes. "Agnes will be proud."

"Why isn't Agnes here?" I ask.

"She's busy. But I'm sure she can't wait to speak to you. I know you both have history."

"We do," I mumble.

I pass the potatoes to David on my right. Then I turn back to Priti.

"What was your challenge?" I ask. "To get into the group?"

"I used to be afraid of heights. So I went bungee jumping with most of the people around this table." She sweeps a hand to gesture to the others.

"Is it always a group process?" I ask.

"No, not always. Sometimes the group just watches. It's different for everyone."

"Why is that?"

She shrugs. "I don't know. I suppose Agnes decides whether or not the participant needs encouragement. Also, some of us prefer to do it alone."

I turn to David. "Can I ask what your initiation looked like?"

He laughs. "Mine is tame compared to some of the stories around this table. I drove over a bridge." His voice has a faint Liverpudlian accent to it.

"Oh," I say.

"I know." He waves a fork, a roast potato swinging back and forth. "It sounds like nothing, but my wife died on a bridge three years ago and I hadn't been on one since."

"I'm so sorry for your loss."

He places the fork down on his plate. "Thank you, Jenny." There's gravitas in the way he speaks my name. As though it's important that I'm here in this room. "My wife, Gemma, committed suicide on a bridge near us, back in Liverpool. I hadn't been near it for years. But this group helped me."

"How did you find out about FREEDM?" I ask.

"I joined a grief counselling group after Gemma died." He takes a sip of mulled wine. "I got friendly with some of the people there and met Frankie." He points to a woman around thirty years old at the other end of the table. "She suggested we try out a seminar. It all started from there."

As I cut my turkey into smaller pieces, I consider what the chances are of Frankie just happening to hear about the seminar. It seems as though FREEDM does not advertise. I haven't seen any social media presence at all, which is strange for a modern-day cult. Half of these dodgy organisations thrive precisely because of social media and how easy it is to radicalise someone. But FREEDM isn't like that. It operates on a word-of-mouth basis. I can't help but wonder whether Frankie was planted in that group therapy session just to try and convert some of the vulnerable people there. I stare down at my food, not hungry anymore.

CHAPTER FORTY-THREE

I drift away from the group after dinner. The last fumes of my adrenaline spiked day are fading away and exhaustion makes my body heavier. Susie, or Agnes as she's known by these people, is a shadowy presence whoever I talk to and wherever I go. But that doesn't stop me from asking questions. What I find is that the members are open about their initiation ceremonies, but they close up when I ask about FREEDM and Agnes in more general terms.

A bland former accountant called Jonas once allowed himself to be buried alive for his initiation. Two members scaled tower blocks at night. Another humiliated themselves by standing in the centre of a circle, naked, while the cult members hurled abuse at them. But when I ask whether they give money to the organisation or when they last saw their family, I often received a thin-lipped smile and a gentle, "I'd rather not talk about that right now."

I slip away. It's all becoming overwhelming. I expect to see Susie every time I turn around.

Even in a small room at the back of the house, decorated as a tiny office, I sense her. Maybe she picked out this chair and this desk. I run my fingertip along the wood, wondering if it's something the Susie I knew would choose. At the end of the day, it's just a desk. There's nothing special or unique about it. Nothing that screams Susie to me. And yet I can't stop thinking about it.

"Oh, sorry."

I turn to face the door. A young woman, perhaps nineteen or twenty, hovers there, her cheeks flushed pink.

"I thought it was empty in here," she says. "I'll leave you alone."

"That's okay," I say. "I was just having a quiet moment."

She smiles. "There are a lot of people here. It gets overwhelming." She tucks a lock of hair behind her ear and drops her gaze.

"I'm Jenny." I take a step forward and reach out.

She's tentative when she takes my hand, her movements furtive and nervous. She reminds me of a mouse searching for a hiding spot. Or of some of the kids I work with at school. The ones with phobias and/or abusive homes.

"Ashley." She smiles shyly.

"Have you been in the group long?" I ask.

She shakes her head. "A few months."

"What made you want to join?"

Her arms fold around her body with her hands gently stroking the tops of her arms. I see she's a lost child seeking comfort.

"Oh, I don't know," she says. "I guess I was scared of everything. I wanted the fear to stop."

"Has it stopped?" I ask.

"Yes." Her smile is bright, lighting up her warm brown eyes.

"Have you met Agnes, too?" I ask.

She drops her hands to her sides and nods. "Once or

twice. After my initiation challenge, she met with me, and she gave me some reassurance that I belong here. My, um, my challenge didn't go so well."

"It didn't? How come?"

One shoulder lifts as her eyes glance away. "I was so scared. I... I only did half of it. I still have to complete the other half. Agnes said I can postpone it. But I am doing better. I'm so much less afraid than before."

"Do you live with the group, Ashley?"

She nods. "I love it here. Everyone is so kind. We're a family. We go to all the challenges together." For the first time, she becomes animated, moving her arms around as she speaks. One of her sleeves drops back showing a bandage running along her forearm.

"Oh no. You've hurt yourself."

She immediately covers it. "Just a scratch."

I purse my lips tightly. I don't want to ask, but I know I have to. "If you don't mind me asking, what was your initiation challenge?"

"I would rather talk about it after it's done." She places a hand on my shoulder. "Hey, maybe you'll be there with me."

"Maybe I will," I say.

We're quiet for a moment, until I ask, "Is there always a group whenever someone is initiated into FREEDM?"

She nods. "Yes. The initiation task needs to be witnessed."

"Is every single task dangerous?"

"No," she says. "Not always."

"But it often is." I let out a little laugh, trying to lighten the mood. "Jonas told me about being buried alive."

"I wasn't there for that one. But I heard about it."

"Ashley, do people ever die?"

I see that the question catches her off guard. "I don't

know." She scratches at her cheek. "But we all know the risks before we do it."

"Of course," I say. "Everyone here is an adult making their own decisions. I'm not blaming anyone. I just... Well, I suppose it's strange to me that FREEDM hasn't attracted more attention. You know, like those Netflix documentaries or long articles online about dangerous organisations."

She leans away from me, frowning. "FREEDM is not dangerous. I have been safe here, it's the only place in the whole world that I feel safe."

"I'm so sorry, Ashely." I reach out to her, but she pulls away. "I didn't mean to offend you. I'm just trying to get my head around everything."

"But don't you feel better after facing your fear? Don't you feel lighter? And look at the faces in this house. They are happy faces, aren't they?"

"Yes," I admit.

"So what's the problem?"

I'm about to ask more questions. But a pretty song chorus drifts in from somewhere deeper inside the house. She grabs my hand and pulls me away. We head back to the living room, which is now sweltering from the heat of the fire. I sit down on the sofa while Ashley joins the group singing.

I don't know the song, but it's melodic and slow with haunting harmonies. I watch the faces of maybe a dozen people, standing in a tight line in front of the fire. Their heads tip back, their mouths open. The sounds fill the room, and my head swims with lyrics.

We are free! We live as one!

I want to be free, too, and I want a family. A pleasant warmth spreads through my limbs. I close my eyes, tilting my head back, and hum along with the tune.

CHAPTER FORTY-FOUR

After the singing ends, I stagger through the house to the kitchen and pour myself a glass of water. Ashley is there, watching me, and Mia. The two of them speak in low voices, their eyes never straying from me. Their images are blurry around the edges, and I blink, frightened by it. I've had a few glasses of mulled wine and a hot chocolate with a shot of whisky. It's not a lot, but I also haven't eaten much today and put my body through an extraordinary task.

I'm drunk. I should probably leave.

I take my phone from my pocket and search through my contacts. It takes all my focus to move the screen up and down with my thumb. The more I scroll, the more I realise how alone I am. Harry is away with his girlfriend, my dad lives too far away and probably won't be sober, which leaves Liam.

I can't turn to Liam for this. I lied to him. Things are civil between us now but he's not a friend.

"Are you okay, Jenny?"

Mia takes the glass of water from my hand. It's only when

she does that, I notice I've spilled at least half of it all over the kitchen floor.

"I should go," I say. "I need to get home. I'll phone for a taxi."

"I'm not sure that's a good idea," she says. "I think you might have had too much mulled wine."

She loops an arm through mine, propping me up, and takes me through to a small bedroom at the back of the house. It's just big enough for a single bed and a wardrobe. The pattern on the walls makes my head hurt. Obnoxious roses glare down at me, giving the room a claustrophobic feel.

"Why don't you have a lie down," she says. "Just relax for a while."

I sink down onto the bed and feel the soft duvet under my weight. It's calling to me. There's nothing I want more than to slip my feet underneath the bedding and go to sleep.

"You're safe here, Jenny. We love you and accept you."

Mia helps me underneath the cover and then tucks it up to my chin. It's a lovely, childlike feeling, and I turn onto my side, thinking about Mum and how she'd do the same thing.

My thoughts fracture and split, unable to focus on one thing. I'm left with an image of Susie's face as I lose consciousness.

Hours later, I wake with a start. Blood pulses through my temples like a throbbing wound. I gaze around the room, disorientated, gaping at the red roses, before it all comes flooding back. I dived underneath the ice and I survived. Every person in this house was initiated into the cult by facing their worst fear.

There's a bottle of water, a packet of ibuprofen, and a bacon sandwich on the bedside table. I eat the food and then swallow the painkiller.

Sipping the water, I take advantage of being alone by

going over the entire evening in my mind, breaking down the dinner and the conversations I had afterwards. I think about all the dangerous stunts performed by these people. I think about Ashley's defensiveness when I asked if anyone had died. I'm not convinced that it's all sweet singing and Christmas dinners together. There is money involved here. Vulnerable people are targeted through group therapy.

I understand the draw. I'm still on my own high after the lake.

"Morning, sleepyhead." Mia's head pops in the room. When she sees I'm awake, she opens the door wide, and steps in, passing me a cup of tea. "Thought you might need this."

"Thanks." I take a sip.

I don't want tea. I want to leave. But I need to play this right. No one knows I'm here and also, I'm basically undercover now. If I slip up, I'm screwed.

"You look tired," she says. Then she laughs. "Sorry, that was a bit rude of me. It's just I'm shattered, too. You were lucky to get a room to yourself."

"Oh, I'm sorry I didn't—"

She waves a hand to cut me off. "You're our guest of honour. You deserve your own room. I ended up on an air mattress in the living room." She sips from her own mug. "We aren't always so crammed in but with it being Christmas, we wanted to have a big get together."

"Of course," I say. "It's weird Agnes didn't come, though. Isn't it? Wouldn't she want to spend Christmas with you all?"

"She's with the six."

I frown. "Who?"

"The six are those chosen as her acolytes. They stay with Agnes in her house."

I take another mental note. The cult is multi-layered. Those at the top of the pyramid live with their leader while the others bunk up in a house that's too small. Susie really has built this thing up. I would be shocked if a portion of these people's salaries weren't going straight to Susie.

I created a monster.

"We're going out today," Mia says. "It's Jabari's initiation."

"I... Actually, I need to go home. I'm so sorry. I just wasn't prepared for all this. I don't have clothes or—"

"We can provide everything you need," she says.

A moment of silence hangs between us.

"But it's okay," she says. "You're not a prisoner here. Of course you can go home."

I'm surprised by two things, how willing she is to let me leave, and how much I want to stay. I chew on my bottom lip. If I stay, I'll get to witness another initiation into the cult.

"Agnes may come," Mia says. "She sometimes does for initiation challenges."

It's a carrot on a stick. I know that. But I still nod my head. I'll still do anything to see her. Swim under ice. Climb a quarry. Whatever it takes. I'll do it all.

Mia gives me a little wave and disappears out of the room. My arms tingle like I'm full of static electricity. This will be my first opportunity to see an initiation into the cult that isn't my own. Butterflies dance in my stomach. I place the tea down on the bedside table and pull in a steadying breath. And then I smile to myself, because I realise that I'm excited.

CHAPTER FORTY-FIVE

Two hours later, and I'm in one of two cars that leaves the cottage. No one has told me what Jabari's initiation will be. I'm in the front seat next to Mia as she drives. Every now and then, I glance up at the rearview mirror to see Jabari rocking back and forth. I don't know much about him except that he is originally from Birmingham, and he told me at dinner that he came to his first seminar five months ago.

"It's going to be okay," Mia says. "Let the fear set you free."

She drives for around thirty minutes before pulling over. I examine the landscape around us. It's barren. There is no snow, no foliage, no people or cars. There aren't even any bare trees. A cold, boggy moor stretches out around us, with one road snaking through the centre.

"It's time, Jabari," Mia says.

I see the second car continue up the road. It's a single track. I wonder if they haven't seen us stop, but they just keep going.

Mia unclips her seatbelt. I'm about to do the same, but

she stops me. Then Mia and Jabari get out of the car. Jabari comes around to the front seat and sits next to me. He's sweating. I see the droplets along his nose. From the way his fingers flex against the steering wheel, I assume his worst fear is driving.

My adrenaline spikes. I don't like driving, either. I've been afraid of it since I passed my test years ago. Now I'm going to be in the passenger seat as a terrified driver faces his fear.

"One, two, three, dare you, dare me," Mia says.

Jabari pulls in a deep breath. He places the car in gear. His hands shake as he presses the ignition button.

There is a chorus coming from the three women in the backseat.

"One, two, three, follow you, follow me."

Jabari revs the engine. The tyres screech against tarmac and he pulls away. His chest heaves up and down, rapid like a pneumatic drill. A roar passes through his lips. I grip the armrest, my chest tightening.

"One, two, three, let the fear set you free."

Jabari screams it solo, "let the fear set you free!"

I watch the speedometer tick upwards. Thirty miles an hour, then forty, then fifty, increasing as fast as my heartbeat.

"That's too fast!" I call. "The bends..."

But Jabari isn't listening. The engine revs. The speedometer goes higher and higher, up to seventy. The three women chant from the backseat. *Let the fear set you free. Let the fear set you free.*

I want out. I want to fling myself from this car, but I'll die if I do that. I press my palm to the window. I long to screw my eyes shut but I also want to keep them open. And then the road opens up to a long, straight stretch. I'm thirteen again, with my arm out of the window, with Susie laughing beside me, freedom a taste on my tongue.

But this is different, not just because Susie isn't here, but because we're not alone on this road. There is a car coming in the opposite direction and this road is not big enough for two lanes. But Jabari isn't slowing down. He opens his mouth, a roar coming from somewhere deep in his body. I'm not sure he can even see with all the sweat dripping down from his forehead.

"Stop!" I scream. "Stop!"

He doesn't stop. I claw against the window, desperate, impotent, facing my death for the second time in forty-eight hours. The car ahead is so close, I see the faces of those inside. Grim, tight faces, not smiling but fixed on their task.

Priti is driving the opposite vehicle. I don't understand at first, and then I do, when the second car swerves onto the verge, sending the car down a ditch. I turn my head, watching it roll and roll until it hits a dry stone wall at the bottom.

"Are they hurt?"

No one answers me. Jabari whoops for joy and the car speeds again. We approach a bend, and he doesn't appear to slow. My heart is a bird flapping its terrified wings. He's out of control now. This is it.

But his foot moves and the brakes screech. The speedometer drops below fifty as we take the bend. Then it continues to drop until it finally comes to a halt. I yank the door handle as soon as it's safe, my feet finding the floor just as the car stops.

There's a field on my left. I climb over the gate and walk through it, striding so fast and pumping my arms with every step. My breath comes out ragged.

"Jenny! Jenny, wait!"

It's Mia's voice behind me, made thin by a strong gust of wind.

"Jenny, there's nothing out here. You're miles away from any villages. Stop!"

I hear the shuffle of her feet against grass as she runs to catch up with me. I turn to face her, thrumming with rage.

"We could have died!" I yell.

"It was all set up safely," she says. "We've tracked movement on this road for weeks. We knew it would be empty."

I lean closer to her. "Bollocks! It's Boxing Day. What if some farmer guy decided to take a short cut visiting his mum. You can never know for sure that a road will be empty."

"We knew there is little chance of—"

"If you think I'm getting back in a car with you lot, you're insane." Then I remember Priti and the car hitting the wall. "Wait, what about the others? Are they okay?"

"Jenny, they're fine. It was a ding, that's all. Priti has already managed to reverse out of the ditch." Mia shrugs. "She's a good driver."

"This is all crazy."

"And yet you feel alive, don't you? For the first time in years, you feel alive. Everything Agnes has given you has been a challenge she knows you'll live up to. She has brought the feeling back into your numb life. She has reawakened you." Mia places a hand over my heart. "That's it. I feel it. The beating of hot blood pumping through your veins. You're reborn, Jenny Woods. You're with us, I know you are."

CHAPTER FORTY-SIX

I let them take me back to the cottage where I call another taxi, but I refuse to let them drive me home. My body crackles with energy and as I wait for my taxi, I pace back and forth in the kitchen, clenching and unclenching my fists.

"I'm sorry."

I spin on one heel, finding Jabari standing in the doorway. I wave a dismissive hand and keep pacing.

"I saw a head on collision when I was a kid. Someone in the backseat flew through the windscreen and it was... it was a horrible thing. I've had nightmares ever since."

"Someone should have warned me!" I snap.

He holds his hands up. "No argument here. I think so, too. But there are rumours that Mia had instructions not to tell you."

I take a step towards him. "Why? From who?"

"I don't know. For all I know, it's a load of rubbish." He turns his head towards a group of other cult members. Someone calls his name. Then he's gone, leaving me pacing up and down.

The taxi arrives while they're in the middle of celebrating with Jabari. Every face is grinning. Wine is flowing. I'm the stick in the mud leaving while everyone rides the high.

"Family visit?"

I look up at the mirror as the driver pulls away from the house. "Yeah."

"Sounds like a good party."

I nod.

"Must be a shame to leave."

"I've got to get home to my baby," I lie. "She's with her dad. Shared custody."

"I get it," he replies. "I'm doing the same thing with my ex."

It's weird that I'm making up stories to the taxi driver. And in them, I force my life to seem more normal than the reality. Maybe it's bold of me to lie. I am Jenny Woods reborn, after all. The anxiety-riddled version of me could still be in that cottage for all I know. Or perhaps she's waiting for me in an empty home.

The envelope waits for me on the doorstep. I kick it away, sending it flying down the hall until it hits Harry's bedroom door. I assume he's still at Hannah's because he doesn't come bursting out to see what the noise is. Then I peel away my clothes and step into the shower, trying to wash away everything I've seen and felt and done.

It's while shampoo rinses out of my hair that the tears come. Gulping sobs that make my naked chest heave up and down, convulsing my abdomen to the point where I think I might throw up. I don't even know what I'm crying for. All I know is that the anger I felt in the field is now fizzling out. I keep picturing Mia standing in front of me, pressing a palm to my heart. *You're reborn, Jenny Woods.*

Sixteen years.

I have lived without Susie in my life for sixteen years. I have lived with this broken brain, desperately searching for the answers, doubting myself, blaming myself, hating myself. Even when I was with Jack, I felt alone, until today.

They made me part of them and for that, I hate them.

Out of the shower, I catch a glimpse of my wet naked body. It's scarlet, like damaged flesh just before it bruises. I dry, putting on my oldest, comfiest clothing, and step back into the hall.

I grab the envelope and take it into the living room. And then I rest it on my knee. I'm not sure I want to know what is inside. The last entry took me to memories that were lost in the accident. This next entry could take me even further along that journey.

I dread it.

Then I tear it open.

CHAPTER FORTY-SEVEN
JENNY'S DIARY

Susie doesn't like Max and Max doesn't like Susie. I mean, of course. It's so predictable, I find myself rolling my eyes every time they're together. It's so awkward. The thing is I like Max a lot and I want them to get along, but it just isn't happening. Max wants to join in with the dares every month. But the thing is, it's mine and Susie's thing and Susie, in particular, is very possessive about that. Which I kinda understand.

I don't want Max to join in. I want to move on. I think. I dunno. I don't like thinking about it too much because sometimes I wonder if Susie and I would stay friends if we didn't do them every time. And... well... Diary, I will explain later. First, our latest dare.

All three of us broke into the abandoned lighthouse and went all the way to the top last week. Susie and I hung from the window for a second. It was only a second, but Max got super pissed off because we *wanted it to be just our thing.*

Also, it was scary! It wasn't the scariest thing we've ever done. Maybe I'm just getting softer as I get older. But none of that matters because if Susie challenges me, I have to do it. Those are the rules established since we were seven years old. Nine years ago. Nine!

Susie has been in remission for so long now. Fuck.

I feel like such a bad friend. For like the last three years, I've considered getting Susie to stop the dares. I figured we were old enough to understand that us jumping off cliffs doesn't stop her cancer coming back. And then I found out the worst news ever.

Susie has to go back to the doctors for tests. There's a chance her cancer is back, and I don't know what I'll do if Susie gets ill. Or worse, if she dies. Did I cause this? Is it because I stopped believing?

Sometimes I think the words I write in this diary are actually insane. I've been learning about sociology, psychology, and religion. Sometimes I think we just made up God because it's too scary to accept there's no meaning. Max says there's no plan, that we control our own destinies. I think so, too. We keep thinking that everything in this world is connected but it isn't. It's all random. Us jumping off the cliff and Susie finding out she's better is just random. A coincidence.

But Susie thinks she can stop the cancer coming

back. I want to feel like that, too. I really do. I want to be a good friend.

We were in her bedroom earlier listening to music. She put The Chemical Brothers on really loud because her mum was at work. We jumped up and down like lunatics. She seemed kind of agitated and even poured out a couple of glasses of vodka then topped up the bottle with water. Her mum checks on the levels.

I downed mine and sat on the carpet. Susie was on her bed. She rolled over and looked down at me. I was reading Q magazine while she did her English homework. She was late handing it in again and I'd helped her by giving her my essay.

"If I do have cancer again, we need to do more challenges," she said. She bit a pen lid before flicking it at me. "Are you listening?"

"Yes," I said, annoyed. "I know you're scared about the cancer."

"But..." Susie rolled her eyes.

"But I know what you're going to suggest, and it isn't worth it."

"How do you?"

"It always comes back to Hangman's Cave with you. But it's counterintuitive."

"Did Max say that?"

This time, I rolled my eyes. "I'm being serious. The challenge at the lighthouse was fun but some of them scare the crap out of me. What if we get hurt? What's the point in doing this to keep you alive when we're constantly almost dying? It makes no sense."

Susie made a face and then went quiet. She stared down at the essay resting against a Just Seventeen magazine.

"Sorry." I raised a hand and offered it to her.

She hesitated but then took my hand and squeezed it. Her mouth lifted at the corner.

"Maybe Max can do it with us."

"Hangman's Cave?"

"Yeah."

I stared down at my Q magazine, not reading a single word.

"Jenny. We have to do it. You have to do it. Look, I know Max hates my guts and everything and that you're starting to hate the challenges, but I need this." Her voice broke. Her eyes filled with tears, and I felt like the shittiest person in the world.

"All right." I threw the magazine to the floor and moved over to the bed. "Okay, I'll do it."

"Do you promise?"

I swallowed before I crossed my heart with my fingers. I knew what I committed myself to. It made her happy.

While I write this now, I keep thinking about the leukaemia coming back. I can't stand the thought of it. I want to scream or throw something, but I guess I haven't done either of those things. I slammed my bedroom door, and I cried like an idiot and shouted at Mum and Dad when they tried to talk to me.

I should do anything to save my best friend. Shouldn't I? No matter what. It's me and Susie *against the world and it always has been. She's always been there for me. She's the only one at school who cares about me. When the other kids tease us, we ignore it because we have each other.*

Dare me, dare you.

Follow me, follow you.

We always said we'd follow each other. That shouldn't change just because I'm in a relationship.

Oh, God, diary, I'm going to do something stupid. Aren't I? I'm going to do it because I feel so fucking guilty.

We're going to end up jumping into Hangman's Cave, because that's the ultimate challenge and the only one I've always said no to.

The worst thing is, I think I want to do it. I know I talk about stopping, and I do think we should, but Hangman's Cave has always been there at the back of my mind. I guess I always assumed we'd do it eventually, as long as I worked up the courage. Besides, we have to go out with a bang, don't we?

CHAPTER FORTY-EIGHT

I let out a long breath. So this is why we jumped into Hangman's Cave. Susie thought she had cancer again. I pull my knees up to my chest for warmth. One more piece of the puzzle slots into place. I was doing it for her.

But why didn't Fiona Patterson mention this during the investigation? Susie had regular check-ups. All cancer patients do. Any change in her test results would be communicated to Fiona as well as Susie.

My heart sinks. Did Susie make it up? Did she tell me just to make me do the challenge?

At this point, it's clear that Max was my boyfriend. At sixteen years old, I break into lighthouses and am in a relationship with an older boy. Because I'm almost certain that Max did not go to our school. I want to track him down, but then I remember I haven't read Susie's next challenge. I turn the page.

I'm proud of you, Jenny. Mia told me about your

bravery in the water. It makes you a fully-fledged member of this humble family.

I know you have questions and I know that you want to see me. I promise that you will get all the answers you require and that you and I will meet.

You more than anyone in this world know what it takes to keep a promise. I will not break it.

I look forward to seeing you soon, Jenny.

Your ever faithful friend.

Agnes

I swipe my hand across my forehead. This is the first time she has called herself Agnes. I wonder how much of her old identity she has scraped away. When I see her for the first time, I'll meet Agnes, not Susie.

I stride into the bedroom and pull out every photo album, yearbook, exercise book, and letter from my school days. Max has to feature in one of them. Maybe if I track him down, he can give me more information about the weeks leading up to Susie's disappearance. And if I know more about Susie's mindset back then, I'll be more prepared for when she summons me.

I flick through the pages, scanning each one. Boys barely exist in my photographs. I don't remember ever taking a boyfriend home. Max wasn't questioned in the aftermath of Susie's disappearance. He didn't even come to visit me in the hospital. My parents must not have known about him, either. Perhaps Susie's disappearance spooked him. I place the photo album down. This is all extremely odd. He never came forward after all these years and there must be a reason for that.

Tired, and in the throes of an awful headache, I decide to

leave all this for now and cook myself a quick meal of pasta and vegetables. Then I text Bob and ask him if they need volunteers tonight.

> If you're free, we'd love to have you here. It's a busy night.

I'm too wired to sleep. I dress and head down to the train station. It's just after seven p.m. and I'll be taking on the night shift that lasts until morning.

Bob isn't there when I arrive. Karen is the manager for the night. I make a coffee and sit down at my usual desk. In between calls, I broaden my search for Max beyond the Chillingham school group. I try every social media app I know, searching for a Max from North Yorkshire. I find a few but none of the ages quite match. There's Max Harrison, Maxwell Leo, Maxim Peters and more. Even after a deep dive, I don't recognise anything about these men. Most are married with children now.

I abandon the social media profiles when I get a call.

"You're through to Solace. My name is Bella, and I am here to listen."

"Hi, Bella. I called the other day and I think I spoke to you."

"It's nice to hear from you again."

"Do you remember me? Do you remember my voice?"

I let out a nervous laugh by accident. "I'm so sorry but no. I speak to a lot of people so please don't take it personally."

"Don't worry, I don't. Last time I called, I told you about how I have terminal cancer."

"Right," I say. "Of course. You told me how you have a large, adopted family. Is that right?"

"Yes," she says brightly. "I hate to leave them. They're my

whole world. They lifted me up and put me back together again. Have you ever known a family to do that?"

Her words force me to think about my own family. I love my dad, but he has no idea how to lift me up.

"I think it's wonderful that you have had that kind of positivity in your life," I say.

"Bella, you didn't answer my question."

"You caught that, did you?" I say.

She laughs. "I get it. You don't want to talk about anything personal. That's okay, I know you must deal with some strange people, and you probably don't want to reveal too much information about yourself."

"It's against the rules to give out personal information," I say.

"Bella isn't even your real name, is it?"

"No," I admit.

"That's okay. I don't want to give out my name, either."

"That's completely fine."

"You're a good person, Bella. I can tell from your deflection that you haven't had a great time of it. Otherwise, you would gush about your family. You'd be vague but you'd say nice things about them. You can't do that, can you?"

For once, I have no answer. I stay silent.

"I've made you uncomfortable."

I want to hang up. I've dealt with curious callers before but there's something about the way this woman controls the conversation that makes my skin crawl. I can't explain it. There's just an odd edge to her voice.

"I'm not uncomfortable," I say. "But I am here to listen." I clear my throat. "You're right, I have had my own struggles. We all do. We're human. We're all together in this world, as it should be."

"I think so, too," she says. "I'm pleased to know it's your philosophy as well."

"I wouldn't be here if I didn't want to help people."

"I have to go now, Bella. I enjoyed our conversation."

The line goes dead, and I take a moment to breathe. She got under my skin, but then some of the calls here do. I go back to the social media profiles of all the men in Chillingham called Max and try to concentrate. But I can't stop thinking about family.

FREEDM offers lonely people a family. There were over a dozen people eating Christmas Dinner together. Breaking bread and drinking wine, talking, singing, touching, kissing. It's what we crave. I am just as lonely as them. I crave family as much as they do.

I think about Mia's palm on my chest.

Jenny Woods. Reborn.

CHAPTER FORTY-NINE

I stand in the centre of Manchester watching the sun rise above shops and apartment blocks and hotels. It is blood red.

I haven't slept but I don't want to go home. Trudy's office doesn't open until January, so while I was at Solace, I booked an appointment with Raj at nine a.m. I walk down to the train station and alight the 8:15 to Harrison Park, not bothering to find my usual seat. I give the coach a quick, cursory scan to check if Susie is around. But she isn't, and I know by now that she will not be coming to me on the train. Her reveal is bound to be something far more dramatic.

Harrison Park is quiet, too. I make my way quickly to Raj's office, keen to get started. I need to uncover more memories. I need to find Max at the back of my brain.

"Did you have a nice Christmas?" Raj asks as I step into his office.

"Yeah," I say, shrugging off my coat. I'm full of anxious energy as my sleeve gets stuck. Shaking the coat in anger, Raj moves around me to help me out of it.

"Did you come for a specific reason?" He hangs my coat on the rack by the door. Tiny rain droplets hit the carpet.

"I want to go back to that night again. I feel like I might be able to remember more." I fold my hands together, pressing my fingers tightly.

"That's great," he says. "Take a seat." He smiles warmly, either ignoring my obvious restlessness or choosing to meet it with a calm composure.

My heart pounds as I sit in the leather recliner. He takes the chair opposite as usual.

"You seem worked up, Jenny," he says. "Do you want to take a moment, just to relax?"

I don't. I want to dive straight into that night, but I'll never get there while I'm like this.

"All right," I say.

Raj guides me through some breathing exercises, and I finally begin to calm. The thundering in my chest becomes a soft padding, still elevated but not about to burst through my ribs.

"I'm going to start the countdown now," he says. "Gently close your eyes for me."

I count along with him.

10.

9.

8...

It can be hard to focus after a traumatic brain injury. You're always more aware of the parts you're missing. But I try as hard as I can to picture the night at Hangman's Cave. I think about the diary entry Susie sent me. The one where I decided I wanted to do it. I wonder if I was nervous. If I asked Susie if I could back out. Or maybe I was confident, feeling that sense of invincibility that Susie sometimes made me feel.

"Jenny, talk to me about the night Susie Patterson went

missing," Raj says, using his soft voice. "You were with her. You were just sixteen years old. Go back to that time and place and talk me through what you remember."

There's a bright white light ahead. The man holding the torch is a police officer and he rescues me from the dark woods. I don't know how I ended up in the woods after the jump into the cave, but that's where I am.

I'm leaving the woods without Susie and I'm afraid. I want to know where Susie is, but I don't know. The man asks me if I'm okay and I nod. Then I tell him my friend is in there somewhere, but I don't know where. I'm aware of the fact I'm leaving Susie behind. But once I get to the hospital, I barely remember a thing. I barely know my own name.

Then I track back. I need to go deeper. Back to standing on the edge of the drop at Hangman's Cave. There's a breeze lifting the hem of my dress. I'm holding her hand.

Black.

A wall shoots up, slapping me in the face.

"Deep breaths, Jenny," Raj says softly.

We're reciting the poem. We're about to jump. Someone is watching me. There's a pair of eyes hidden in the shadows. A prickling sensation spreads across my scalp moving from the front to back. I think I turn my head before we jump. But what do I see? I don't know.

I'm cold. Freezing. I can't breathe.

Then nothing.

I wake. I'm alone and I don't know where I am. My head is pounding. I see water churning. Black water. Everything goes dark. Then I wake again. I feel like I need to find her, it's the first thought that pops into my head. So I wander around. I trip. There's blood on my hands. I scream and I run.

I don't stop running until I see that white light.

And then I wake for a third time. My mum is holding my

hand. She's crying. I'm poked and prodded and questioned and whatever I say, it's the wrong answer. I want to see Susie because I know she'll make me laugh. She'll say something bitchy about the doctors and nurses. She'll tell me how she had it worse and I should stop being a wimp. But most of all, I want to see her to tell her what a stupid idea it was. Because if we hadn't jumped into Hangman's Cave, she would still be here. We'd be at home listening to her free NME mix CD and trying to write an essay about Of Mice and Men.

I want to say I told you so.

Susie's mum visits and she has only one question.

"Where is my daughter?"

I try to answer her, but I can't. Something is missing from my brain.

Raj counts again and I come back to the present, but I don't want to. I want to stay there, sixteen years ago and find the missing parts to make it all make sense. The churning water. The running. The blood. The eyes watching me from the shadows. What does it mean? I wish I could see Max's face, but I still can't picture him.

He's the key to everything, I can feel it.

CHAPTER FIFTY

I finally sleep.

My body collapses into it. And when I wake, it's with a start. I hear voices in the house. I move over to my bedroom door and listen. Harry and Hannah giggle together from somewhere in the house. I wipe my sweaty forehead with relief and then jump in the shower to freshen up.

I completely forgot he was coming home today. I dress quickly and make my way out to say hello. It seems as though they've just arrived. There's a hold-all on the dining table and the two of them are hovering in the kitchen.

"Hey, Jenny." Harry pulls me into a hug. "Did you have a nice Christmas?

"It was fine, thanks," I say. "Hi, Hannah."

"Hey." She grabs me and plants a kiss on my cheek. "Oh, you have a letter. I put it on the table."

Hoping they don't notice the blood draining from my face, I quickly snatch up the envelope. But it's different this time. The envelope is smaller and handwritten. I don't recognise the handwriting.

"I hope it isn't something bad," Hannah says, frowning at my intense reaction.

I try to laugh it off. "Oh, no. Probably just my aunty. She likes to write letters around Christmas. Anyway, I'll leave you to it."

"Do you want a cup of tea?" Harry asks. "I just put the kettle on."

"No thanks. I have one in my room going cold. See you both in a bit." I stumble back away from them, almost knocking my shoulder against the door frame.

I'm positive Harry knows I'm lying. He would have noticed the kettle was warm when he refilled it. I shake my head as I head into my room. I need to keep my cool if I don't want to come across as a psycho. Though I guess that ship sailed quite a while ago.

I rip open the envelope and remove the contents. This isn't the same as before. There's no diary entry. Instead, I really do find a letter but it isn't from my fake aunty, it's from Mia.

Dear Jenny,

I hope you don't mind me writing to you. Agnes sent me your address and gave me permission to contact you. I don't have your phone number otherwise I would call. I'm sorry I forgot to ask you for your phone number. In all the excitement, it slipped my mind.

I know that you found the experience at FREEDM to be quite intense. That's okay. It is an intensive experience. Fear is the hardest of all emotions to face.

If you are willing, I would like to show you another side of our humble organisation. I've left some contact details at the end of this note. I would love to hear from you again, Jenny Woods, you left a lasting impression on me. I am, and always will be, floored by your bravery.

Mia

This is all so strange. It's like I'm being headhunted for a new job. There's so much flattery packed into such a short note. But it doesn't matter because I already know I'm going to text Mia. I need to know more about FREEDM and that isn't going to happen unless I spend time with members of the cult.

I fire off a message.

> It's Jenny. I got your letter, and I am interested in meeting you again.

She responds quickly:

> I am so thrilled to hear that! I've felt so bad about Jabari's initiation and how it upset you. Can you stay at the cottage this weekend? For NYE?

I consider it for a moment, pacing back and forth in my bedroom. God, I hate this set up with a housemate. At thirty-two, I should have my own space that's bigger than one room. I'm itching to get away from these four walls. But I have no idea what is in store for me at the cottage.

Nerves jangling, I reply back to Mia and tell her I'll be there.

I hate to admit it to myself, but knowing I have this waiting for me, makes me feel even more alive.

There's no easy way to pack for New Year's Eve with an adrenaline junkie fear cult. I could be jumping out of a plane for all I know. I take jeans, jumpers, boots, and one smart casual outfit in case we end up at a pub. Then I agonise over whether to take some sort of gift. A bottle of wine or a box of chocolates. But considering there are so many people living in the cottage, nothing seems adequate.

Mia picks me up from outside the house early on Saturday morning. I won't be home until Monday. Harry and Hannah are out, but I've let them know I'll be away with friends. I can't help but wonder if Harry buys that, considering I've never mentioned any friends outside my work friends. I also had to skip a shift at Solace, but considering I took the night shift earlier this week, Bob doesn't care.

Mia helps me with my bag and then gives me a long hug. "It's so good to see you again."

"Thanks. I'm glad we don't have to dive into a frozen lake together today. Unless you're going to make me do that again."

She laughs and we get into the car.

"There's no lake this time," she says. "Actually, we're going on a hike today. Did you bring boots?"

"I actually did. I guess being an overthinker who plans for every eventuality finally paid off."

"You know, there are some benefits to fear. Like you said, it helps us plan for different scenarios. Humans have evolved based on our fears, right?" She looks at me like she expects an answer.

"Based on survival," I say.

"Right. But that's connected to fear. The fear of becoming prey."

"Yeah, I guess so."

"But it also holds us back." She pats me on the knee as we make our way out of Harrison Park. I see the train station on my left, the place where all of this began. "You know that more than anyone, Jenny. Agnes told me about your anxiety disorder."

I shake my head slightly. I can't get used to Susie being referred to as Agnes. "How does she know about my anxiety disorder? I was diagnosed after she disappeared."

"That's the power of Agnes," Mia says.

Her perfect smile should put me at ease, but it doesn't. There is something in Mia's voice, and her smile, that makes my stomach squirm. *The power of Agnes.* It almost sounds preternatural. How does Agnes know intimate details about my life? According to Mia, it's because of some sort of mysterious power, not because Agnes has sent someone to follow me, to watch me, to find out everything about me.

Mia drives past the city and out into the countryside and I wonder how many lies Agnes has told her and the other followers. And then I wonder why she believes those lies.

CHAPTER FIFTY-ONE

I change into thicker jeans and socks for the hike. But when I emerge from the spare room at the cottage, I see Mia and Jabari carrying large packs and tents into the living room.

"Are we camping?" I ask.

"It's going to be a mild night," Mia says. "We thought it would be fun."

"Okay," I say. "I haven't been camping since I was ten."

"Don't worry. We have a sleeping bag for you, and you can share my tent. Here." She tosses me a pack. "Some supplies for the walk. Come on."

I pull on a coat and sling the bag over my shoulder before following the others out of the cottage. There's a footpath leading out past the back garden that snakes through a wood. We use stepping stones to cross a stream and Jabari helps me up a steep bank on the other side. From there the woods open up and we're soon on the edge of Saddleworth Moor. I pull in a deep breath, enjoying the fresh air away from the city suburbs.

For some reason, I expect everyone to be chattier, but we

all seem in our own little worlds. I think about the last camping trip I went on. It was me, Susie and my parents. We ate bacon sandwiches and beans from the tin. Dad got annoyed when Susie ate two Kendal mint cakes to herself. I got annoyed when she farted all night in our tent.

It's like a lifetime ago.

The moors rise and fall. It's colder on the peaks, and my boots trample through the last of the snow. Every time we're high up, I gaze out at the landscape beyond. This is what I've needed for a long time. An opportunity to clear my head.

When the group stops and I see some of the FREEDM members setting up the tents, I make my way through the small cluster of people until I find Mia.

"Are we allowed to camp here?" I ask. "Aren't there rules about camping in some of these places?"

She shrugs. "No land is truly owned. Every human being on the planet is simply borrowing a piece of the world."

I'm not entirely sure what to say to that so I decide to allow it to happen. After almost dying in a car collision and swimming through a frozen lake, camping where we're not supposed to be camping seems pretty tame.

David and Priti get a fire going. I wander away from the group. I know I should ask everyone questions about FREEDM but right now all I want to do is stare at the view before me. It's almost three and the sun is low. I feel my hair blowing behind me, and the tips of my ears are freezing cold. Susie seems so far away. As does Liam. And Harry. And Jack.

"Hey."

I turn away from the view to find Ashley a few feet away. She approaches slowly, as though she isn't sure whether to talk to me or not.

"I heard about Jabari's initiation. Sorry it spooked you."

"Are they all like that?" I ask. "I understand that the group is there to bear witness, but throwing us in harm's way like that?" I shake my head.

"I know you probably won't believe me, but they really did plan everything super carefully. We never want anyone to get hurt."

I glance over at Ashley, and she averts her eyes. I still believe that people are injured or even worse during these challenges. Maybe the cult forgets this, but I used to partake in them as a stupid kid. I know how close we came to hurting ourselves more than once.

Close. Susie would tell me that nothing ever happened. We never actually hurt ourselves. She'd tell me that I exaggerate, that I overthink, that I want to look for the negatives instead of the positives.

"How old are you?" I ask Ashley.

"Twenty," she says.

I look at her. She could be twenty. She could also be fifteen. I can't exactly demand to see identification, so I don't press the issue.

"What happened during your initiation?" I ask.

She shakes her head slightly. "I backed out. They had it all planned out and I couldn't go through with it."

"Why not?"

"I was too scared." She brushes a tear from her cheek.

"What was it?"

She shakes her head. She still won't tell me. I want to pull her into a hug, but I don't. Instead, I ask, "Has the group made you feel bad for not wanting to go through with the challenge? Are they pressuring you?"

She sniffs. "No. Nothing like that. I just want to do it. I want to be like the others."

She's so young. She reminds me of how I felt at twenty, still figuring out my broken brain and how to live with it, falling in love with Jack, grieving the loss of Susie and not quite sure how to handle so many emotions all at once.

"Hey, you two. Do you want bacon or sausages?" Mia calls.

It breaks the moment. Ashley and I walk back to the group and her tears stop. She smiles at the people who are probably the only family she has right now.

CHAPTER FIFTY-TWO

As the sun sets, I sit down on a blanket next to a man called Gerry and eat sausages with beans. We make small talk at first, remarking on the clear night sky and the coldness of the night. I learn that he's retired and used to teach geography at a secondary school in Oldham.

"How did you join FREEDM?" I ask.

"Well, my wife died last year," he tells me. "She had dementia and wandered out of the house one night." He pauses, his lips slightly parted. I can tell he's considering how much to say. "She suffered a horrible accident that night."

"I'm so sorry for your loss."

He nods and takes a bite of baked beans. These people all remind me of my calls at Solace. The loneliness. The loss. The vulnerability.

"I wasn't sure what to do," he says. "I have a son, who's forty now. He helped me but with practical things. He made sure I had food. He fixed things around the house and lent me money. But he wasn't there..." Gerry drifts off, staring out into the dark.

"He didn't give you emotional support," I say, slipping into my role as a volunteer listener.

"That's right. So I tried a few different support groups. Then I met Mia, and she told me to come to a seminar."

I feel like I need to experience one of these seminars. That I need to know what they say to these lost and lonely souls.

"I tried a few group sessions with Mia and the others," Gerry continues. "And then I moved into the cottage."

"You moved in?" I ask. "Did you sell your house? What about your son?"

"I gave the house to my son. It's better this way. I have a family again."

I'm about to ask more questions about finances because I need to know if these people are giving the cult money. I'm convinced that they are. Even organised religions ask for donations. It could be a percentage of their wages. There might be pressure to donate. Something is going on.

But then Mia stands, and all of our eyes are drawn to her.

She raises her flask. "I wanted to say something and toast our newest member, Jenny Woods." There are some whoops and cheers. A few people lift their flasks.

Gerry elbows me and passes me a small hip flask. I lift it to the others and take a sip.

"We all know Jenny is one of the reasons why we're even here. If it wasn't for her and Agnes's bravery as children, FREEDM would not exist. Jenny, you are an agitator. A trailblazer. We know how much you have suffered and how you must have so many questions about what has been happening these sixteen years. I want to tell you that I admire you, and I love you, and that I am so glad you are here with an open heart and an open mind." Earnestly, Mia drinks from her flask, then raises it towards the stars.

Everyone around the fire drinks and raises their flasks. I follow suit.

"One. Two. Three," Mia says. "Dare you. Dare Me."

We all say the words. Even me.

"One. Two. Three. Follow you. Follow me. One. Two. Three. Let the fear set you free."

We drink. Whisky warms my bones. Someone plays music through a portable speaker and Mia drags me up on my feet, spinning me around until my hair flies out behind me, and I laugh. Then I'm passed to someone else. David, I think. I twirl so fast, I can barely make out faces. I drink more whisky. Someone plays '90s dance music and I picture myself back in Susie's bedroom creating dance moves to our favourite songs.

We warm up the cold air with our drinking and dancing. Some of the older members soon retire to their tents but I'm arm in arm with Mia, swinging around. My flask is refilled, and I keep going. When I start to sweat and my vision blurs, someone hands me a bottle of water, then I'm guided back to the campfire. Jabari sits next to me on a blanket and the others follow suit. But Mia remains standing.

"It's time to release," Mia says.

For the first time, I see a pot over the fire. David is spooning the contents into tin mugs. He passes the first mug to Priti who passes it on.

"This isn't compulsory, but it is encouraged. We all drink the tea, which contains a small dose of Ayahuasca, and then we go around the circle and utter one thought that we have never told anyone before. It must be something that makes us feel vulnerable. A deep, dark confession. It has to matter." Mia takes a mug and drinks deep. Then she passes it back to David.

I stare at the palms of my hands. I've never taken drugs aside from alcohol and caffeine. I've heard of Ayahuasca, and

I know it can be microdosed. I also know it can cause hallucinations and a lot of vomiting. I mainly know this from following celebrity gossip after it became the latest fad.

Jabari presses the mug into my open hands. I stare down at it. Am I really going to do this?

I am not the same Jenny Woods I was back when I saw Susie on the train. Like Mia said, I have been reborn. I want to do this. I want to know what the Ayahuasca can pull out of my brain. I go to hypnosis at least once a week, why not also try hallucinogenic drugs. Why the fuck not?

I tip the tin mug and drink deeply.

Jabari claps me on the back and there are cheers around the circle. Mia stands ahead of me, smiling and clapping her hands. In the centre, the fire crackles, spitting embers into the grass beneath our feet.

Then she sits in the circle. I take a good look at all the faces around me. Some people are sweating already. Others seem giggly but nervous. David rocks back and forth slightly, his jaw tense. I find myself losing focus. Someone mentions their secret and I don't even hear it, I have to pull my focus back to the group.

"I lived in fear," Mia says. "On top of my arachnophobia, I was agoraphobic for over three years and my house was a mess. I was a hoarder. I couldn't throw away a chocolate wrapper, I was so bad. My sister had to drag me out of that house before I'd make any changes. FREEDM saved my life."

Guilt and shame burns away as each of us confesses our darkest secrets. I close my eyes. I don't want to put a face to the words. I hear how relationships were broken by pettiness, about abusive family members, revenge that made someone sick to their stomach, confessions of crippling depression that made people not want to live, the murderous thoughts of misanthropes. I've heard it all before. I've been the confessional to so many troubled souls who call Solace in their hour of need. But I have never confessed to anyone. Never. Then Mia says my name.

I don't open my eyes.

"For the last sixteen years, I thought I killed my best friend. For this whole time, I have believed that I am a terrible person and that I don't deserve love. Because my ex-boyfriend, when he was drunk, told me I probably killed her out of jealousy. He said I was in love with her, and he mocked me for it, and I have carried that with me always. But now I'm just furious at her, because she wasn't even dead this whole time. She could have spared me so much pain, but she chose not to. She is the terrible one. And when I see her again, I don't know what I'll do."

CHAPTER FIFTY-THREE

I stumble away from the circle and throw up at the top of a steep hill. The world is spinning. I drop to my knees and press my forehead against damp grass, trying to find a way back to reality. Then I lie flat, turning over onto my back so that I can gaze up at the stars. This year is almost over. I ended my long-term relationship, moved in with a stranger, and then went through everything that has happened since I saw Susie on the train.

Now I'm off my tits, watching the stars move across the sky—they should not be moving—and find it all amusing. I shake my head and check my phone, wondering what the time is. To my surprise, Liam sent me a message.

> Can't go into details but there are some accidental deaths to look into. Have you heard from Susie? Seems weird to not hear from her for so long.

Without thinking, I text:

> Can't talk. Taken Ayahuasca with the cult. Watching stars.

The reply is instant.

> Wtf?

I send him a shooting star emoji and text:

> I miss you.

Then I slap my forehead. "Oh no. Oh no, no, no, Jenny. What are you doing?"

The phone rings. I throw it away from me and sit upright, my heart beating fast.

"Shit."

It carries on, the jingling tune like nails on a chalkboard. I get on my hands and knees, scrabbling around for it. Finally, it's in the palm of my hand.

"Hello," I say.

"What the hell is going on?"

"Oh, hi, Liam. Sorry about the crazy text—"

"Where are you?"

I laugh. "I have no idea."

"What are you doing with the cult? Are you mad? Cults are dangerous. I thought you knew that. I thought you were smarter than that."

"I can't tell if you like me, hate me, or just completely underestimate me," I say. "Sometimes I think you believe I'm a delusional idiot sending myself my own diary entries. Sometimes it feels like you think I'm a cold, calculated murderer who got away with it sixteen years ago. And sometimes I think you want to fuck me. Which is it, DS Harding?"

He hangs up.

"Well, I guess I'll never know." I lean back and stare up at the stars.

This was never about him anyway. This is about me and Susie. He inserted himself in it because this case is a draw for him. I'm sure he remembers our pretty, sixteen-year-old faces. He would have been a teenager himself, fantasising about us. Picturing himself finding Susie, carrying her to safety, being a knight in shining armour.

I don't need him.

I get up on my own two feet and stumble down to the tents. Mia waits with her arms open, ready to embrace me.

"How are you doing, Jenny?" she asks.

"I think the drug kicked in," I say. "I just did something I'm probably going to regret in the morning."

"You won't," she says. "Because you have faith in yourself now. You know that every instinct, every choice is the right one. You are right here." She touches my chest again. "You live here. And you will always live here from this moment on."

I nod my head. She's right. I'm finally open.

I sit with the group again but this time I've forgotten all my questions. I just listen. I hear strong voices speaking from the heart. After a while, I walk away and sit, watching dawn break as the birds sing. I see myself with Susie. We're standing on the edge of Hangman's Cave. We're holding hands. I'm scared. I've always been scared. But she isn't.

The hike back to the cottage is quiet. The effects of the drugs and alcohol are wearing off. I haven't slept, but I don't feel as exhausted as I thought I would. Ashley walks in step by my side. I see Mia at the front, with the others in small groups of two or three.

I remember Ashley's confession from last night. Even with my eyes closed, I recognised her soft voice. She talked about her abusive uncle and the fantasies she had about killing him.

"How are you today?" she asks.

"Well, I have the worst headache of my life, and I yelled at a police officer on the phone, but—"

"A police officer?" She turns to me sharply, her face pale.

"It's not like that." I bite my lip because it sort of is like that. "Back when I thought Susie, I mean Agnes, contacted me out of the blue, I went to the police because she was a missing person. I kind of made friends with the police officer and he called me last night while I was tripping on Ayahuasca. Which was not great timing."

"Oh. Okay. Only we're not supposed to talk to anyone about this."

I smile. "You mean an organisation called FREEDM has rules?"

She laughs. "Yeah, I guess. It's for protection. Not everyone understands our way of life."

"I know," I say. "I get it."

"Are you looking forward to tonight?" she asks.

"New Year's Eve? I guess so. What does everyone do for it?"

"Not New Year, something else," she says. "I'm retrying my initiation tonight."

"Oh, wow. Are you nervous?"

"A little." She clasps her hands together tightly. "I'm terrified, actually."

"What do you have to do?" I ask.

She looks at me, her eyes flashing. "You'll see."

CHAPTER FIFTY-FOUR

We take turns showering and go for naps once we're back at the cottage. Mia had told me that I wouldn't regret anything that happened because it was the right choice at the moment. I still want to believe her, but my anxious brain won't stop going over the phone call with Liam Harding. He hasn't checked in with me today which means he's mad at me. Which bothers me more than it should. I'm here for a whole other reason. I need to concentrate. What I don't need is to worry about what Liam Harding thinks of me.

Once the alcohol and drugs are out of my system, I finally slip into a deep sleep. By the time Mia shakes my shoulder, it's dark again. My stomach rumbles and I'm groggy.

"It's time for Ashley's initiation. Are you ready?"

"I just need to—"

"No, Jenny. I don't mean are you ready to go. I mean are you ready for this, because you're about to experience something you've never experienced before."

I sit up straighter. "What do you mean?"

Mia sits on the edge of the bed. "There's a reason why

we're called FREEDM. We mean it. We don't live within the constraints of normal society. We push boundaries. We are—"

"The agitators," I finish. "I know."

Mia shakes her head. "You don't know. Not yet. But you will know tonight." She stands. "Oh, and Agnes is going to be there."

"Susie?"

"Yep."

Then I have to be there. I have to be. As Mia leaves the room, I swing my legs out of the bed and pull on my clothes. Shivers run up and down my arms and legs. I hurry through to the rest of the house to find a cluster of people around Ashley. She's sitting with her head between her knees, her skin like milk.

I don't know what to think or feel. Someone hands me a shot of alcohol.

"We're all taking one tonight," he says, still holding onto my hand with the shot glass inside. "We'll need it." Two greying eyebrows shoot up his forehead.

They are warning me that whatever happens tonight it will be intense. But none of them are telling me what is about to happen. None of them.

What is going on?

I down the shot without even thinking about it. For all I know, it's spiked, but I do it anyway because I'm scared of what I'm about to witness. I need the warmth of alcohol running down my throat. I need the extra courage.

There are several cars outside the cottage and we each break into small groups. David drives the car I end up in. Mia stays with Ashley. I want to be closer to Ashley. I don't like seeing her out of my sight. I feel like I might be the only one looking out for her, who considers the fact that she might not even be an adult, and she's gone, just like that.

"Where are we going?" I ask David.

"Sorry, Jen, I can't say. But try not to worry, okay?"

I lean back against the car headrest and sense the alcohol spreading through my veins. About thirty minutes into the drive, I'm convinced there was more in the drink than whisky. My muscles slowly unclench. A strange, chemical sense of happiness makes my chest lighter. It is in conflict with my thoughts.

"Take a deep breath, Jenny," David says.

Streetlights blur past the car. We're back in the city now. It's raining again and the bars are overflowing with partygoers. I smudge my finger over the glass, touching their staggering high heels and rainbow of dresses. Then David switches to the sat nav. The landscape changes from the overflowing bars to an industrial area filled with garages and factories. I look up at the mirror to see the other cars behind us.

FREEDM is taking over this quiet area on New Year's Eve. There are no pubs here, no restaurants or apartment blocks. It is dark and covered in graffiti and not a place I'd want to be at night.

He parks the car, and we get out. I pull up my hood against the rain. David takes hold of my arm and leads me towards a huge warehouse behind iron wrought gates. They are unlocked, swinging open on high-pitched hinges. I feel the sound in my teeth and run my tongue over them.

"I don't like this," I whisper.

"Don't fight it," he says. "Listen to your body."

He means the drug. He wants me to give into it, to let the good feelings wash over me. Maybe he's right. I don't want to have a panic attack.

There's a *clunk* and the lights come on. I squint against the brightness, momentarily transported back to the moment at the quarry. It takes me a few seconds to adjust to the sudden wash of light, and once I open my eyes, I see what's going on.

Every light points down to a clear, circular space in the centre of tiered seats. It reminds me of a theatre I once visited where the stage was ground level with the seats all around the actors. Or, alternatively, it resembles a coliseum, and we are about to be the audience waiting for the gladiators to arrive.

What are they going to make Ashley do?

Sourness comes up from the pit of my stomach. I almost gag but manage to keep my composure. Then David leads me over to the seats. A few others are already sitting. He shows me where to sit before taking his place next to me. A tall man I've not spoken to much sits on the other side. There's a reason why I'm being flanked by the tallest, strongest men in FREEDM. They don't want me to make a fuss.

"Drink this." David hands me a flask.

I shake my head.

"Unless you want to leave, drink it."

I take the flask and tip it. I try to only take the smallest of sips, but David lifts the bottom, and the spiked whisky floods my mouth. It spills out of the corners of my lips, but I still end up swallowing a large mouthful. I shove the flask against his chest to show him my disdain.

"It's for your own good," he says.

"Fuck you."

The warehouse is freezing cold but the whisky and the many bodies around me soon warm the air. I pull my coat off and place it underneath my seat. My knees bounce up and down, on edge.

The crowd shushes and silence descends. I check every face, searching for Susie again. She isn't there and neither is Ashley, but Mia has taken her place opposite me. She seems as calm and serene as always. I can't help but wonder if she's just constantly high. Maybe drugs are the answer after all.

A door scrapes open and cold air floods into the open space. There's a second scraping sound and a bang as the door closes again. The lights go off and gasps spread around the seated crowd. All I feel is the effects of the drug on my body. I place my hands on my knees and pull in a deep breath. I need to stay sharp. I need to watch this, every moment of it. I need to remember these faces.

I need to see Susie once and for all.

And then the lights come back on.

I blink several times. The powerful spotlights reveal pasty, yellowing flesh. It shows the pink splotches of a heat rash. The thin lips and wrinkles of a smoker. The stained underpants of a scared man.

He stands in the centre of the stage with his hands over his eyes. He is naked apart from the white cotton Y-fronts. His pot belly sticks out over the waistband. I fold my hands together, uncomfortable looking at this man in his vulnerable state.

"Who are you? What's going on? I don't understand." The man wanders back and forth, squinting into the light.

When he moves his hands away from his face, I see he is around fifty years old. His hair is sandy blond with grey peppered in. His mouth gapes open to show the saliva coating his yellowing teeth. I look away.

"Why... why are you all sitting there?" he asks.

His voice has a whining tone to it. Like a toddler about to throw a tantrum.

At the exact same moment, everyone in the crowd stomps

against the metal frames of the seats. I turn my head to find two figures emerging from between the stands. One is Ashley, but the other...

I gasp. My hand flies to my face.

It's *her*.

My heart beats hard against my ribs. I pull my hands away and lean back in my chair, then I close my eyes, before opening them again. I look at her for a second time, this one is to make sure.

She stares right at me. Our eyes meet. Her sky-blue eyes find mine and she smiles.

CHAPTER FIFTY-FIVE

Susie.

After all this time. Sixteen years of holding onto the horrific belief that I may have killed her. Sixteen years of living with a broken mind, one I blamed myself for, because I thought I'd committed a crime so heinous that I'd blocked out an entire year of my life. But it was all a lie because my best friend is standing there in the centre of this makeshift stage.

She is the woman in coach D. I know now that she placed her bag in the aisle on purpose. She wanted me to see her. She wanted to pretend not to know me. Susie always knew how to manipulate me. But she has taken it to an extreme that I never thought possible. Not only did she orchestrate our meeting, but she played with me for weeks.

I wipe tears from my eyes. I can't believe it. Part of me wishes Liam was here so he could see her, too.

"Ashley?"

It's the man speaking. He stumbles towards Ashley but Susie—Agnes—steps between them.

"She will speak to you in her own time." Susie's voice easily commands the room.

She is wearing a smart, figure-hugging dress that reaches her knees. Her shoes are low-heeled pumps. Her hair has been styled and blown out. The last time I saw her, her hair had been lank and greasy.

Her face has changed slightly over the years. Her lips appear fuller, and her eyebrows are thinner. It could be make-up and contouring or plastic surgery. But it's her, I'm sure of it.

My eyes drift down to Susie's hands, where I notice she's holding a baseball bat.

Shit.

I'm about to witness something extremely fucked up.

"Jeremy Nicholls," Susie says. "You sexually abused your niece from the age of seven years old."

My stomach lurches. I'm scared I might throw up. I glance across at David, he frowns at me, but he doesn't move. I lean back in my seat, lifting my eyes up to the roof, pulling in a deep breath. I know what's coming and I don't know if I can watch it.

"Hold it together, Jenny," David whispers. "This is important."

I redirect my attention back to the three people at the centre of the warehouse.

"That's a lie. I loved you, baby. I treated you like you were my own daughter." The man reaches out to Ashley, but Susie pushes his hand away.

"You molested and raped your niece," Susie says. "You told her not to say anything to anyone because you said her mummy wouldn't love her anymore. You told her that you would kill her family pet if she said anything. You made many threats over the years. Sometimes you told Ashley that you would murder her mother."

"You're lying. She's lying. Let me out of here!" He turns to run. Two large men block his exit from the circle stage. "Fuck you all!" He points at people in the crowd. "Fuck you and you and you. Fuck all of you and especially *you*." He turns to Susie. "I'm going to have fun with you once this is over. I'm going to cut your tits off."

The stomping begins again. I'm worked up. The sound of that man's voice brings all my inner rage to the surface. I stomp. I bang my feet.

Susie turns to Ashley, passing her the bat.

And now I know what fear Ashley faces and I know exactly what she is about to do to it.

She's going to beat the shit out of that fear.

The crowd begins to chant. *Let the fear set you free. Let the fear set you free.* Susie finds me in the crowd, smiling slightly.

This is what we did. These are our words.

Here she is, my best friend, as powerful as she was when we were seven years old. She was never Susie. She has always been Agnes, but she had to fake her own death to get here.

"You're not going to hit me with that bat, baby." Jeremy holds his hands out. "You can't. You're too sweet. You're too good and pure. I know you can't do it."

Ashley sobs. She holds the bat limply and I'm terrified Jeremy will rush forward and snatch it from her. I want to go to her and hold her in my arms. I want to tell her that everything is going to be okay and that I'll save her. I'll adopt her. I'll raise her. I think of all the suicidal people I haven't been able to save at Solace. If Ashley becomes one of them, I will never forgive myself.

He steps towards her.

"Stay away from me!" she screams, swinging the bat towards him.

It's not a convincing swing. Ashley's eyes are full of tears, her hands are shaking, she looks like a dog about to run away with its tail between its legs.

I hold my breath.

"You're worthless," Jeremy says.

Every word that comes out of his mouth makes me want to run down there and beat him myself.

"You're pathetic."

She folds over.

I turn towards Susie who now sits in the front row. There's no smile on her face anymore, she's sitting with a rigid back and a tight but neutral expression.

"And you were a terrible lay," Jeremy spits.

Ashley lifts the bat above her head and brings it crashing down. The older man makes an attempt to dodge, but the bat connects with his shoulder. He lets out a yelp and staggers back. My fingers grip the edge of the seat. Now there's fear in that man's bloodshot eyes. Now he knows what is going to happen to him. Now he feels just the tiniest percent of what Ashley felt every single day for years.

"Please." He places his palms together, begging.

We stomp. We chant.

Jeremy runs but there's nowhere to go. Ashley chases him with the bat above her head. She lets out a roar, bringing her weapon crashing down.

I don't flinch away. I lean forward to see the blood splash along the stone floor. Ashley connects with the side of his head. When he drops onto the ground and pisses himself, she beats his ribs and his abdomen.

Let the fear set you free.

Ashley is free and she is wild. She wears her abuser's blood across her face.

CHAPTER FIFTY-SIX

It's over.

Ashley drops the bat and Susie steps up. She folds Ashley into a hug while we cheer. I'm aware of the barbaric nature of what I just saw. It was the coliseum. Ashley is the gladiator, and she knows it. She grins from ear to ear.

I push sweaty hair from my face as Susie leads Ashley away from the crowds.

"No!" I shout, getting to my feet.

David grabs hold of my forearm.

"Susie!"

But they're gone.

The two large men pick up Jeremy and carry him away. I think he's dead at first, but then I see his eyelashes flutter.

"Where are they taking him?" I ask David, sitting back down. There's no point making a scene trying to get to Susie. She obviously has her guards here.

"They'll pump him so full of drugs he won't remember what happened to him, then drop him outside a pub or something."

I turn to David. "Does this kind of thing happen a lot?"

"No," he says. "This is the second one I've seen. We rarely find people who are afraid of a specific person. But some survivors of abuse do want to confront their abuser as part of the programme."

I rub my palms against my jeans. I want to run. What I saw was barbaric. I can't see how Ashley beating a grown man could ever help with her trauma. And yet I witnessed the expression on her face. I saw the pleasure she took in it and saw how free she was.

And I leaned closer.

The crowd filters down to the stage area. A small group points to the blood on the stones. It's sick. What happened tonight has no place in a civilised society. But my heart thumps and, for some strange reason, there's a smile on my face. Jesus. Am I like these people? Am I turned on by violence?

"Hey, Jenny, are you okay?"

I didn't notice Mia approach. She stands with her hands on her hips like she's stopped for a chat in the middle of a supermarket. Not at a literal battle royale.

"I honestly don't know."

Before I say anything else, Ashley comes back into the warehouse. There are blood splatters across her clothes, but someone wiped the blood from her face. She lifts her arms and the crowd cheers. She's lifted up onto a man's shoulders and carried around the warehouse. My heart surges for her because I'm *happy* for her. Despite everything, I admire her.

It's easy to say I could never do that. I could be in denial or egotistical enough to think I'm so special that I would never take revenge like Ashley did. But I honestly don't know. I have no idea what her life has been like. If I'd been through what she suffered, I may have kept going until his brains were on the stone.

I look for Susie outside the warehouse, but she's gone. Mia pulls me into her car. We speed back to the cottage where the drinks flow and we celebrate Ashley, then the new year and then pass out.

I wake abruptly in the small hours of the night and drag myself up from the sleeping bag on the floor. I stumble through to the kitchen to pour a glass of water. But Ashley has the hot tap running. Her hands are working to wash something in the sink. I take a step forward and notice that she's scrubbing the blood out of her top. I watch her standing there in the moonlight in her bra, steam rising from the running water.

"Hey," I say. "Would you like me to put that in the washing machine?"

When she turns to me, I see the tracks of her tears down her cheeks. "I don't think the stain is going to come out."

I feel like it should be Susie here trying to wash out the stain. She's Lady Macbeth in this scenario, goading Ashley to violence.

"That's okay. Why don't we get you a new t-shirt? Do you have any others?"

"Yes," she says.

Her eyes are wide and afraid. I gently guide her by the shoulders, pulling her away from the sink. I spot someone's abandoned hoodie on a kitchen chair and grab it.

"Here, why don't you put this on for now."

"Okay," she says, pulling it over her head.

I help her straighten it out and then I take the bloody top and shove it in the kitchen bin.

"Everything is going to be okay," I say.

"Is it?" she asks.

I nod. "I promise."

CHAPTER FIFTY-SEVEN

Mia takes me home the next day. It surprises me that they're so willing to let me go after everything I've seen. Especially considering my relationship with Liam Harding. But she must have orders from Susie to allow me back into my regular life.

Susie.

Agnes.

I want to know where one starts and the other begins.

I say goodbye to Mia and drag myself into the house. My head is still spinning from all the drugs and alcohol David fed me. I fill a water bottle and check the house to see if Harry is home. He isn't. I head into my bedroom and lie down.

There's a chance that I could get the cult for this. I made a mental note of the make and model of some of the cars used to transport us to the warehouse. I know the name of the man who was beaten. There has to be a hospital record and there should be CCTV footage of the cars driving through the city. Then there's the baseball bat but I don't know if Susie will have destroyed it.

They could twist the story somehow. Call me paranoid

and a drunk. They could allege the meeting was nothing more than an organised group therapy session and that I'm sabotaging them with tall tales of some underground fight club.

I probably don't have enough evidence, but I already know I'm not going to tell Liam any of it. If I tell the police, Ashley will be arrested. Susie might be able to squirm out of it and the cult will probably live on, but Ashley's life will be ruined. She's a traumatised kid. I can't do that to her.

The other reason for not wanting to tell Liam is that Susie will withdraw from me. After weeks of playing her game, I'm so close to the end. If I stop now, it'll all be for nothing. If I push on for the last stretch, I'll have my answers at last.

No. Susie knows I won't go to the police now. She knows that she has me wrapped around her little finger. I'm deep in FREEDM's mud, right up to my neck, and there's no one around to haul me out.

The next few days go by in a blur. Harry comes home. He gushes about his new year with Hannah in London watching the fireworks. I'm a zombie and each morning before work, he passes me a coffee. I spend some time at Solace, answering the usual calls. January is a tough time for lonely people. I start to recognise voices and they also recognise me. That isn't unusual. We get a lot of regulars. Bob even has a list of regular callers who we have to hang up on after forty-five minutes because they take up so much of our time.

For the first time since I started volunteering at Solace, I find myself feeling impatient with the callers. I ask the usual questions and say as many comforting things as I can, but at the back of my mind, I wonder why they don't just face their fears.

At the end of each Solace shift, I get on the train and sit anywhere I want. I don't check for Susie anymore. I don't have that sense of creeping panic working its way through my chest and my muscles and my brain. I don't bother reserving a seat.

"Did you get your haircut this week?" Harry asks after I return from work one day.

"No, why?"

"No reason." He smiles. "You look good, Jenny."

I glance down at the dress I'm wearing. "Thanks!"

It's the first time Harry has commented on my appearance since we moved in together. I'd always assumed I was some non-sexual sister-like being to him, which is pretty much what you want when you're housemates. But now he's starting to notice me.

On the first Friday of the year, I get a phone call on the way home from work. I walk quickly as the rain patters down on my hood. Fumbling with gloves, I check the caller and stop.

"Hello," I say.

"Hey," Liam says.

I start walking again, albeit slower this time. "How are you?"

"Fine. How are you?"

"Fine."

There's a long, stretching silence. I'd be lying if I said I hadn't thought about him this week. But not enough to send him a text.

"Okay, well, I guess you're alive. That's all I wanted to know."

"No, it isn't," I say. "You could probably have just followed me or whatever detectives do. You didn't need to call me to find out if I'm alive. You wanted to know more about FREEDM, didn't you?"

He sighs. "Well, what did you learn?"

I pause. "Are the police looking into them?"

"I thought I was helping you find Susie," he says.

"And I thought you'd decided this wasn't a police matter anymore."

"Well, I changed my mind."

"Why?" I ask.

I hop over a puddle and cross the road towards home. He's still silent.

"I just want to help, Jenny. I'm worried about you. What the fuck do you think you're doing infiltrating a cult like this?"

"I'm finding my friend," I say. "That's what I'm doing."

"No. You're playing her game. You're lost, Jenny. You don't see them converting you but it's happening."

I stop again, standing opposite a line of terraced houses. "How dare you! How dare you say that I'm weak enough to fall for their tricks. I'm not being converted, I'm there undercover—"

"Undercover? You're not a police officer. Undercover officers go through extensive—"

"Shut up, Liam. Just shut up. I've made my choice."

"Fuck!" he yells. "Fuck you, Jenny."

"Fuck you, too," I shout back.

"You're going to get yourself killed, you fucking stupid—"

I hang up, shaking. Every part of me, trembling. I stride across the road not paying attention to my surroundings and a driver blares his horn at me. I run the rest of the way, still shaking on the other side of the road. I lean my hip against the low wall in front of the line of houses, wondering how the hell our conversation turned out like that.

The problem is, Liam continues to see me as the Jenny Woods from sixteen years ago. He can't see me as I want him to see me. I get up and walk the last few feet home. I'm going to show him who I really am. I swear it.

When I open the door to the house, I call out to Harry. He calls back. Then I dump my coat, bag, and shoes. I turn to the kettle to fill it, when I see the letter waiting for me on the table.

CHAPTER FIFTY-EIGHT
JENNY'S DIARY

I wanted to go to Hangman's Cave and see how far the drop goes. Susie wouldn't let me. She said I'd chicken out if I researched it too hard. I don't know, maybe she's right. Even Mum says I think about things too much.

Susie told me about her blood test while we were at the beach. She fainted. Which is weird because I've been in the hospital with Susie while she's getting her chemotherapy and she's always been fine with needles. She said it hurt so much this time and she kept sobbing.

"It's because I don't want to go through it again," she said. "It's all the dread about it. And Mum isn't being much help. She just keeps telling me that everything is going to be okay, but I don't believe her. She's said that before and now look at me." She showed me the plaster on her arm. "I'm back where I started. I'm going to lose my hair again."

"She just doesn't know what else to say. I guess I don't know what to say either except that it's not fair."

She took my hand and squeezed it. "You're the only one who gets it."

It made me feel good to hear her say that. We are more like sisters, and I want to be the one who understands her.

"How's the freak?"

I dropped Susie's hand when she says that. For some reason, she calls Max a freak now, but I don't understand why. They don't even spend that much time together because they hate each other so much.

"Don't use that word!" I said.

But Susie just laughed. "Why?"

"It's mean."

"Is the freak jumping into Hangman's Cave with us?"

I shake my head. "That's just you and me, you know that. It's our thing."

She nodded. "That's right. They're our challenges and no freak is going to stop that."

"That's exactly why Max hates you. Why can't you just be nice?" I got up then and walked towards the sea.

I hate how much they hate each other. Sometimes I think they're going to actually start fighting. And then sometimes I think Max has other feelings for Susie. The kind that makes me jealous because it's like sparks are flying between them.

There was an icky feeling in my tummy as I stepped into the sea. But I know the final challenge will make me feel better. All I need to do is be there for Susie one more time. And then we'll both be going into sixth form, and we'll be like adults. This is the last bit of teenage girl shit before life really begins.

If life is just beginning for Susie. I hope so. I don't want her to be ill again.

God, it's so messed up.

I just need to get through these last few weeks and then I will help my best friend face whatever it is she needs to face. I may have a life outside Susie now but she's still my number one.

I'm with you Susie. I always will be.

Let the fear set you free.

CHAPTER FIFTY-NINE

Tears run down my cheeks, gathering under my chin. The diary entry lays on top of the desk in the corner of my room, and I don't want to look at it. I don't want to go any closer, not after reading what I assume is the last entry before Susie went missing.

I step over to the desk and stare down at the page. I have no memory of this day at the beach. But I imagine Susie's tears as though they really happened. I see the patchy sunshine filtered out by long stretches of clouds. And as I imagine the entire conversation, something hits me.

Susie is lying.

She never went for a blood test. She stuck a plaster on the crook of her elbow and told me how hard it was. Thirty-two-year-old me knows what sixteen-year-old me likely missed. Susie is making up the cancer scare for attention and to get me back into the challenges. That's why Fiona Patterson never mentioned a scare. That's why it wasn't reported in the media after she disappeared. They would have used every iota of sob story to sell more copies of their papers. There's no way they would have missed this opportunity.

Susie, what did you do?

She risked it all for nothing.

I wipe my tears away and grab the sheet of paper. With a deep breath, I turn it over.

> *We're going back to Yorkshire. Meet me at this address tomorrow at midday. Wear comfortable clothing and sensible shoes. Come ALONE. Leave your police officer behind.*
>
> *Dare me, dare you.*
> *Follow me, follow you.*
> *Let the fear set you free.*
> *Agnes*

I take the paper back to the bed and place it down on the pillow. Then I put the address into Google Maps. It takes me to a large, modern mansion surrounded by green fields and the stretch of the North Yorkshire coastline behind it. Susie's mansion is in between Chillingham and Whitby. It's so brazen, I almost laugh. There she is, right back where it all started. I'll need to get the train to Whitby and a taxi to Susie's house.

Something else gives me pause. Tomorrow is the anniversary of my mother's death. It's a day I always take off work and I usually either go for a long walk or spend it drinking wine while watching sad movies.

She knows that. She chose this day because she knows.

I let out a whistling breath. Susie is powerful now. She's Agnes, the leader of FREEDM. She's rich. She's above the law. She has security to take care of her. She has acolytes who worship her. She's a God.

My stomach is in knots, but I decide to try to eat. My toast pops up as Harry steps into the kitchen to make spaghetti.

"Do you want some?" he asks.

I shake my head.

"Is everything okay?"

I decide to give him a half-truth. "It's the anniversary of Mum's death tomorrow. I'm a little wobbly today."

He immediately pulls me into a hug. "Oh, Jen. I'm sorry. Do you want me to stay home tomorrow? We can get some ice cream and veg on the sofa."

I pat his arm, thinking about how lucky Hannah is to know an emotionally intuitive man. "No. I'm going out, actually. I'll be gone all day."

"Oh, cool. Where are you heading?"

"Near home," I say. "I want to visit somewhere near to where I grew up."

"That sounds like a good idea." He stirs his sauce. "I'm not one for revisiting the past but there are times it helps."

I butter my bread. "I hope so."

Halfway through eating my toast, I get a text from Liam.

> I know you hate me, but you should know there's chatter about FREEDM. They're suspected of covering up deaths. They're bad people. Be careful.

I almost text back a snippy comment about how obvious he's being, but I don't. Then I lean back on the bed, considering his words. If there are rumours, FREEDM is probably being investigated, either by someone in the media, or someone with the police. Which makes sense, because every single member of the cult has a family somewhere. If someone dies accidentally, family members will want to know what happened to their loved one.

I know how tight-lipped people in FREEDM can be. I've asked them direct questions and watched them avoid answering. But surely the family members get a better idea of what's going on. I've seen documentaries where the families of cult members are desperate to get them out. It's one of the reasons why these documentaries are made. Some cults are still ongoing despite the fact they have been outed as run by terrible people.

Even the best people in the world can lash out when they're backed into a corner. That could be happening to Susie and FREEDM right now. Liam is right, I do need to watch my back. But I also don't believe that all of those people are bad. My thoughts pull left and right. FREEDM is manipulative and gives out drugs to keep people happy. But I've experienced my own initiation, and I can't deny that I am a stronger person after going through it.

For so long, I have fantasised about coming face to face with Susie. I pictured hugging her, telling her everything is going to be okay. But I never thought it would be like this. She has changed me again, shaping me into a new person by pulling the right strings at the right time.

Who is she? And who am I? And what has her fear cult done to me?

CHAPTER SIXTY

It's difficult for me to ignore how far I've come in such a short space of time. From frequent panic attacks travelling to and from work, to infiltrating a dangerous cult in order to clear up a mystery from my past. I've faced heights, icy lakes, a dangerous railway line and speeding cars. I've confronted my past, lived through my nightmares and come out stronger on the other side.

When I step on the train, I'm fully aware that I am not the same person I was before I saw Susie sitting in coach D. But now it's all coming full circle. After weeks of dares, of getting my hopes up, of believing that the answers lie right around the corner, I am finally going to see her.

I will finally get the answers I want.

There's a woman with blonde hair and a backpack about three seats in front of me. My stomach flips, but when she turns her head and I see her in profile, I know it isn't Susie.

The scenery rushes past in a blur. I have a feeling that when I see her for the first time in sixteen years, I will be a whole other person yet again. What will that be? The third or fourth Jenny? Perhaps we are all reborn several times over the course of our lives. I'm nothing special. I'm simply human.

The hours slip by. Before I know it, the salty coastal air hits me at Whitby. I exit the station and find a good spot for an Uber pick up when a black SUV pulls up. The window rolls down.

"Jenny Woods?"

I take a cautious step towards the vehicle to find a man with dark, cropped hair driving. He wears a black hoodie and jeans.

"Yes."

"Agnes sent me to collect you."

Pulling in a deep breath, I open the back door and get in. I pull the seatbelt across my chest and clutch my hands together to stop them from shaking.

The man driving says nothing. He simply drives through the town, gets onto the A71 and crosses the River Esk. After about fifteen minutes, he turns off the main road and we go down several narrow and twisting lanes heading closer to the coast. I wind the window down and fill my lungs with sea air. It has been so long since I came back to the coast.

All too quickly, the driver turns across the right-hand lane and pulls up on the drive next to a wrought iron fence. He speaks into an intercom box on the gate post and a moment later, the gates swing open. The SUV moves slowly along a smooth, tarmac drive.

Up ahead is a two-story, red brick mansion. It has four columns spanned across its width and is capped off with a glass, pyramid-shaped roof peeking out from the traditional slates. A spacious yard and elaborate gardens stretch down to the front gate. The mansion seems new, but there's an air of age about it.

A light and crisp breeze tickles my skin. The scent of honeysuckle hangs in the air.

"No going back now," I mutter.

The driver chuckles from the front seat.

As I step out of the car, my stomach lurches at the thought of what is to come. Liam tried to warn me. He said this could be dangerous, but turning back isn't an option now. I've come too far. I'm in the middle of this. My heart beats faster with each step closer to the front door. I pause for a moment to take a breath. A sense of dread washes over me.

The driver opens the mansion door and I pull air deep into my lungs, trying to calm my thundering heart. A man stands on the threshold. He's older, around forty, with a thin beard and round glasses. He smiles at me.

"Welcome to you, Jenny. Please come into the Sanctum. My name is Ryan, and I will show you around today." He steps back to allow me in.

The driver walks back to the car.

"Where is Susi—I mean Agnes?" I ask, not giving a single flying fuck about the tour.

"There's a cupboard here for shoes," Ryan says, completely ignoring my question.

I step in and slip off my trainers. There's something oddly intimate about removing shoes and now I feel vulnerable in front of this stranger.

"Do you like the artwork, Jenny?" Ryan asks. "The entire house was designed specifically for rest and relaxation. These murals of blossom trees transport all visitors to a wonderfully peaceful location."

"What happened to the fear?" I quip. "Shouldn't we all be on edge?"

"Oh, no," Ryan says. "Once a member reaches The Sanctum, they have already faced all of their fears."

"I haven't," I say.

"You're Agnes's visitor today. That changes the rules," he says with a stiff smile.

Ryan opens a door, and the corridor leads into a large ballroom. As soon as I see the mural on the walls, I hiss through my teeth. It's a perfect depiction of the cliff above the cove at Chillingham-by-the-Sea. The place Susie and I leapt into the sea when we were just eight years old.

"We all know of your bravery," Ryan says. "We're fans of your fearlessness."

"We were reckless kids putting our lives in danger," I say.

"This way," Ryan says, leading me through to another room.

This one has no mural. It's painted completely black. The effect is unnerving, and I wrap my arms around my body.

"This is where we come for sensory deprivation. It's good for meditation," Ryan explains.

We cross the small space quickly and move on to a flight of stairs. I gaze upwards, where the glass pyramid reflects light against the walls. We've reached the centre of the house now, and a spiral staircase winds its way up to the second floor. Ryan goes first, with me following. I'm sweating once we reach the next floor. It isn't hot inside the house but there's so much anticipation clogging the air.

I should take a mental note of the layout, but it's hard to concentrate as my heart hammers away at my ribs. The familiar sense of panic washes over me. I'm cold and numb, disassociating from my body as we approach the final door at the end of a long hallway. The walls narrow around me, pressing in. I wipe sweat from my forehead.

"Agnes wanted you to come straight to her," Ryan says. "She's anxious to meet you."

"Yeah, well she can't be as anxious as I am to meet her," I say.

I press my palms together. This is what I've been waiting for ever since I saw her on the train. And now that it's happening, pure panic runs through my veins.

Ryan knocks softly on the door. A quiet voice answers.

"Send Jenny in alone."

CHAPTER SIXTY-ONE

The room is a white canvas with floorboards polished to a glossy sheen and walls that stretch up to the high ceiling. A large window lets in soft beams of sunlight and the scent of freshly mown grass hangs in the air. Beyond the window is a lawn lined with neat flowerbeds leading down into the grandeur of the mansion's grounds. In the centre of the room stands the only piece of furniture in the entire space. A desk.

She waits for me there, her palms down on the glossy surface.

I tighten and release my hands, flexing fingers, letting go of all the anxiety curled inside my body.

Susie is dressed in a white suit. She's completely transformed from the woman I saw on the train. Her hair is not greasy, and she doesn't look tired. Her perfectly highlighted, golden hair falls down to her shoulders in waves. Expertly applied make-up exaggerates her cheekbones and large eyes. She smiles at me.

"Come in, Jenny, don't be shy." When she speaks, her entire body remains still.

The Susie I knew had too much energy to sit like this.

I walk into the centre of the room. My socked feet pad softly against the wood. As soon as I sit, she reaches across the desk and takes hold of my hand.

I'm not sure what I expected. Tears. A hug. Something more. But at this point, it's not even a part of me that I want to give to her.

"Is it really you?" she murmurs.

Her voice is so familiar to me. The sound transports me back to Chillingham. I feel the pale northern sun on my skin, the sand between my toes.

"Shouldn't I say that?" I turn away from her as I speak, embarrassed or shy, I'm not sure which. Whatever resolve I had to hate her fades away by the second.

"Yes," she says. "That's fair." A single tear falls from her left eye, but her expression never shifts, nor does she blink. She squeezes my hand tightly. "I've missed you so much, my wonderful friend."

When I try to speak, my throat catches and I hold back a sob instead. I want to tell her how much pain she's put me through. To explain how I've spent sixteen years being stared at by strangers who think I'm a murderer. By Susie Patterson Truthers like Kevin, the toothpick man. I want to tell her about the death of my mother. My father's fall from grace. *Her mother*. She has been so selfish for so long. I don't know where to begin or how to say what ought to be said.

She lets go of my hand. "You've done so well, Jenny. I'm proud of you. I know you've had some anxiety issues over the years. I did wonder if you'd be able to complete the challenges." She grins, revealing straight, white teeth. "But I knew the fearless side of you still exists."

She's had work done, I realise. Her teeth used to be crooked. These might even be veneers.

I shake my head slightly. "What are you doing, Susie? This place is..." I trail off. "I saw a teenage girl beat her uncle until he was unconscious. I saw a crowd egging her on. What are you doing here?"

"I'm not sorry you witnessed any of those events," she says. There's no hint of emotion on her blank face. "The lost souls who come to us made a choice. Ashley made her choice, and it was one to help her heal."

I shake my head. "You didn't see her later that night. She was traumatised, Susie. You added to her trauma."

Her lips twitch. "I almost forgot that you have a psychology degree. You may need to shed that way of thinking if you are going to join us here."

"I'm just here to see you. To get answers." My voice raises. Some of that suppressed anger is eking out.

She's silent. I blink, trying to control the conflicting emotions wrestling beneath the surface. She waits, impassively, for me to speak again. She knows me well enough to understand that I'm building up to something.

Finally, I release. "I'm so glad you're alive. I've wanted to find you for so long." I let out a long, steadying breath. "There have been so many times in my life when I've been through a rough patch, and I just wanted my best friend to talk to. I've missed you so much, Susie. But it is hard for me to reconcile seeing you here. Knowing everything you've put me through. I spent hours in the police station trying to tell my story. I suffered a brain injury. Your mother thinks you're dead and she has asked me every week for the last sixteen years if I remember what happened to you. I've been through therapy, hypnosis, rehabilitation, and more trying to piece together what happened to you." I pause, brushing away tears. "And all this time you've been building up a cult."

"Is that what we are?" she asks coolly.

"Yes! You know exactly what you've done. Look at where you *live*. I... I don't know what to say. Either you've become something I never thought possible, or you've always been this person and I never saw the signs. Either way, my heart is broken. It's... it's just broken, like..." I trail off, wanting to say like my brain is broken. Like my fractured memories.

I sit back in my chair, gasping for breath. The words came from a deep, primal urge to rid my body of the heavy weight it has carried for sixteen years. All Susie can do is reach into a desk drawer and produce a pack of tissues.

"I have all the answers you've been waiting for," she says. "But you're going to have to open yourself up to fear and conflict and much, much more."

Dabbing away tears, I nod my head. "How much worse can it get?"

The first real flicker of emotion crosses her face. She winces. "It does get worse. There is a lot to talk about, but you need to see it for yourself first. We need to go back."

"What do you mean? Figuratively? Like meditation?"

She shakes her head. "Back to Hangman's Cave. I need to show you something."

CHAPTER SIXTY-TWO

She rises from behind the desk and steps towards me. I swallow, watching her, the moment stretching out as though she's moving in slow motion. My mouth is dry. I turn away from her and cough, suddenly self-conscious.

"Jenny? Are you okay?"

"What about your mum? Are we really going to go on a trip to Hangman's Cave before you tell her you're alive?"

She smooths wrinkles from her perfectly tailored trousers and smiles. "You must think I'm a monster."

"The thought has crossed my mind," I admit.

She aligns herself with me so that we're face to face, and places her hands on my shoulders. "Whatever you feel right now is valid. Whatever choice you make is the right choice. You are no longer afraid because you have been reborn." She places her hand over my heart, just like Mia did. "You are free."

Then she hugs me briefly before brushing a lock of hair from my face. "Don't you trust me?"

"I used to. But I don't trust Agnes, that's for sure."

She moves back to her desk and presses a button hidden

underneath the surface. Ryan must have been waiting in the corridor because less than twenty seconds later, he's in the room.

"Ask the driver to bring the car around."

Ryan nods and backs out of the room like Susie is royalty. I shake my head.

"My followers like to embellish our interactions," Susie says. "To be clear, I did not ask them to do that."

There's something about the tone of her voice that makes me wonder if she's finally coming to see things from my point of view. That she's understanding what it was like to walk into this house and be confronted with all this grandeur. To see her at the head of it all. The empress of this house of fear. It's baffling in its scope. How did a damaged teenage girl do all of this when there were literal search parties out there looking for her?

I watch Susie move in her perfectly fitted white suit. Her appearance on the train was as perfectly sculpted as her appearance is now. She faked vulnerability that day. She didn't wash her hair. She wore clothing too big for her. She wanted me to believe she needed help. If I'd seen her like this, dressed in this way, I may not have worked so hard to find her. I might have assumed she didn't need me.

Step by step. Inch by inch. That's how she played this. The first glimpse, the diary pages, the slow introduction to her cult members before bringing me here.

What comes next?

"You used the Chillingham cliffs as a mural," I say, nodding to the intricate painting as we reach that particular room.

"Of course," she says. She grins. "Dare me, dare you."

An electric shock jolts down my spine. I haven't heard her speak those words for so long. It's surreal.

Back at the front door, Ryan helps her into a long trench coat. She slips her feet into a pair of pristine trainers. Susie doesn't even open the door for herself, Ryan does that, too. There's a man waiting on the front step to escort her out. In a suit, tie, and sunglasses, I'm pretty sure he's a bodyguard. The breadth of this operation is confirmed when the same black SUV pulls up next to the door. The man in the suit opens the door for us and lets us in the back. Then the bodyguard climbs in. When Susie gives a signal, the driver sets off.

"Does he know where we're going?" I ask.

"Of course," she says.

She slips a pair of sunglasses over her eyes and smiles.

"Why are we going back to Chillingham?" I ask. "What do you want to show me?"

She gazes out of the window as though she hasn't heard me.

I'm restless. I want more.

"Why did you send me the diary pages?" I ask her.

"I wanted to remind you of all the things we did together."

"But I don't understand why you even had it."

"You gave it to me, Jenny. About a week before we jumped into the cave. You told me that your mum had found it, and you needed a new hiding place. She would've killed you if she'd known about our challenges. Remember the car we stole?"

"Yes. You sent that entry to me," I say.

She smiles. "We were so happy that day."

"But you still read my diary. Wasn't that a betrayal of trust?"

Her smile fades. "So much time has passed. I'm surprised it still bothers you. I needed a way to reconnect with you and I remembered that on a whim I'd taken the diary with me. So

I flicked through it looking for good memories. Ways to tell our story."

I still feel like she's holding something back. There has to be more to it than that. It's just so odd that she felt the need to take my diary with her when she fled.

"You went home after we jumped into the cave? You didn't stop to help me?" I ask.

"Jenny, there's so much more to it. Please wait until we're there. I'll explain everything. I promise."

I watch the sea from the SUV window. The winter sun is low and bright. Seagulls dip and swoop. I shake my head.

"Is there something in my diary you didn't want anyone to see?" I ask. "Is that why you took it?"

She reaches out and places a hand on my knee. "Jenny, please relax. I just wanted something to remember you by. I wanted a piece of my best friend."

"Then why did you leave?" I ask.

"I had to," she says.

It's infuriating. Like I'm going round and round in circles.

"Just tell me," I say.

"I swear I'm going to. It's just so much better for us both if you see it for yourself," Susie says. "You've waited sixteen years. Thirty minutes isn't so much to ask for. Is it?"

CHAPTER SIXTY-THREE

It's the squawk of the seagulls that bring the memories flooding back. The childhood memories that weren't taken away by my brain injury. Bacon sandwiches on the beach with mum. Football in the back garden with Dad. Walking along the cliffs with Susie and Mrs Patterson. Cool smooth stones found on the beach. Daisies we picked in the fields at the top of the cliffs.

Susie rolls down the car window and the salty air hits the back of my throat. I'm in the water again by the cove, paddling desperately. I can't find Susie. Then she laughs and we're grabbing our clothes before running back to Susie's house. Her mother tells us she's in remission and we hug each other, squealing for joy. I look over at the cult leader who used to be my best friend and I want to ask her if the cancer ever returned.

"Have you missed home?" she asks.

"Yes," I say.

It's not the whole truth. I miss the way it was before she ran away. There are two versions of Chillingham in my head. The one after is cold and unforgiving.

"We can't come here and not see your mum, Susie," I say, staring at the turning that would lead her home.

A flicker of tension flashes across her face. "Not yet."

Her face is so familiar to me and yet so different. It's hard to quantify it all. I can't pinpoint what has changed or even what I recognise.

The driver heads inland and we travel through Chillingham to the other side of the town. I recognise the long, straight road immediately.

"We drove down here when we stole that car," Susie says. "Why don't you drive, Jenny?"

"I just never wanted to," I say.

"There's more to it than that isn't there?" Her eyes narrow. She watches me, gauging my reaction.

"No, I don't think so," I reply.

"Yes, there is. You've held yourself back by not driving. You could have trained to be a social worker or a counsellor by now, but you won't do it because you know you'll need a car. You have a fear holding you back."

Susie instructs the driver to stop. Then she opens her door and gestures for me to get out, too. She walks over to the driver's door and asks him to get out.

"You, too, George," she says, looking at the bodyguard.

"Agnes, I—" George starts to protest.

"Jenny and I will be alone from this point," Susie says. "It's okay. We won't be going far."

I make my way round to the passenger door, but Susie stops me.

"You're driving, Jenny," she says.

"What? No, I can't drive."

"Yes, you can," she says. "Come on. I'll show you how." When I still don't move, she puts a hand on her hip in a gesture that seems so familiar to me. "Jenny Woods, if you don't drive this car, we aren't going anywhere."

I sigh and walk across to the driving seat. She smiles, happy to have won.

"Do you remember all the pedals?" she asks, climbing in.

I pull the seatbelt across my body and check under the wheel. My heart is beating fast. Considering I don't even remember the last time I drove, this is a lot to take in.

"You look pale, sweetie," Susie says. "Take it slowly. Put your foot on the clutch."

"Susie, I don't want to do this." My voice trembles with fear.

"I know you don't," she says. "This is your last challenge. There's a reason why you're so afraid. It's all about that night, isn't it? Everything comes back to that night. All your fears and anxiety started with us at Hangman's Cave."

Shaking, I put my foot on the pedal and push the gear stick. It's only when an old memory of dad letting me drive his truck around the field at the back of our house pops into my head that I finally think to find the biting point.

"No, it's because I have an anxiety disorder and a brain injury," I snap. "Where the fuck is the handbrake?"

"Oh, cars have little switches now." Susie pulls the switch and the car shoots forward.

I squeal, but somehow manage to keep it going without stalling.

"Up to third, Jenny," Susie says, laughing.

My knuckles turn white as I grip the steering wheel. We're going about twenty miles an hour, but it feels like a hundred. "Fucking hell, what am I doing?"

"Living your life," she says. "Let's face it. Before I came back, you weren't living at all. You were existing. Faster,

Jenny. Come on!" She bangs her hands against the glove box, and I cringe.

It's the first time I've seen Susie show any kind of emotion. She's been so well kept together. Creepily so. Now there's chaotic energy emanating from her body. It's a sudden change that makes me nervous.

"Just follow the road," she instructs.

The road curves and I slow slightly to follow it. My gear changes are clunky, and the car complains, but it doesn't stall. Susie tips forward as I brake too hard.

"Sorry," I say.

"Don't apologise. You always apologised too much."

"I'm not sure that's true." I glance over at her but she's staring out of the window at the sea. "If anything, I'm unapologetically honest. Or at least, I am now. Maybe not when you knew me."

She doesn't reply. I slow the car, looking out for the path through the woods. I know it's around here somewhere, but it's been so long that I'm not sure.

"Do you remember us coming here when we were about twelve?" I ask.

"I think so," she says.

"We just came for a walk with your mum. She got mad when you kept asking inappropriate questions about Hangman's Cave."

"Right," she says, almost absentmindedly. "I think I do remember that. Was it during the summer holidays?"

"No. Just one Saturday. It rained."

Susie points to a layby on the left. "Stop here."

I jab the brake and we both pitch forward. "Sorry." When I try to drive the last few feet the car judders and stalls.

"Close enough," she says. And then she directs me to put the weird little switch handbrake on and turn the car off. "Are you proud of yourself, Jen? You drove us here, just like you did that night."

"That night? I drove that night?"

She nods.

I unclip my seatbelt. "I just want answers. I need you to tell me everything."

She grins. "You'd better follow me then."

CHAPTER SIXTY-FOUR

We tread a familiar path through the woods. One that isn't used by tourists, with overgrown thorn bushes poking themselves between the beeches. Breath vapours float between us and everything smells cold, like there's been a recent frost. Susie pulls her coat closer to her throat.

"You were scared that night," she says. "You didn't want to go through with it, and I don't think you would have if it hadn't been for my blood test."

I let out a humourless laugh. "Which was a lie."

Her eyebrows bunch together.

"Come on," I say. "I read the diary entry, but you were obviously bullshitting me back then to get me to jump. Otherwise, your mum would have mentioned the cancer scare to the police."

Her expression morphs into a wry smile. "You're smarter than you look, Jen."

I roll my eyes. It's exactly the kind of thing my dad would say when I got an A at school.

"Have you stayed cancer free all these years?"

She flashes me a look, one that's hard and soft at the same time. Her lips are thin, and her face is in shadow, but her eyes well with moisture. I almost gasp. There's so much pain in her expression that I already understand the answer. I'm hit by another sensation, one of déjà vu.

"This way," she says.

"I remember the way," I say, almost to myself. "Which is weird because I don't even remember that night. Maybe I'm remembering that walk with your mum. Did you know that many of my memories are gone?"

"Yes," she says.

"Were you watching me on the news? Did you see the way they hounded my dad? Did you read the articles insinuating I killed you?"

"Some," she says. There's no hint of remorse in her voice.

A thorn snags my coat and I stop to unhook myself. Susie barely slows down and once I'm free, I hurry to keep up. But it was always like that. Always me trying to keep up with her, even though she was the vulnerable one. The sick one.

She takes a quick left and I stumble as I follow. She speeds up as we come to the clearing that leads to Hangman's Cave.

The mouth of the cave isn't much to look at. It's round, craggy, covered in moss and sticks up out of the ground slightly. You have to climb up onto the stones to look down. There's a fence and a sign telling people to stay away. Children aren't allowed near the cave, it's too easy to fall straight in. We heft ourselves over the fence. Susie is far nimbler than I am. I land awkwardly, almost twisting my ankle.

"I haven't been here for sixteen years," Susie says, placing one foot on the mossy stone.

Unlike her, I hang back, the sight of the place already quickening my pulse.

"Why did you bring me here?" I ask. "Are you trying to get me to remember?"

"Yes," she says. "I want you to put the pieces of the puzzle in place all by yourself."

I shake my head. "That's not how a brain injury works. Those memories are lost."

"If you really believe that, why have you been going to a hypnotherapist for all these years? Why even try to get them back?"

"Because I was trying to find you!" I shout. "Why do you think? I'm the one who sees your mother in pain. I'm the one who gets her emails begging me for information. They accused me of your murder. People stalk me because they think I deserve to be in prison. I even... I even thought maybe I did kill you." Suddenly exhausted, I drop to my knees. "How could you? You're a sociopath, Susie. You have to be. You've hurt... You're a fucking bitch!"

Susie sits down on the rocks and allows her legs to swing over the drop. It makes my stomach lurch. Those rocks could give way at any moment. But then she's already survived the drop once. We both have.

"I'm not a sociopath. I'm a survivor. The universe decided to give me a difficult start in life. I reached a point where I wanted—needed—to start again. So I did."

I shake my head, disgusted.

"I might give you the bitch part, though," she says. "Maybe I am a bitch."

"You had a loving mother and a best friend," I say bitterly. "You chose to leave us behind. And then you moved into your mansion thirty minutes away!"

"It was selfish, I know. But it had to be done."

"Why?"

She sighs. "What do you remember about Max, Jenny?"

"Nothing," I say. I scramble back onto my feet and move closer to the cave. I'm not ready to climb up the stones but I stay closer to her. "Those memories are gone, remember? So all I know is what was in the diary you sent me. I met him on the beach. I got talking to him while you were with another boy. Then we exchanged numbers and dated. But I don't know what happened to him after you ran away."

She picks up a pebble and tosses it into the mouth of the cave. "Did you know Max was there that night?"

"I suspected it, but I wasn't sure. I read in my diary that he wanted to come with us."

Susie climbs down from the stones. "Come on."

We walk in a line following the downward slope of the woods. It's steep here, and my boots slip across the uneven ground. After a few minutes, it starts to rain. Susie grabs hold of my hand, her trainer slipping in the mud.

"You didn't like Max," I say. "You both argued."

"You and Max argued quite a bit, too," she says.

"I wish I remembered him. Did something happen? Was he hurt?"

She doesn't say anything. I think about the dark water I saw while hypnotised. The closer we get to the cave, the more I dread being there. The more I think that the churning water is about death. But no one died the night we jumped into the cave. The police brought cadaver dogs to the area. Divers checked the standing water at the bottom of the drop. There was no body. The dogs picked up the scent of my blood from where I hit my head, but that was it. Some police officers had speculated that Susie's body had fallen into the heavy stream at the bottom of the woods and made its way out to sea, but they never found evidence of it. They thought that perhaps the water at the bottom of the cave diluted the scent of Susie's blood so that the dogs didn't pick it up.

Maybe that happened to Max instead. I glance at Susie as we stumble down the last of the slope. Her face is flushed, her eyes shining. Am I looking at a murderer? Did she kill Max and then run to save her own skin? Or am I missing something?

CHAPTER SIXTY-FIVE

We enter the cave from the bottom exit, by the murky stream that flows out from the underground lake. It's a wide body of water, nowhere near as big as a river, but still fast enough to move a dead person. We walk towards the still pool of clear-blue water sitting directly underneath the mouth of the cave. I see my reflection shimmering within its depths, clear under the winter sun. Do I know the feel of that cold water on my skin? Or am I imagining it right now? Long lost memories stir inside. I'm on the edge of knowing. When I turn to my friend, I see her watching and waiting.

She lingers in her spot by the pool, her eyes searching mine as if she has something more to say. But then she turns away and starts walking, her fingers brushing against the cold, wet walls of the cave.

"When we jumped," she says, "I couldn't breathe. I swallowed so much water that it felt like my lungs were burning." Her voice catches. "You hit your head on the rocks, and it took me a while before I could get you out."

"Then what happened?" I ask. "You're holding something back. I can tell."

The smile she gives me is weak.

"Why now, Susie?" I ask. "Why did you track me down after all this time?"

"I have my reasons," she says.

She takes my hand and pulls me away.

"Are you dying?" I ask.

She stops, her hand brushing over the layers of thick make-up and concealer that highlights her sunken cheeks. The long blonde curls seem too perfect to be natural, and I am now convinced they are extensions. She looks at me, her eyes glimmering with amusement beneath her mascara-laden lashes as she asks, "Do I look like I'm dying?"

"No," I say. "You look amazing. But maybe you're a little thin." I think back to how tired she appeared on the train. Maybe it wasn't quite as curated as I thought. Maybe her real vulnerability did emerge that day.

Susie smiles. "Come here. Let's follow the stream. I have so much to tell you."

"Start with what happened that night. Please."

"Well," she says. "Do you remember that there'd been a lot of rain the day before the jump? It was one of the reasons why..." She pauses and licks her lips. "Why I wanted to do it then. I knew there'd be plenty of water in the cave. The person who died here did so because there'd been a drought and they hit rocks. I thought it would be safer."

"I don't remember that but go on."

We slip along the muddy path, watching rain droplets hit the water surface.

"The body washed into the stream. It was full of water and moving more quickly than usual. On any other day, a body would get tangled in rocks or tree roots, but it just washed straight down through the woods out of sight. I guess it hit the estuary before the police found us." She stops and pulls in a deep breath. When she sits down on the wet grass, I join her.

"The body," I say. "Max. Did you kill him? Did you kill Max?"

"It wasn't safe for me to stay." Susie stares at her knees. "Tell me why it wasn't safe for me to stay."

"Because you'd killed someone."

"There's more to it than that," she says. "Think, Jenny. Really think about it. Think about me and everything you know about me. Please. You need to try harder." She grasps hold of my hands. "If we're going to do this, you need to remember. I know you can. The head trauma didn't erase those memories, you did. You, Jenny. You blocked them out because you didn't want to know. But you're strong now. I know you can do it."

I close my eyes.

CHAPTER SIXTY-SIX
JENNY

SIXTEEN YEARS AGO

"I think I'm having a heart attack."

Susie laughs. "You're so dramatic, Jen. Here. Just put your foot there. Now change the gear. Rev the engine. Good!"

"Why did we have to steal a car anyway?" I ask, pouting.

"It's too far to walk, dumbass."

When the car starts to roll, I'm convinced my heart is going to break through my rib cage. A *whoop* comes from the back seat, and I glance up at the mirror to smile at Max.

"Okay, I'm getting the hang of it," I say.

Susie cranks up the radio and we bop along to S Club 7. We wouldn't normally listen to such babyish music, but the beat is fun, and we know all the words.

"Here!" Susie shouts. "Stop the car!"

When I slam down the brake, Max hits the back of my seat.

"Jesus Christ, Jenny!"

"Sorry!"

"Come on." Susie opens her door. "Max, grab that bag from the back. It has our towels in it." She grins, and it's good to see her smiling for the first time in a few days. The latest tests have really taken it out of her.

Susie's hair still shines golden in the dim moonlight. Such a contrast to Max and I with our dark hair. I reach back to grab Max's hand. I need warmth.

"I've got butterflies about this," Max admits. "Are you guys sure it's safe?"

Susie is in front of us, but I can practically hear the roll of her eyes as she responds. "Like I've said a thousand times. Everything is safe. It rained so hard yesterday the cave will be overflowing with water and we'll be fine. Stop shitting on everyone's cornflakes." As she turns her eyes narrow. I feel Max's body tense beside me.

"Don't fall out, you two." I laugh nervously.

The constant bickering between Susie and Max heightens my anxiety. They hate each other. Even though they're making an effort to get along, you could cut the atmosphere with a knife.

Susie sings more S Club 7 songs as we make our way through the woods. I can tell she's a bit tipsy. The light from her torch bobs around, bouncing from tree to tree. The surface is rough and bumpy beneath my feet. I almost fall a few times, but Max is a sturdy presence next to me.

"Here it is," Susie says. "Jenny, come here. You need to hold my hand when we jump." She turns to Max. "This is our thing."

Max lets me go. "I know that."

"Just checking."

I hate the malice dripping from Susie's voice. She's only like this when she's drunk.

Following the light, I make my way over to the mouth of

the cave. We climb up the stone together and stand over the hole. Susie directs the torch down into the abyss. It's not our biggest jump, but it's definitely the most dangerous. Even with the recent downpour, I see the jagged rocks ringing the edge of the water pool.

"You have to really jump, Jenny," Susie warns. "You need to clear those rocks. Don't just step off, actually push yourself forwards."

"She'll be fine," Max says from behind us. "Stop babying her. She knows what she's doing."

Susie turns. "Shut up." Then she grabs my damp face with her free hand. "We can do this. I promise you. We always come out the other side. We're fucking invincible, Jenny."

Susie places the torch down and pulls off her shoes and coat. I do the same. Behind me, I sense Max pacing back and forth. Then Susie nods at me, a question in her eyes. *Am I with her?* I nod back. *Always.*

The abyss yawns beneath our toes. Somewhere, deep down, in the throat of that black hole awaits freezing cold water. But the drop will be long before our bodies hit the water. I look at Susie and see fear written across her young features. We clasp hands, both letting out a nervous giggle.

This is the one. The challenge to end it all. This is what we've both waited for. And now we've finally dug deep enough to mine out the bravery needed.

Or stupidity.

People have died in this spot. I know that. It's closed to the public for that very reason. We are trespassing in a place that doesn't belong to us, but I don't care.

I look at my best friend in the entire world and know I'm doing the right thing. Susie looks back, long hair flowing in the wind, tears formed in the corners of her eyes. Maybe from the wind, maybe not.

We say the words in unison.

One, two, three

Dare you, dare me.

My body trembles, my toes tense around the crumbling edge of the drop.

One, two, three

Let the fear set you free.

I pull in a deep breath, redirecting my eyes to the hole below.

One, two, three

Follow you, follow me.

I tremble in fear.

One, two, three

Let the fear set you free.

Let the fear set you free.

Susie steps first. I hesitate. Only for a split second. And then my knees are bent. I'm flying into the air. Our fingers loosen from each other's grip and the darkness swallows us both. I hang there for just the briefest of moments before gravity pulls me into the abyss.

I break the freezing cold water. It isn't the first time I've hit water like this, but I immediately know something is wrong. The back of my head is hot. Blazing hot. My body isn't responding in the way it usually does. I can't control my limbs.

I sink down until my back hits the bottom of the pool. Then I somehow push myself up. There's another huge splash somewhere near me but I hardly hear it because I'm trying to swim to the edge.

A bright light hurts my eyes. Just for a moment. It flits away and bounces around the cave. The cave goes dark. I find a rock to rest on, keeping my head above the water. I close my eyes for a second. Then open them again. The torch is back, near Susie, only this time there's a girl standing over her, holding her down. The water around them is dark, almost black, and churning where Susie is struggling, kicking her feet. I try to cry out, to tell her to stop, but unconsciousness seeps over me.

The next time I wake, I'm alone in the woods.

CHAPTER SIXTY-SEVEN

"Max," I say.

Three letters. So easy to say, mouth and tongue travelling over the sound "axe". Each letter is a whisper on my lips as I turn to the woman I thought was my best friend.

She is not Susie. She is Max, my girlfriend. The girlfriend taken from my mind along with the rest of my memories from the months leading up to Hangman's Cave. Memories I have repressed because I didn't want to see that moment again. The moment where Max held Susie under the water.

Max used to hang out with the kids on the beach. She lived in Chillingham, but she wasn't from here. She was a runaway. She slept in a tent, either on the beach or in the woods somewhere. One night, after a few beers on the beach, she told me about how she'd escaped an abusive home about six months before I met her. She'd drifted around the coast, working in cafes and fish and chip shops for minimum wage, but she hadn't managed to save up for a place of her own. She was sixteen when I met her, but she pretended to be eighteen.

She murdered Susie.

"It wasn't safe for you to stay because of your stepfather," I say. "He was looking for you."

Her eyes fill with tears.

"But you killed Susie. You *killed* her. Why?"

The tears fall. "Jenny, she was almost dead. I just finished it."

"You held her under the water! She was struggling! She was kicking the water!" I step back, my hand flying up to my mouth. I'm standing here with a murderer. With a cold, sociopathic killer.

"I didn't know you saw that," she admits. "I thought you were unconscious at the time."

"I blocked it all out." I think of the dark, thrashing water imagery. It was always there, under the surface, waiting to come out. It just didn't have a form. "You left and you stole her identity for your cult. That's sick!"

All of this. The searching for answers, the playing with my memories and making me believe she was Susie... All of it has come to this. And I can't tell if I'm sad, angry, terrified, or something in between.

I walk out of the cave, stumbling away from the underground lake. Finally, the tears come. I crouch down on the wet ground, pressing my face against my knees as I sob. Rain patters down on the back of my skull.

She follows me. Without turning around I hear her approach. "You were right about one thing, though. I am dying. I have ovarian cancer."

I lift my head. "What?"

"It's true."

"But you're a liar," I say. "I can't trust you."

She clasps her hands together. "I think you know it's true. Deep down."

She's right. *Max* is right. I can see it. Beneath all that

make-up is the face of an ill woman. "I'm sorry. Truly. Maybe I shouldn't be, but I am."

She nods. "And I'm sorry, too. For... For everything."

I sniff and wipe tears from my eyes. "I don't understand how... How you got away with it."

Max shrugs. "You hit your head on the rocks jutting out of the water pool, but Susie went under the surface and half-drowned before she floated back up."

I tense my hands into fists. "I can't believe you took her away from me. I can't believe any of this."

"I made sure you were okay first," Max says. "I moved you out of the water. Susie bobbed back up after at least five minutes. I thought she was dead already. But..." She shakes her head. "I was so angry. I thought you were going to die, and it was all for that bitch who didn't deserve you as a friend. I ended it that night. I held her down until she stopped breathing. Then I carried her body over to the mouth of the stream and tossed her in." She wipes her nose. "The next day, I took my tent somewhere near Whitby and set it up in the woods. Then I waited for someone to find the body. I saw a news report about you and how you were in hospital. But no one was talking about me so I figured you were either covering for me or you genuinely couldn't remember. I also knew you'd never told your parents about me. Then I saw a newspaper article about how you had lost some of your memories. I figured you might have forgotten me. So I broke into your house and stole your diary to make sure that the police never found me." She pats my hand. "I'd seen you writing in it while we were hanging out. You can have it back by the way."

"No one knew you existed. No one knew you were in Chillingham at all."

She nods. "And no one found Susie's body. She washed straight out to sea."

Suddenly disgusted, I get to my feet. "I need to get away from you. You're a murderer, Max! You killed my best friend!"

"Calm down, Jenny." She lifts her hands, trying to placate me. "I'm not going to harm you, I swear. Aside from that night, I've never committed a violent act. It was a one off. It wasn't me."

I scan the landscape around me. Where can I run? Another memory flashes through my mind. Pulling myself up from the rocks, I staggered through the woods searching for Max and Susie. But then I collapsed. When I woke up for the second time that night, I was somewhere deeper inside the woods. I was bleeding and in pain. My legs had been wobbly, but I'd managed to stumble into a run. Then I'd seen the light of the police officer's torch. He'd placed his jacket on my shoulders.

"I need to go," I say, searching for a path away from Max. I can either follow the stream down to the estuary or climb the hill we just came from and make my way back to the road.

"I'm giving it all to you," Max says. "The empire I've built. You're the only one they'll follow after me. That's why I came to you." She climbs to her feet and takes a step towards me. "I know I lied to them. I made them believe that I was Susie Patterson and that I kept cancer away by facing my fears. I know I've done wrong."

I shake my head in disbelief. "Of all people, why did you become *her?*"

"I don't know," she says. "Maybe I wanted to be you, more than her. I wanted to be part of the sisterhood you both had. But I also wanted *you* and she was the only one who truly had you."

I stop and turn to her. "Yet you never came for me. You hid from me."

She stumbles down a slope and stands before me, tucking a lock of my hair behind my ears. I'm taken back to another time. Sitting in a tent with the girl I can't stop thinking about. Her tucking a lock of hair behind my ear and kissing me.

"I left it too late. I thought I had all the time in the world." Her shoulders sag with sadness. "Don't you see what I've made? There are thousands of people all over the world following my teachings, listening to *me*." She grasps hold of my upper arms and it's like my body is in a vice. I try to step back but she holds me tight. "You saw the house. The land. You know what all of this is worth." She laughs. "They give me their money and thank me for it. I could sell my blood to these people. My bathwater. They'd eat shit if I told them to. I'm *Agnes* now. Max is dead." Her eyes burn. "I'm Agnes and it means something for the first time in my life."

Her fingernails dig into my flesh through my coat. Every time I try to wrench away from her, she digs deeper. But she can't hold on forever. The fight seeps out of her and she steps back, suddenly exhausted.

"But it's slipping away from me," Max says. "I didn't grow up with much. I made what I have all by myself, and God—or the universe or whatever—has chosen to take it away from me." Her voice drips with bitterness. "I don't even care what you do with what I've built. All I know is that you're the only one who could take it on, and I owe you. You're getting it whether you like it or not."

I rub my sore arms.

"Tell me why you killed her," I say. "Tell me the real truth."

Max looks up. There's no remorse in her eyes. "I hated her. She had a hold on you that would have lasted for years.

She was a user and she only liked you because you followed." Max rests against a rock and folds her arms. "Imagine Susie lived that night. You both would have assumed that jumping into Hangman's Cave saved her from cancer. How dangerous were your stunts going to become in time? And for how long? Were you going to be eighty years old running in front of a moving train? She would have demanded you go to the same university, told you who to date, manipulated you into staying around her because she needed you. I did you a favour. Without her, you've flourished."

"I'm a nervous wreck with amnesia," I say. "Fuck this and you. I'm going back to the road."

"And I'm coming with you," she says.

Max closes the space between us surprisingly quickly and grips hold of my arm.

"I may be dying," she says breathlessly, "but I'm still strong. And I'm not letting you out of my sight. We're finishing this once and for all."

CHAPTER SIXTY-EIGHT

Numb from all the revelations, I let Max lead me back up the hill. We're muddy and soaking wet by the time we make it back to the road. Rain smudges Max's make-up, her perfect veneer sliding down her face. I can't look at her. Every time I do, I try to conjure up the feeling of knowing her intimately, of being her girlfriend, but I can't find those emotions. All I see is a murderer.

She doesn't tell me to drive this time, she gets in the driver's seat and takes control. A few minutes later, we collect Max's driver and both of us move to the back.

I redirect my thoughts away from Susie's death to a new revelation about myself. I loved a girl. As far as I know, Max is the only girl I've ever had romantic feelings for. But knowing I was with her makes a few things about myself click into place. Jigsaw pieces reveal more of the story that is me. I've always thought women were beautiful. But I think my co-dependent relationship with Jack stopped me from exploring those feelings any further. I remember his drunken taunt, suggesting I had romantic feelings for Susie. Maybe I internalised that.

As we approach Max's house, my stomach growls. The sea view is grey now that the mist has crawled in. She's greeted by Ryan again. Once we make our way inside, he leads us through to an enormous dining room with a table laid out with platters of meats, cheeses and fruit.

"I'm going to shower before eating," Max says. "If you'd also like to freshen up, Ryan will show you where to go."

It seems so surreal. I see a group of devoted followers bowing to Max as we leave. Liam was right. I've walked into the dragon's den and there's no way they're going to let me go.

Ryan shows me through to a guest room with an ensuite. I note the clean clothes folded neatly on top of the plush, king size bed. I peel away damp layers of clothing and hop into the shower, only to consider hidden cameras after I'm naked.

It seems like the least of my worries, to be honest.

Scalding water hits my skin. I rub shampoo into my damp hair and scrub my arms with body wash. I want to clean it all away. Now that I know everything, I want to go back to not knowing. Then at least there was the possibility that Susie was alive. Now I know the awful truth.

I scrub and I scrub, squeezing handfuls of lime perfumed wash out of the bottle. But I still feel filthy. My best friend is dead. I couldn't help her. I thought she set up a cult. I thought she was a horrible person. I believed the people telling me she was.

And then I'm on the floor of the shower, tears washing down the drain along with the soap bubbles. I wrap my arms around my knees, thinking about Max's reasoning for murder. She's right, Susie did see me as a follower. Susie always liked it that way. But is Max right about my life if Susie had lived? Would Susie still control me, or would I have developed a backbone?

Most childhood friendships fizzle out, no matter how intense they are. People grow. They evolve. Max robbed Susie of the opportunity to become a better person. Reading my old diaries and talking to my father, Max, and Mrs Patterson has made me realise that Susie was a user. But she was also traumatised by her illness. In a way, I was, too. Susie never had the chance to face her emotional demons and become a better person. It breaks my heart.

I need to get out of here.

I don't want this cult. I don't want this responsibility.

But I have no choice but to get out of the shower, dry, and dress in the clothes left for me. In slippered feet, I make my way back down to the dining room.

"Please sit here, Jenny." Ryan shows me to a chair. He places me halfway along the table.

"It's so nice to meet you," says a woman. She smiles, and her full lips part to reveal a missing tooth on the left side of her mouth. "You're very important to us."

"Thanks," I say.

"I'm Anita," she says.

"Nice to meet you."

We cordially shake hands. The man on my other side introduces himself as Nate. I feel like I'm floating up in the clouds somewhere. It's all so weird. The food smells delicious. I see some of my favourite cheeses in there alongside pots of chutney, cooked meats, potato salad, and bowls of fruit.

Suddenly, everyone at the table stands. I follow suit, and Max walks in. The others bow. I don't. I sit.

"Today is a special day," Max says. "My best friend in the world is here. The only other person who knows what it is to let the fear set her free. Jenny Woods."

A spattering of applause breaks out around the table.

Max holds up a glass of champagne. "This is for you,

Jenny. I'm sorry I didn't find you sooner but I'm so happy to have you here with us."

"Happy to be here," I say through gritted teeth, raising my glass.

"Let's eat!" Max says, and the group laughs.

They have no idea, I think. She's a fraud and they have no idea.

My gaze drifts over to the door where one of Max's bodyguards stands. How devoted are these people? Are they willing to die for her? I consider what might happen if I pull rank. I should be as important as "Susie". After all, I am one of the founding members even if I didn't know about FREEDM until recently. Would these people follow me? Max seems to think so.

I need to get out of here, but I need to be smart about it. I load my plate with food, trying to fit in.

"How long have you been with FREEDM, Anita?" I ask, back in investigator mode. If I'm stuck here, I might as well learn more about the cult.

"Three years," she says.

"You're part of Sanctum here. Do you live here permanently?"

She cuts a slice of ham and nods her head. "I live here and work in Whitby."

"Oh, what do you do?"

"I'm an accountant," she says, smiling.

I nod to myself. An accountant would come in useful. I glance across the table. I wonder who these other people are. Solicitors. Financial advisors. Doctors. Maybe even politicians. People to help her keep this cult running.

"What was it like jumping into Hangman's Cave and saving Agnes from cancer?" she asks.

It makes me cringe that these people believe our rash actions cured Susie of her terminal illness.

"I don't remember it," I tell her. "I have a brain injury." I try not to think about what I learned today. "What did you do for your initiation?"

Anita smiles as she slices a potato in half. "Confronted my abusive husband. Agnes arranged it herself. She got him to walk down an alley with her. He was such a pig; he'd never turn down a pretty woman offering him sex. Then I came into the alley with the others tasked with witnessing my initiation. Agnes gave me the bat and I did the rest."

"You hit him?"

She pops the potato into her mouth and chews. "I did. Over and over again."

"And the police never worked out you beat him?"

"Agnes made sure he was drugged up. He didn't remember a thing. I moved out while he was unconscious in that alley and never spoke to him again."

That's another occasion where members of the FREEDM cult resorted to violence. I place a chunk of bread back on my plate, sickened.

"How did it make you feel?" I ask.

"Like a queen," she says. "Like a rockstar on ecstasy in front of a hundred thousand adoring fans."

"You don't think what you did was morally wrong?"

For the first time, her tone turns hard. "If you saw what he did to me, you wouldn't ask me that question."

"Sorry," I say. "I'm trying to get my head around all this."

"I think Agnes brought you here too soon," Anita says, her eyes narrowing. "What was your initiation?"

"Swimming underneath ice," I say.

She nods. "Then you're still as brave as you were when you were a kid."

"I am," I say, meaning it.

"And it's all thanks to that woman there." Anita raises her fork towards Max. "I would be dead without her."

"You really believe that?" I ask.

She nods. "I know it. She saved my life."

CHAPTER SIXTY-NINE

I wake in luxury. I had the best night's sleep possibly for the last sixteen years. When I open the curtains, I see that the grey mist has dissipated revealing the sea stretching out along the horizon.

It doesn't seem normal to feel rested and content. Not after all the revelations from yesterday. Perhaps it hasn't hit me yet, but I should be grieving Susie. Instead, I feel more alive than ever.

It's after eight a.m. so there's no way I can make it into work on time. That's if Max even lets me leave the Sanctum. I send Trudy a text message telling her my anxiety is bad and I'll need a few days off next week. Then I shower and find more clothes inside a wardrobe that I can wear.

The clothes fit me perfectly and even match my complexion. The jumper is a hazelnut shade similar to my eye colour. The jeans are indigo blue that somehow fit my awkward pear-shaped body.

My phone pings and I'm surprised to see a message from Liam.

> Everything okay? You haven't done anything stupid with FREEDM have you?

I enjoy not responding. For so long he had the upper hand in our "relationship". Him as the police officer. The one who rejected me because of his ethics. The one who would come along and save me, letting me lean on him, letting me become dependent. Maybe he was nothing more than a Jack all along.

Or maybe he's a good man.

I push the thought away and head downstairs. There's already a group gathered around a buffet breakfast table. The food here is good. I grab an almond croissant and a cup of tea.

A few of the others come over to chat. I get a few names, and some tell me where they're from. It gives me a good idea of how large FREEDM is. There are people here who attended seminars in London, Manchester, York, and Leeds. I hear of rented houses full of FREEDM members in these areas. Many members still work, whereas others have quit their jobs.

And then I see a familiar face.

It's just for a second as she walks past the open doorway along a corridor. But I'm sure it's her.

Hannah.

I jump up from the table and hurry towards the door. Someone steps in my way asking me how I slept. I whisper an apology and dodge around them, jogging out into the hallway. I see a ponytail disappearing around a corner.

"Hannah!" I call.

"Jenny, what are you doing?"

I turn around to see Max standing behind me. "I saw Hannah."

She frowns. "Who's Hannah?"

"My housemate's girlfriend." I step towards my ex-girlfriend and jab a finger at her chest. "You've had people in my life keeping tabs on me. Don't lie to me! I know you have."

She shakes her head. "Jenny, I don't know a Hannah and I don't know what you're talking about. No one has infiltrated your life. Our research has all been conducted from afar." She takes hold of my arm, pulling me away. "Come on. Have a cup of coffee and calm down. I know it's all very strange being here. I know you feel out of sorts. That's normal, I promise."

The room clears leaving us alone. I accept a cappuccino made from the fancy barista machine the cult owns. Then I stare at it, wondering what kind of drugs they put in the coffee here. Max sits next to me at the table, angling her chair so that we're face to face.

"How are you?" Max asks.

"When can I leave?" I snap back.

"Whenever you want," she says. "I'm not keeping you prisoner here."

I let out a derisive snort at that. "Coming from the person telling me Hannah isn't in the cult when I saw her."

"As far as I know, there is no Hannah at the Sanctum," she reiterates. "Whether Hannah goes by another name here, I don't know, but I certainly didn't plant her in your life."

"I think you're a liar."

She shakes her golden curls slightly. "I can't argue with that." She sighs. "Jenny, I don't want to fight. I just want to spend time with you before I have to go into a hospice. It won't be long now. I've decided not to seek treatment. It's too widespread to do much anyway. So we can either end this as friends or enemies, but I would prefer it to be friends."

In the wan of her smile, I see the cracks forming. There are dark circles just visible beneath layers of concealer. A few beads of sweat break out across her forehead. She's tired and doesn't want to show it.

It could be the passing of time, or it could be the amnesia keeping my memories muddled, but she sounds like Susie to me now. As I break away, I try to remember the dark-haired, blue-eyed girl I'd fallen for. There's so little of her in my mind and that's so sad to me.

"I want you to remember the good times we had," Max says. "I loved you. It breaks my heart that you forgot me so easily." She takes my hand. Her skin is cool, her fingers are skinny and long.

"I forgot because of what you did," I say. "I obviously loved you because seeing you kill Susie traumatised me so much, I put up a wall and blocked it all out. You broke my heart."

She drops my hand in shock. Her mouth opens and she lets out a strangled sob. "Oh my God, you're right. I did break your heart."

"And then you stole my diary and Susie's tapes. Why did you take them?"

"I thought you and Susie might have talked about me on them."

"Even the ones from when we were children?"

She shrugs. "There were no dates on them. I had no time. I just grabbed whatever I could."

"Mrs Patterson never noticed," I say.

"You saw Susie's room," Max says with a laugh. "There was shit everywhere. Piles of crap. Luckily, I remembered you once saying Susie kept the tapes in a box under her bed."

"Why did I tell you that?"

"We were in my tent one night. I told you about my stepfather and how he used to hit me and tell me I was worthless. You said we should get a tape recorder and say all of our deepest, darkest secrets because that's what you and Susie do. Then you put them in a box and under her bed so that her parents don't listen to them."

And there it is, the memory, fresh in my mind. We're in our underwear with the sleeping bags tangled beneath us. The canvas above us is blue. Max has a camping light dangling from one of the tent poles. Every now and then, I push it with my finger so that it sways back and forth. Her skin is warm next to mine. Our fingers are entwined, and her palm is damp.

"Come on." Max rises, holding out a hand.

I don't take it, but I do follow her out of the room.

Yes, I remember her. I see aspects of myself I didn't know existed. But those hands murdered my friend, and I cannot let myself forget it.

CHAPTER SEVENTY

Max's bodyguard follows us as we make our way through the Sanctum. She's moving more slowly today. I wonder if she took some painkillers or other medication to help her get through yesterday.

"Do you find this display of wealth unseemly?" she asks out of the blue.

"Who paid for this house, Max?"

"It's not what you think. Yes, members donate a small portion of their wages, but we have some wealthy donors, and the seminars pay for a lot of expenses. The money trickles down to those who need it. People like Ashley. She hasn't paid rent at the cottage, and she doesn't donate to FREEDM. Without us, she would be homeless, or still living with her abusive family."

Max unlocks a door and takes me through to what appears to be a storage room. I take a mental note of the boxes of files stacked on the shelves. Could these contain hard copies of financial details? Or information about the members here?

She notices me looking. "This is where we keep all of our seminar notes. Booklets about the organisation, notes for presentations, and so on. We usually have some left over and the various areas send them back here after a while."

She tries to pull down one box but struggles to hold the weight. I step in, taking the box from her. It's not heavy. Max staggers back and wipes sweat from her forehead.

"I keep forgetting what I can't manage." She shakes her head slightly. "Anyway, you can have these. I don't need them anymore and they are more yours than mine. Maybe you can take them back to Mrs Patterson and tell her what I did. I don't care. Why would I care now? I'm dying."

I look for the lie, but I can't find it. Max truly doesn't care about being outed as a murderer.

"What about your legacy?" I ask. "Wouldn't FREEDM fall apart if everyone found out what you did?"

She smiles. "It doesn't matter. I did what I set out to do. I helped people. If it comes crumbling down now, then so be it."

I find it hard to believe but she's compelling.

"I know how long you've volunteered at Solace, and I know you have helped some callers there. Imagine if you could do it on a huge scale. That's what I did." Her eyes widen, glistening with emotion. "You could be the head of this family. You could continue my legacy—"

"Wait." I place the box down at my feet. "You're the mother with the adopted children. It was *you*."

"It was me."

"You told me about your diagnosis. You told me you were worried about who would replace you and look after your kids. But you didn't mean kids, you meant *cult* members."

"It isn't a cult, Jen. Stop saying that—"

"It is!" I throw my hands up in the air, exasperated.

Max sighs and leans heavily against the shelves behind her. "Let's go."

I pick up the box and carry it out of the small space. As Max locks the door, I flip open the top flap. Small plastic boxes stand in a neat line with Susie's untidy handwriting along the spines. Most are just dates. Some have our names on with hearts around them. Others say things like *Don't listen! Stay away! Private!*

It shouldn't surprise me that Max phoned in like that. Many callers have a favourite operator and will hang up until they hear the voice they want. It does surprise me that Max recognised my voice after all these years, but maybe that's because my own memory is so bad it seems impossible to me. Voices don't tend to change too much. Maybe if someone moves around, they pick up new accents, but the tone, depth, and volume often stays the same.

"Take the tapes home," Max says, pulling me from my thoughts. "Listen to them. There might be things you've forgotten." She walks away from me. "I'll have my driver take you to Whitby train station." She places a hand on my shoulder. Every time she touches me, I think about what she did to Susie. She may not have spilled Susie's blood, but she took away her life. "I made a mistake, Jenny. You can't inherit FREEDM. You don't have what it takes to lead them."

The words come out of left field. Since I arrived at the Sanctum, she has tried to persuade me that this place belongs to me. And now, so abruptly, she has changed her mind.

"Then who will—"

"I have other options," she calls.

The man in the suit comes closer, placing a hand on my elbow, and turns me around. I glance back, hoping for one more look at Max, but she's gone.

The train journey home goes by in a blur. I place the box of tapes on my lap and lean my head against the glass. Mundane weather alerts tell me that we're about to go into a cold snap. I text Liam back.

> I'm fine. They haven't had me whacked, so don't worry.

I consider that this is where it ends. I know what happened to Susie and I finally know that it wasn't my fault. The person who killed her may not have been brought to justice, but she is dying. Or so she wants me to believe.

I can't trust her.

The Wi-Fi signal is patchy on the train but this time I put in the name Maxine Graham. The girl I knew. The one who is hazy in my mind, but there, like a ghost or a hologram.

To my surprise, she has an Instagram account set to private. The profile picture is her, only without the blonde extensions. It's Max in her mid-twenties, her hair still dark, her eyes startlingly blue. Something thuds in my chest. A reminder of what I found attractive about her in the first place.

I request access to her private profile page. I don't expect a response, but it's approved after only a moment or two. Max saw the notification right away. She's still active on this account.

Max has a handful of followers, but no one I recognise. This tells me there are a small number of people that know she isn't Susie. It's remarkable that Max has built up this cult and not one of them has reported the sighting of Susie to the police. I know she goes by "Agnes", but it appears to be an open secret that she is Susie Patterson, even though they don't know it's a lie.

Still, Max could simply call it a misunderstanding. With nothing linking her to Chillingham at all, I doubt the police would put the pieces together even if they did speak to Max. She's so brazen and so cunning that if she hadn't murdered someone, I might admire her.

Scrolling through Max's private account, I see dozens of photographs of her without the Agnes styling. With no make-up, no hair extensions, and no pristine white suits, she is a thirty-two year old woman in a bed receiving treatment. She isn't in a hospital in any of these pictures, she is in a bed, presumably in the Sanctum, with IV drips and nurses around her.

I lean back against the train chair. She could still be lying, I remind myself. For all I know, she's receiving a vitamin boost in these photos. My head is a mess. I don't know what to do or what to think about all this.

CHAPTER SEVENTY-ONE

I step into the house and Hannah waves to me from the kitchen. I pause.

"Hey, Jen," she says. "Harry said you were visiting home. Did you have a nice time?"

I gape at her for a moment, rewinding the moment I thought I saw her at the Sanctum. And then finally speak. "Yes, thank you. Did you stay over?"

"No, I came to meet Harry for lunch. He's just in the bathroom right now. Do you want a hot drink?"

I shake my head. "No thanks."

"It's good to see you," she calls, as I make my way through to my room.

My legs are shaking by the time I get to my room. I place the box down on the end of my bed and go over the moment again. I saw her just for a second, from a distance, but I was so sure it was her. But she must have left the Sanctum immediately, and either caught an earlier train, or drove straight here. It's possible. But is it likely?

I dig through the box, pulling out tapes to arrange in some sort of order. There must be hours and hours of our conversations here. At the very bottom, there's an old cassette player. I turn it over in my hands, remembering Susie walking down the street with the player attached to her waistband, headphones on. It was out of date then. Most people had portable CD players. A few years later, she got a CD player for Christmas, and I never saw the tape player again, until now.

I grab a tape, shove it in the player, and put on the headphones. But there's no power. I unclip the piece of plastic keeping the batteries in, remove old ones and head into the house to hunt out a pair of fresh AA batteries. From the living room, I hear Hannah and Harry giggling together.

If Hannah is in the cult, then she must have seduced Harry and started a relationship with him just to get to me. Maybe it's crazy to believe that. She even took him home to meet her parents at Christmas. Could she really do something like that?

I find a packet of batteries in our junk drawer in the kitchen and hurry back to my bedroom. Slightly out of breath from rushing around the house, I plug in the batteries and put the headphones back on. This time, the player comes to life.

"Rebecca James is a bitch," Susie says.

There's a brief silence. "She laughed at me during hockey practice today. Like she's any better in goal. And she has fat thighs."

My voice comes in. "Yeah."

I'm quieter than Susie. My one word has far less conviction.

Our conversation continues about Rebecca James. I remember her. She played hockey with Susie but I didn't have much to do with her. But she wasn't overweight in the slightest, Susie is just being bitchy.

Now I remember that Susie's comment about Rebecca's

thighs made me feel bad because I was stockier than Rebecca. I know why I sound so quiet on the tape. I'm feeling shit about myself. We were eleven here. I'd felt self-conscious about puberty and the way my body changed. I want to hug eleven-year-old me.

I keep listening, unable to fast forward even the most mundane conversations about maths homework and our form tutor. I'm addicted.

Eight inches of snow falls overnight, and I haven't slept. I've listened to hours of our conversations, from people Susie doesn't like, to made up lyrics to All Saints songs, to us talking about our challenges and which cliff to jump into the sea from, to the boys we liked or hated.

When I go back to our years as children, not long after Susie's battle with leukaemia, I'm transported back to the night in the woods with Liam. When I listen to us as teenagers, I think about our first bikinis, Susie's boyfriends changing weekly, and Hangman's Cave hovering in our future.

Hearing her makes me sob at times. I press my face into a pillow so that Harry doesn't hear. At other times, I feel angry. Or afraid. Or amused.

I check the website for the counselling centre and Trudy has announced that it's closed. I am still off sick anyway but considered going in just to give me a break from the tapes. In the end, I pull myself out of bed, put the tapes back in the box, and leave the house. All of the buses and trains have been cancelled. There's nowhere to go but I just want to walk.

As I trudge along icy pavements, I realise I haven't had a panic attack in a while. Bad weather, compacted snow on the pavements, public transport cancelled, and everything else that comes along with a sudden snowstorm usually sends me spiralling. Aside from the sleep deprivation, I feel completely fine.

I wouldn't recommend swimming under ice to try and "fix" my anxiety, but everything that has happened over the last couple of months has resulted in a shift. I can't deny it. Being part of FREEDM has actually helped me.

And it makes me sick to my stomach to admit it.

CHAPTER SEVENTY-TWO
JENNY

SIXTEEN YEARS AGO

I'm at the beach, soaking wet. Susie is lying on her back on a towel, pushing up her breasts in the tiny bikini. Every now and then, she glances over to the group of older teens around a fire. There's one particularly arrogant-looking boy she has her eye on. He is handsome but it's clear he's cocky with it. His hyperactive energy frightens me, but I can tell it excites Susie.

Once the boy invites us both to join him and his friends, Susie gets cosy with him, and I watch from the other side of the circle. It's a lonely feeling seeing your best friend get with a guy when you're in a group of strangers. But then a girl comes over and sits next to me.

"Hey, I'm Max," she says.

"Jenny." I sip my bottle of beer. It's sour but refreshing.

"You live round here, don't you? I think I've seen you and your friend in the town," she says.

"Yeah. Just down the road."

"It's nice here." She smiles. She has a lovely smile, but her teeth are off-white, beginning to yellow.

"Where do you live?" I ask.

"Oh, all over the place really. On Owen's bedroom floor at the moment," she says.

I don't really understand what that means but it sounds very grown up.

"Cool," I say.

She grabs a book from her back pocket and moves it out the way so she can sit more comfortably.

"Carrie," I say, reading the title. "I liked that one. Have you read The Shining? I had nightmares."

"Yes," she says. "And, controversial opinion, but it's better than the film."

"Oh, that is controversial. I love both, though. I can't choose."

She laughs. "Are you always that diplomatic?"

I shake my head. "I don't know. Maybe."

It's then that I realise I like the sound of her laugh, and she has gorgeous, tanned skin. Her blue eyes are so strange but alluring next to her dark hair.

"Looks like your friend, Susie, gets on well with Owen." Max sips her beer.

I glance over to see Susie on Owen's lap. "Yeah, how old is he?"

"Nineteen," Max says.

I make a face. Mrs Patterson won't like that.

"How old are you?" Max asks. Her eyes are focused on me, and it makes me blush.

"Sixteen. You?"

Max takes another sip of beer. "Younger than I tell people."

"Why is that?"

She gives me this knowing smile. "Because when you're sixteen and you don't have a family to go home to, people tend to ask a lot of questions."

Now I understand why she said that about sleeping on Owen's floor. It hadn't even occurred to me that she didn't have parents like most kids my age. She must not go to school, either. That's probably why I haven't seen her there.

"Sorry," I say, not sure how to answer.

She shrugs. "It's okay. I like the independence. It's cool. I get to do what I want. And I get to meet cool people." She nudges me with her shoulder. "Like you."

There's a fluttering sensation in my stomach. Max has a really pretty smile that lights up her eyes. They're almost the same shade of blue as Susie's but slightly lighter. Her knee keeps touching mine and her skin is so soft. I want to keep talking to her about books and movies and all the things we like and dislike. I want to get to know her more because I think I might like her, and I haven't felt that way about a girl before.

CHAPTER SEVENTY-THREE
RECORDING BETWEEN JENNY WOODS AND SUSIE PATTERSON

SIXTEEN YEARS AGO

Susie: What's it like, being with a girl?
Jenny: It's like being with a boy but there's no... you know.
Susie: You can say penis, Jenny! Christ!
Susie: So you and her have had sex then.
Jenny: OMG! Shut up! I'm not talking about that!
Susie: Why not? I fucked Owen.
Jenny: You did? When?
Susie: After that disco at school. Remember how I said I was going home early? Well, I didn't. I met him at the park, and we went behind the trees.
Jenny: Wow, that sounds romantic.
Susie: Oh, like you and Max touching each other in a tent is any more romantic.
Jenny: Fuck you!
Susie: Fuck you!
Susie: Do you love her?

Susie: Oh my god, you do love her!
Jenny: I wish you two wouldn't fight so much. It's so annoying that you always argue when we're around.
Susie: Well, I don't like how she treats you. She's always around and she's always touching you like you're her property or something. Don't you think it's weird that she's cut her hair? It's like yours now.
Jenny: You think?
Susie: Yeah, she has no personality of her own. She just wants to be like us all the time. That's why she wants to do our challenges because she hasn't got anything else to do. She has no friends, no school, and no family. She's a freak.
Jenny: That's not fair. And way too harsh. She's basically homeless.
Susie: I get that, but it doesn't change anything. I think you need to be careful around her, that's all I'm saying. You're a bit...
Jenny: What?
Susie: A bit naïve, Jen.
Jenny: Yeah, and Dad says you take advantage of me. He thinks you're a manipulative little madam.
Susie: So what? I like getting my way. But it's different with Max. She's... oh, I don't know.
Jenny: What?
Susie: I don't know. There's just something sneaky about her, that's all. I keep seeing her watching me and it creeps me out.
Jenny: [inaudible]
Susie: What?
Jenny: Nothing.
Susie: Tell me or I'm stealing this lipstick.
Jenny: You can have it for all I care. Mum doesn't like

me wearing make-up anyway. Neither does Max. She says I'm prettier without it.
Susie: Nah, you need the lipstick.
Jenny: Ow! You threw it at me. You know what I said? I said you're jealous. Owen is a selfish dick who kissed Rebecca James at a beach party and Max is good to me. So you're just jealous. I'm going home.
Susie: Fine.
Jenny: Fine.

CHAPTER SEVENTY-FOUR

Tears run down my cheeks as I listen to an argument between me and Susie. One that ends in her throwing lipstick at me. She was jealous. Max took up more of my time and I think Susie used me as an emotional crutch. She needed me and didn't want to share me.

But was there more to it? I loved Susie. She was my best friend and I've considered our friendship a sisterly love. But could that have changed after we entered our teenage years? Now that I know I'm bisexual, I wonder if there was some sexual tension between us, too. Maybe Susie never got a chance to explore those feelings and maybe it explains why our friendship was quite so intense.

Jack's taunt comes back to me. He was being a homophobic dick, but he may have seen what I wasn't able to see because I was too close to the situation for clarity.

One other aspect of the taped argument stands out to me. Even then, Max demonstrated a tendency to morph herself into another person. She has never wanted to be Max. I bring up her Instagram profile again. This is Max. Vulnerable and ill in bed. This is the Max she prefers to hide behind make-up and bodyguards and a huge mansion by the sea.

Towards the end of the day, it rains, washing away the snow. I have dinner with Harry and Hannah, feeling lighter. I'm still unsure whether to trust Hannah but her behaviour has been completely normal over the last few days. She and Harry still seem like the perfect couple, telling funny stories about how the cat stole some turkey over Christmas and how Harry fell over in the mud playing with Hannah's nephew.

I sleep well that night and decide to put in a shift at Solace the next day.

The train is busy. People in damp coats and hats brush up against one another in the aisles. I lean against the carriage wall near the toilets, trying not to breathe in. My eyes drift towards coach D, towards my usual seat, and the place I saw Max posing as Susie.

I'm officially done. I don't need any more closure. The one part of all this I need to figure out is what I tell Susie's mother. And then it's over.

Reliable as always, Bob hands me a cup of hot tea as I walk in. I shed my coat, sit down at my desk, and wait for the first call.

"You're through to Solace. My name is Bella and I'm here to listen."

The lady on the line sobs.

"Take your time. I'm here when you're ready."

I wait patiently as she gets out all of her tears and then she tells me all about her cat who died that day. By the end of the conversation, I have tears in my eyes that I blink away. She thanks me for listening and hangs up. Then I speak to a lonely older man who misses his wife. I think his voice is familiar but I'm not sure. Then a defensive younger man tells me about how much he hates his family. I try not to judge, simply listen.

At the end of my shift, I feel emotionally drained and raw after the angry man. But I take one more call.

"Bella. I don't have much time left. I'm going into a hospice next week."

I freeze.

The person on the other end of the line is Max. I recognise her voice now.

"I'm sorry to hear that," I say.

I can't say more. I can't tell Max that I know it's her because if I do, Bob will notice. He'll want to know if I'm okay if there's a change in my demeanour.

"I'm still concerned about who will look after my family. I keep having a change of heart. What do you think?"

"I'm afraid I can't give you advice, it goes against our policies here at Solace. But if you want to talk about it more, I'm here to listen."

"There is someone I have in mind," Max says. "He's my number two, and my best confidante. I trust him and I know he will protect my family at all costs. But will they love him? Because I'm not sure. I think there's someone else that they will embrace, who they will love because that person is so similar to me."

"Why are you so sure they will love this person?"

"Because she is everything I'm not. I'm just a fraud but she is the real deal. She is the bravest person I know as well as the kindest. But she's also not a pushover and she can be brutally honest. She's had a tough life and hasn't always stood on her own two feet. She may have leant on others too much at times. But now she has become the person I knew she could be."

I lower my voice. "That isn't what you said before."

"Like I said, I've gone back and forth about this. She is also resistant to my gift. I think she doesn't believe she's worthy of it. And no matter how much I tell her I'm helping people, she doesn't believe me."

I don't respond. There's so much I want to say but I can't say it here in public.

You are a murderer, Max! FREEDM is a cult!

She lets the silence stretch. The back of my neck itches. The air in the room clogs. I know what I should do. I should tell her to leave me alone and go away and die. I cannot be bought. I am a good person who wants to live a simple life. I want love and a house and some pets I love as much as the first caller loved her cat. Maybe I want kids, I'm not sure but I think I do.

Those are the things I *should* want right now as a thirty-two-year-old woman who is coasting through life.

But I want something else more.

I cup my hand around the phone receiver. "Give me FREEDM."

CHAPTER SEVENTY-FIVE

As one day moves into the next, I'm never quite sure what to expect. I'm never sure if a police officer investigating FREEDM is going to knock on my door, or whether a solicitor will ring me to tell me I've inherited Max's estate. I ignore another message from Susie's mum, because I still don't know what to say. And at night, I fall asleep listening to the tapes.

About a week after my phone call with Max, Liam rings me out of the blue. I'm not paying attention and answer it quickly, still stirring the stew I have cooking on the hob.

"Do you know Gerry Turner?"

"Who is this?" I blurt.

"It's DS Harding."

My first thought is surprise. I hadn't expected to hear from him. After nothing for over a week, I had figured that our communication had ended.

"No, I don't know Gerry Turner, why?"

"His body was found near a lake on the edge of Saddleworth Moor."

I lower the heat and walk away from the hob. Slowly, I sit down in one of the dining chairs.

"You did know him, didn't you?" he says. "I knew he was part of that cult."

"How do you know that?"

"Well, he was a retired guy. Sixty-six years old. And he decided to climb a tree in the middle of nowhere. Oh, and according to his son, the old geezer gave him the house and moved away to live with this commune on the moors. His son hasn't been in touch with him for months."

"Oh."

I rub a hand over my face thinking about the night I spent camping with the group. Gerry had told me about his wife dying in an accident. Now I think I understand. She had dementia and she climbed a tree, falling to her death. Gerry's biggest fear was confronting the way his wife died. He repeated the action and the same thing happened. He died.

"Do you want me to tell you about the other accidental deaths connected to FREEDM?" he asks.

"No. I don't. I didn't know Gerry and I don't have anything to do with FREEDM."

The breath he exhales whistles through his teeth. "Okay."

"Okay," I repeat.

"Then we don't have anything to discuss."

"Nope."

The line goes dead.

I knock on the door and wait. The cottage is as busy as always. I hear voices coming from inside the house. The door opens and the sounds intensify. There's laughter emanating from a room deep inside the house.

Mia takes one look at me and flings her arms around me. "Jenny! It's so good to see you. Come in!"

I'm hesitant, but I also can't have this conversation on the doorstep, so I make my way in. Soon, a group of people gathers around me. Ashley hugs me. David shakes my hand. I say hello to others. The reception is warm and welcoming. It's early afternoon on a Saturday. The television is on. Someone is cooking in the kitchen.

I pull Mia to one side. "Can we talk privately?"

"Sure."

She's exactly how I remember her. Perfectly calm and composed. There isn't the slightest sign that she might be anxious about what I'm going to say. There's no trace of mourning going on in that house. Do they even know that Gerry is dead?

Mia takes me through to the office at the back of the house. I remember this room. Back then I still thought Susie was alive and imagined her decorating it.

We sit in a pair of armchairs on one side of the room, a large bookcase stretching across the opposite side of the wall.

"I heard about Gerry," I say.

She frowns. "Gerry?"

I press the palm of my hands into my knees. "Don't play dumb, Mia. I met Gerry the night we went camping and took Ayahuasca."

"Oh, hun. There's never been anyone called Gerry here at the cottage. Are you sure it was Gerry and not Gary? There's a Gary here. I'll call him in if you want."

"No. I spoke to Gerry. Gerry Turner. He died near the lake we swam through." Heat rises up to my cheeks. I feel like I can't look her in the eye. If I do, I might lose my composure altogether. "He was there. He told me about his wife's accident."

Mia holds up her palms. "I'm so sorry but I think you might be mistaken. Look, Ayahuasca is different for everyone. You may have—"

"I didn't hallucinate it. Why would I make up a man called Gerry whose wife died?"

"I don't know. I'm so sorry, Jenny, but I don't know any Gerry. Look, maybe someone joined our group for that night and then left. Sometimes it happens. Maybe I just don't remember him. What were you going to say about him, anyway? He died?"

"Yes," I say, my tone sharpened by frustration. "He climbed a tree near the lake, fell, and died. Doesn't that sound like an initiation to you?"

"Not really," she says. "We plan the initiations carefully."

Her expression is impassive. I know I'm not going to get another answer from her. I'm tempted to tell her about my last conversation with Max, but I leave it. Mia is lying to me to save her back. She fucked up. She let an initiate die.

"Well, it sounds like there's going to be an inquest," I say. "Hopefully Gerry's family will get the answers they need."

"I hope they do," she agrees. "It sounds like a terrible tragedy."

CHAPTER SEVENTY-SIX

The donations begin about a week later. It's how I know Max doesn't have long left.

Floral displays, baskets of treats, and vouchers for pamper sessions. All addressed to me but with some sort of message directed at Agnes or the future Agnes. Each one makes me queasy.

"Wow, someone has an admirer," Harry says, eyeing another vase of pink roses. "Is it that police guy?"

I make a non-committal sound as I trim the stems on the roses. "How are things with Hannah?"

"Great." He leans against the kitchen counter and a slow grin spreads across his face. "I'm thinking of proposing soon."

"That's awesome!"

"She's amazing. I'm so lucky to have her." He steps over and loops an arm around my shoulder. "Look at us both in love."

I toss in the last rose. "Yep!"

It's almost funny to me that he has absolutely no idea what's going on. The last time he asked me for updates about my "crazy friend", I told him that she'd stopped trying to get in touch. I didn't think he'd believe me at first, but—presents aside—everything else has gone back to normal. I'm at work every weekday and at Solace some evenings. Harry is busy with Hannah. She's often over at the house watching reality TV with us both when we flake out.

He saunters back to his room, and I stare at the flowers. The sycophantic nature of it makes me feel like I've rolled around in grease. I need another shower.

I turn my back on the kitchen table loaded with flowers. I finally managed to get through to Mia at the cottage and she agreed to give me the details of Max's hospice. I check the time. I have a train to catch.

I'm surprised she didn't stay at the Sanctum with nurses around her. But I wonder if she wanted to maintain her image with her acolytes. I don't think Max wants them to see Agnes dying.

The hospice is small and obviously well-funded. I imagine it is private and Max pays a lot of money for the best care. I'm taken down well-lit corridors until I reach the last door.

I don't have a gift. Maybe I should. What do you give an ex-girlfriend and murderer?

I open the door.

It's like seeing Susie tucked up in that bed. Max is bald now and there is no make-up on her face. She's thinner than the last time I saw her, and even though she's propped up with pillows, she seems barely able to sit up.

Despite everything that has happened, tears prick the backs of my eyes. I look at her, and I see the Max I met on the beach. The girl who talked to me about books and made my tummy flutter with new feelings.

"You came," she says, smiling.

I move over to the chair by the bed. When we were at the Sanctum, I didn't want to hold her hand. But I take it now, because I know once and for all that she isn't lying. You can't fake this. You can't fake the smell in this room. Death hangs over us like a low-lying cloud.

"Are you comfortable?" I ask. "Would you like water? More pillows?"

"You sound like Bella," she says. "You have a slightly softer voice when you are at Solace. And now you're using it on me again because you see that I'm a goner."

"Sorry, I didn't mean to make you feel like that."

"Why? It's true." She squeezes my hand lightly. "Well, the cancer is everywhere now. Blood, brain, bum. I'm on borrowed time so you'd better get yourself ready."

"Ready for FREEDM?"

"Yes."

"I'm not sure I'm ready, Max. I don't think I can lead FREEDM like you have all these years."

She smiles. "You can. You were born for this, Jenny."

I return the smile. "I hope you're right." I sigh. "The last few weeks have messed me up, Max. Sometimes I feel like I've dreamt parts of what happened. Can you tell me about that night at Hangman's Cave again? I'm sorry, I know you're tired, but I still don't remember it all."

"You jumped and hit your head, Jenny. Susie drowned."

I look at her. "But that isn't everything. Is it?"

"No. I suppose not."

"You held her under."

"I did."

"And then?" I prompt.

"Then I took her body out to the stream and watched it float away. She looked so beautiful in the water with her golden hair spreading out. Maybe that's why I went blonde. And why I had my nose altered to look like hers. She had many flaws, but she was beautiful. Just like you." Max's head flops back against the pillow. "Can I have some water, please?"

I pour some out into a plastic cup and help her get the straw in her mouth.

"Thank you," she says.

"Thank you for saying it one more time. I needed to hear it. Now I know it was real." I stroke the back of her hand. "I remember more now. Like how you and I met. You were reading Carrie."

"That's right."

"And I remember our nights in the blue tent."

Her eyes mist over. "The best nights of my life."

"I wish you hadn't done that to Susie," I say. "We might have had a future together otherwise. You let your temper get the best of you."

"I had a wicked temper. I always have." She smiles. "But I learned how to control it eventually."

"How?"

She shrugs. "You'll see one day."

It's an odd response but I decide not to grill her further. I see that she's tiring, and I have one more question to ask her.

"Max, I found out that a member of FREEDM died not long ago. His name was Gerry Turner. It sounds like he died during his initiation. I met him and we had a conversation about his wife. Then I found out that he fell out of a tree next to the same lake where I swam under the ice. When I went to see Mia, she told me no one called Gerry was in the organisation. Is that true? Why did she lie to me?"

Max pulls in a deep breath. It rattles out of her. I give her some more water so that she can concentrate.

"Mia is good at things like this. You'll know when you take over. She knows when to protect FREEDM and when to keep her mouth shut. I suspect that's what she's doing now. She's keeping her mouth shut."

CHAPTER SEVENTY-SEVEN

As the year rolls into February, ice-cold rain hammers against my umbrella. It was a long day at work and my feet are full of blisters. I'm half-limping when I get to the house. My hair is soaked against my forehead and every part of my body aches.

I unlock the door and stop.

Hannah is kneeling on the hallway carpet. Her head is bowed as though in reverence.

I drop my keys.

Then I take a step forward to ask her if she's okay, because a part of me wonders if she tripped and fell. But of course she hasn't. This is deliberate.

"Hannah," I say cautiously. "What are you doing?"

She doesn't move a single muscle.

"Can you look at me and tell me what you're doing?"

She lifts her chin then. "Yes, Agnes."

I stagger back. I'm not sure what hits me first. If I'm Agnes, then Max is dead. And if Hannah has called me that name then that means she's part of FREEDM and always has been. Hannah has watched me this entire time. I *did* see her at Sanctum.

"Is Ma—Susie dead?"

"Yes, Agnes."

I gasp. Max still feels like a dream to me, but she was real, she lived, and she died.

"Do you know what happens now?" I ask.

"I can take you to the six," she says.

"What about Harry?" I ask. "He wants to propose to you."

"Harry is very nice," she says. "But he isn't part of FREEDM and I'm not sure he ever will be."

"You wouldn't want to give up FREEDM for him?"

She shakes her head.

"Did you ever love him?" I ask.

Her silence is the answer. I sigh. Then I tell her to get up while I pack my belongings. I have a feeling I'm not going to be coming back to the house for a while. After I've thrown together a suitcase, I grab my phone and stare at it for at least thirty seconds. I pull up Liam's number. All I have to do is tap dial. I can tell him that the cult has come for me. Maybe he'll help me deal with this. Maybe he won't.

I place the phone back in my pocket.

Then I have another thought, and I grab an envelope and a pen.

Hannah smiles widely as I step back into the living room. She holds out her hand to take my suitcase. I pass it to her in silence.

When we step out of the house, there's a car waiting for us. Another sleek, black SUV with a driver ready to take us to our destination. Hannah hefts the suitcase into the car and I get in.

"What can you tell me about the six?" I ask, as soon as the car starts moving. "Are they powerful? Will they accept me?"

"I don't know a lot," she says. "I'm not one of them and they tend to keep to themselves. But they run all the day to day things."

"Day to day things?"

"Yes. They file taxes, keep on top of the bills and make sure we receive payment from members."

"Do the six still have jobs outside the organisation?" I ask.

"Yes, some of them do. Some dedicate themselves completely to Agnes."

I'm not sure I like the way that sounds, as though these people are her personal playthings.

"Does FREEDM employ a lot of people?" I ask.

"In a way," Hannah says. "Most dedicate their time."

"What about you, Hannah? You seem to have a life outside of FREEDM. You even took Harry to stay with your parents. How do you manage both?"

"My parents knew I lived with a commune for a while but once I went home, they assumed that was the end of it. But what really happened is Agnes gave me a job. She wanted me to meet Harry."

"And you were okay with this?" I ask.

"I knew Agnes would never put me in a situation that would cause me pain. I trust her." She shakes her head and wipes away a tear. "I'm so sorry, Agnes. I don't mean any disrespect when I talk about Agnes in her previous form."

Her words make me cringe. It's like I'm some sort of supernatural being.

"That's okay," I say.

Hannah sniffs loudly. "I enjoyed my time with Harry."

"He deserved better than being tricked."

"It was all for the greater good. You have a destiny, Agnes. It was my job to help bring you to that destiny."

I want to grind my teeth, but I finger the sleeve of my shirt instead. Any mention of doing bad things to achieve good pisses me off. It's an easy step towards dehumanisation. I wonder if such things can be corrected. Can amending future mistakes erase the past?

"Tell me about your initiation, Hannah." I lean back against the car headrest. The grey smudge of a passing town blurs against the damp window.

"Well, when I was little, I had a recurring nightmare. It was about this monster that I called Mr Bad Man." She laughs. "I know. I wasn't the most creative child. But he was tall, wore a bowler hat, had prominent veins running across his face and yellow teeth. So for my initiation I took hallucinogenic mushrooms and lots of FREEDM members dressed as Mr Bad Man. I woke up in the warehouse alone and naked with the others running around me dressed as my nightmare."

"That sounds like torture," I say.

"It was at first. I crawled into a corner and cried for hours. But they stayed in their costumes just sitting around not doing much. In the end, it didn't bother me at all. We were together in that warehouse all night. I came out a new person. Nothing else touched it. Not therapy. Nothing."

I close my eyes. I wonder where Hannah's nightmare came from, whether her mysterious monster is based on someone she knew in real life. Someone who hurt her. But I don't bring it up because that would be unkind. And then I wonder if these people really are better or if the kind of healing FREEDM offers is a temporary fix. I still don't know the answers to any of these questions and now I am their leader.

My stomach churns. I have a multitude of possibilities in the palm of my hand, from ruling over the cult members like a queen, to dismantling it from the inside out. I think I have an idea of which direction I'm going to take. But first I need to see the six.

CHAPTER SEVENTY-EIGHT

There is a line of people greeting me as I step out of the car. One by one, each acolyte falls to their knees as I pass. My breath comes out quickly and ragged. The scene before me is so surreal that I sense myself disassociating. But I need to concentrate. Somehow, I manage to pull myself back. A tall woman opens the door to the Sanctum and lets me inside. I follow Hannah through the strange hallways and rooms as more people fall to their knees when I walk past them.

I imagine Max walking these halls. I wonder what she said and did to command this amount of respect. The thought makes my insides squirm. I could never achieve this on my own. The more I think about it, the more the idea of disbanding this organisation without upset seems less and less likely. These people dropping to their knees are fanatics. Liam was right. You can pull out a tooth, but a new one will grow back. If I refuse to become their leader, they will simply appoint a new one. Maybe that leader will be even worse.

"This way, Agnes," Hannah says, taking me through to a large office.

There are six people waiting for me, each in an armchair. I'm relieved to see that I don't recognise any of their faces. At least none of the six have turned out to be people in my life. I half expected Harry to be here, too, or someone from work, or —plot twist—my father. They bow slightly in deference, but none kneel like the others.

"Agnes," Hannah says. "The former Agnes recorded a video for you. Would you like me to play it?"

"Yes."

Hannah gestures for me to sit in the large chair in the centre of the circle. I take my place, wondering what the six are like. Four men and two women. All expressionless.

Hannah rolls down a screen and lifts a remote. A projector whirrs to life and Max's image appears. She looks very similar to the first time I saw her, with perfectly coiffed hair and a thick layer of make-up. She smiles.

"I have now been reborn," she says. "And the vessel is among you. We all knew this time was coming and have prepared for it well. My six closest friends: Robin, Michael, Sasha, Francis, Veronica, and Eric, you must guide the new Agnes to lead our people. And, Jenny." She sighs and I feel like she's staring right at me. I feel like she's in the room. "You have the greatest responsibility of all, and the greatest rewards come with it. You are now the matriarch of our family. I believe in you, Jenny. I know you will see my vision through."

I shiver, sensing the heavy weight of responsibility transferring to me. This house, these people, the house by the lake, so many other things are now under my control. *Mine*.

The video goes on, explaining the legalities of the transfer. How a solicitor will come to see me about inheriting the house and the business. At one point, I feel like running out of the room. She discusses her funeral and where she will be buried. Then Max speaks directly to me again.

"Jenny, there may be some temptation to reject Agnes. I urge you not to allow that to happen. Agnes belongs in you. I know she does, and I know you believe in her. Deep down. Remember those days sixteen years ago when you were so brave you jumped into Hangman's Cave. Don't let yourself slip back into the frightened version of yourself. The person who was alone and depressed in a small, terraced house, allowing men to walk all over you. Don't go back to that, Jenny. You can do real good with what I'm giving you. Think of all those people in pain who call you on a daily basis. Imagine if they faced their fears in the same way these people here did. Some of these people wanted to die before they came to FREEDM. We have saved lives. You may find yourself focusing on the extremely rare cases of initiations going wrong. The accidents. They are few. And every single one of our members chooses to go through with their initiation knowing the risks. They *choose* this with a sound body and mind.

"I never told you which fear I faced, did I? Obviously, as Agnes, I need to face the greatest of fears in order to take my place at the helm of this family. It's funny that you never asked me about it. Didn't you want to know?

"I leave this video with a request that you go with Hannah to see for yourself. It shows you the breadth of what we do here. I warn you, it's hard to look at. You may even feel angry at me. But dig deep, Jenny. Don't go back. Go forward with us."

And with that she signs off. I glance over at Hannah who nods towards the door.

"It was nice to meet you all," I say quietly to the six. They bow.

Something in my heart tells me that Max's six closest members aren't ready to accept me. It almost feels like a challenge. I wrap my arms around my body, wishing this responsibility didn't fall on my shoulders.

Hannah takes me down two flights of stairs to what I assume is an underground bunker. The air cools with each step. I rub my upper arms for warmth. Hannah unlocks a large, steel door and we walk into some sort of chamber.

There's a thump, and the sound of heavy breathing. I startle when I see a man throw himself at a sheet of glass.

"Reinforced," Hannah says. "Don't worry he can't get out."

"Help me," the man says.

He must be around sixty years old. His hair is ragged and filthy, grown out below his equally scruffy beard. He's wearing a grey tracksuit stained with sweat. His damp palms leave misty marks on the glass.

I gasp.

The greying, filthy man is trapped in a cell with a mattress, a toilet, and a chair. On the wall behind him written in red are the words:

THE STEPFATHER.

CHAPTER SEVENTY-NINE

This is Max's fear. The stepfather she was terrified of, who she ran away from. Here he is, beating the glass with his fists. A caged animal at the zoo. She kept him here to watch him. My mouth fills with bile and I turn away from Hannah to throw it up.

But that's when I see the cage on the far side of the basement. Another reinforced glass enclosure with another person inside. I rush over to the tall, thin man. I see the words in red on the wall behind him:

THE STALKER

"Kevin?" I whisper.

He rushes over to the glass. "Jenny. I don't know why I'm here. What did I do wrong? What did I do?"

"I... I don't..." I take a step back.

"Help me! Please help me!"

"Get me out of here," I say to Hannah. I can't process this right now. I can't think with these two prisoners staring at me with their pleading expressions.

Hannah leads me back out of the locked area.

"What the fuck was that?" I demand. "Are there more down there?"

"I don't know," Hannah says. "All I know is that I was instructed to give you this after you saw them." Hannah hands me an envelope.

I take it from her and walk up the steps to the main floor. Then I find a quiet corner in an empty room to sit. It's a light, airy room at a pleasant temperature. I find a chair by the window and stare out at the manicured gardens. This is all too much. What have I done?

I wipe a sheen of sweat from my forehead and tear open the envelope. A familiar sheet of paper falls onto my lap. Another diary entry.

Max told me about her stepfather today. How he hurt her. How he hurt her mother. But also, how her mother let him hurt her. I've never wanted to kill someone before, but I do today.

He belongs in prison for the rest of his life, but Max says no one would believe her. She told a teacher at school that he was hurting her, but the teacher didn't do anything about it. She said all she could do was run away. And now she has nothing, and her life is ruined all because of one person. How is that fair?

If God exists and makes everyone equal, why is it that some people are more powerful than others? It makes no sense.

We talked about what we'd do to him if we ever saw her stepfather but we both know that we can't do anything. Max is too scared. I am too, I guess. I just think we're two teenage girls and we have no power. Like, Susie has no power over whether she's ill or not. It's not fair, but it's the way the world works.

It ends abruptly. I turn the page over. Max has scribbled one last note.

I found one of the men who has made your life a misery over the last sixteen years. He knows where you work. He knows where you live. He has followed you. He has talked about you online and called you a murderer when you had nothing to do with Susie's death.

Who else would you punish if you had the chance? What about your dad for giving up on you? What about Jack who cheated on you with one of your friends?

What about the men in your life who have taken advantage of you?

Men. Plural.

Check the USB.

I delve back into the envelope to find the small USB. Then I hurry out of the room to find Hannah. She's waiting right outside for me.

"I need a computer," I say.

She doesn't ask why. She takes me up to Max's office. My office now.

"I'll give you some privacy, Agnes," she says, smiling. She bows before leaving.

I walk around the desk, sit down in Max's large, leather chair, and pull the laptop towards me. My pulse quickens as I push the USB stick into its slot and open the lid. It's clear that FREEDM's influence is far reaching, and I hate to think what she has found.

The battery is low, so I rummage through the desk drawers before finding a charger. Then go on the hunt for a plug socket. And when I sit back down my heart is pounding, with the blood rushing through my ears. I quickly double tap on the USB icon and wait.

A folder pops up with a few files inside it. One is CCTV footage that appears to have been taken outside my house. In it, I see a car on the other side of the road. Two people are inside the car. I lean in. It's not great quality, but I know that profile. The person in the driver's seat is Liam. But there's a woman with him. The woman is probably another police officer.

I fast forward through the video. It goes on for a few hours during which he doesn't move. When I check the date, I see that it's not long after I went to the police station about seeing Susie—or Max as I now know—on the train. It's exactly as I suspected. Liam didn't trust me.

Next, I open an audio file and quickly turn up the volume.

"...she's lying. For sure."

It's Liam's voice but I don't know who he's talking to.

"Jenny Woods?"

"Yep. Look, I still think a lot of evidence suggests Jenny murdered Susie Patterson. That's always been the theory, right? She murdered her friend and got lucky when the body washed out to sea. Without Susie's body, no one has been able to charge her. I'm hoping I'll get her to confess. This whole story she told me about Susie being alive is total bullshit. I think she's sending herself those diary entries. Every time I meet her, she tries to convince me otherwise but it's pretty clear she's an attention seeker. The world has moved on. There hasn't been much in the news about Susie Patterson's disappearance so she's looking for other ways to get attention. We need to act fast—"

The file ends.

I think about Liam coming to my rescue at the quarry. His fingers entwining with mine on the roof of the apartment block. I think about him taking me for lunch, meeting me for breakfast, drinking with me in the pub, and walking me home. I think about him letting me stay at his house, the kiss he reciprocated. The professional barrier he put up between us but the carrot he dangled, that maybe one day we could connect as more than friends. It was all a lie. Liam never liked me. He used me.

He thought I sent those diary entries to myself. He never, not once, believed me.

CHAPTER EIGHTY

I take the USB stick and roll it over in my fingers. The betrayal cuts deep, I can't deny it. I send Hannah away and get up from the chair, walking over to the window. Spring will be here soon. The gardens at the Sanctum will be beautiful. I could live here, looking out at the sea, watching the waves coming and going, erasing footprints on the sand.

This is Max's gift to me. This is her apology.

I go back to the computer and reinsert the USB. There's still quite a bit of memory left on it. Max gave me this so that I would know that I have been betrayed one more time. I've had a fear of police officers since the traumatic interviews following Susie's disappearance. Her death, as I know now.

I look through all of Max's folders on her computer. These are mine now. I can do whatever I want with them. But for now, I simply read.

And then I make a phone call.

George wants to follow me in, but I won't allow it. This is something I need to do alone. He goes back to the SUV and waits in the back. I'm not sure I'll ever get used to having a bodyguard. I press the doorbell and wait.

I'm dressed in a pristine white suit and my hair has been braided by Hannah. She pinned it up for me before expertly applying make-up.

It has been a week since I found out I was Agnes. During that week, I have learned how FREEDM works. I've met with the six on several occasions, talked through the healthy finances, and all the different accounts. I've seen the various properties owned by FREEDM all around the country. I've visited some of the communes and talked to the members, asking them about their initiations. I've even been given an approximation of how many accidental deaths there have been since FREEDM began.

Fifty.

It's a lot. I've seen the records about the people who died. Some families were paid to sign NDAs. Some of the victims did not have families.

There are over forty thousand members with the vast majority paying between ten and twenty percent of their income to FREEDM. Then there are the seminars which cost upwards of three hundred pounds per session. After the seminars, some people go on a course. Then after the course they stay in the communes. And eventually, they go through their initiation.

I learn that FREEDM is being investigated by several journalists. The six think it will be a while until there is an expose. They also believe FREEDM will weather the course and as long as we don't comment, there's not enough evidence to bring the organisation down.

It has been a long week. But I am still glad that I arranged this meeting.

Fiona Patterson opens the door, and her eyes widen in surprise.

"Jenny? You look different."

I smile. "Can I come in?"

She waves me in. "I bought a coffee cake. I know you and Susie both used to like it."

"Thanks, that sounds lovely."

"Gosh, it's been so long since you last visited the house. Would you like to see her room? I've kept it how it was."

Fiona walks me upstairs and then gives me a moment alone in Susie's room. I run my fingers along the posters and concert ticket stubs taped on the wall. We used to buy our CDs at car boot sales and save our pocket money to go to gigs in York. Most of her CDs are bootlegs.

I sit down on her bed, remembering the way it felt. I look at my feet against her pink carpet, remembering how jealous I was that her carpet was pink. I inhale and almost believe I smell the scent of her coconut shampoo. And then I open my eyes. I see her sitting on the floor looking up at me with her maths homework spread out around her tanned legs.

I ball up the bedding in my fists before I leave.

Fiona has a slice of cake waiting for me in the living room. Her eyes are wet.

"I don't think I can wait any longer," she says. "I know you've remembered something. I can tell. You're holding yourself differently. You know what happened to my Susie, don't you? Is she... is she..."

I hold her before she collapses. And then I tell her everything. I tell her that her precious daughter has been dead for sixteen years.

CHAPTER EIGHTY-ONE
LIAM HARDING

Liam watches DS Stroud pacing up and down outside the interview room. She bites her thumb nail and then sighs.

"Look, it's going to take some time," he says. "This cult is big and protected by a lot of money. We're not going to get to them from the first witness statement. What was the girl's name again?"

"Ashley Nicholls. She still says that the cult had nothing to do with her uncle's assault. And what she has told us makes no sense."

Stroud walks me through to the incident room and grabs a desk chair. Liam sits opposite.

"So, Ashley Nicholls says that Susie Patterson set up the cult after she disappeared sixteen years ago. Apparently, Patterson went by the name Maxine Graham. She spent a lot of time homeless but turned her life around. She became some sort of motivational speaker. But apparently, this Maxine, who is really Susie, died last week. And now they have a new leader, but she won't say who it is."

"Then there might be some truth to what Jenny Woods claimed." He always cringes slightly as he says Jenny's name. He isn't proud of what he did to get close to her. He may have crossed a few lines there, though he was careful not to let Jenny's crush on him go too far. And he hates to admit it, but he liked being around the girl. He didn't trust her as far as he could throw her, but she was funny. She was interesting. Argumentative and defensive, sure, but in a way that intrigued him.

"We need to look into this Maxine Graham. Either she really was Susie Patterson, or she pretended to be." Stroud stands. "But we need to keep in touch with Ashley Nicholls, too. I get the impression she knows more than she's letting on. Have you heard anything from the families you contacted?"

He shakes his head. "Some are working with a journalist, and they seem a bit cagey. I don't know if they're getting paid or what, but I get the impression there's a deal of some kind being made. At this point, we might have to wait until the journalists are done with the story. The families might talk to us afterwards."

"Meanwhile, people are dying to get into this cult. Literally. Talk to you later." Stroud walks away and Liam heads back to his office.

He spent over a month monitoring Jenny Woods and never got anywhere. There were times he was so sure she was behind Susie Patterson's death, and other times he believed every word Jenny said.

But there was always an attention-seeking aspect to her that gave him pause. She was a woman who had been in and out of the newspapers for years. And then nothing. He'd always suspected that she wanted that attention back. After all, a few stories about the possibility of Susie Patterson being alive and seen on a train made a few headlines. Only, it all fizzled out. He made sure that the diary and the dares didn't leak to the press. He wanted to study this one himself. He wanted to be sure.

There's an envelope on his desk when he gets back. He sits down and examines the padded packet tearing it open at one end. A USB stick spills out. He reaches in and pulls out a sheet of paper. To his surprise, it's a handwritten note.

He reads the note first.

You're a liar, Liam. I hope you know that. I hope you think about that as you examine what I have sent you. Have your experts analyse them. They're all real.

You underestimated me from the start. I should never have trusted you. But I also know you have an ego the size of a house and closing this case as well as bringing down a huge cult like FREEDM will definitely get you all the attention you crave.

Goodbye, DS Harding. I hope you have a nice life.

Jenny Woods.

Well, shit. She read him to filth, as his seventeen-year-old niece says.

He plugs the USB into his laptop and works through the files. For some reason, there is CCTV footage of him and Stroud staking out Jenny's house. Then there is a cut off phone conversation between the two of them. These have been put into a folder called "Pants on Fire."

Then he checks through a folder called "The underestimation of Jenny Woods" and discovers an audio file of a woman called Max confessing to the murder of Susie Patterson. She then goes on to talk about FREEDM concealing the accidental death of Gerry Turner. He comes out of those files and goes through several financial documents and screenshots of accounts. There are even a couple of transactions to some low-level officers in his own department. The cult bribed two PCs to look the other way. He whistles slightly through his teeth.

"I think I owe you an apology, Jenny," he whispers.

CHAPTER EIGHTY-TWO

Agnes died with Max.

I've done what I needed to do. I only wish I'd seen the look on Liam's face as he worked his way through the USB stick. During my visit to Fiona Patterson, after I showed her the contents of the USB stick and let her listen to the recording of Max admitting what she did to Susie, I gave her an envelope with a copy of everything and asked her to get it to DS Harding. It was the only way to get the information out of the cult without them knowing what I was doing. Now Liam has everything he needs to close the case of Susie Patterson's disappearance and bring down FREEDM, too. He'll certainly get all the accolades and promotions that I suspect he desires.

Now I need to get out.

I make my way down the stairs and through the Sanctum. I watch acolytes bow to me as I hurry through the corridors. They have no idea what I've done and what I'm about to do.

"Agnes! Can I have a word?"

I stop, my skin crawling from the sickeningly sickly tone

Veronica uses to get my attention. As one of the six, she has helped me this week, particularly with accounting. A few times I've had to pull rank on the six, forcing them to follow my specific instructions. But I can tell they are suspicious.

"Not right now," I say with a smile. "I'm..." I try to think up an excuse but there's so much adrenaline coursing through my veins that I can't think straight.

Veronica takes hold of my arm and leads me into a small room to our right. A study, filled with books. I don't have time to peruse the spines before she begins talking.

"You haven't signed the papers yet," Veronica says. "You haven't formally inherited FREEDM."

"I know that," I reply, keeping my voice as smooth as possible. "Like I said, I want to wait until after Susie's funeral." I'm careful not to say Max. I suspect that the six know her true identity but also don't want to acknowledge it. It's best to follow their lead. "The funeral is three days from now. So I will sign the papers then."

She clasps my upper arm. "We trust in Susie's judgement. That means we believe *you* are our new Agnes. But there is a limit to how long we will wait for you to accept it yourself."

Smiling, I place my own hand over hers. "I have accepted it. I know who I am and why I'm here. There's nothing to worry about, Veronica. We are the agitators. We are free, and I cannot wait to be the guiding light taking FREEDM to the next level."

My heart pounds as I lie to her. I'm sure she senses it. Perhaps she sees the beads of sweat forming at my hairline. But I squeeze her hand tightly and maintain the smile.

"There's an initiation tonight," she says. "A new acolyte. I think you should be there."

I nod. "I think I should, too." Then, spontaneously, I kiss

her cheek. "Susie was right to trust you, to bring you into her inner circle. You, and the rest of the six, have been my support. I appreciate that I have asked a lot of you over the last week. I understand that I have already tested your loyalty with my demands, but I will repay it in kind." I lower my chin and give her a knowing smile.

She grins smugly. She thinks she understands. In her mind, I will give her preferential treatment once I've formally inherited everything. She thinks she's about to become very rich and powerful.

"Thank you, Agnes." She bows slightly and walks out of the study.

I stand by the window, collecting my thoughts. I wipe away the sheen of sweat from my forehead. This is the hardest part. Getting out of here when there are so many eyes on me. But I swam under the ice. I jumped into Hangman's Cave. I can do this. I know I can.

I take my phone, which I'm relieved to find that the cult has allowed me to keep, and call Dad.

"It's me," I say.

"Jenny."

His voice sounds the same as it always does. Initial happiness tinged with sadness. Slurring slightly at the edges.

"How are you?" I ask.

"Same old. Are you okay? You sounded upset the last time we spoke."

"I'm fine," I say. "I'm good, actually."

"Did you have a nice Christmas?"

"Yeah. I spent it with friends. Sorry I didn't come."

He sighs. "That's okay, I understand. Maybe next year, eh?"

I laugh slightly. "Yeah. Actually, I promise. I'll definitely come next year."

"You promise? Well, now you'll have to keep it. Remember how I said I'd never break any promise I made to you."

"I do remember," I say. "And you didn't, because you never made me any promises."

"I didn't?"

"No. You didn't."

"All right, well how's this? I promise to always pick up the phone when you call."

I smile. "I like that promise."

We say our goodbyes and I hang up the phone feeling lighter. Then I walk out of the study to find George, Max's bodyguard and now mine, waiting for me.

I clear my throat. "I'd like to take a drive."

"I'll get the driver—"

"No," I interrupt. "I want to drive myself and I want to go alone."

George frowns and tiny wrinkles appear in the corners of his eyes. It's the smallest amount of vulnerability I've ever seen from the man.

"Are you sure, Agnes?" he asks.

"I am sure. In fact, it's a direct order," I say. "I would like to drive a car alone. I'm sure your previous Agnes had private challenges she would set herself in order to do her job. This is mine. You must allow me to do it. Do you understand?"

"Yes, Agnes."

"And you cannot follow me."

"Very well. There are cars in the underground garage. Choose which one you would like, and I'll have someone bring you the key."

I choose the smallest car in the garage and one that I hope I'll be able to drive. George tells me it's a brand new BMW M3. My hands shake as I place them on the wheel. The garage door opens slowly, and I press down the accelerator, moving gently away from the line of sports cars. George watches me with an impassive expression. I say a silent prayer to whoever will listen and leave the Sanctum compound.

CHAPTER EIGHTY-THREE

Sweat tumbles down my face, dripping onto the pristine white suit. I touch the seam of my bra through the satin blouse. It's where I sewed in several diamonds I found in the vault at the Sanctum. Distracted, I stall at a junction and a man in a Nissan beeps me. Waving at the rearview mirror, I get the car going again and drive too slowly down a long, narrow road. The man overtakes me, and I let out a long, relieved breath.

On Google Maps, this journey is less than ten minutes. It has been fifteen and I finally approach the lay-by I needed to find. He's there, waiting for me, in his old Volvo. I swing the steering wheel too harshly, hitting a patch of grass verge, and then slam on the brake. Every part of my body shakes when I apply the handbrake and take hold of the door handle.

I rush out of the car and head towards the Volvo. He steps out and hurries towards me, worry etched across his face, the scrunched expression making him seem older.

"Jenny, what the fuck is going on?"

I fling my arms around his shoulders, holding back tears.

Part of me had worried he wouldn't come, but throughout all of this, Harry has proved himself a good person.

"Did you bring it?" I ask, breaking away.

He lifts the holdall. "Your passport is in the inner pocket along with some cash and the credit card you mentioned in your note. Jenny, I'm scared. What's going on? I haven't heard from you or Hannah for a week!"

"We need to go," I say. "I might be being followed."

I get into the backseat while Harry puts the car in gear. Rummaging through the holdall, I find my passport, a baseball cap, jeans, and a hoodie. I pull the white blazer from my body and drag the hoodie over the blouse.

"So we're going to the train station, right?" he asks. "You're running away from someone?"

I fiddle with the zip on the trousers as I speak, "Harry, listen to me. You can't trust Hannah."

His mouth gapes in the mirror. "What?"

"Do not tell Hannah where I'm going."

He shrugs. "I can't. I don't even know. I'm just taking you to the train station, remember? I guess you're going abroad because you have your passport, but I don't know where."

"The less you know the better. Sorry I have to be so vague, but it is what it is."

He shakes his head slightly. I can't even imagine what is going through his mind right now. A few weeks ago, I was just Jenny. A homebody without much of a life aside from a dark past and some volunteer work.

"Shit," Harry says.

"What is it?"

"There's a black SUV behind us looking suspicious as fuck."

I tug the baseball cap over my hair and duck down. "You have to get rid of him."

"Jesus," Harry mutters.

He takes a sharp left. We're on twisty, countryside roads. The Volvo swerves around bends, snaking down a hill. At the bottom, he takes a right and then another left. I keep hold of my seatbelt, sliding across the seat. The car climbs up a rise and comes out near the coast, with the sea over my shoulder.

"Is he gone?" I ask.

Harry looks up at the mirror and bites his lip. Then he shakes his head. "He's back. He's speeding up. Fuck!"

I'm pinned back as Harry presses the accelerator down. I allow myself one glance back. I see George driving. I see the determined expression on his face.

This is it. He knows that I am not loyal to FREEDM. He knows I'm escaping from them, that I'm leaving them without an Agnes. And he isn't going to let me go without a fight.

"He's on my fucking bumper!" Harry yells.

The Volvo lurches forward. That familiar surge of adrenaline rushes through me, heightening every one of my senses. George rams the car again. Harry almost loses control around a bend. There's just a small barrier between us and the long drop down. We're going far too fast.

"He's trying to kill me," I mutter. It hits me with perfect clarity. George wants me dead. But if he kills me, he kills Harry, too, and I can't stand that thought.

When the next junction comes up, Harry swings the car, just managing the turn. Then he stops dead. To avoid a collision that could potentially kill him, George swerves the SUV around us. As the SUV stops, Harry reverses back around the corner and slams the accelerator on. We head in the opposite direction. It gives us a few seconds lead.

The road widens and Harry takes another turn, heading

away from the coast. I see a few properties coming up, with farmland stretching out behind.

"Turn into that farm," I say, pointing to the closest.

Harry does as he's told, swerving into the courtyard. I don't care if I piss off a farmer right now, there are bigger things to worry about.

"Behind that old caravan!"

Harry pulls the Volvo behind a dilapidated caravan and kills the engine. Slowly, we slip out of the car. I grab the holdall and clutch it to my chest. In the distance, I hear the sound of an engine.

Harry turns to me. His brown eyes, usually so warm, have turned dark. His fists clench at his sides. "Run, Jenny. Run!"

I have no time to even thank him. I run.

EPILOGUE

I don't know if Max genuinely believed I would continue her legacy or if she wanted me to burn it to the ground, but I lit the match and tossed it. As soon as it left my fingers, I knew I was in danger. But I didn't care. If I'm honest with myself, there is even a part of me that enjoyed it, and for that, I blame both Max and Susie.

After leaving Harry behind that day, I ran as fast as I could, zigzagging through fields and woods. Climbing over fences. Dragging myself through the mud. Every time I was on the brink of collapsing, I took a break, cowering behind trees with my limbs shaking and my teeth chattering. Then I'd limp on, determined to survive.

By the time I found a village, I needed water, food, and a shower. But I had no time for that. I bought a new pair of shoes from a charity shop, a box of plasters for the blisters on my heels, a bottle of water, and found a local taxi service that took me to a small town on the way to Manchester. There, I rented a room in a B&B, finally showering and eating. Then I planned a route down to London using meandering rail services that stopped at all the tiny stations. I had a feeling

George would check the main service that runs straight to Euston Station. But I figured I had a good chance with my route. I disembarked at a small town near Stanstead before going to the airport in a taxi.

It was strange, checking the train again. Walking up and down the aisle, looking for a thickset, pale man in a black suit. At every stop, I examined the platform, searching faces, just like I did after I saw Max in coach D.

During those moments, I had no idea what had happened to Harry. I feared the worst. I left him behind. The guilt made my stomach churn.

I'd lost my power to help Harry at that point. In the interim week where I was Agnes, I had money and security. As soon as I sent that USB stick to DS Harding, I had nothing.

Which is why I'd been careful to plan everything.

When I reached Stanstead airport, I used what was left in my bank account to get me to Singapore. It wiped everything out.

But that didn't matter because of the plan. While FREEDM believed I was Agnes, I used the power at my fingertips to have the FREEDM accountants set up a bank account in my name in Singapore. As soon as I got there, I moved the money into a different account just to be sure they had no access to it.

It contained millions.

Then I moved again. And again. And I still had the diamonds to sell. After never leaving the country for thirty-two years, and suffering from panic attacks even on trains, I managed to move around the world until finally settling in Australia. It's surprising—or maybe not—how the world opens up when you have money. From the best flights to the ease with which you can buy property and settle in a new country. But the best part is the security team I hired once I'd bought my house in Sydney.

The exposé of FREEDM finally hit streaming services a week ago. I saw DS Harding on my television talking about how he received a "tip off" and obtained a warrant to search the Sanctum. The police were shocked to find people imprisoned in the basement. Three men in total. The stepfather, the stalker and... the saviour. Harry.

Then I watched Ashley tearfully recount the way Max pressured her into beating her own abuser. Even Harry himself ended up interviewed by the documentary makers, though he was blurred out and his voice altered. I cried as I listened to how he was beaten and imprisoned by the cult. But by the time the documentary came out, I had already mailed him the key to a security deposit box where he would find a few more diamonds I managed to remove from the Sanctum vaults before tossing that match.

Hannah, Mia, and the six were arrested and charged with various crimes, including fraud, blackmail, bribery, and manslaughter. I did not feel sympathy for them. They preyed on vulnerable people. They organised dangerous events and pressured people to join in. They forced families to sign NDAs.

There was one name spoken throughout the documentary. Maxine Graham. The murderer. The fraud. The copycat. The face of FREEDM. Not me, her. Because I slipped away before she was even in the ground.

But there is no mention of a man called George and I am sure that he is out there somewhere, looking for me. Whenever I'm alone, I look over my shoulder expecting to see a bulky, suited man staring at me. I dream of him grabbing me from the shadows and forcing me into one of their glass-fronted prison cells.

There's no real reason for him to continue hunting me.

FREEDM has been dismantled like a car stripped for parts. But there is something about that man that makes me think it's personal for him. I imagine him never giving up until he finds me. Yet part of me doesn't care about that. I have lived with fear for years. I know the shape of it, the smell of it, and how to get through it. I know I will always be afraid. At least here, I can live with that fear where the sun shines and the water is clear.

I am Jenny Woods reborn.

In fact, I'm experimenting with new names and identities. Jenny doesn't cut it anymore. Maybe Bella is more me.

Then there is the matter of the millions in my bank account. I've already sent an anonymous donation to Solace, which I hope put a smile on Bob's face. I'm not sure what I will do with the rest of the money. There's enough to live comfortably plus some extra. Perhaps I can set up something good for the world.

Max was right about one thing, there were some positive stories at FREEDM. It wasn't all bad. Some of the members genuinely did come away from the organisation feeling lighter. I know I did. But nothing is worth the exploitation of vulnerable people. The robbing of their hard-earned money. Members went into debt just to donate money directly to Max. They bought tokens blessed by her. They spent thousands on seminars that didn't help them. FREEDM wasn't good at its core, it was built on Max's greed.

And now I need to pay it forward. But not yet. First, I'm going to bask under the hot sun.

I lie back on my lounger on the beach, listening to the waves crashing against the shore. This is true solitude. My parents' faces pop into my mind. Mum when she was young. Dad before his addictions took over. The breath that leaves my chest is long and slow, exhaling many dark thoughts and fears. The breath that fills my lungs brings with it possibilities that stretch out like the ocean. I stay where I am until the sound of the waves bores me. Then, squinting underneath my sun hat, I follow the stone steps that lead up towards my house, nodding politely to the people I recognise from my neighbourhood.

The sun beats down. Flip flop soles slap against stone with each lazy step. I think about Chillingham during heatwaves. I think about Max on the beach nursing a warm beer as she talks about books. Then Susie with her freckles and her head tipped back in laughter. Susie younger, running ahead with a bucket and spade, collecting shells. She always gave me the prettiest ones.

I walk slowly along the coast until I find the perfect spot. High up on a cliff overlooking calm water. I drop my beach cover up to the ground and then kick off my flip flops and remove the sun hat. I leave my beach bag next to the pile. I pull a deep breath into my lungs, reach out, and feel her fingers in mine.

One, two, three
Dare you, dare me.
One, two, three
Follow you, follow me.
One, two, three
Let the fear set you free.
Let the fear set you free.
We jump.

ABOUT THE AUTHOR

Sarah A. Denzil is a British suspense writer from Derbyshire. Her books include *Silent Child*, which has topped Kindle charts in the UK, US, and Australia. *Saving April* and *The Broken Ones* are both top-thirty bestsellers in the US and UK Amazon charts.

Combined, her self-published and published books—along with audiobooks and foreign translations—have sold over one million copies worldwide.

Sarah lives in Yorkshire with her husband, enjoying the scenic countryside and rather unpredictable weather. She loves to write moody, psychological books with plenty of twists and turns.

To stay updated, join the [mailing list](#) for new release announcements and special offers.

ALSO BY SARAH A. DENZIL

Standalone Psychological Suspense

Saving April

The Broken Ones

Only Daughter

The Liar's Sister

Poison Orchids

Little One

The Housemaid

My Perfect Daughter

Find Her

The Stranger in Our House

The Nice Guy

The Silent Child Series

Silent Child, Book One

Stolen Girl, Book Two

Aiden's Story, a novella

Crime Fiction

One For Sorrow (Isabel Fielding book one)

Two For Joy (Isabel Fielding book two)

Three For A Girl (Isabel Fielding book three)

The Isabel Fielding Boxed Set

Supernatural Suspense

You Are Invited

Short suspenseful reads

They Are Liars: A novella

Aiden's Story (a SILENT CHILD short story)

Harborside Hatred (A Liars Island novella)

A Quiet Wife

Printed in Great Britain
by Amazon